Rush Home Road

Rush Home Road

A NOVEL

LORI LANSENS

LITTLE, BROWN AND COMPANY
BOSTON   NEW YORK   LONDON

First U.S. Edition

The characters and events in this book are fictitious. Any similarity to real persons,
living or dead, is coincidental and not intended by the author.

First published in Canada by Knopf

Library of Congress Cataloging-in-Publication Data

Lansens, Lori.

Rush Home Road : a novel / Lori Lansens. — 1st American ed.

p.   cm.

ISBN 0-316-06902-7

1. Women, Black — Ontario — Fiction.   2. Racially mixed children — Fiction.
3. Abandoned children — Fiction.   4. Blacks — Ontario — Fiction.
5. Ontario — Fiction.   6. Girls — Fiction.   I. Title.

PR9199.4.L36R87 2002

813'.6 — dc21   2001050194

10 9 8 7 6 5 4 3 2 1

Q-FF

Designed by Iris Weinstein

Printed in the United States of America

For Milan

AUTHOR'S NOTE

I wish to acknowledge a number of writers whose books were important to my research. They are, in no particular order: A. C. Robbins, Gwendolyn and John W. Robinson, John Rhodes, G. H. Gervais, Stanley G. Grizzle, John Cooper, Elaine Latzman Moon, Robin W. Winks, Victor Lauriston and Victor Ullman.

I also wish to thank my mother and father, and my family, for things too numerous to mention.

Rush Home Road

Indian Corn

It stinks of piss in the room. Sharla Cody breathes it in, thinking it's a sweet stink. Reminds her of the little white flowers Mum Addy planted instead of grass on the square out front of her trailer. They keep coming up, those little flowers, year after year. Sharla likes the notion of seeing them each spring, like an expected but unreliable guest.

Sharla forgets the name of that piss-stink flower. *Alyssum,* Mum Addy had told her, and said though it was not technically a perennial it would surely come back, and it did. Mum Addy said that's nature. Some flowers self-seed and *that's just what is.* Only a fool would take the time to wonder about *what is.*

Once Sharla made a bride's bouquet out of the white flowers. Mum Addy shook a yellowed curtain from her mending bin and fastened it to Sharla's hair with wooden clothespins. They walked down the mud lane like Sharla was the princess bride and Mum Addy was the lady holding her train, doing that step then stop, step then stop, like brides do. Mum Addy sang some pretty love song Sharla never heard before or since.

At five years old Sharla still pissed the bed when she got lonely. Mum Addy'd cluck her tongue but never smack her. Both of them half asleep, she'd wipe down Sharla's parts with a scratchy wet rag that used to be a brown sock, then she'd take her back down the skinny hall to her own musky bed to sleep the rest of the night.

Mum Addy wasn't Sharla's Mum. She wasn't even a relation. She was an old, cigarette-smoking colored lady from the mud lane of the Lakeview trailer park, twenty miles outside of Chatham, Ontario. Sharla was sent to live with the old woman when Emilio moved in with her real Mum, Collette. Emilio said if Sharla gave him a thimble more grief he'd set her fat ass on the stove. After that, Collette walked over to the mud lane and started knocking on doors. At the third place she tried, old Addy Shadd said she'd take the child in if Collette would give her a few dollars for food and such.

They never did get to the Kmart for new summer sandals like Collette had promised. Collette stuffed a white plastic bag with Sharla's bunched-up shorts and a couple of tops, a too-small swimsuit, and the pajamas with the kitten on it. Collette said, "Mothers send their kids to camp, don't they? And boarding school if they got the money. No difference, so."

"Yeah, but it ain't camp," her neighbor friend Krystal said.

"I could give a shit, Krystal. Anyways, it's only till September and Emilio's car accident money runs out."

Sharla knew her numbers, so there was no good reason why Collette had to walk her all the way over to Addy Shadd's. If she wasn't retarded, though Emilio suspected she was, she'd find number four on the mud lane. Besides, Emilio couldn't wait to fuck Collette on that green velveteen La-Z-Boy in the living room without worrying Sharla'd walk in on them again.

Collette lived off welfare and whatever boyfriend. You'd guess her about seventeen if you didn't know she was twenty-two. She was shapely, with creamy white skin, dyed blond hair, and rare-colored eyes that men said things about sincerely. She fucked Emilio good after she found out how much he'd be getting from the settlement. Emilio knew he'd be gone when his money was gone. He didn't care. Just looking at her mouth made him throb.

When it was time to leave for Addy Shadd's, Emilio hustled Sharla out the door. "Have fun swinging with them porch monkeys."

Sharla was confused because she hadn't been told there'd be monkeys. Collette waved, whispering sad things about sending off her baby girl. Emilio patted her shoulder and pretended he didn't think she was full of shit.

In spite of the name of the place, there was no view of Lake Erie from the trailer park. And in spite of the claims, no way you could see across the lake to Cleveland on the American side, even on the clearest of days. Addy Shadd had settled at the trailer park in the late fifties because it was as close to the water as she could get on the money she had. She thought it'd just be a temporary address, but after twenty years at the park she accepted that she'd never have a real lake view.

The weather'd been dry. Sun baked the mud lane where Mum Addy and most of the other colored people lived and formed it into rivulets of hard earth. Hurt to walk on in bare feet and no good for a bicycle tire. Between the evenly spaced white and silver trailers, tomato and cucumber plants got ready to choke up cages of rusty chicken wire. On most of the squares in front there were old wood chairs and dented trashcans, a patch of crabgrass or nothing. But Mum Addy grew those tiny, white, piss-smelling flowers on her square and felt the better for beautifying her neighborhood.

Sharla was squatting on her haunches, picking up kernels of hard Indian corn from a pile near a shabby trailer somewhere on the way to Addy Shadd's. She knew she was stealing the makings of some child's necklace because each red or purple or golden kernel already had a neat hole in the middle from a needle pierce. She wanted the kernels and meant to make her own pretty necklace, maybe for Collette.

As Sharla pinched the corn gems out of the dust and dropped them into her white plastic bag, she imagined her necklace and how it'd be admired. She saw the shadow, but not soon enough. The foot caught her in the small of her back and drove her into the ground. She turned around to see who'd kicked her, blocking the sun with her hand. "What, Fawn?"

Fawn Trochaud was seven years old and lived with her Aunt Krystal in the trailer across from Sharla and Collette. Fawn had curly yellow hair and cloud white skin and big blue eyes like a picture-Bible angel. Sharla knew the Indian corn didn't belong to Fawn. She also knew it didn't matter.

Sharla got up, clutching the white plastic bag, watching Fawn. She didn't dare speak. Fawn took a step closer, kicking dust at Sharla with her dog-chewed flip-flops. Sharla flinched, thinking Fawn meant to hit her. But Fawn didn't strike again. She just ripped the plastic bag from Sharla's clutches and ran away.

A couple of bored mutts started a fight on the road. Sharla watched them, thinking she'd feel better and know what to do next if she could cry. But Sharla didn't cry, ever, and she had no sense of why.

Collette knew why. It happened when Sharla was almost two years old. She'd been an early walker but didn't get out of her crib much so she'd lost her head start. She had a few words: *Mummy, bottle, stinky, lighter, juice.* Collette's boyfriend at the time, Wally, was a huge man with shoulders so wide he had to duck and go sideways to fit through the trailer door. Sharla recalled him coming into her tiny baby room, filling it up like water in a glass, with his yeasty breath and cigarette hair.

It was a late fall day, smelling of McIntosh apples and maple-leaf fire. Baby Sharla shuffled to the back of the crib, grinding the nipple of her empty bottle with her tiny white teeth. Wally'd come to get something from the room. He stumbled in, in all his bigness, and banged his shin hard on the edge of the old crib. He screamed, *Jesus Fuck, Collette!*, raised his leg and kicked the rickety crib like he wanted to send it through the wall.

Little Sharla'd been steadying herself with her hand on the edge of the crib, and when Wally kicked it, her chubby brown fingers got slammed between the crib and the wall. Collette came in, fierce about the noise and the screaming. "Shit, Wally! You fucking asshole! Why'd you get her going?!"

"I never laid a finger! I never fucking touched her!"

Collette threw a "Shh" Sharla's way and pushed Wally out of the room, banging the door shut behind her.

Baby Sharla screamed and tried to pull her mashed fingers out from between the wall and the crib. She used her words. "Mummy. Hand. Mummy. Hand. Mummy. Mummy! Mummy! Mum-my!"

Collette only came back into the room to yell, "Shut up! Shut up and go to sleep!"

An hour passed while Sharla cried. She puked up sour milk and Chef Boyardee supper, chewed the rubber nipple off her empty bottle and cried some more. The sound of the television in the living room went up, then off. There was no sound, then a *click-click* and banging metal noise. Baby Sharla knew her mother and Wally'd gone out the door and there was no one left to hear her. She stopped crying then and never did again for a long, long time.

After a while, Sharla's fingers went numb. The quiet made her sleepy. She wanted to sink down into her sour, puked-on blanket but she couldn't sink down because of her hand being jammed, so she rested her forehead on the soft part of her arm and closed her puffy eyes.

In the morning, Collette was sick from too much Southern Comfort, grateful that Sharla was quiet and letting her sleep in. Around noon she thought she better go check though because her daughter had never slept that late before. Baby Sharla was standing up in the crib, her head turned to the window, runny shit spilling out the edges of her diaper. She acted like she didn't hear her mother open the door. Collette knew Sharla was mad about last night and going to be a brat all day to make her pay for it.

The smell in the room made Collette gag, then she saw the puke on the blankets and decided Sharla was going to get a smack so she'd learn. Collette reached into the crib with her fingernails. She took Sharla by the armpits to lift her out but she was stuck. That's when Collette saw the arm, purple and blue up to the elbow, the smashed fingers swollen like sausages. Collette said, "Shit," and pulled the crib from the wall. Sharla didn't move her hand. She couldn't. Collette said, "Shit" again and called for Wally.

Wally was gone forever the next day. Collette took care to change the bandage on Sharla's hand and let her have a bottle whenever she wanted. She let her out of her crib more too, with Wally gone and being lonely for company. Collette even brought Sharla a present — a fat, mewling, orange and white kitten from the box under Krystal's porch. Collette called the kitten Trixie and thought of getting her fixed but never did. Sharla fell on Trixie twice the first day, pulled her tail and fed her Cracker Jacks. Trixie learned early to make herself scarce.

When a few weeks passed and Sharla could pick up a banana with the mashed fingers, Collette felt satisfied she was healed and that was the end of it. They never saw much of Trixie, though the bowls of cat food kept disappearing. Collette was sorry she brought the cat home at all, because now she had to put up with Trixie's heat screaming in the middle of the night and all the Toms squirting on her broken screen door.

*A*nd so Sharla stood now in the hot sun somewhere on the way to the stranger Addy Shadd's, wishing she could cry and that someone would tell her what to do. There was no point in going after Fawn and the white plastic bag. The only thing she missed out of it was the Indian corn anyway. But she felt funny showing up at Addy Shadd's without her bag of summer clothes and didn't want to be asked questions about why Collette would send her empty-handed.

Sharla started walking toward the mud lane hoping some idea would jump in her head, and when she saw some ladies' clothes hanging from a clothesline, one did. Sharla could hear the TV on in the trailer beside the clothesline so she snuck over quietly and pulled off three things fast — a pair of big underpants, a shiny triangle-print blouse, and a blue-flower housedress with square pockets on the front.

There was something churning in Sharla's stomach. Maybe it was her shame at stealing the clothes, maybe it was because she was getting closer to Addy Shadd's trailer, or maybe it was that she hadn't had any breakfast. Sharla made a bundle out of the ladies' clothes and squinted at the sun. She kicked up dust to amuse herself but wished she hadn't because of the way it stuck to her damp shins. Her shoes made *scuffa scuffa* sounds as she went along.

Except for the fact it wasn't paved, the mud lane was pretty much like the rest of the park, lined with white and silver trailers, most permanent, some ready to hitch and go. Little space to play or have a catch except the road. Cars, some better, some worse, parked everywhere. Sharla started at the bottom of the lane, looking up at the numbers, knowing that twenty-eight was a lot bigger than four. Up ahead, she could see two colored children she knew. Nedda was the girl and Lionel Chase was the boy.

Nedda looked up at Sharla and smalled her eyes. "What do *you* want?"

Sharla clutched the clothes in her hands and said, "Hi, Lionel."

Lionel looked up and said nothing. Lionel Chase hardly ever said anything and Sharla liked him best of all the children in the trailer park. He had eyelashes nearly as long as Fawn's, and his lips smiled even when he wasn't happy or thinking something's funny.

Sharla pointed at the bouquet of yellow dandelions in Nedda's hand and said, "Know what?"

Nedda sneered. "What?"

"Know how you can tell if you like your butter?"

Nedda was curious. "How?"

"You put a dandelion here, under your chin, and if it shines yellow, you like your butter. If it don't shine nothing you like your margereen."

Nedda put the dandelion under her chin and turned to Lionel, asking in a furry purry way, "Do I like my butter?"

Lionel didn't say anything. Nedda shrugged and dropped the dandelion bouquet, dragging Lionel Chase away from Sharla Cody.

Her stomach was empty and her legs were achy, so Sharla thought she better sit on the big pink rock out front of the slick silver trailer no one lived in. Sharla liked to sit on the pink rock when she came down the mud lane. It was shaped like a catcher's mitt and her bum felt good nestled against the hot smooth stone. She could sit there all day if nobody chased her off.

She might have fallen asleep because of the sun and the smooth pink rock. Maybe she didn't sleep at all and she'd only blinked, but she thought the sun had moved in the sky and she felt shivery when she opened her eyes and saw Lionel Chase standing there with his long lashes and smiling lips. Lionel looked different though, a big welt on the side of his head like he'd recently got a smack. He turned to look up the road, and Sharla looked too.

There was a big old colored lady moving toward them, huffing and wheezing and smoking and blowing. *Addy Shadd,* Sharla said in her head. Lionel stood in front of Sharla, both of them watching the lady get closer and closer, no one saying anything till the lady reached the pink rock.

Sharla looked up and smiled but the lady didn't smile back. Instead she reached down, yanked the clothes bundle away with one hand and raised the other to give Sharla a slap. The little girl cowered. Lionel said just one thing: "Don't."

The big smoking lady put her hand down. Then just like that she started back down the lane with the clothes, blowing her smoke and shaking her head.

Sharla looked at Lionel, but before she could ask, "That Addy Shadd?" he turned and walked away.

Sharla was afraid. What if Addy Shadd was going to tell Emilio and Collette that no little clothes thief was going to live with her now or ever? She ran, fast as her splayed legs would allow, all the way back to Collette's trailer. She didn't know what to do when she got there though. *Hide,* was all she could think.

Sharla crouched in the trash shed behind the trailer, waving fat black flies off the rusty pail beside her. There was a broken chair that came from the kitchen set, some old bushel baskets for apples in the fall, a busted-up suitcase, and a push lawnmower she never saw get used before. Sharla kept the shed door open a crack so she could see if Addy Shadd was gonna come smoking down the road and go tell Collette what she'd done.

Careful and quiet, Sharla opened the metal door a little more, to see better and to let out the garbage smell. She could hear Emilio fart inside the trailer and a more distant sound of Collette banging pots and dishes. She jolted when she heard Emilio shout, "Fucking thing! You fucking cocksmoking thing!" He kicked something hard. Whatever it was he kicked, she hoped he broke his toe.

After a while Sharla knew it must be suppertime because she started to smell fried bologna and potatoes and orange cheese from Kraft Dinner. She thought of her last meal, the end of the groceries so they just had cream of mushroom soup from a can. She wished she had a little of that gluey soup now. The push lawnmower was digging into her back. Sharla moved the thing away, leaned up against the garbage can, and shut her eyes.

When she woke up it was night and quiet. At first Sharla didn't know where she was. She knew she'd had a bad dream but she didn't know she'd missed a storm, thunder and lightning but hardly any rain, that took out the power at the trailer park. The moon shone full and silvery through the cracked-open door and fell on the garbage pail. That's when Sharla realized she was still in the shed.

It was just a little red boot, but when she saw it in the moon-light, stuck between the bushel baskets and the broken chair, Sharla felt like laughing. She hadn't seen the boot there before, and to see something in the dark that you didn't see in the light was magic. She picked up the rubber boot and held it like a doll while she looked around for its mate. There was no second red boot to be found, but that didn't matter because Sharla's feet were too big now and she couldn't wear them anyway. She pulled out the busted-up suitcase, opened it, and put the boot inside. The little red boot gave her courage. She opened the shed door and stepped into the night. Emilio's big gray van was gone from the driveway but it was just as well if he and Collette were out. Sharla'd already decided she couldn't ask to come home.

She knew it had rained. She could smell the dampness in the air, and as she dragged her suitcase with the red boot down the mud lane, her feet sank a little and there was no dust left to kick up on her shins. There was no television sound and no radio sound and no lights in any of the trailers. It made Sharla feel like she was in a dream. She wondered if she'd wake up and still be smelling garbage in the shed.

She was counting the trailer numbers in her head, number seven, number six, number five, and right then a breeze snuck up behind her and she smelled that sweet piss smell. She didn't know it was the little white flowers. She thought it was a dog, or maybe a trailer tank was broken because that happened sometimes. She even put her fingers to her own parts to see if she'd pissed herself and just didn't know it.

The moon pushed aside a cloud and it was suddenly so bright it might have been day if it weren't night. The moonglow pointed out Addy Shadd's long white trailer, number four, and the prim square of white flowers in front. Sharla looked at the trailer, hoping it was real.

There were three metal mesh steps up to the door, and Sharla could see them clearly in the bright night. She parked her suitcase on the ground and counted as she climbed, *one, two, three.* She put her ear up against the door. There was no sound at all. Sharla'd been told never to knock when a grown-up was sleeping, so she settled on the top mesh step, thinking how it'd mark a pattern on her thighs. She looked at the night sky and breathed in the piss smell she was already starting to feel fond of. She noticed the trailer beside, smaller than this one with torn sheets for curtains and a rusty old stove outside that kids kept plastic toys inside.

That old stove made her think of Emilio and the first time he came to the trailer. It was only a few months ago, Easter Sunday, but it seemed longer. The groundhog had lied because there was enough snow on the ground to make an angel and more flakes coming down. Collette was mad because her new shoes were white sandals and she'd taken the time to paint her toenails with the Reckless Red polish her friend Krystal scoffed for her at the drugstore.

Collette washed her hair with fruity shampoo, painted stripes of pink on her cheeks, and drew blue on her eyelids. Sharla thought her mother looked like a clown but didn't say so. She watched Collette pull on her soft purple sweater with the wide-open neck. Her mother said, "Fuck Fuck Fuck," when she squeezed into the blue jeans she used to wear before she had Sharla.

Krystal Trochaud came over from across the road to see how Collette looked. Krystal liked to be the boss and acted more like Collette's mother than her friend. She'd had a baby of her own last year but it died in the night. She called it "my crib death baby" and didn't seem as sad as you might expect.

Krystal looked Collette up and down as she puffed a Kool. "Them jeans give you camel toe."

Collette looked between her legs at the way the seam split her pussy lips like a cloven hoof and knew what Krystal meant. She went to change into a different pair, but put on her new sandals because they were just going to stay in the house all day anyway. Her heels went *click-clickety-click* on the linoleum.

Sharla was watching TV and eating chocolate malt balls shaped like Easter eggs. Krystal sat down beside her on the couch. She said, "Emilio's got a good job. Got a van too. Wouldn't that make a difference for getting groceries and whatever?"

Sharla pressed a malt ball to the roof of her mouth.

"You better be nice to him, Sharla. Your butt's gonna be at foster care if Collette loses this trailer."

Sharla didn't want to be at foster care, so she sat up straight on the couch and stopped eating the malt balls, deciding she should give the rest to Collette's new boyfriend with the van.

The inside part of the oven was on and that was unusual because Collette mostly used the burners. It made the trailer hot, and when Sharla complained, Collette set her teeth and said, "Go put your fucking shorts on then."

Emilio was late. The trailer got hotter and hotter. Whatever was inside the oven was still pink. Sharla'd never seen it before but it smelled good, like something cooked in one of the red brick houses in Chatham. Sharla hoped they wouldn't have to wait till dark to eat the meat because the only thing in her stomach were a few chocolate malt balls.

There was no knock at the door. It scared Sharla when Emilio just walked right in and stood on the mat looking at her like *she* shouldn't be there. Emilio wasn't short but neither did he have to duck to get in the door. His head was shiny black waves and his face was a good one with round dark eyes and a not-too-big nose and thick red lips you might see on a pretty girl. Sharla liked the look of him, but he didn't like the look of her and she knew it.

Sharla made room for him on the sofa, and when he sat down, she gave him what was left of her malt balls, only four or five melty ones because she'd gotten so hungry waiting. Emilio looked in the bag and scratched his head, and he didn't say *thank you* or *wasn't that thoughtful*. He called, "Collette?! Hey, Collette, you know your kid's out here dressed like an idiot? There's snow on the ground and she's in goddamned summer shorts!"

When Collette came down the hall, Emilio got up off the couch. There was a mean look on his face but Collette didn't look scared. She kissed his mouth and said she was glad he was getting to know Sharla a little. Emilio and Collette kept on kissing, and when Emilio's tongue wormed out between his lips, Sharla turned away.

All the sudden, after waiting all day, that pink meat was coming out of the oven and set on the table with nothing else. Sharla was hungry. "We gonna eat?"

Collette's cheeks were red under the pink stripes. She hardly looked at her daughter. "Have a little ham to tide you over. We'll be back in a bit."

Sharla watched Emilio go down the long hall to Collette's bedroom and waited till the door closed. She turned the channel on the television, wishing for cartoons but there was only sports and news. She sat down at the table and tore at the ham with her fingers, loving the sweet burnt taste of it.

*S*harla *didn't know how long* she'd been sitting there on Addy Shadd's step when the metal door screeched open behind her. She held her breath. She couldn't see any person in the trailer, but a voice came through the screen, deep as a man's and like she'd just swallowed pudding.

"You Sharla Cody?" was all the voice said before it opened the screen door to let her in. Sharla rose, but her legs buckled because of sitting so still and quiet for so long. She felt queasy, but the feeling eased up when she stepped inside.

The trailer was dark, but warm and thick with some smell Sharla didn't know. Sharla heard the sound of a match being struck and then there was a flame on a candle and a big shadow on the wall. The candle was set on the table and a chair dragged across the floor. The lady who sat down in the chair was not the one whose clothes she'd stolen from the line, and Sharla felt relieved.

Addy Shadd leaned her face toward the light and lit a long slim cigarette on the candle, saying, "You don't look atall like your Mama."

"I got a Dad. He just don't live with us" was all Sharla could think to respond.

The old lady crooked her finger at a chair across from her and said, "Sit down, Honey," in that thick pudding voice. Sharla took the chair and stared.

Addy Shadd's skin was the color of root beer, so wrinkled and stretched it looked like there was enough of it to cover two people. Her hair was sparkly white and unpinned to make a halo around her long face. On each side of that halo was the well of her ears, which were not just enormous, but stuck out from her head like wings. Her eyes were hooded and rheumy. Her nose was broad, with round nostrils that made flute sounds when she breathed out. The lines around her lips puckered like a bum when she smoked her cigarette.

Sharla liked the looks of Addy Shadd and thought how no one ever called her Honey before. She felt like she'd like to pat down Addy Shadd's sparkly white hair. She felt like she'd like to kiss Addy Shadd's pucker bum mouth and to sit in her skinny lap and bury her nose in the folds of her neck.

Addy Shadd took a long puff and blew the words out with the smoke. "Where you been, Honey?"

Sharla was puzzled by the question because Addy Shadd had just seen her sitting on the top step of the porch. Maybe the question was a trick. Sharla knew about tricks and getting smacked for the wrong answer. "Out there on the porch?"

Addy Shadd couldn't tell if Sharla was sassing but suspected she was so she didn't say Honey this time. "Where you been before that?"

Sharla recalled slowly. "The shed?"

"You suppose to come this afternoon."

"I know."

"I figured you'd be coming along tomorrow. I'd have called if I had a telephone."

"We don't got no telephone too."

"That right?"

Sharla nodded. "We're getting it back though."

"Where's your Mama?"

Sharla shrugged. "In Emilio's van?"

"Who brung you here?"

"She said I could go by myself."

"All by yourself?"

"I know my numbers."

"That may be, but I never knew a Mama to send a child out in the middle of the night like that, did I?"

Sharla didn't answer because she didn't know what all Addy Shadd knew of mothers and their children. The old woman brought her cigarette to her mouth but a wracking cough stopped her from sucking on it.

Sharla allowed her eyes to leave the candle glow on the face of Addy Shadd and roam around the trailer. The walls were paneled in gray barn board and there were pictures here and there but she couldn't make them out in the dim light. There was a skinny hallway, not as long as Collette's, that led to a bathroom and back bedroom. The living room was up front, the kitchen in the middle, and that was about it.

On the shelf that separated the kitchen from the living room, there was a collection of salt'n'pepper shakers — cornstalks and green apples and red lobsters and entwined dolphins and Mounted Police and dancing ladies and pairs of everything under the sun. Sharla noticed the pullout couch with a big soft pillow and blue plaid blanket. She said out loud with a marvel Addy Shadd didn't quite catch, "I'm gonna live here."

"Did your Mama give you the envelope?"

Sharla thought of what Collette put inside the white plastic bag. "I don't think so."

"You're suppose to have an envelope for me."

"I don't have no envelope."

Addy Shadd suspected she was being played and didn't care for that, especially not at half past midnight when she'd waited and worried and wondered all day. She was not at all sure she wanted this fat sassy child living in her home.

"Well, you was suppose to bring an envelope with money for your food and your whatnot."

Sharla shrugged and tried to recall if Collette put a money envelope in that white plastic bag, and if she did, Fawn Trochaud was rich.

Addy Shadd coiled her lips around her cigarette. "Where's your things, Child?"

"What things?"

Addy Shadd's patience was used up. "Your things. Your things. Don't you have no suitcase, Miss Sassafrass?"

Sharla felt sick again. It took a full minute for her to remember she left her suitcase outside. She stood up and started out the door but came right back because she had to know, "You gonna let me back in though?"

Addy Shadd truly did not know what to make of this child and decided she was either simple or strange. Then she supposed simple or strange was all right as long as she wasn't sassy. She stood at the door and watched Sharla in the moonlight.

The child was school age, five or six. Addy couldn't quite recall what that white trash mother told her when she came knocking on her door just a few days ago. Collette sat down in the chair, crossed her pretty legs, folded her arms under her substantial bosom, and told Addy Shadd all about herself and her foreigner boyfriend but little about the child she wished to lodge. She said her boyfriend had been busted up in a car accident and needed time to recover. She said, "I just can't have Sharla around making noise all day when alls Emilio needs to do is sleep."

Looking at the young woman sitting across from her, Addy had a sudden, staggering recollection of her own youth. She remembered her own pretty legs and ample bosom and the certain way she'd walk to show herself off. How long had it been, she wondered, since she'd been admired, or done the admiring herself? "I understand," Addy'd said about Collette's situation, though she was naturally suspicious of the woman and her intentions.

Collette said, "I can give you a hundred dollars for two summer months. That's my baby bonus plus. Emilio's got his rugby Sundays so I can take her then, but not overnight."

"Rugby? How can your man play rugby if he's all busted up?"

Collette fumbled, "Oh. Yeah. Well, he's just scorekeeping now. Anyways, it's just till Sharla starts school and I promise she won't bother you. Give her a bag of chips and send her outside."

All Addy Shadd could think is *what kind of Mama asks a stranger to take care of her own baby girl?* Collette knew what she was thinking, and she put her eyes on the floor. "I don't have family to go to or I would. My Mum died when I was nine years old and last time I saw my Dad he got the hose out after me, so."

"Why'd he get the hose out after you?"

"Him and Delia said I stole twenty dollars from the flour jar, which I did not."

"Mmm-hmm."

Collette glanced at her watch and knew Emilio was waiting to go look for packing boxes. "I could probably find another fifteen dollars being there's still a few days left in June. I was hoping to move her over just as soon as you say. I could probably find another twenty."

Addy Shadd had already decided to take the child, and though it's true she could use the money, mostly she saw the child as a gift. She was seventy years old and had been alone for decades. She liked the idea of having a sweet little thing running in and out of her trailer.

But, Addy Shadd thought looking at her now, *Sharla Cody was no sweet little thing.* She was tall for her age with a funny shape to her. Her fat legs touched at the top and splayed out at her feet. She had a big rolly stomach and shorter-than-usual arms that stuck out instead of hanging from her shoulders. Her heavy head was propped up by a short thick neck, and her small eyes hid in a cave of lid and cheek. There was no sign of sweetness whatever in her expression. The one thing you might say was cute on Sharla was her nose, a little round button set just right over her plush crooked lips.

Collette never mentioned to Addy Shadd what Sharla looked like and it never occurred to her to ask. Collette also never mentioned that Sharla was mixed, but there was no question her Daddy was colored. Sharla's caramel skin didn't come from Collette, and neither did her tight coils of black hair. Addy Shadd knew first-hand about half-and-half children.

Sharla got her suitcase from where she parked it on the ground, and Addy Shadd watched her turn around in the moon-light and start back up the stairs. Sharla swayed on her legs. She had bubbles of sweat on her lip and was feeling all the hotter because she just came in from a breeze. She set the suitcase down and it fell over on its side. "Shit."

Addy Shadd felt her smacking hand itch. "Didn't your Mama teach you not to cuss?"

Sharla shook her head but it made her feel dizzy and confused.

The old woman pointed at the suitcase. "Open it up, Child. Likely your Mama put my envelope in there."

Sharla shook her head. "There ain't no envelope in there."

Addy Shadd got serious. "If you did something with that money and you are lying to me now, you're going straight back to your Mama and that boyfriend of hers and I won't never think of you again. You understand?"

Sharla said nothing, so Addy Shadd lifted the suitcase up to the table, unbuckled the strap and opened it up. She looked at the red rubber boot and she looked at Sharla and back at the boot. Collette Cody was either simple or just dog mean.

"That's all she sent you with? That's all you brung? One dirty old red boot?"

Sharla was much too tired to explain about the white plastic bag and the clothesline and the smoking lady. She hadn't eaten a thing all day and she could feel her kneecaps shifting on her leg bones. She looked at Addy Shadd's foggy eyes in the candlelight and opened her mouth to speak, but she must have blown the candle out because everything went dark.

Addy Shadd didn't have the quickness in her old body to catch the little girl before she fell unconscious and hit her head on the salt'n'pepper shaker shelf. She cursed Collette for knocking on her door and cursed herself for thinking a stranger's child could bring her anything but grief. She nearly cursed Sharla too, but when she saw the little girl's head was bleeding, she winched herself up on her lean old legs.

It was just a habit that Addy Shadd flipped the switch in the tiny bathroom, but when the light came on she realized the power was back and it felt like a miracle. She grabbed a soft, embroidered hand towel from under the sink, then opened the medicine cabinet and found a box of bandages and the orange iodine.

Back in the kitchen the old woman turned on the light and saw that her Mountie pepper shaker, her wheatsheaf salt, and her dolphin pair were all broken on the ground near Sharla's head. She got to her knees, took Sharla's little brown hand, and was relieved to find a strong steady pulse.

Addy Shadd guided the big head of springy curls onto her own narrow lap, not caring about the blood on her thin nightdress. She tunneled through the thick coils with her nicotine fingers and stopped when she found a goose egg. There was a gash on the swell, small but deep. She held the edge of her good towel there until the bleeding stopped, then she dabbed some orange iodine and tried to cover it with a medium-size bandage that wouldn't stick.

Addy Shadd stayed on the floor, absently stroking Sharla's soft cheek. She thought of her whole long life and all the times she'd seen a person go unconscious and tried to remember what all got done for them. She recalled when her brother Leam got kicked in the head by that ugly horse on Mr. Kenny's farm in Rusholme. He slept two days straight then woke up smelling asparagus, which wasn't even in season. She recalled when she fell out of the apple tree in the backyard and lost her sense of words for a full day. She also recalled, though she wished she hadn't, what happened at the river with Chester Monk. She quickly pushed Chester Monk and Rusholme from her mind and focused on the child.

Sharla's wound wasn't too serious but she shouldn't be moved, was the conclusion Addy came to. The other conclusion was that she was taking Sharla Cody back to her mother in the morning. She'd been crazy to accept responsibility for the child, and she could see now it would never work.

Addy Shadd rose again, and with all the up and down tonight, she was glad she'd gotten the winter rust out of her bones working her little garden out back and tending her white flowers in the square out front. She gathered up the blue plaid blanket and the soft pillow from the pullout couch and brought them to where Sharla lay still and quiet on the kitchen floor. She tucked the pillow under Sharla's head and put the blanket over her.

As Addy Shadd was set to rise, Sharla opened her eyes. "Mum?"

"Shh. Close your eyes now."

"It's hot."

"I know. Close your eyes, Honey."

"Smells like Ivory soap."

"Shh now, Honey. Shh."

Sharla looked at the old woman directly. "I wish you was my Mum."

"You got a Mama, little girl."

"You could be my Mum though. Mum." Sharla closed her eyes, and because it felt good rolling off her sleepy tongue, said it once more, "Mum."

Addy Shadd cleaned the broken china pieces from beside Sharla's slumbering head. When she was finished, the old woman pushed herself up and sat down in a hardback kitchen chair. She watched the big little girl sleeping on the floor, and though she knew she might regret it, she allowed her thoughts to return to Rusholme.

Rusholme

There were mostly colored families in Rusholme when Adelaide Shadd was a young girl. The town had been settled entirely by colored people, fugitive slaves from the United States, in the mid-1800s. In the red brick schoolhouse on King Street, they taught their children the rare history of the land and how it came to be theirs. It was told to each generation, like a storybook legend, how the Good Lord came to an American man, a white reverend called Mills. The Lord spoke to him in his sleep, telling him to rise with the sun and set his fourteen slaves free. The Reverend Mills understood the word of the Lord and he rose and set the people free. But to further atone for his grave sins against them, the Lord said deliver those people to the North, from the hateful and ignorant, to a land that shall be theirs.

Like all the children of Rusholme, Addy Shadd learned about Reverend Mills, who brought those fourteen and more across the border to freedom in Canada. She learned that after enduring a long winter and much hardship, they found the land by the lake. She was taught how Reverend Mills disregarded the people in neighboring Chatham who said it was wrong and organized the many who knew it was right. How they set aside a tract of ten thousand acres and sold it to the colored settlers for whatever they could pay. She imagined how the land had been, thick with woods of oak and hickory and maple and ash, and how her people cleared the trees, revealed the dark soil, and became tillers of their own rich earth.

Those first people of Rusholme felt like they were born to the place and knew it was a better world than the one they'd left. In Chatham and other nearby towns such as Dresden, Amherstburg, and Shrewsbury, there were a thousand fugitive slaves and more coming North every day on the Underground Railroad. The railroad was not one of steel rails and wood ties, but a series of routes on which the slaves could find safe places to hide, and men and women to conduct them.

The slaves escaped their captors at night, guided by the stars, hiding in the southern swamps and bayous, then farther north in the forests and waterways, helped by the Quakers and other friends of freedom, hunted by federal marshals, bounty seekers, and mad dogs. There were no maps. The fugitives passed information by mouth, in stories and in song.

Rusholme was a terminus on the Underground Railroad. The town rejoiced when men found freedom, grieved when they perished, and worried when they were expected but had not yet arrived. All of Rusholme suspected, when Harriet Beecher Stowe's *Uncle Tom's Cabin* appeared in 1852, that *Uncle Tom* was really one of the Railroad's most famous conductors, Josiah Henson, and his *cabin* really that shack in the woods in neighboring Dresden. Reverend Henson had published his autobiography years earlier and believed it was the inspiration for Stowe's novel. His fame spread, and when the Reverend was sent to England to see Queen Victoria, Rusholme celebrated. It was quite a thing for a black man to meet the Queen.

Generations later, when Adelaide Shadd was a girl in the early 1920s, Josiah Henson and the Underground Railroad were but a memory and booze-toting bootleggers ruled the day. Rusholme was clear-cut and you could see all the way to the clean blue lake. Larger and grander farms flanked the smaller original ones, a few owned by white farmers, but still mostly colored. A new network of roads conveyed the freshly spawned black Ford trucks and autos through the township, and the Libby's canning factory in neighboring Chatham was expanding to meet the bounty of the land.

Addy's father, Wallace Shadd, got a good position in construction on the Libby's factory site that paid him more money in one week than he made in two weeks being handyman for Theodore Bishop. Wallace hadn't liked his former employer much, even though, or maybe because, Bishop was the richest black man in Rusholme. Addy and her brother, L'il Leam, didn't have to work in the fields that summer because of Wallace doing so well, but their mother, Laisa, said "idle hands," and wrung her own, imagining what mischief her near-grown children might be getting up to in a long hot summer.

Addy and L'il Leam, who'd complained bitterly about the farmwork last summer, begged to return to Mr. Kenny's fields in spite of the family not needing the money. Mr. Kenny was a fat white man with a twisted red nose and a farm nearly big as Teddy Bishop's. Addy and L'il Leam couldn't remember a summer they didn't work Mr. Kenny's fields and though neither thought of him in a fatherly way, they did think of his farm as a second home.

Laisa liked to have the little house on Fowell Street to herself anyway and was relieved her children cared to work. Wallace said though he'd have to approve how they spent it, Addy and L'il Leam could keep whatever money they earned and not put it in the family coffer. Addy dreamed of a wool coat for winter and a gold-filled hat-pin from the Sears catalogue. L'il Leam dreamed of Birdie Brown.

The winter'd been long and Addy was eager to return to the fields with the spicy smelling foreign ladies and the whole gang of boys and men from last year. They'd start on asparagus, then do peas, strawberries, tomatoes, and corn. In between the picking there were horses and pigs and chickens to tend and all of it done under the good blazing sun.

Addy loved to feel her bones and muscles as she bent and stretched over the neat green rows. She'd hitch the back of her long cotton skirt through her legs and tuck it up into the front.

She did that for ease of movement and to let the smooth skin of her calves enjoy the glances of the men beside her in the field. She was aware the men admired her strength and speed and how she could fill baskets all day and never resort to sitting on her behind and dragging it through the dirt like some of the foreign ladies did. But the real reason she chose the field this year, and she'd confess it to him soon enough, was to be near Chester Monk.

At fifteen years old Addy was womanly, with full breasts, a smallish waist, and a high round behind. Laisa noted unhappily that Addy'd grown the curves over winter and knew, because she was a mother and a woman, that her daughter would be thinking thoughts this spring. The time had come to sit her down and Laisa wrung her hands at the thought of it.

It was a gray May afternoon and they'd had an unpleasant walk back from church. Addy'd been dreamy and vacant during the service and never joined in with but one hymn. Laisa scolded her daughter for her posture and propriety, and Addy felt wicked for hating her mother on a Sunday.

Laisa found Addy on the back porch of their tidy brick home and forgot to bring the walnut squares she'd made as a gesture of forgiveness. She ensured they were out of earshot of her father and brother before she took one of Addy's strong working hands and said, "I'm gonna give you a gift and it's the truth, and the kind only comes from a Mama that loves you."

Laisa took a long breath, wishing her voice were softer. "You ain't no beauty, Adelaide Shadd, and it's just as well to know that now. You got stick-out ears and hood eyes, and a long face like your Daddy and go ask yourself if he a looker."

Addy didn't want her mother's gift. She pulled her hand away and itched to run when she realized there was more.

"I see the way the men put eyes on your behind and don't get a smirk, Little Girl, because I see the way you move that behind to keep them eyes looking."

Addy felt thrilled and shamed by the talk and fixed her sight on a black squirrel sniffing around the apple tree at the far end of the yard.

"You know you got the holes betwix your legs, and you know what they for because we talk about that when your blood come. But Addy, look at me, you move that behind the way you do and you just asking for the men to go digging your hole. 'Specially them white boys 'cause they think you think they best. You understand?"

Addy hated her mother and thought she was mean to talk about her stick-out ears and un-Christian to speak of her holes on a Sunday. She watched the squirrel drag itself up the apple tree like it was still hungry but tired of looking.

"If you get a man go sticking hisself there, you know you can get a baby outta that. You understand? I ask if you understand me, Daughter?"

"Yes, Ma'am."

"Yes, Ma'am. And I'm here to tell you, that you ain't got the beauty of a girl like Beatrice Brown and no boy's gonna fall in love and take you for his wife just because you got a baby from him. You understand that?"

"Yes, Ma'am."

"And if you don't listen to the truth I'm telling you, and if you go lifting up your skirt for some boy, do not bring no baby back here to this good home of ours."

Addy had no intention of bringing a baby home, and she thought she'd like to strike her mother and run away forever for the suggestion. She barely whispered, "I hate you."

Laisa's eyebrows lifted her lips to her nose. "I do beg your pardon?"

Addy said nothing and was surprised she didn't get a pinch.

"Now you get, and think on what I said. And Adelaide, Child, look at me, don't never say a mean thing against your own Mama because you bring the Lord's vengeance down on your head and I can't save you from that."

By trying not to think on what Laisa told her, Addy could not think on much else. Only one thing could distract her mind and that was a glimpse of Chester Monk. Didn't matter if he had a shovel full of horseshit and a hard face from the stink, or if he was laughing in that throaty way and wiping the field dust off a big red berry before taking it in his teeth. Addy thought if anyone could see beauty in her hood eyes and stick-out ears, it was Chester Monk. She knew if she got a baby outta that with him, he'd walk her down the long church aisle and promise to be her man forever and a day.

Chester Monk had been in Rusholme three summers and before that Addy didn't know. He had smooth brown skin, a fine square head and thick strong neck. His black pupils floated in oval ponds shaded by curled-up lashes. His mouth was wide with straight white teeth. He smiled well and often, teased all the girls equal, and said he didn't love only one. Addy knew he just meant to be kind, but thought it was wrong in the end, to give the others false hope.

Chester was only sixteen years old but he was already bigger than most men and twice the size of L'il Leam, who'd been sickly and near passed as a child. Leam would never grow to proper size and that's why he got the Little in front of his name. Sometimes, when the farmhands were finished and stretched out on the soft grass near Mr. Kenny's barn, L'il Leam'd get an old horse blanket and climb up on the huge shoulders of Chester Monk. They'd fix that big blanket so you couldn't see Chester's head and make it look like L'il Leam was some funny giant with thin stick arms and thick strong legs. They'd laugh to sore stomachs and say do it again, do it again, when Chester Monk complained it's too hot and get off now.

Chester Monk was nowhere near done growing. It was speculated he might get as tall as Big Zach Heron, the oldest of the farmhands and a boyhood friend of Wallace Shadd. So far Mr. Heron was the biggest man, colored or white, in the whole lake region, and that was proven in the contest at the Harvest Fair last year. Heron was a man who could be counted on, and L'il Leam admired him above all others. He was still Wallace Shadd's closest friend. He had a tiny, frightened wife called Isobel, and he liked to whistle a tune when he walked.

On the third Sunday in June, all of Rusholme was gathering for the annual Strawberry Supper. They'd be having the picnic on the church lawn after service since the Lord was good and there was no rain in sight. The winter'd been bitter with a short, sharp spring and the berries were not large and luscious like last year but small and hard and densely sweet. They spread the tables with white lace cloth from home and laid them with platters of roasted meats and fish and fowl, and bread and pickled eggs and the end of the root vegetables they put up last fall. There was a whole table just for the berries, tarts and pies and cakes and jams, and bowls and bowls of them just simple, hulled, with sugar.

The lake wasn't warm enough for swimming yet, but the young people could cross the road to splash their feet as long as a few stern adults went along to keep an eye. The Pastor'd preach about temptation because of how the boys and girls'd be mixing around the campfire later on. The adults knew all about those strokes stolen behind the flames and no one wanted to see an impropriety done on Strawberry Sunday.

Addy had felt sick all morning. She thought it to be excitement because of the church supper. She'd nearly brought up her break-fast when she went to take the pie from the oven and the smell got up her nose. She asked L'il Leam to do it for her so she didn't risk the ruin of her new Sunday dress. Her older brother didn't balk at using an oven cloth and touching a pie plate like some boys would. He set the pie by the window to cool and knew that Addy wanted Chester Monk to have a slice of it and admire her touch with the pastry.

L'il Leam had his own heart set on the day. He was in love with Birdie Brown and even though she was the most beautiful girl in Rusholme, it was Leam she chose to love, because he was special and didn't know it. She was small like him, and they came eye to eye with each other when her Mama wasn't around and they had the chance, and he the courage, to have a word.

They shared a kiss when the snow melted in April and it lingered still on L'il Leam's lips. He'd been fixing his bicycle out back of the schoolhouse and Birdie'd come around the corner expressly to find him. She bent down, watching him through the wheel. "L'il Leam?"

"Why, hello, Beatrice Brown."

She pooched her lips and squinched her nose and L'il Leam thought that was the sweetest face and the only reason he called her Beatrice at all.

"Don't call me Beatrice, Leam. I don't like Beatrice and I told you so before."

He acted contrite. "I'm sorry, Birdie."

She leaned in and pressed her face through the spokes. "I ate maple sugar. Smell it?"

L'il Leam could smell the maple. He could also smell her hair and neck and the perfume of her young girl skin. He nodded and swallowed and didn't know what to do about the closeness of her pretty face.

Birdie leaned in further. Quick as a hummer and light as its feather, she brushed her cold mouth against his. "Taste it?"

L'il Leam could taste the maple sugar, and her soft mouth and smooth skin and wanted her to do it again, but he worried she might see how quick his pecker had sprung up in his trousers and be afraid of that. "You better get on now, Birdie."

Birdie smiled prettily and stood, swinging the top half of herself on the hinge of her hips. "Mama told me I get Aunt Aeline's dishes that come from London England and that's got a serving platter and a soup tureen."

L'il Leam nodded and Birdie Brown skipped off.

Birdie was Addy's age and that was one year younger than Leam and Chester. All the girls of fifteen were best friends and the best reason was there were only four of them. There was Addy and Birdie and the twins, Josephine and Camille Bishop. Josephine and Camille were soft girls, fat and spoiled, and couldn't have stood the labor of the fields even if their Daddy did think it fit work for a young woman.

The twins' Daddy, Theodore Bishop, had the biggest house and fanciest suits and a sleek new motor car he took over on the ferry to Detroit every other day. When Wallace left his employ, Addy heard her father say that Teddy Bishop was running bootleg whiskey for the Purple Gang out of Detroit. Laisa clucked her tongue. "Let us thank the Lord the good folks of this town don't take that devil's juice."

When Laisa said that, Wallace and Addy knew she meant the colored folks because Mr. Kenny was known to take whiskey every night including Sunday. And nearly all the French folks in the region liked to take bourbon and gin and whatever else they could get their hands on. The truth was, even Addy tried a taste of some burning amber fluid behind the barn with L'il Leam and the rest of the farmhands last summer. Everyone knew it had been brought there by Zach Heron. And Addy knew it was devil's juice, not the sun, that made her father's eyes shine after a day out fishing with the big man. If her mother ever found out, she'd have to wring her hands right off.

The four girls spread out a blanket under the big willow near the church graveyard, distant from the food tables and chittering children and worn-out women in their fresh spring hats. The girls caught a breeze from the east and with it the scent of Dillon's pig farm. Camille and Josephine made hostile faces at a trio of sea-gulls looking for charity. The girls knew better than to offer so much as a peach pit to a begging bird because no one needed a whole flock swooping down and spoiling the lawn.

On the grass nearby, L'il Leam was doing handstands. Birdie knew Leam was showing off for her and made sure he could tell she was impressed. When Leam finally toppled over, it was his friend Jonas Johnson's turn. Jonas was short like Leam, but pear-shaped and heavy and when he tried to stand on his hands he fell forward onto his face. Leam didn't laugh when his friend fell and that impressed Birdie most of all.

Addy didn't mean to stare, but sometimes she felt green about Birdie Brown's heart-shaped face and lay-back ears and wide almond eyes. She'd catch Chester Monk looking Birdie's way and imagine he thought of lifting that pretty girl up and pressing his lips on her little round mouth. Addy was comforted to know that Birdie loved L'il Leam. Her friend had long ago confessed she thought a man as big as Chester might well crush a girl to death.

Addy was lost in Birdie's profile, and they were under the willow so there was no shadow when Chester Monk appeared. He startled Addy when he leaned against the tree and bit into one of Isobel Heron's berry tarts. He wasn't much of a talker and hardly looked Addy's way in the field, but she knew how he felt like she knew her own name. Addy wondered if Chester'd yet sampled her pie and was sure L'il Leam would've pointed it out. She could count on her brother for such things as that.

Josephine and Camille were lost in their peas and butter, fretting about seconds on the stewed rhubarb before it all went to the Pastor's cousins. Addy dared to glance up at silent Chester leaning against the tree. She liked the way his Adam's apple rose and fell when he swallowed. She smiled to herself when his tongue found the berry lost on the ledge of his lip. She let her gaze drop further and noted that his church trousers were much too small this year and stretched tight over the lump between his legs. She was a proper young lady, but Addy felt a surge nonetheless.

Even though it was Sunday and she knew it was a sin, Addy encouraged her thoughts to roam. She imagined herself pressed against the willow, lips parted and ready to be swallowed up by Chester Monk's. She imagined his big hands creeping up from her waist, daring to touch her breasts through her new Sunday dress. She imagined leaning against him, feeling his body, his hot breath on her neck. Addy glanced at the sky briefly, hoping God was too busy to see what she was thinking.

She was still lost in her imaginings when Chester tossed his final bite of berry tart out to the gulls. The trio snapped and flapped around the morsel as all four girls looked up. Chester Monk shrugged like he didn't know what he'd done wrong and Birdie said he'd be reckoned with if the flock appeared now and they had to move from under the willow. Chester dropped down on the blanket next to Addy and acted like he hadn't meant for his arm to brush hers. He tilted his head at Birdie Brown. "Your Sunday dress is pretty, Birdie."

"Thank you, Chester."

He glanced at Addy. "Yours is too, Adelaide. Ain't from last year."

Addy smoothed the folds of her dress. "No, Chester, this here's from the catalogue bought new for today."

Chester Monk nodded and released a willow leaf snared in the hair on his arm. "Good day for the supper, wouldn't you girls say?"

The other girls stayed quiet and pretended not to be holding their breath. Addy nodded. "Yes it is. It's a very good day. Last year we had that storm."

Chester Monk nodded and was silent again. Addy stole a glimpse of his face and thought how one day they would lay naked and unashamed in their marriage bed and she would confess her wicked thoughts about him on this Strawberry Sunday. She wanted to ask him if he'd sampled her pie and was thinking how to phrase it right, when Chester took a deep breath and said, "Would you care to go for a stroll, Camille?"

The girls' jaws came unhinged all at once. Camille knew about Addy's plans for Chester but she nodded just the same, letting him take her hand and heft her to her feet.

As they walked out from under the willow, Camille looped her arm through Chester's and flashed her collection of long white teeth. She didn't look away, even when it was clear that Chester had his sights fixed on her father, Teddy, in the distance, with his black calf boot set up on the runner of his shiny new automobile.

Birdie grasped Addy's arm. Addy didn't cry but neither did she smile bravely. Josephine shook her head from side to side and said, "My sister's been thieving my possessions all my life and my Daddy never did believe me and now look she's thieving Addy Shadd's man." She crammed a boiled egg in her mouth and secretly wondered why Chester chose her twin and not her.

"Never mind about Chester." Birdie whispered softly, "There's better and more deserving boys in Rusholme. He'd never be sincere to just one girl and he's much too big anyway. *Much too big.*"

Addy felt stung. "I never saw him look sideways at Camille before. Never."

Birdie cupped her hands and whispered into Addy's ear, "We could follow them and see what."

Josephine squinted at both girls. When neither looked her way, she shrugged and headed off to the lake. Addy wanted to go home. Birdie said she'd go too and they could both have a good cry. Though Addy did want Birdie's company, she thought it'd be a good deed to tell her to stay.

Laisa didn't like the look of Addy and felt her forehead and cheeks with the back of her hand. It could be fever, but it could just be excitement and if she wanted to go home and lay herself down that was fine with Laisa if it was fine with Wallace. If she could locate her father, that is.

"We'll be singing hymns around the fire come evening if you feel well enough to come back," Laisa told her.

Addy found her father out near the cornfield with Big Zach Heron and a couple of other men. They were snickering over some bawdy joke of Mr. Heron's, Addy knew, because she'd heard a few of the same jokes and the same snickers around the farm. Wallace didn't feel her forehead and cheeks. His eyes were a certain brand of shiny, and he hadn't heard Addy or just wasn't listening because he said, "Sure. Go on and have yourself a good time, Daughter."

Home was less than a mile from the church. Addy walked slowly, her head hung low, hoping she'd been noticed and pitied. But all of Rusholme was at the supper and she passed no one on the road. She was damp and dusty by the time she got home, so she peeled off her pretty Sunday dress and draped it over the chair behind the head of her bed.

Addy pulled her cotton nightdress over her naked body and lay flat on the narrow bed. She folded her arms over her chest and pictured herself stone dead and how it would be when they found her in the morning. She thought how Chester'd feel sorry he missed the chance to sample her soft lips. How her Mama'd think she was so very beautiful and did not in fact resemble Wallace one bit. And how her Daddy'd feel guilty he never paid her much mind, and now it was too late. Then Addy realized her thoughts were sins and she'd already committed a lifetime's worth today. She watched the sheer white curtain wave back and forth at her window.

It didn't matter what picture she conjured up, it'd fog over and whip itself back into Chester Monk. She could see Chester under the shade of that willow by the graveyard, doing all the things to Camille Bishop that Addy wished he'd do to her. That made her want to cry and touch between her legs all at once and she knew truly she was going to Hell.

Chester Monk had no honest affection for Camille Bishop, and Addy knew that in her heart. But Camille's father was wealthy and powerful and she could understand why a young man might care to be in his favor. It occurred to Addy that maybe the stroll was nothing more than a way to get Teddy Bishop's attention. The thought of that made Addy hopeful and she resolved to give Chester a second chance when she saw him in the field the next day.

The white curtain in the window began to flutter and flap. The breeze became wind and the birds warbled warnings to their kin. Addy hoped they'd have a mean June storm and vengeance would rain down but hard on Camille Bishop's head. She turned her long face into the soft pillow and forced herself to cry a little longer before she fell into a deep sleep.

Some time later Addy woke groggy and confused with the feeling that someone had shaken her. It was dark in the room and must not have rained after all because there was no sense of it in the air. She could hear the voices of those gathered around the church fire rising splendidly into the night, swept up by the breeze and into her bedroom window. There was some foul yeasty smell that snuck in behind the singing, but Addy didn't think much of it, except to notice. She listened to the hymn for a time, then joined in because she knew the words and enjoyed the vibration of song in her throat.

A voice came from the chair behind her bed. "Pretty," it said, and scared the devil out of her.

Addy had but a second to turn and recognize Zach Heron rising up from the chair like a giant and no time to scream before he pounced on her and crushed her body with the enormous weight of his own. The giant held one huge salty hand over her mouth and nose. With the other hand he lifted her nightdress and wrenched her legs apart. He hissed and grunted and stabbed at her thighs. Addy thought, as she struggled for air, that he meant to kill her at one end or the other. He found her spot and jammed himself inside it. The pain was white and scalding. Her teeth tried to clamp down on his palm but she bit her own tongue and tasted blood. He dug her deep, breathing his whiskey breath into her ear, humming, "Honey, Honey, Honey, Honey, Honey, Honey, Honey." He shivered and shuddered and stopped.

Addy was taken by surprise when it was finished, much as when it began. The huge man removed his hand from her bloody mouth, pulled himself to standing, hitched up his trousers and stumbled from the room and the house, whistling some friendly tune, like it was just another day.

The faithful in the churchyard took up another hymn and their voices rose in harmony to praise the Lord, who Addy knew had already turned away.

It was a struggle to get her breath back at all and she could coax only a shallow in and out from her lungs that whole long night. She lay stiff and shivering, her hands crossed over her breasts, having resumed the death pose unaware. She heard the church singing stop and knew they'd be dousing the fire with buckets of water from the lake. She thought of the steam smoke gilding the moon.

Addy didn't stir when she heard her family return. When the door to her bedroom creaked open and her mother whispered, "Are you awake, Daughter? Are you all right?" Addy heard a tiny voice rush up from her throat to answer, "Yes, Mama. G'night."

The blood had soaked clean through the thin cotton mattress and left a pea size spot on the floor beneath the bed. Wallace was confounded at having to replace the thing and said Addy could use the money she'd earned from Kenny's or sleep on the stain, he didn't care which. Laisa didn't tell her husband the linen was ruined too. She hid the sheet in her scrap chest and would find a good use for it someday.

Laisa bled heavy like that when she was young too. You couldn't blame a woman if her cycle came early, especially when the woman was only fifteen years old and it happened in her sleep. Besides, Addy looked so sickly when Laisa went to rouse her for work Monday morning she felt nothing but tenderness and was hardly annoyed about the bed. It put her in mind of when L'il Leam nearly passed and made her wring her hands.

Addy didn't go to work at the Kenny farm that morning and never would again. She bled spots for three days and stayed in the house or yard after that. She only said a few words to her mother and L'il Leam and found a way not to speak to her father at all. She didn't believe Wallace had known or allowed what happened, but she felt betrayed by him all the same.

Though she knew the doctor'd say melancholy and prescribe castor oil and sunshine, Laisa thought they should have him come around anyway. Wallace thought it was a poor idea to indulge any female too much, and he'd already noticed a weakness for emotion in his daughter's character and didn't like it. Wallace said though it was true a woman's balance went off every month, it always came back and Addy's would too.

Laisa didn't think so. It seemed to her that Addy was so mad or sad she'd like to wring her own neck. She wasn't eating but a little bread each meal and could have been taken for consumptive. Laisa doubted by the look of her eyes that Addy was sleeping much either. If she'd known about Addy's affection for Chester Monk, Laisa might have suspected it was love sickness. But she would never believe, even if she was told it outright, the true thing that had crushed her daughter.

Birdie and Josephine came around at first but Addy would pretend she was asleep or pick up some neglected sewing and beg her Mama to send them away. Camille stayed away altogether, feeling responsible for Addy's grief. She wanted Josephine to tell Addy that Chester Monk only took her for a stroll to ask was it true her father was looking for a few men to expand his business? And was it true he'd pay twice what Mr. Kenny would? And if so, could she walk him on over there to her Daddy's shiny new auto and introduce him as a friend?

Addy was rocking quietly in a chair set back from the window, feeling hot and parched and suddenly hungry, hungrier than she'd felt in some time. The hunger alone lifted her spirit, and she wondered if she might come back to herself after all. She wondered if she might eat a biscuit, or a chicken leg, or one of the blood ripe tomatoes L'il Leam brought home from the farm, and feel altogether different.

And for the hundredth time since Strawberry Sunday, Addy thought of Chester Monk. She thought of him in the field, having stripped the shirt from his strong brown back, bending over the tomato plants, working in a steady rhythm to fill the bushel baskets. She imagined him rising to full height, maybe he'd grown even taller over the summer, stretching out and biting into a tomato like it was an apple. She thought how he'd wipe the juice off his chin with the back of his hand, if he cared about it at all. The idea of Chester Monk made her smile, surprised she remembered how.

Addy rocked and rocked and soon a pleasant hum rose up to tease her tongue. Though she could never forgive him his trespass, maybe she could take the memory of Mr. Heron and what he'd done to her in those few wrong moments, put them in a boat and sail that boat out to the middle of the lake. Maybe she could imagine it all happened to someone else, and maybe it did, because she was nowhere near the same girl now. Maybe to help her put it out of her mind, she'd ask L'il Leam if Chester was well and how he was finding the fields this summer. Was the corn high? Was the lake warm? Did it look like the pumpkins would be early or late?

When finally Addy did ask her brother about Chester Monk, she was unprepared for his response. "Chester's gone, Addy. He's over in Sandwich bootlegging for Teddy Bishop." Leam had added darkly, "I wouldn't count on him coming back."

Her legs had seized upon hearing the news. Her tongue too. She stood, numb and dumb, watching her brother watch her. Was it possible she'd been wrong about Chester? Could it be he hadn't loved her after all? If she could be wrong about something she felt so certain, how could she ever trust her judgment again?

When it was clear to Leam that Addy had no reply to the subject of Chester Monk, he hefted a bushel basket of tomatoes up to the table and suggested she clean a few for supper. Addy was glad of the chore until the tomatoes reminded her of the season, and she was overcome by the sudden and terrifying awareness that it had been six weeks since strawberries and more than that since she last bled from her cycle.

*A*t first she thought to starve herself and maybe it wouldn't sprout. But by the time the apples bent their branches, and the north wind claimed the night, there was a gentle swell to her stomach and her nipples were big as saucers. Addy knew there'd be a child before the trilliums poked up in the ditch, and it horrified her that, being Mr. Heron's child, it might grow gigantic in her womb.

Once Addy started eating she could not stop. Though her daughter's spirit was still dull, Laisa was relieved to see Addy finish a third corncob and reach for a fourth on one ordinary Tuesday. And she was reassured when her daughter's interest in baking was revived. Addy even let Birdie Brown come around for a visit to show her the new books they'd been learning from in school. Addy politely inquired about the Bishop twins and Birdie thought it an honor to have such a pure saint as a best friend.

Wallace had never concerned himself much about Addy, and though he didn't notice she hadn't said a word directly to him since June, he did notice he was coming home to warm apple or pumpkin pie each night, and quietly thought his daughter a finer baker than his wife.

It was L'il Leam who changed the course of all their lives. L'il Leam had suspected that Addy's hunger for corncobs and pumpkin pies was more than just good appetite. And though it was not proper for a brother to do, he'd studied her changing body mindfully. He was distracted from his schoolbooks in the morning as he envisioned the complicated web of events, and his rage simmered afternoons at the farm. By evening he was puzzled all over again, sure he could not be right in his thinking.

After he saw Addy consider her reflection in the window and move her hands in a circle over her swollen belly, L'il Leam screwed up his courage and asked Mr. Heron if he could have a word when the day's work was done.

When the sun fell, Big Zach Heron brought a pint of bourbon down to the cold barn, feeling very sorry indeed. He took several long pulls on the bottle and blew steam out his nostrils as he strode from one end of the barn to the other. At last he stopped, having set his sights on an old broken manger. He let the alcohol numb his throat as he considered the manger. It was the right size, Leam being such a small boy, and could be covered easily with a few seed bags or some hay.

Zach Heron took another drink and another walk around the barn to ensure the manger was well hidden from all angles. He'd find a reason to send one of the boys back there in a week or so if the smell didn't alert anyone sooner, or an animal didn't get there first. He thought forward to how he'd hang his head and shake it when he got told the news.

L'il Leam showed up with his hands in his pockets and a look on his face. Zach Heron asked did he want to sit down and L'il Leam said no. He asked did he want a belt of bourbon and L'il Leam said yes. Leam gulped twice before handing back the bottle.

Zach Heron had his actions fairly well planned and the boy didn't have a knife or gun, but he thought to ask anyway, "What's this about, Son?"

The small boy drew himself up like a young man and said, "First, let me say what I got to say, then I'll tell you what I got to do about it." Then the words spilled out of his mouth like they'd been drowning him and it was nothing but a relief.

"I can trace it back to Strawberry Sunday. It's a puzzle, Mr. Heron, but I know it started there. What I remember most on that day was how Addy was feeling poorly and decided to go home and lay herself down. Nothing in that is very unusual, being women up and start feeling poorly at surprising times, but I knew how much she been looking forward to that supper and I thought it were a shame she got ill.

"My Daddy'd gone off to work in Chatham so it were me my mother called to drag my sister's old mattress out that Monday morning. She said put it in the backyard so the sun can get at it, but clean out of sight because no one needs to know the girl's on her cycle. When I saw how much blood was in the middle of it and how it soaked clean through I understood why Mama was wringing her hands the way she was and I near lost my breakfast.

"And now, I do apologize to you, Mr. Heron, for being indelicate, but the thing is, I happen to know for a fact my sister had her cycle blood a full two weeks before that day. And the reason I know is I found one of her blood rags in the commode and I was ashamed to find it, but of course I didn't speak to her about such a thing.

"And though I truly wished I didn't know this, that blood rag did not belong to my mother because I overheard her tell the Pastor's wife that her monthly had stopped altogether."

Zach Heron nodded but he was hardly listening because he already knew the truth and hated the cagey, breathless way the boy was baiting him. He thought how simple it'd be to reach out and snap L'il Leam's twig neck. He reckoned he could do it with one hand and not have to set down his bottle. He thought to do it now and get it over with, but L'il Leam was agitated and started pacing.

"Again, I apologize to you for my crudeness and wouldn't say any of this if I didn't feel I had to, but the blood on the mattress was such a quantity that it just don't make sense it were cycle blood. Even if, like my Mama, I could believe Addy's moon just come on early, it looked more like the blood from when a person gets cut. Do you understand what I'm saying, Mr. Heron?"

Zach Heron nodded slowly and kept his eyes to the ground as he advanced on the boy, but L'il Leam was shaking his head now and maybe even feeling the bourbon.

"I know now that I was right in my suspicion. It appears like my sister has got herself in a condition."

Zach Heron blinked five times and had to make himself stop. He hadn't seen the girl since that night and didn't know she was in a condition. He started toward L'il Leam again, but now he felt fear.

L'il Leam went on before the big man could reach him and just in time. "I was thinking on it one day a few weeks back and it hit me like a storm. The only other person gone from the fire and hymn singing that night was Chester Monk. Addy's in love with Chester and baked a berry pie expressly for him. I saw them together under the willow near the graveyard. It started to make sense that Chester arranged it so Addy'd say she's sickly and come back to the house. I know she done it willingly. And though she likely expected a little kiss or tender word, she could not have expected what he done to her. No sir."

L'il Leam looked up into the huge man's wide, stunned eyes and said, "I know I shocked you here and I'm sorry for it. But if you had seen the blood on that bed, Mr. Heron, and the look of Addy the next day and all the days since, you'd have thought the devil himself drove his pecker into that poor sister of mine."

Zach Heron took a long slow pull on the bourbon and told L'il Leam to finish it off, which he did.

"Remember the next day, how Chester never showed up at the farm and word was him and Jonas Johnson gone off to work for Teddy Bishop and that Frenchman running booze over to Michigan?"

Zach Heron nodded and stopped himself from glancing at the broken manger behind the wheelbarrows.

"I was surprised he never said nothing to me about Teddy Bishop because Chester was a good friend, or so I thought. I went around to his house that night but his Mama wouldn't come to the door. A few weeks later, when I started having my suspicions, I went back and knocked till she come. She was bitter and told me Chester's a bootlegger now and gone from the Lord. She didn't even know how right she was. She said though he never had the decency to tell her hisself, she heard he and a few like him was living in a house in Sandwich and God have mercy on his soul."

Zach Heron thought he better sit down and did.

"There's a dock near Sandwich where the liquor boats come and go at night. I'm told Chester does a good deal of the rowboat work, being so big and strong as he is and able to fight the current. I don't think it's right that Chester Monk get away with what he done and no action whatever against him. My sister's life is spoiled now and she'll likely be sent down to South Carolina to live with Aunt Myrtle. First she'll get beat though, my mother, my father, likely both.

"Course I don't have a chance against a boy big as Chester Monk, but I didn't want to go to the younger men for help. Everyone'll know soon enough. But it was my hope, Mr. Heron, what with you being a friend of my Daddy's, and mine, that you might assist me a little. Hold him back just so I can get a fist or two on his chin and maybe his gut. That ain't gonna change nothing for Addy, but I'll feel a little better. Least I won't feel no worse."

Zach Heron reckoned many things quickly. The girl had not told the shameful thing he'd done to anyone and would not. Even if she did, Wallace and Laisa would never believe her. Her own brother suspected another man. Of all the people in Zach Heron's life, it was only his wife, Isobel, who'd believe it, and she'd never find out, at least not if Chester Monk stood accused. If Addy Shadd got sent away, it'd be the best thing for them all.

Rum

*T*he water was murky and cold and it wouldn't be long before it froze over completely. Chester Monk stroked it with his battered oar, glad it was calm tonight and he could think his thoughts without fighting the current and fretting he'd miss the dock. He thought how it could be a short trip from the Detroit shore, or long, depending on the whims of the river and the men who patrolled her.

At his feet was a slat wood case filled with premium liquor making its way back to the dock. There'd been no one to take the pickup on the other side and Bishop wouldn't be happy, but Chester wouldn't be blamed. Looped through the box of liquor was a long heavy cord connected to a sheave on the underside of the boat. If the Patrol came by, over the box'd go like an anchor, and even if they searched, they wouldn't see the cord, the box, or where all it was hitched to the bottom.

Chester had in his trouser pocket several ten-dollar bills given to him by Teddy Bishop's man, Mr. Remillard, who was called Remy to get his attention and Frenchie to get his goat. Remy'd shown Chester how to fold the bill and the right way to pass it to the patrolmen when they stopped his boat. If they asked how the fish were biting, he should pass the bill. If they asked to search, he should let them. And no matter what, he should remember he's colored and know his place.

Chester didn't care for Teddy Bishop and his meanness and frippery, but he liked Remy just fine. The Frenchman put Chester in mind of a Pastor he knew when he was a boy, before he moved to Rusholme. Remy wore simple cloth suits, kept his old boots shined, and held many deep convictions. He made opining on bootlegging whiskey sound like testifying at the pulpit. "Bad laws make criminals of good people!" Remy'd slam a fist and say. And when he invoked the Holy Spirit, he meant *imported* whiskey and everyone knew it.

Remy called Chester "*Mon ami le Noir Gros.*" He told him it meant *black giant,* and patted as high on his back as the wiry little man could reach. Chester didn't mind the French sound of that. Remy didn't suggest an ounce of discourtesy, but only had a different way of talking. It's something Chester'd learned, how a person's words did not always disclose the intention of his heart. He'd been called fine things by people who feared and loathed him, and slanderous things by people who thought well on him but were ignorant.

It had been months since he'd been home, but Rusholme was never far from his thoughts. *Rush home,* he'd think, like it was a commandment, *Thou Shalt Rush Home.* He thought of his mother infrequently because she was fanatical and cold. Mostly he thought of the land, and the lay of the streets and the smell of the lake and the soil, and in a frame beside any thought of Rusholme was a picture of his one true love.

Chester loved all of Addy Shadd. Her heavy lid eyes put him in mind of a hound he'd had as a boy, and he thought to tease her about that one day in the future. Like that hound, there was something in her gaze, loyal and loving and saying they belonged to each other and always would. He saw that look the last time he was with her, when she peered at him under the willow at the church supper in June.

He'd been surprised Teddy Bishop wanted to put him to work that very night and sorry he couldn't find Addy to explain his departure and his plan. Birdie Brown was cool to Chester when he inquired as to Addy's whereabouts, but she did inform him that Mizz Shadd was feeling poorly and went on home. He'd worried some, but as Teddy Bishop was driving him and Jonas Johnson out of the town after dark, he'd seen Big Zach Heron coming through the front door of Shadd's little brick home and felt better that the family friend had been sent to check on her.

It was not the beauty of Addy Shadd, though he found her charms considerable, that compelled Chester to devotion. It was the unspoken communion of their spirits he could not deny or explain. Since the first day he saw her, when she was twelve years old and minding the babies at the Kenny farm, Chester knew she'd be his mate. He never told her that was the case, naturally. Having the soulship they did, he knew she understood and felt the same.

Chester looked down into the frigid river under his sturdy boat and thought of the watery world below. He'd been told come winter the ice'd freeze thick, some said ten feet and some said two. Didn't matter how many feet down that river froze, he'd be travelling back and forth on it because the rum had to run. That was business.

Remy described the jalopy they'd get for him and how the best thing was to drive with the car door open. If the ice started to crack, a man had a chance in Hell of jumping to safety and not ending up fathoms deep on the silt bottom with the automobiles and corpses and cases of liquor from winters past. When he thought of the river bottom, Chester felt a shudder and could hardly force the picture of ruination from his mind.

Chester paddled a little harder when he looked up and saw the dock approaching. He began wondering if he could use that old jalopy one Sunday to drive the fifty or so miles back to Rusholme to see Addy Shadd. He'd ask Remy when he saw him tonight. He smiled to think of how Addy's face might look when he came motoring up to her little house on Fowell Street.

He missed her like a limb. He thought of Addy in the schoolhouse on King Street. How she'd help the younger children sound out words and never be smug. He regretted he didn't have the chance to spend the whole long summer in the field beside her, watching her bent over the neat green rows.

Some day in the future Chester'd tell Addy in a whisper how often he thought of her like that, bent over in the sunshine, her perfect bottom waving back and forth and how he longed to touch her there. If she had a notion it wasn't a sweet way to be, he'd tell her there was nothing they couldn't do to each other that wouldn't be sweet, because of the true nature of their love.

At night, he'd lay down in his too-short bed and work his fist up and down his shaft, imagining that Addy Shadd was his wife. He'd caress her face and tell her she was beautiful and a treasure to him. He'd kiss her and feel her slick teeth with his tongue. He'd dip his mouth into the valley of her ear and chew the round lobe before he turned her to face away from him. He'd plant his hands on her hips and press himself into the cleave of her bottom, then reach up to fill his palms with her breasts. He'd whisper, "Bend over," and she would, because he asked. He'd pull up her nightdress, exposing the halves of soft flesh and guide himself between them, gently thrusting until she pushed back and he knew she was ready to buck as hard and fast as he would like. Chester would explode with his imaginings and remind himself to start going back to church.

He'd have a good deal of money by spring and with what his father gave him secretly before he passed, Chester'd have enough for payment on a little acreage near the old Rusholme crick to start a small farm of his own. He'd ask Wallace Shadd for his daughter's hand and soon as they were old enough, they'd be joined in the church as husband and wife.

Chester's boat floated up and struck the dock. He took a quiet moment to ensure there were no police to give him trouble and no temperance types to give him grief, before he hauled up the case of liquor. He shifted the load to his shoulder and started walking through the dark night. Thinking on Addy Shadd and a trip back to Rusholme, he began to sing. He was wishing he knew a better song than the one that came to his mind, though, as it was something lewd he learned at the blind pig in LaSalle.

Remy had yet to arrive. Chester deposited the crate in a small shanty near the water and sat back on his heels to wait. He listened to the river lap the bank and mused on the sharp white stars in the big black sky before the clouds moved in and hid the moon.

It was a Ford truck and not an automobile whose round beams flashed in his eyes a short time later. Chester stood and knew right off the driver was not Teddy Bishop or his friend Remillard. He stuck his hands in his pockets and felt the folds of the ten-dollar bills. If it came to that, he'd pass them over, but maybe the truck never saw him at all and he could just creep downriver into the tall bulrushes and wait till whoever it was left.

He heard the truck stop and two doors open and close, but he didn't turn to look as he put some distance between himself and the shanty. After a moment, he heard his name and knew by the tone that whoever called it was uncertain. "Chester Monk? That you, Chester?"

Chester turned, the voice sounding familiar, but he didn't know it was Leam Shadd until his old friend stepped into the truck's headlamps and revealed himself. A chill went through Chester at the strangeness of seeing Addy's brother, all the way from Rusholme, standing there in front of him now. His heart skipped at the idea Addy herself might be in the darkness of the truck, but he quickly reckoned that wouldn't be the case. It was more likely that L'il Leam had come to work for Teddy Bishop too.

It was no less than a thrill to see him there. "L'il Leam Shadd!" Chester let go a howl like he'd seen men do after a snort of jack. He liked the feel of it in his chest and howled again to show off a little as he strode toward the vehicle. "Like an apple on a pear tree! I can't hardly believe my eyes to see you out of Rusholme!"

L'il Leam stood in the bright headlamps, astonished by Chester Monk's manner. Was it possible the big fool didn't know what he'd come for? He shifted his weight from one leg to the other, suddenly unsure. "I didn't expect you'd be pleased to see me, Chester Monk."

"Pleased to see you?! Why, you felt like a brother to me since I known you. What's that look on your face for? Leam?" Chester nearly lost his legs. "Addy?"

L'il Leam flinched, remembering the blood on the mattress and thought his friend must be a fiend to appear so innocent. He walked forward, distracting the bigger boy from seeing Big Zach Heron climb out of the truck. "How do you dare ask about my sister after what you done, Chester? How can you look me in the eye?"

For the first time, Chester allowed for the possibility that Addy might have thought he abandoned her. It suddenly occurred to him that he should have sent those letters he'd written after all, and not been so ashamed of his childish scribble and sorry poetics. Or that he should have found a way, any way, to return to Rusholme to see her over these weeks past. He'd have kicked himself if he could, for being such a fool. It pained him greatly to know he caused Addy enough distress to have her brother come hunt him down.

"I love your sister well and truly and if—" Chester didn't have the breath to finish as Zach Heron snuck up behind him and used his big hamhock arm to put a choke-hold on the boy's neck.

It was disturbing to L'il Leam that Chester didn't seem to understand how wrong he'd been to pluck Addy in the brutal way he must have. And a further wrong to run away like he had and never to inquire about her spirit or condition. But looking into the choking boy's wide bewildered eyes, it was clear Chester thought himself without fault. L'il Leam's blood boiled at his disregard. Zach Heron hissed, "Do it. Do it."

The knife had been Zach Heron's idea. He thought to mark Chester's face, a slash on his cheek or above his eye, to brand him as the one that had done Addy wrong and to keep him away from Rusholme forever. L'il Leam agreed. It seemed a right and fair thing to do, and more lasting than whatever minor discomfort his own small fists might inflict. Slowly, L'il Leam pulled the long blade from his pocket.

Chester Monk looked at him, not comprehending why this boy he called brother might have come here with a knife, nor what exactly he intended to do with it. He tried to cry out, but Zach Heron clamped his huge salty hand over his mouth. L'il

Leam raised the knife and caught the glint of the automobile light. A north wind kicked up a maelstrom of dry maple leaves at their feet. Chester tried to shake his head. Zach Heron throttled him, shouting, "Do it, Boy! Do it!"

L'il Leam couldn't cut his friend, but it wasn't because he thought Chester was innocent. He couldn't do it because he had not the spirit to make a man suffer no matter what suffering that man made. L'il Leam stood there, watching Chester's eyes bulge and redden, listening to the sickening quiver of air stuck in his closed-off throat. Zach Heron sucked his teeth, feeling powerful, tightening his grip.

With some extraordinary effort, for his fight was fading and he could sense peace in some near place, Chester Monk decided he would not die like this. It was his foot he thought to use, and wished he'd thought it sooner. With the scant strength he still possessed, he lifted his leg, then brought the full force of his heel into the kneecap of the huge man behind him. Heron yelped in pain and lost his hold and that was enough for Chester to break free.

It was not that Chester planned it as such, but L'il Leam was standing only a foot away with the knife. Chester snatched the knife when he was clear of Zach Heron and held it up against both men as he struggled to fill his lungs with air.

Zach Heron sneered at L'il Leam and spit mightily. "Coward! After what that devil done to your sister?! How you gonna live with yourself, Leam?"

Chester Monk turned to L'il Leam, his chest heaving as he spoke. "I don't know what you think I done, or what Addy told you I done, or even *what* been done. But I'll tell you brother, and may I be struck by the Almighty's hand, that I never hurt your sister in any way I know, except to suppose she'd understand I'd come back for her. That's all. And I don't see you stabbing me for that. And I don't see why you come all the way here to hurt me and brung him along to help."

L'il Leam didn't care he was crying like a baby. He didn't care Zach Heron would lose respect forever. He only knew he was betrayed by his friend and deeply grievous for his younger sister. He couldn't think what to do then, except to recount for Chester his crime, like he was standing on a hanging platform, waiting to hear why he's got to die.

Chester had a hard time grasping, at first, what L'il Leam was saying through his blubber and sorrow. But when he finally understood, though it was beyond understanding, that someone had gone to Addy, his Addy, and defiled her and now she had a baby coming and was ruined, Chester Monk lost his soul. He had a flash in his head and a picture of Big Zach Heron stumbling out the door of Shadd's house on Fowell Street. In that instant, he knew.

When Chester lifted his face and trained his fire eyes on the bigger man, Heron could see that he knew. It did not occur to Chester to share the truth with L'il Leam. The only thing that came to Chester's mind was that Zach Heron would die for what he'd done.

With an animal roar, his long blade primed, the boy attacked the man, seeking his heart or liver or lung. L'il Leam, not know-ing that Chester was the friend and Zach Heron the fiend, jumped into the melee to wrest the knife from Chester's hand.

To explain the struggle of the man and two boys is to describe the chase of an eddy, or the melding of sand into glass, or the frenzy of wild dogs shredding one of their own. It was one set upon another, set upon another, thrashing and stabbing, biting and clawing, shouting and gasping and finally rolling back toward the river.

In the end it was silent and still and the moon felt safe to come out again. Zach Heron lay crumpled on the ground, a small twig stranded in the cave of his nostril and twenty-four stab wounds patterned on his huge dead body. Chester sat soaked and freezing on the river's edge, looking down into the deep murky water.

Chester'd heard the splash when L'il Leam fell and left Zach Heron bleeding on the riverbank to dive in after him. He couldn't see anything under the surface. He rose for a gasp of air and went back under, and up he came and back down again, but he couldn't find Addy's brother in the black water, and after a while, he was too cold to keep looking. He didn't have to wonder what happened because he knew.

L'il Leam's arms had been broken in the clash of bodies, his legs were weak and bruised. He'd fallen and stumbled into the cold grim river and was unable to rise back to the surface. The poor wrong boy floated down to the bottom and got lost among the sunk jalopies and wasted whiskey. Chester couldn't believe, though he knew it to be true, that that was the last of L'il Leam, who had more courage than most grown men, and such goodness that Birdie Brown chose him alone to love. Chester wished he still believed in Heaven, so he'd have a place to put his small, dead friend.

Remillard had seen many things in his day and understood men's rage too well, so when the Frenchman pulled his automobile down to the river a short time later, he was not shocked by what he saw, only concerned for his friend Noir Gros. Chester tried to explain, but what had happened was indescribable. He could only say how he ached at the loss of L'il Leam and wasn't sorry he killed Zach Heron after what he'd done, and that he had to return to Rusholme and explain it all to Addy himself.

Remillard knew, even as he said this, that Chester could never return to Rusholme and never explain what had happened to anyone. He'd go to prison when the police found Zach Heron's body, and if L'il Leam ever drifted back, he'd be blamed for that death too. Remillard looked at him squarely. "Mon ami, you must go."

Tears came to Chester's eyes but he would not let them pass. "Addy . . . ?"

Remillard understood because he knew of Chester's love for the girl back home, and he was sorry for his young friend. "C'est fini. It cannot be, Chester. Better for her to think you are dead. You must go. Go now before the Patrol comes by. First help me dump this pig in the water."

Each man took a huge foot and dragged the animal to the river. Together they rolled him in and were soaked by the great splash. Chester shuddered, watching the river swallow Big Zach Heron. Remy remembered an overcoat in his automobile and went to retrieve it. He put the coat around his young friend's shoulders and gave him a roll of ten-dollar bills and the name and address of an American man who would help. He saw him to the rowboat and embraced Chester before he set down in it. Remy said he would take care of things, though neither was sure then what he meant.

Chester knew he was leaving Remillard and Rusholme and Addy Shadd and even his country forever. His heart rose to his throat as he pushed away from the dock. He heard, or thought he heard, his name, whispered like a curse from the river's edge. Chester turned to look but Remillard was gone, and though he knew it wasn't possible that L'il Leam was alive, he wished it was him cursing from the bulrushes and not just the wind bemoaning his fate. He drove his oar through the water, his face hard as he set out toward the near shore of a new country and an uncertain future.

Mum

*T*he sun peered in from behind the white eyelet curtain and kissed the little girl sleeping on the trailer floor. Sharla wasn't afraid. She knew where she was because the first things she saw when she opened her eyes were the salt'n'pepper shakers way up on the shelf above. She turned her palms over to feel the cool of the floor and recalled falling last night and Addy Shadd's good face and Ivory soap smell. It was the softest pillow Sharla's head had ever been laid on, but she still felt a headache between her eyes. She reached up, found the goose egg on the back of her head and tried to push it back where it came from but that hurt too much so she stopped.

The trailer floor had the look of creamy gray marble, same as in the busy place where Collette took her to try to get their telephone back. Sharla put her cheek on the sun square part of the floor and watched a line of teeny ants coming toward her from a spot under the sink. She thought how the ants looked like babies and wondered where was the Mum that should be leading them.

The sound of Sharla's crusty breathing made a concert with the morning dove outside Addy Shadd's trailer. Sharla used her feet to turn herself around on her back so she could see down the skinny hallway. The bedroom door was closed, but Sharla wanted to go see what Addy Shadd looked like in her bed. Then all of the sudden she got a squeeze in her gut because she remembered she was in trouble for two things: she broke the china salt'n'pepper shakers and never brought the envelope with money.

Sharla sat up, fingering the soft blue plaid blanket, rubbing it against her cheek a while before she felt ready to stand. She pulled herself up and looked at the butt-filled ashtray on the little kitchen table. She blew a short gust at the ashtray and watched the white and gray ashes scatter like snowflakes. She wiped the ashes off the table then sniffed the cigarette smell on her hand.

There were three kitchen cupboards but none could be reached without a chair. Sharla was hungry so she dragged a chair over to the cupboards and climbed up, losing a heartbeat when she nearly tipped and fell. The cupboard door made a *sceerauk* sound and it was all just pots and dishes inside. Sharla was mad at that and because she couldn't reach the next door without getting down and moving the chair again.

The next cupboard had bags of flour and sugar and cornmeal and a loaf of bread that was not soft and white but hard and black and something Sharla'd never seen before. On the bottom shelf was a large tin her pudgy fingers struggled to open. Inside the tin was a package of cookies, chocolate-covered coconut logs. Sharla's favorite. She lifted the cellophane, careful not to let it crinkle. She stuffed two cookies into her mouth, and the taste of the chocolate and coconut made her feel smooth and right. She put two cookies in one pocket of her shorts and three in the other pocket, and that was the end of the package.

Sharla stepped off the chair, pressing the gritty bits of coconut to the roof of her mouth. She took up her soft pillow and blue plaid blanket and brought them to the couch that was pulled out like a bed. She wished she could watch a cartoon, but after having a good look around, she saw there was no television. Sharla kept reaching into her pockets until all those good cookies were gone and just a smear of chocolate left on her shorts to pick at and lick off her fingers.

They weren't toys, they were china things and she knew that, but Sharla thought how the dancing lady looked like something she could pretend was a toy. Sharla dragged the chair to the salt'n'pepper shelf, snatched the dancing lady and held it like a doll.

She checked down the skinny hallway then whispered to the doll, in Collette's voice, "I'm gonna have a date, so the babysitter's coming and that's Greg what's visiting his Aunt Krystal. You can have some chips but don't be a brat."

Sharla acted mad and shook the doll. Pepper sprinkled out the holes in her head and fell on the bed. "See what you done now you little bugger? Spilt pepper all over the shittin' place. Don't make another mess or Emilio's gonna take care of that."

Sharla didn't like how Emilio came up and soured her play, so she decided that she would sing a song to the pepper-shaker doll instead. She tried to recall the words for the Elmer Safety Elephant Song, which was taught to her by Collette's boyfriend from a while ago, Claude, who said criticizing things when Collette fed Sharla just cheezies for supper.

Claude was the janitor at the school in Chatham where Sharla'd be going this fall. He had flat yellow hair and red spots on his chin, and Collette had said he was going to be Sharla's new Daddy. Claude drove Sharla by the school in his blue truck and said it was a religion school so she'd have to get acquainted with God and Mary and Jesus, who died on the cross for our sins. Claude paid the tickets for the boat to Boblo Island, and he never took away Sharla's corn dog when she was only half done.

There was a smell about Claude: vinegar and Ajax bleach and Peter Jackson cigarettes. Collette had to have a talk with him about a bath and not so much VO5 grooming lotion in his hair. But Sharla liked the smell of Claude and thought she'd be proud to say that's her Daddy and to eat her jam sandwich in his janitor room with the rusty buckets and tall gray mops. He taught Sharla a funny way to count. "One, two, skip a few, ninety-nine, one hundred," and he sang the Elmer Safety Elephant Song for her whenever she asked him to, even when you could tell he'd just rather smoke his Jacksons and watch the sky.

Claude liked the looks of Collette, and he said she must be the devil herself the way she could lead a man to temptation. He came by the trailer after work most nights and Collette fed him supper from the cans in the cupboards. For a treat on Fridays he'd bring a bucket of Kentucky Fried Chicken, promising the drumsticks to Sharla. He said his old Mum was moving out of her red brick house on the Thames River and it was time he found a wife to move in there with him. He never felt so strong about anyone as he did about Collette, and when she saw that house on the Thames River she never felt so strong about anyone either.

On Collette's birthday Claude showed up with his truck and two of the best things Sharla'd ever seen: a brand-new green velveteen La-Z-Boy that you could lay back in like a bed, and a curvy coffee table with not one scratch. Collette cried because they were beautiful things and she deserved them. After that, Claude came every night.

When supper was done, Claude'd give Sharla her bath and teach her songs. Collette would roll her eyes when Claude said Sharla had to have a bath *every* night, even when she wasn't very dirty. Mostly Claude and Collette got along fine, until Collette got mad one night because he wouldn't ever sleep over.

"I don't get it, Claude," Collette said after she thought Sharla'd fallen asleep between them on the sofa. "You can *fuck* me in my bed, but you can't *sleep* in my bed?"

"Don't you think you've had enough?" Claude gestured at the beer in her hand and the empty bottles on the table. He didn't imbibe and didn't approve.

Collette took a long swig. "I'm sick of this. When we moving out to River Road?"

"After we get married."

"When we getting married?"

"After you meet my Mum."

"When am I meeting your Mum?"

"When you stop saying the *f* word."

"Does your Mum say you can't sleep here? That it?"

Claude didn't answer.

"You're twenty-fucking-four years old! Fuck your mother!"

"Shut up about my Mum, Collette. It's not just my Mum. What about Father Charlie at the school?"

"Who gives a shit what Father Charlie thinks?"

"You knew when we started I got religion and that's important to me. *I* give a shit. *God* gives a shit. And keep your voice down. Your daughter's sleeping right there."

Collette laughed and pointed at him with her beer bottle. "*You* know what *God* thinks?"

Claude rose, pulling on his skunky cowboy boots, saying, "I'm going now." He bent to kiss her but she pulled away. "I'll swing by tomorrow."

Collette shook the beer bottle at him, not laughing this time. "What does God think about me sucking your cock, Claude?"

Claude's face turned red then white then red again. He snatched his vinegary coat from the kitchen chair and he was gone. He never swung by the next night or any other night. Collette was sorry about missing out on the River Road but she told Krystal she'd have likely choked him in his sleep anyway and didn't she just save herself a peck of grief.

Sharla knew she wasn't getting the words right as she reached up with her voice, remembering the way Claude sounded and how she wished he were her Daddy and singing along with her. "Be just good and right and you'll see tonight. Have a happy safety day."

It wasn't the singing that woke Addy Shadd. She couldn't hear the child in the other room, didn't know she was singing, or that she'd eaten all the coconut cookies Addy kept for when her sweet tooth acted up. What woke Addy Shadd was a dream she wasn't anxious to get back to. Still, she wasn't ready to get out of bed just yet and didn't know how she was going to tell this child she had to go back to her mother.

When the bedroom door opened, Sharla stuffed her peppershaker doll into her pocket and sat still on the sofa bed. She watched Addy Shadd grow from small to large as she moved forward down the hall. Sharla wanted to say many things but she learned it was best not to say too much in the morning because there was usually a hand nearby to smack you and sometimes you had a smart mouth when you never even knew. She smiled at Addy Shadd though, and couldn't help it.

Addy Shadd had pulled her hair back in pins like she always wore it in daytime. Her head looked smooth and her ears stuck out like they ought to have faces of their own. She was wearing a starchy yellow plaid housedress and short baby blue socks with nurse-looking white shoes. She was silent as she neared the sofa bed and Sharla flinched, wondering if she could smell the cookies. Addy Shadd sat on the sofa bed and reached out gently to touch the goose egg on her head. "Mmm–hmm. Guess you're gonna live."

Sharla let her touch and didn't care it hurt.

"Suppose we should have iced it."

Sharla just looked at her.

"What's wrong, Child?"

Sharla tugged at her own ears with her fingers. "You got ears like a mouse."

Addy Shadd nodded and laughed inside her head. To be told such a thing was humorous when you were old and long past caring about your looks. "You think I look like a mouse?"

"Wish I can make mine stick out."

"Need a well for all that wishing, Little Girl."

Sharla squinched her nose. "Emilio says I'm a pig."

Addy Shadd hid her concern. "That right?"

"Emilio give me a Dilly Bar but he said that's enough now Pig and he throwed it in the garbage when I only ate half. Claude never done that."

"Who's Claude?"

"The janitor what teached me songs."

"That right?"

"I don't like it when Emilio throws my Dilly Bar in the garbage. I'll get it back out next time."

"No, don't do that, Child. Don't get food out the garbage."

"My Mum said we're gonna live in a cottage on the lake."

"Mmm–hmm."

"How am I getting to school in Chatham?"

"Suppose the bus'll take you."

"Emilio said he won't drive me."

"Well, you don't pay any mind to Emilio. You are what you are and that's that and that's for you to figure out."

"Mum Addy . . . ?"

Addy Shadd took a long look at the child and had not the heart to say don't call me that. "What, Child?"

Sharla surprised them both when she put her little brown hand inside Addy Shadd's crinkled old one. Addy cleared some thought out of her throat and said, "Let's get you some breakfast now."

Addy rose and cleared her throat again, moving to the kitchen to study the cereal boxes in the third cupboard. She needed a moment to collect herself and couldn't look at Sharla when she said, "But then we're gonna get you on home to your Mama, Honey."

Sharla knew that Addy Shadd had made a mistake and because she was old she likely didn't know it. "I'm living here though."

"I think we better be getting you on home."

"My Mum said though."

"I think the best place for any child is with their Mama and that's where I'm taking you."

"I'm living *here* for summer though."

"Well, I think it's gonna be better to get you on home," Addy Shadd said. Her decision was partly to do what's right for the child and partly because she knew it'd be too much for her to have this sad, unusual child in her home all summer long.

The old woman turned around, sick at the look on the child's face and the calm way she said, "My Mum'll hate me though, because I'm bad and I broke them chinas and I ate them cookies and Fawn stolt my envelope and now you don't want me."

Addy opened her mouth to speak but it was too late. All the suffering in Sharla's gut came up and out; no tears but a sob as deep and sorry as any the old woman had ever heard. She went to the child, gathering her bulk in her spindly arms, and though Sharla was heavy and smelled of dirt and piss, Addy kissed her cheek and stroked her thick back, saying, "It's gonna be all right, Honey. It's gonna be all right," even though she knew it wasn't.

She wasn't a child to cuddle and the awkward feel of her told Addy Shadd that Sharla hadn't been touched much in her life. Sharla went stiff, tore away from the old woman, and was out the door without a word.

There were some days when there was no peace to be had and what you thought might happen didn't and what you never dreamed of did. Addy knew this would be one of those days. She shook a cigarette from her package and lit it while she wondered what to do. The child had either gone to hide or gone back home. If she's gone back home that's the end of it. Addy never did get her envelope and long as she never had to see that little girl's pitiful face once more in her life she could pretend she never knew her at all. But if she's gone to hide, it's Addy who's responsible. No one else would know to go looking.

Addy didn't cuss and she wasn't even cross, she just thought here's what she ought to do and she set out to do it. She plugged the cigarette into her mouth, squinting to keep the smoke out of her eyes, and found her black vinyl purse in the cupboard. She left the trailer, trying to remember where Collette lived and the shortest way to get there. She turned to lock the door, then thinking twice left it open, in case the child returned.

The dry of the lane had been redeemed by the rain and Addy could smell the onions under the earth in her garden. She didn't leave her trailer much and hadn't in the nearly twenty years since she moved there from Chatham. She had her groceries delivered and took taxicabs to the Kmart and to see Dr. Zimmer when her legs and lungs gave her trouble.

She'd have liked to chat with the neighbors, but none seemed eager for a visit. Addy was confused in the present, secretive about the past, and she didn't share trailer-park gossip. Last time she stopped to talk to Nedda Berry's young mama she'd insulted the woman and didn't understand how. Bonita Berry was sitting out the front on a broken lawn chair. To Addy it was just an idle comment. "Another colored family moving out down the road."

Bonita tapped the ash from her long, brown cigarette, object-ing, "It's almost nineteen-eighty, Mizz Shadd. We don't say col-ored anymore. We say black."

Addy'd laughed at the young woman's serious face and said, "*I* been *colored* all my life."

"Colored is an ignorant word. Black is proud."

"Never thought to see a day a Negro can't be called colored."

Bonita winced. "Don't say Negro. Black. Just black."

"So happens I'm proud to be Negro and to be colored."

Bonita Berry wagged her finger, saying, "Those are racial words, Mizz Shadd. Never too old to get with the times."

Addy Shadd remembered that conversation now and won-dered if it was possible to be racial against your own. She inhaled deeply and coughed up a quantity of brown sputum on her hanky. She coughed a little more, trying to be quiet as it seemed the whole mud lane was still asleep. She looked around, thinking she used to know the names of everyone in the nearby trailers, but they came and went now and some weren't even colored.

The trailer park was never meant to be separated, but it worked out that a few colored folks bought up some of the cheaper lots and trailers on the unpaved lane in the sixties. More came and more, and even those who could afford to buy on the paved lanes came to the mud lane instead. It was just natural to want to be near your people. She noticed the same thing hap-pened in Chatham with the Italians settling in that subdivision near the Southside arena. She used to see them when she was working her delivery job for the bakery. They ate strange cold cuts with unpronounceable names and they pierced the lobes of their baby girls and hung grown-up earrings in the holes. The women didn't think themselves too good for fieldwork come spring though and Addy admired them for that.

And there were Chinese in Chatham now too. There was just the one family with the buffet restaurant way back when, but then a whole other family showed up that were not even related. More and more came and pretty soon it wasn't unusual to see them on the streets and in the schools. Addy remembered when

she was a child, how the bootleggers'd get paid for running Chinamen across the border into America. That made her think of
Chester Monk. She made herself wonder why the Chinamen
didn't want to stay in Canada, just to get Chester out of her head.

Addy's eyesight wasn't what it used to be but she knew she'd
spot Sharla if the big little girl were on the road. Her knees ached
and her spine shifted in a troubling way. Dr. Zimmer had given
her a smooth cherry-wood cane last time she saw him and said
her bones were getting brittle. He said an old woman could die
from a broken hip so be careful. Addy hadn't used the cane yet
and was sorry now she hadn't thought to bring it along.

There was a collection of tears buried in Addy Shadd's throat
and she couldn't say exactly why. Young Sharla, she guessed, and
the sad way about her. But something else too, and when Addy
came upon it, it surprised her. Addy Shadd missed her mother.
Even after all these years. Even after what Laisa did. Addy longed
to watch Laisa's wrinkled fingers turn a crust for apple pie. To
hear her hard voice and look into her soft eyes. To kiss her cheek
and smell her throat and say, "I'm sorry, Mama. I'm so sorry."

As she walked, Addy recalled the lullaby her mother had sung
when she was too young to know, then crooned to L'il Leam that
whole summer and fall when he lay in bed, sick and near dead. She
sang it now, under her breath, hoping it would make her feel better:

> Sleep Child, deep Child, Mama holds you near.
> Sleep Child, keep Child, nothing need you fear.
> May all your dreams be sweet,
> And all your days be bright,
> Sleep until the sunrise,
> My little one, good night.

The storm had swept away the muggy heat, leaving the sky
blue and high. The moon was still hanging there, like it forgot it
was on night shift and done for the day. Addy thought, *it's a sign,
when the moon and sun share the sky, that change is coming, and change
isn't always good.*

Chestnuts

*T**he wind warned Rusholme of the storm's approach.* The last of the
leaves fled their branches. The grass went brown and the sky
grew gray and the squirrels hid nuts they'd never find again.

Laisa woke in her bed with a shudder and it wasn't from the
cold. She'd been shaken and was startled when she turned to look
for the hand on her shoulder. No person had touched her. Wallace
was still asleep beside her. His body was hot, his breath steady and
even. Laisa was afraid. *Addy* was all she could think, and she rose
and hurried to her daughter's room.

The door to Addy's bedroom was closed. Laisa, in bare feet,
made no sound at all as she approached from the hallway. She was
biting her lip because she knew. She was wringing her hands
because she knew. It had been whispered to her in her mother's
heart and forewarned by that phantom hand. Laisa held her breath,
sure she'd find her girl stiff and cold and laid out on her bed,
drowned in a river of blood. How could she forgive herself then,
for pretending she hadn't seen?

She pushed the creaky door open. Addy was not cold and stiff
and laid out on her bed, but dressing in the corner of the small
frosty room. It was the first time in years Laisa'd seen Addy in her
immodesty. Her bloomers were hanging low beneath the growing
swell of her belly and her breasts spilled forward, tipped by black
plum nipples. Laisa knew, and realized she'd known for some
time, that her child was carrying a child. She nodded again and

again and thought to strike the girl on her head and her stomach and never stop till she beat them both to death.

Laisa raised her hand and stepped forward, but just then a howl came from somewhere outdoors and took her breath away. She stood still a moment, listening to the sound, only turning when the howl became a word and she could hear her name. "Laisa. Lais-saaaa."

Again she felt a phantom touch. This time the devil hands pulled Laisa out of Addy's room and pushed her down the little hallway. She could see the front door was open. There was a crowd gathered on her lawn, exhaling clouds in the cool, crisp air. *Why all the neighbors come to my dream?* Laisa wondered. Her mind searched her kitchen. Was she expected to feed all those dream people? All she had was a little milk and tea, though she could bring out the preserves if it came to that. Jars and jars of strawberry left over, her children having gone off it for some mysterious reason. And there was bread. Addy making fine bread these days. Though it hurt to admit, her daughter had a better touch with her dough than Laisa ever had.

It was Wallace whose face first appeared to her out of the crowd. Laisa was vexed to see him dressed in nothing but his under-garments and pulled-on, but not buttoned-up, trousers. Dream or no dream, it was disgraceful of Wallace to be weeping — was he weeping? — on the lawn with the rest of the sleepy town, and not even dressed. He had good work in Chatham he ought to be getting ready for, and she'd have a talk with him about that when she woke.

Laisa peered out from behind the front door. It was then she saw Jonas Johnson, a friend of her son's, and another man, a stranger — the two of them standing over what appeared to be a giant baby swaddled in an old brown blanket.

She made her way through the crowd toward the bundle in the blanket. She felt the dream hand again, squeezing, painful, and turned to see Wallace's fingers compressing her shoulder. "It's Leam," he said slowly. "It's L'il Leam."

Laisa shook her head. "Leam is asleep. Leam is in his bed." She shouted in the direction of the house, "Leam! L'il Leam?!"

Laisa waited, but it was Addy who appeared on the porch. Addy was dressed and had composed herself, but when she saw the spectacle on her lawn, she knew to prepare for some horror she never even dreamed of. She did not stop to catch her breath and she did not look at her mother's face. She turned to the crowd, aware they were staring at the swollen stomach under her skirt, pleading, "Will y'all kindly go home now. Leave us to this. Please. Leave us to this."

And the neighbors did, all at once, pull each other away from the awful scene. The five were left there, silent and afraid, Addy and Laisa and Wallace and Jonas Johnson and the stranger who introduced himself to them simply as *Remy*.

Remy and Jonas had agreed on the way to Rusholme that since he was a town boy, and a friend of Leam's, Jonas should be the one to tell the story. Jonas spoke quietly. "Mr. Shadd, Mrs. Shadd. I'm sorry to tell you a terrible thing happened up at the Detroit River last night." He paused to check with the Frenchman. "I believe it was all a misunderstanding." He cleared his throat so he wouldn't cry. "L'il Leam, Ma'am. He . . ."

Addy watched as Jonas pulled the blanket from the face of her dead, bloated brother. She did not cover her mouth with her hand or gasp or cry out. Her pain was too deep for such gestures. She listened to Jonas explain how Remy had woken him in the night and told him about the *misunderstanding* at the river. She heard how the Frenchman had come upon Chester Monk and Leam and Zach Heron fighting at the water's edge. How he'd witnessed Zach Heron topple into the water and how he'd searched and found L'il Leam's body floating in the bulrushes. She watched as her mother and father sank to their knees to touch the corpse, not hearing the rest of what was said, for it was said in a whisper. She drew one horrified breath after another, felt Zach Heron's baby kick, and asked silently, *What about Chester?*

Jonas came to the end of his terrible tale, and Addy knew when her mother and father turned to look at her that what had happened at the river had happened because of her. It didn't matter what Laisa and Wallace had been told. It didn't matter what they believed. The only truth was that Addy was to blame. She watched her father cast his eyes over her round stomach and saw how he hated her. She looked down at her good brother, then back up at Jonas, and shouted once more in her head, *But what about Chester?*

The stranger, Rémy, must have heard her silent scream, for he turned to her and answered, "Chester was stabbed. When I find him, he is clinging to the dock. He has only a few breaths left. Before he slip under the water, Chester say tell you he's sorry." Jonas opened his mouth to say more but Wallace wouldn't hear it. He stood, gathering up his son's body, and made his way to the house. Laisa followed, not meeting Addy's eyes as she passed. Rémy and Jonas, with nothing left to say or do, returned to their automobile and left.

Addy thought *Leam,* and then *Chester,* and sank to the brown grass, shivering. She bent her head to vomit, then wiped her mouth with the sleeve of her dress. She didn't move away though the mess was steaming and stunk. She knew there were eyes watching from behind curtains in all the nearby windows. And she knew the devil was waiting to see what she'd do next. She tried to stand, but couldn't. She spread her palms over the cold hard earth and closed her eyes.

Addy thought of L'il Leam and how he'd be buried in the church graveyard in view of the lake, trod upon by the geese and gulls and sheltered by the willow. And she thought of Birdie Brown and how she'd like to die too when she learned the news of her only love. She had an idea to go to Birdie and comfort her, but she didn't think she could stand her own grief and her friend's too.

The little being in her body struggled and kicked and pushed against her womb. Addy set her hand on her stomach and made a circle. She begged her baby to be a boy and thought to call him Leam so her Daddy would feel tender and disposed to care. She'd live in disgrace and not be welcome at church, she knew, but she was comforted that at least Zach Heron was dead and would never try to claim her child.

The Lord shook the gray blanket sky, scattering a hard cold rain on the ground below. Addy lifted herself from the ground and found shelter on the porch. She sat down in the old rocking chair to watch the rain pelt the earth. It occurred to her that she might be sent South to live with her Aunt Myrtle, and she nearly threw up again at the thought.

Addy prayed that the Lord'd take the pain away. She sat on the porch most of the day, rocking in the chair, avoiding the curious glances from people passing in the rain, nodding to the Pastor with his hard hateful eyes as he hurried by her into her father's house. Addy tried to make pictures of the future, but could never imagine what she might see, where she might go, who she'd become, or how one day she would die.

It was hard to think forward past her next breath, for nothing seemed right or true or believable. Even now, it was not to be believed that L'il Leam, who only yesterday had grasped her arm as he went out the door grinning and said, "Your sugar pie was good, Addy. Better than Mama's but don't say I said," was dead and laid out in the parlor. And Chester. She could see Chester under the willow that June Sunday in his tight church pants with the berry on his lip. But no matter how she tried, Addy couldn't picture him clinging to the dock, pierced by the hand of that devil. And no matter that she knew it was true, she could not accept that at winter's end, Big Zach Heron's baby would come out that little hole between her legs.

Wallace'd be wishing it was his daughter and not his son drowned in the river and Addy knew that. Her Mama was gentler though. She loved babies and would set him right. Elizabeth Duncan from two streets over was sixteen years old when she had that fat James Cox's baby and he ran away to Amherstburg and never was seen again. Elizabeth played with her baby all summer in the yard of her home and Addy'd seen Laisa give a kind smile to both as they walked on by.

Addy rocked on the porch until the middle of the afternoon. The rain stopped and the sky lifted to let winter in full. She shivered but didn't hate the numbing cold. She was hungry though, and felt shame for that with her brother dead in the house. She had an idea to scrounge out back for a rotten apple she might get a decent bite from, but decided against it, thinking of the little white worms and how they might find a way to her baby.

It was with some effort that Addy stood, being heavy and grievous and hungry and sore from rocking all day long. It would not be possible to describe to Wallace and Laisa the truth of what happened. But in time they might forgive her if she could work hard and do for them, and help bury L'il Leam and make food for the mourners to come. Addy tried the door but it was locked. She tried again. She knocked and waited but there was no answer. She knocked again, louder. Still no one came.

Addy reasoned she must be dreaming. Her dreams were mostly frightening since what Zach Heron had done, and she nearly always woke feeling relieved. She realized she must still be sitting in that rocking chair, dead asleep, and not standing here with the door locked against her. Better, she must still be in her bed, and it not yet sunrise, and not this, not any of it, really happening. And even better, it must still be June, and the day before Strawberry Sunday, and won't Chester Monk enjoy her berry pie?

She lumbered back to the rocking chair, sinking down and closing her eyes. *Let me wake in bed,* she begged. *Let L'il Leam be alive. Let it be June and me not ruined and Chester Monk to love me forever.* But she had not a moment to beg anything more as a sharp pain struck her in the forehead. She opened her eyes and saw the neighbor children gathered on the lawn. There was Isaac Williams and Junior and Martin, and Davis and Gertie, all rearing back to fire on her, armed with handfuls of chestnuts.

Addy knew then she was awake and not dreaming at all. She rose again and tried the door, but it was still locked. She knocked on it as the children grew brave and drew closer, and the hard nuts struck her shoulders and head. She tried to keep the panic from her voice. "Mama? Mama? Daddy?" She knocked and called, but they did not answer. She knocked again, and again, but no one came. Addy covered her stomach with her arms as the shower of nuts continued to rain on the porch. She stepped down and didn't look at the children as she ran around to the back of the house.

The backyard was quiet and empty, but for a black squirrel not ashamed of Addy and willing to share his land. The children didn't follow and she was grateful for that. Through the window she saw her father light a lamp, and in the glow of the lamp she saw her father turn from her mother's embrace. Wallace drew the curtains and she knew he'd seen her there.

The rain returned. Addy could not find shelter under the leaf-less apple tree, so, drenched, shivering, and hugging her arms across her chest, she began to walk. Though it was not possible, it was true. And though it was unthinkable, it would be done. Addy was alone. Her brother dead. Her mother and father no longer themselves. Chester drowned in the river. And she, Addy Shadd, would leave Rusholme and find some other place and some other way to live.

Addy'd never left Rusholme before, not even to go to nearby Chatham. She'd think it all the rest of her life, like a commandment. *Rush home,* she'd think, *Thou Shalt Rush Home.*

La-Z-Boy

Sharla Cody hardly glanced at Collette's trailer as she passed. She knew her mother wouldn't be happy to see her and Emilio might even give her a swat for coming back before the scheduled Sunday visit. Sharla didn't much want to see Collette either. There were just two things she wanted. She wanted to get the money envelope back from Fawn Trochaud, and she wanted to live with Addy Shadd in that prim little trailer and sleep every night on the soft pillow, under the blue plaid blanket.

Fawn's Aunt Krystal opened her trailer door wearing a man's big white tank shirt and sloppy blue jeans. Her titties were drooping so low Sharla couldn't stop herself from staring. One nipple pointed to the ground and the other pointed to the sky. She thought at any moment one of those titties might swing out of the armhole opening and if it did Sharla wanted to see it.

Krystal held the door open but didn't say come inside. Her armpits stunk like burned green pepper and her lighter wouldn't work on the cigarette between her lips. She said "Fuck" through her closed mouth, then whipped the lighter on the ground. She sneered at Sharla like the lighter was her fault. "Why aren't you at the old lady's place?"

Sharla didn't even try a smile. "Is Fawn here?"

Krystal shouted, "Fawn!"

Fawn came to the door with her hand deep inside a box of Puffa Puffa Rice. She grinned and Sharla could tell she was looking forward to this. "I want my bag, Fawn."

Fawn shrugged. "Don't got it."

"Liar. Who gots it?"

Fawn checked to make sure her Aunt Krystal couldn't hear. She sneered, "The garbage got it, Cooty Girl."

"That's my bag."

"So."

"So get it."

"It's just a bunch of smelly shorts."

"It's not just shorts."

Fawn pulled her hand out of the cereal box and waggled her wrist. "What do you want, Sharla? This?"

Fawn shook her Indian-corn bracelet in Sharla's face. Sharla didn't care about the corn anymore.

"Where's my envelope, Fawn?"

"What envelope?"

"My envelope for Addy Shadd."

Fawn sniffed. "You stink, Sharla. Keep them Cody coots outside. I don't got no envelope."

Krystal appeared at the door once again, her cigarette lit now. "What's she want?"

"I want my envelope for Addy Shadd."

"You got her envelope, Fawn?"

Fawn shook her head. Krystal shrugged in Sharla's direction and was about to close the door when something caught her eye. She looked across the road at Collette's trailer and noticed the big gray van was not parked out front, which was no surprise in itself, except the curtains were gone from all the trailer windows too.

Krystal made a face like something was wrong. She didn't stop to put on shoes but spread her arms like wings and said, "Ouch, ouch, ouch," stepping over sharp stones as she crossed the road to Collette's trailer.

Sharla and Fawn followed and watched as Krystal heaved herself up the stairs to the door. She flicked her cigarette toward the back shed and banged hard. "Collette? Col . . . ?"

When no one answered, Krystal tried the door but it was locked. She leaned over the stair rail to see into the tiny kitchen window. The kitchen cupboards were open and bare. The green velveteen La-Z-Boy was gone, along with the good coffee table. Krystal remembered hearing banging noises the night before and wished she'd looked out the window instead of pouring herself a fourth rye and Coke. Krystal shook her head. "Hosebag. That fucking hosebag!" She turned on Sharla, asking, "Where'd she go?"

Sharla thought for a minute. "Is it Sunday?"

"Don't act stupid, Sharla. Where'd she go? She owes me a hundred bucks! She's got my leather jacket and half my fucking records!"

"Emilio gots rugby on Sunday," Sharla said. She wasn't a good climber, but she wanted to see inside the trailer too. She shoved Fawn out of her way, climbed onto the railing, and leaned over. She looked through the little window and saw that everything was gone. She turned to Krystal, her left eye twitching. "Where's my Mum?"

"That's what I'd like to know. She never said nothing to me. Not a fucking word."

Fawn skipped down the bottom step. Krystal leaned over to look in the window again. It was then that Addy Shadd rounded the corner, appearing tiny and breathless on the ragged stone road. Sharla saw her, but was afraid to move.

Addy's relief was short. Even from a distance, she could see that something was wrong. She called, "Sharla? Sharla, what's wrong, Honey?" No one answered as Addy approached the derelict trailer and stood at the bottom of the steps. She held the railing, wishing she had a hanky to wipe the perspiration from her face. She looked at Krystal with her no-bra titties and angry face and when she caught her breath, said politely, "I'm Adelaide Shadd."

Krystal hardly glanced at Addy. "You know where she went?"

Addy shook her head and shrugged, not understanding. Sharla bounced down the steps and stood behind Addy, taking her hand and holding it tight. Sharla whispered, "She took the La-Z-Boy."

Addy still didn't understand, thinking Sharla must be talking about that foreigner boyfriend of her mother's.

Addy watched Krystal tug at the door a moment. "Sure they'll be back."

Krystal closed one eye. "They took the fucking furniture."

"Took the furniture where?"

"Up North, I bet. Emilio got a cousin in Kingston."

Addy could not believe it. "They just up and left? What about the child?"

"Don't look at me, Lady."

"But . . ."

"Collette told me she give you money for the whole summer."

Addy didn't care to explain about not getting the money. She didn't know what to do but climb the stairs and try the door herself, thinking that if they could get inside the trailer, the mystery might be solved. She tugged and pulled at the handle, then thought to look under the mat. She kicked the mat over, surprised to find the key there, but she couldn't bend fast enough to scoop it up.

When Krystal opened the door they were slapped by a hot wave of putrid, oddly sweet stink. Addy'd smelled that smell many times in her life and knew what it meant. She glanced down the steps at Sharla and smiled tenderly. "Honey, you go play with your little friend there and we be back in a minute."

Fawn thought the old woman must be crazy to imagine she and Sharla were friends. She squinched her nose. "Puke. What's that smell?"

Krystal had no idea what the odor was except bad. She turned to the old woman. "Jesus effin' Christ, eh?"

Addy and Krystal stepped inside the trailer, breathing out their mouths. The old sofa was still in place in front of the window but so ravaged it'd fall apart if you tried to move it. A green garbage bag was full to bursting in the corner of the living room. Krystal gestured at it. "Pigs."

Addy glanced down the long hallway. "That man a violent man?"

Krystal shrugged as she went to check the green garbage bag, only to find it filled mostly with newspapers and broken dishes. "Smell ain't coming from the trash."

Addy started down the hall slowly. Krystal followed. Addy pushed open the first door. The bathroom. The room was empty, a damp towel on the floor, the garbage full, the tub filthy. They moved further down the hall. Sharla's room was next. A pitiful room, Addy thought, with a few broken toys and a sunken, pee-stained mattress on the floor.

Addy swallowed as they pushed on down the hall. She could hear the buzzing flies. She turned to Krystal. "There's something dead in that room, Young Lady. Maybe we outta call the police."

Krystal's eyes danced. "Let's see. Let's just see." She put her hand over her mouth and nose. Addy did the same and they moved forward. The door was open a crack. Addy steadied herself and pushed it with her foot.

They saw Trixie's body immediately. There was a long shit hanging out between her stiff splayed legs, blood congealing on the carpet near her head. Krystal made a gagging sound and ran for the door. Addy looked at the cat's body, feeling sick and sorry.

When Addy went back outside, Krystal was making her way across the stones, still shoeless, with a cigarette in her mouth and the package of Kools in her hand. Addy motioned at the package. "You mind?"

Krystal passed a smoke to the old woman and lit it with shaking hands. Addy could tell Krystal was disappointed it was a big dead cat in that back bedroom and not her old friend Collette. That would be a story to tell, and human nature to want to tell it.

Sharla was waiting on the bottom step. Fawn was nowhere in sight. Sharla watched Addy take a few puffs of her cigarette. "My Mum in there?"

Addy shook her head. "Nothing atall in there, Honey. Nothing atall."

Krystal inhaled and took a look around. "Where's —?" Before she could finish, Fawn came around the side of the trailer looking pleased.

"I climbed on top the shed. I seen in the back window."

Addy tried to stop the girl. "Shh. Don't matter what you seen, Child."

"Dead Trixie."

Sharla smalled her eyes at Fawn. "You never saw dead Trixie."

"I did too!"

"Trixie's been gone since Easter."

"Well now she's back, 'cept she's dead like this." Fawn let her eyes roll back and stiffened her limbs to show. "With a big poo stuck out her butt."

Sharla looked at Addy Shadd. "Trixie dead?"

Addy ground her back teeth and took another long puff on the Kool. Krystal wondered if the old woman would lie.

"Looks like your Trixie had a accident, Honey," Addy said.

"Can't fix her?"

"Can't fix her."

"Really she got a poo stuck out her butt?"

Addy understood Sharla was just curious. "Yes. Yes she does."

"Can I go look?"

"No. No you can't."

"Fawn looked."

"Your Mama say anything to you about going somewhere with that boyfriend of hers?"

Sharla shook her head.

Krystal flicked her butt and lit another, turning to Addy. "We should have looked for a note. Maybe there was a note."

Addy just shrugged. Like so many things in her life, Sharla had just happened to Addy. All she could do now was live with the unexpected turn. She smiled at Sharla. "Well, Young Miss, I think that's enough excitement for one day. Let's go on back home."

Krystal wagged her finger. "Wait a minute. Wait a minute. What about *that?* You just gonna *leave* that there?"

"You want to bury that animal you go on ahead. Me, I gotta get this child home and fed some lunch."

Sharla wanted to smile but thought she better not. She knew that to appear too happy meant the thing you were happy about might get taken away. She went to Addy Shadd's side. Seeing it was painful for Addy to walk, she lifted the old woman's spidery brown hand and placed it on her own small shoulder, saying, "Here. Lean on me."

Fish

Addy didn't know where to go. The rain had stopped, but she was still soaked and shivering and her clothes grew stiff in the ill wind. She imagined the child inside her was shivering too, so she wrapped her arms across her stomach, whispering, "We gonna be fine. We gonna be fine," even though she knew they weren't. She looked into the black night and was grateful she was bone cold and so hungry she could think of nothing beyond food and shelter.

All but one of the houses in Rusholme were dark and silent. Addy had wandered in circles for a time, then found herself standing in front of the little house on Fowell Street. She could see Laisa sitting in a hardback chair near the window. Her mother's lamplight flickered, and a dark oil cloud settled above her head. She was mending a good white-collar shirt of her husband's, ashamed her son had not a good shirt of his own to be buried in. Addy remembered how Laisa'd scolded Leam for the grass stains on his Sunday shirt after the church supper in June when he'd been showing off for Beatrice Brown. Laisa had hated his love for the pretty young girl, believing it was drawn from the same well as his Mama love, and she'd go thirsty if he loved Birdie too much. She'd said, "Fine, you keep your coat on then, Leam, no matter how hot it gets this summer, 'cause them grass stains never coming out them elbows and that teach you about showing off." But she couldn't bury her son with grass stains on his elbows, and she was glad to have a chore and to do for him this one last time. Laisa's hands had stopped shaking when she picked up her needle and thread, and there was comfort in the dance of her fingers and the tiny perfect stitches they made. Addy watched her through the window for some time before she willed her feet to move in the direction of the church.

In the mile between her home and the church, Addy felt the shroud of darkness settle on her shoulders. The rain was hard and lashed her face. The doors to the church would not be locked but Addy could not go inside. It wasn't God she feared but the fat Pastor and the way his eyes had hated her. The old shed near the graveyard was unlocked and although Addy was afraid of the restless spirits, she opened the door, squatted on the ground, and was glad to be out of the wind. She leaned up against the shovels, telling her teeth to stop chattering and her baby to be still. Then Addy told herself, as she would tell herself all her life, that although she was the cause of what happened, she did not cause what happened.

It was then she thought of the lake and the cliff across the road and how simple to raise her arms like Jesus and spiral down. She imagined what it'd be like under the water, walking on the deep sandy bottom, seeing Chester and Leam swimming there like fish. She thought how they'd wave and say, "Glad you come, Addy. We can all be together now and it ain't even so bad down here." But she felt terror at the notion of gulping for air and finding water instead.

Near dawn Addy woke, remembering the horror of the previous day and that it was not a dream and time to go. The grave diggers would be along any time now, and her brother put to rest by sundown. She stood with some effort and opened the shed door to the dark November sky.

The graves of her ancestors were grouped together at the far end of the yard and she went there now, for it'd be Leam's final home and her last chance to say good-bye. She looked at the gravestones of her father's people, unknown to her, feeling little for their dead souls. She looked up to Heaven and saw sky. She looked at the ground and saw earth. She closed her eyes and whispered, "Leam? L'il Leam? Are you there?" And because she couldn't hear him, but was certain he was there, Addy imagined a talk with his ghost, and whispered it out loud to make it feel real.

"L'il Leam?"

"Yes, Adelaide?"

"When we was children and you got sick and near died, I prayed the Lord take me instead and leave you to grow to a man. Did you know that, Leam?"

"I knew that, Little Sister. I know you loved me well."

"We never did fight and hate each other like other brothers and sisters. I always felt proud of that."

"I did too, Addy. You were always my good friend."

"And I told Birdie Brown all the good things about you and never said how you chewed your fingers and weren't fond of a bath."

"I know that too."

"It weren't Chester done me wrong, Leam. Do you know that?"

"Chester told me how he loved you. He's sorry he never got to say so. Don't worry, Addy. The Lord knows the truth."

"But if the Lord knows the truth, why am I here in the graveyard instead of shaking you awake for your day's work? Why can't the Lord tell Daddy the truth so he can take me back in his house?"

"That's all a mystery, Addy. It's just what is."

"I got to go now before the grave diggers come."

"I know."

"You cold?"

"I'm not cold."

"Good-bye, Leam."

"Good-bye, Addy. I'll be with you."

Addy opened her eyes, felt the wind whip up around her, and heard a gull scream overhead. She knew the bird was Leam, showing off his new flying spirit, and felt better. The trees were bare but the woods were thick and gave enough cover to hide. Addy couldn't walk on the road for fear of being seen. She couldn't stand the shame. Besides, she didn't yet know where she'd go or what she'd do. She ached from the cold and felt dizzy as she crouched near a fragrant evergreen.

Addy was surprised when she awoke that she'd fallen asleep. She could not feel the tip of her nose. She was poised to come out of the bush when she saw the first of the mourners arrive for her brother's funeral. She moved through the trees, closer to the church, so she could watch and listen and even join in a hymn. Leam Shadd had been a loved boy and all of Rusholme showed up to send him on his way to the Lord.

Addy shivered, wishing she were inside the big warm church. She imagined the Pastor telling the congregation that the best thing to do was pray for the souls of the sinners, exalt the righteous, and never speak to each other about what had happened. God moves in mysterious ways, Addy knew, and today, she thought, that was true.

Split-Pea Soup

Sharla had not seemed as troubled by Collette's disappearance as Addy thought she might be, but children were good at coping and Sharla'd learned the skill early. She had to go to school, Addy thought. Take the bus to Chatham like the rest of the children from the trailer park. Addy'd have to see to that somehow, without arousing too much suspicion about where the child's mother had gone or what all arrangements had been made. As much as Addy'd been sure she couldn't keep Sharla, she knew now that she had to. A homely little girl like that'd end up in a foster home and never get any attention. Strange as it was, Addy felt a rush of love for the child.

Sharla had run ahead of Addy and was skipping in a funny way with her fat splayed legs. The strawberry patch at the end of the lane would be fruitless soon, but there were still a few berries reaching for the sun. Sharla squeezed through a hole in the gate and bent to pick them.

"Don't be picking them berries, Honey," Addy called.

Sharla stood, puzzled. "Why?"

"They don't belong to you."

Sharla looked at the berries in her palm. "But I wanna eat some."

"Don't matter what you want. They don't belong to you."

"I already got them though."

Addy coughed. "Well, eat the ones you got in your hand but don't go in that field again. If you want berries, you go to the Loblaws and you buy some."

"My Mum don't get them at the Loblaws, though."

"Them berries belong to a farmer, Child. That's stealing same as if you go in the store and put a thing in your pocket without paying."

Sharla stuffed the berries into her mouth before they could get taken away.

"Ain't right to steal, Sharla."

Sharla left the berry patch and scuffed back to Addy's side. They walked in silence. As they rounded the corner onto the mud lane, Addy became aware of the neighbors watching from their yards and windows and the way their eyes judged Sharla. She looked down at the girl, dusted with dirt, too-small shorts, top stained and torn at the shoulder, her face grim and grimy. She reached for Sharla's hand but the child pulled away. "What's wrong, Honey?"

Sharla's voice was small. "I stolt them coconut cookies this morning. Them ones in your tin."

"That right?"

Sharla nodded and waited. "You gonna smack me?"

"I'm not gonna smack you. But you know you did wrong, don't you?"

Sharla shrugged.

"You want something, you ask me."

Sharla reached up for Addy's hand. Addy nodded to Bonita Berry, sitting on a broken chair in her yard. "Fine day, Bonita."

Bonita gestured at Sharla. "Got yourself a new friend there, Mizz Shadd?"

Addy squeezed Sharla's hand. "Yes. Yes I do."

Addy had decided on the walk back that the first thing they needed to do was get Sharla Cody into the bath. She wondered how long it'd been and the picture of Collette's filthy tub made her shudder. She liked to make her own tub sparkle, and though it hurt her arms, she took out the rag and baking soda after every soak and wiped the porcelain to gleaming.

Sharla sat on the toilet seat, watching Addy draw the water and sniffing a little rose-shaped soap from a dish on the sink.

"Let's get them clothes off you."

Sharla stood and pulled her top over her head. Addy tried not to make a face when she saw the dirt on her plush breasts. She helped the little girl pull down her shorts and winced at the pee and shit smell. The elastic on her underpants was broken and the crotch was streaked and soiled. Addy cursed Collette.

Sharla swung her arms from side to side, feeling awkward to be naked. Addy thought, looking at her round stomach and full thighs, she looked like an overgrown baby. Addy ached to rock the poor child, sing her a lullaby, and let her drift off to sleep. But Addy knew she had to teach Sharla what's right. She held out the soiled underpants and made her voice go soft. "Honey, you got some stains here on your unders. You see that?"

Sharla stopped swinging and flinched as she looked at the shit streak on her underpants.

"You wipe your bum clean, you won't get no leftovers here." Addy reached for the toilet roll and tore off a long strip.

"You take this much, Sharla. Look at me, Child. You take this much and you have a good hard wipe at your bum. You wipe where the pee comes out too. All right?"

Sharla nodded.

"Then you take another piece, 'bout this much, and you have another wipe. Then one more, and you look at it, see did you get everything, and if you did, then you're clean."

Sharla counted in her head. "Three?"

"Three. Or many as it takes. Don't your Mama teach you about that?"

Sharla remembered something and said, "My Mum got blood come out where she pees."

"Mmm-hmm."

"I don't got blood though."

Addy looked at the child, not knowing what to say. She was only five years old and couldn't understand the mystery of her body. Addy decided the best thing to do was tell the truth and try not to scare her too much.

"A lady gets blood come out when she gets nearly grown-up, Honey. You don't have to worry about that for a long, long time."

"It hurt?"

Addy thought it was best not to be *too* truthful. "No. Don't hurt atall."

"It come out your bum too?"

"It come out your privates, Honey. You know why it's called privates?"

Sharla thought, then shook her head.

"Private means it's just for you. Means you don't let nobody see and you don't let nobody touch."

"Not even Claude?"

Addy tried not to be shocked. "Claude touch you there between your legs?"

"Just after supper when he give me my bath."

Addy ground her teeth, telling herself to be calm. "Sharla, Claude was bad to touch you like that."

"I like Claude."

"Don't matter that you like him. That's a bad thing what he done. You're just a little girl and no grown person needs to be touching a little girl in your private place. You don't let nobody do that again."

"I say I'll tell my Mum Addy?"

"That's right. Now come on. Let's get you in the tub."

The tub was not freezing like the baths at Collette's where there was always a boyfriend to use up the hot water. Sharla slipped into the warm water and showed the little rose soap in her hand, which she'd thought to steal, then remembered what Mum Addy had said. "Can I use this, Mum Addy?"

Addy nodded, watching Sharla dunk the rose soap and run it over her arms. Addy took the soap from Sharla, rubbed it into a wet washcloth, and handed it back. "Most important thing is to get all the smelly parts, Honey. Like your feet and your privates. And when you get older, under your arms here."

Sharla reached over her tummy and rubbed the cloth between her dirty toes. Then, glancing at Addy, she tucked the cloth between her legs and moved it back and forth. "Like this?"

"That's right. Few more times." She added, "Best to do your toes last though."

When the water turned brown and cloudy and Sharla looked clean enough, Addy pulled the plug and started the water again. She guided Sharla's head beneath the tap, soaked her hair and squirted shampoo into the curls. Gently, and carefully avoiding the goose-egg spot, she scrubbed her scalp clean and rinsed out the shampoo.

Sharla stepped out of the bathtub. Addy wrapped her up in a big soft towel and held it around her body. Sharla felt like she could stay there, wrapped in the towel and in Addy Shadd's arms for the rest of the day. But too soon, Addy let go the towel and reached for the baking soda under the sink.

Naked, feeling sweet and clean and precious, Sharla watched Addy bend her old bones over the tub to shake the white powder over the dirty porcelain. Addy's arm worked the rag for a moment, then she had to stop to cough. She turned to Sharla, thinking she looked like an entirely different child.

"Get another rag out from under the sink, Sharla. You can help me."

Addy showed Sharla how to make circles with the rag and scrub at the dirt ring. They worked side by side, naked Sharla and old Addy Shadd, until the tub was clean and sparkled. Sharla was pleased with herself. "Want me clean something else?"

"First we got some errands to do."

Sharla clapped her hands. Addy Shadd might have said they were going to Disney World for the way Sharla felt.

It was not possible to put Sharla's filthy clothes back on that clean body, and Addy only thought about that now as she dumped the shorts and top into the trash. Or maybe she'd thought about it sooner and not let herself dwell. The fact was she did have something in her closet that the child could wear, a little white dress, which it pained her to think of, for she hadn't laid eyes on it in decades.

The box was at the back of her closet beneath bags of winter sweaters and extra blankets. Addy pulled it out, flicking off a mothball that was stuck to the side. She sat on the bed with the box in her lap. She'd told Sharla to wait in the bathroom, not wanting the child to see her see the dress.

She opened the box slowly and removed the old sheet in which she'd wrapped the dress for protection. *Oh,* was all she could think, *Oh.* The dress was not yellow with age as Addy had expected and the cotton looked as fresh and white as the day she'd selected it at the dry goods store. The eyelet lace, which she'd thought too dear and then gone back for later, trimmed the collar prettily, and the pink ribbon around the empire waste and hem was as shiny as when she'd sewed it on. Addy'd been late finishing the dress and worried she wouldn't have enough to trim the hem too, but there'd been six inches left to fashion a little bow for her six-year-old daughter's hair.

Addy'd been proud of the dress and the neat stitches and the way it hung just right. She'd shown it to her husband half-finished and said, "Look here. Who's gonna be the prettiest little girl on her birthday?" He had whistled long and low, though she'd told him time and again she didn't care for the sound of whistling, and said, "And you say *I'm* the one spoils that child, Adelaide." He was teasing her, she knew, and she also knew he was impressed with her skill and her good taste.

The dress had been wrapped and folded so nicely before she set it in the box all those years ago that when Addy shook it out, it looked almost like it had just been pressed. She thought of Laisa and the hours at the kitchen table with the sewing basket and how her mother'd made her rip stitches till she got them right. Addy couldn't sew well anymore, with her crippled claw hands, but she wished her mother could see this dress and know her teaching had counted.

Addy dug further into the box and was relieved to find the matching bloomers, for she couldn't recall if she'd saved them and she couldn't think what all she might put on Sharla's bottom. Sharla was peering around the doorway, her damp hair coiled tight against her scalp. She looked at the dress like it was a princess gown and couldn't imagine that Mum Addy meant for her to wear it. Addy said, "Come here, Honey."

Sharla walked into the room slowly, her finger pinching her belly button.

"Put your hands up, Sharla."

Sharla did as she was told, and Addy pulled the dress down over her naked body. Addy turned her around, fastened the little pearl buttons at the collar, and turned her around again.

"Mmm-hmm."

The dress was too long, as she'd expected, and tight across the waist. Her own daughter, Beatrice, had been stick thin with long legs and knobby knees. Her husband had called Beatrice "Chicken," *Chick* for short, because of her skinny chicken legs, but also because of the peculiar web of skin that joined her big toe to the second toe on both feet. Addy'd laughed when her husband remarked on their daughter's chicken feet and told him, "Chickens don't have webbed feet! You're thinking of ducks!" He'd had to think about that and she'd teased, "I can't believe I married myself such a city boy!"

Sharla caught sight of herself in the mirror over Addy's dresser. She walked toward it, watching herself like she was meeting a stranger. "Whose dress is this?"

"That belonged to a little girl a long time ago," Addy said, knowing she could not say *my* little girl without breaking into a thousand pieces.

Sharla twirled and watched the pink ribbon on the hem. Addy smiled and held out the bloomers for her to step into.

"Them shorts?"

Addy nodded, pulling the bloomers up on Sharla's waist. They were a little tight, but they'd do. Addy went to her dresser drawer. She found some elastics and gathered Sharla's hair into two fluffy black pigtails on top of her head. Sharla couldn't look away from her reflection.

There were no shoes in the box. Addy couldn't recall what Chick wore on her feet that day of her sixth birthday. But she could remember the three-layer white cake with butter cream frosting she'd made and decorated with candy rosebuds. And she remembered that Chick's father brought the blond Shetland pony from the farm so the children could have rides. "You have to wear your old shoes, Honey. Let's clean them up a bit and get ourselves going."

They'd walk to the gates of the trailer park and get Warren or Peggy Souchuck, the caretaker couple, to call a taxicab the way Addy always did when she went into Chatham. First she looked in the money tin on her refrigerator. She counted nearly thirty-seven paper dollars and a weight of quarters and dimes that'd add up to a few more. She took her black vinyl purse from the closet, stuck a small white hat on her head, and took Sharla's hand in hers.

It was a twenty-five-minute drive into Chatham, longer in the summer if you got stuck behind a tractor. Thankfully, the taxi company gave Lakeview residents a reduced flat rate. It wasn't cheap, but Addy had no other means of getting from here to there. In the taxi, Sharla'd worried about the dress. "What if I get it dirty though?"

"We'll wash it."

"I won't get in trouble?"

"Long as it's not because you're careless."

Sharla seemed satisfied with that and relaxed a little. They watched the green farms roll by with their big red barns and century-old brick homes and then, as they neared town, the fancier homes with no fields but beautiful manicured lawns and heavy peony bushes. Addy'd been in a few of those homes, just at the door really, on her deliveries for the bakery. She liked to get a look in the living rooms and was often surprised how rich people'd fill their rooms with clumsy sofas and cheap pine tables and let their pets up on the upholstery. *If I was rich,* she'd think, *I'd have everything oak and mahogany and no cat hair on my pretty brocade chairs.*

"Where we going, Mum Addy?"

"Going to the Kmart to get you some clothes."

Sharla smiled. "And summer sandals?"

"That be a good idea. New sneakers too."

The Kmart was busy, it being Friday and there being a sidewalk sale out front. Addy didn't care much for shopping and didn't like to be tempted by something she wasn't there to buy. As she made her way to the children's section, she saw several women, especially the older ones, notice Sharla Cody. She imagined they were feeling nostalgic, looking at the cut and style of the pretty hand-sewn dress. She also supposed they were admiring it and maybe even thinking, *Don't that little fat girl look sweet?*

Addy found sets of summer shorts and tops at a good price and three bags of white underpants in girls' large. She chose a nightdress with a kitten on it because Sharla said it was just like her old one, and after some debate they settled on a pair of white T-strap sandals and pink canvas sneakers. Addy'd put the return cab fare in a small compartment in her purse so she wouldn't forget and spend it, and when all was bought and paid for, they had just enough for lunch in the cafeteria.

The orange plastic trays were greasy. Sharla and Addy took one to share and got in line behind a tired young family. Sharla pointed at some smooth chocolate Whip'n'Chill in a tall fluted glass. Addy shook her head, then remembered what Sharla told her about Emilio taking away her Dilly Bar. She put the dessert on the tray, saying, "But you're gonna have a samwich too."

When they got to the steam table section, Addy looked up and told the scrawny woman behind the counter, "I'll have the split-pea soup, please."

The woman chewed some dirt in her thumbnail and glanced over her shoulder into the kitchen. "Have to wait. It's just coming off the stove." They waited. People moved around them in the line. Sharla looked at the dessert on the orange tray. "Can't we go?"

"Have to be patient, Child. They're getting my soup off the stove."

Sharla watched her feet in the new white T-strap sandals, which Addy'd asked if she could wear right away. More people moved around them and the scrawny woman seemed to have forgotten why they were waiting. "Excuse me, Miss. Miss? I'm still waiting on that soup."

The woman rolled her eyes and went around the corner into the kitchen. Addy could see her approach the cook and everyone in the cafeteria line heard her say, "Will one of yas get that nigger woman her split-pea soup?"

People turned. Sharla looked worried. The pea soup came, the woman smiling falsely and unaware. Addy felt weary as she paid for the lunch and led Sharla to an empty booth.

"That's a bad word," Sharla said quietly.

"Mmm-hmm. She's a ignorant woman."

"Emilio said I'm half that word."

Addy took a long look at Sharla, wanting to ask if she knew her Daddy was colored, then she remembered what Bonita Berry said and changed her mind. "Only ignorant people say that word, Sharla. The right word to say is black."

"Black?"

"That's right."

Sharla ran her fingers over Mum Addy's hand. "You ain't black but brown though." The little girl looked concerned when she found a long dark spike buried in the flesh of Mum Addy's palm. "What's that?"

"Just a wood splinter."

"Can't you get it out?"

"No."

"Not with a needle?"

"Too late for a needle, Sharla. Skin's grown over it twenty times. The splinter's a part of me now."

"Still hurt?"

"Sometimes. Mmm-hmm."

Sharla shrugged and dug her spoon into her chocolate fluff. Addy lit a cigarette and didn't say eat the sandwich first.

Kidney Pie

Rusholme Road was the only main road that led out of town. The road forked and a small signpost with arrows pointed the way: Chatham to the northeast, Windsor and Sandwich to the west. Addy could just barely read the words in the dusk. She had already decided on Windsor because her father worked in Chatham and she couldn't bear the thought that she might run into him there. When she heard a coyote yowl in the distance, she would not let herself be afraid. She had to move forward and only under cover of darkness.

Addy had stayed in the bushes until the final hymn was sung for Leam, and though she was exhausted, her stomach cramping and sore, she couldn't move on before she had seen her brother's body committed to the ground. She'd watched the Pastor sprinkle Leam's casket with earth and thought how oddly pretty the scene was. The mourners were a cluster of small black trees, swaying with grief, then floating away, one by one, until only her mother remained, alone at the graveside, puny and stooped, her eyes on the fresh dug earth.

As she watched her mother, Addy summoned all her strength not to run to Laisa. She knew it would make no difference anyway. She'd never turn away a child the way Laisa had done. And never hate a child like her father had done. She stayed hidden in the bush and smoothed her hands over the baby in her belly.

When finally her mother left the graveyard and started her long walk back home, Addy rose from her hiding place and made her way to the Pastor's residence beside the church. She knew the Pastor'd be at the little house on Fowell Street, feasting on the pies and cakes the neighbors would have brought. She also knew that his own pantry would be fuller than most.

As she let herself in the back door and crept into the Pastor's house, Addy felt strangely unafraid. Leam would warn her if she were in danger of being found gnawing on a hamhock or munching an apple. She filled her mouth with bread and butter and found a cloth sack near the back door. She crammed the sack to bursting with biscuits and jars of peaches and thick smoked meat and potatoes. She tried to lift the bag, but it was much too heavy so she took out the peaches and most of the potatoes, then hoisted the thing over her shoulder. Realizing she was already cold and that when night fell she was likely to freeze to death, Addy took one of the Pastor's black wool coats and one of his dark hats from a hook by the door. She did not think to ask forgiveness for her thieving as she set out from the house, warm and sated and dressed like a man of God.

The north wind was sharp and dark clouds rolled overhead as Addy put one foot in front of the other on the long road to Windsor. There were ditches on either side of the road, deep and muddy from yesterday's heavy rain. Addy was prepared to duck into the ditches in the unlikely event she encountered an automobile. At this time of year, with the last of the crops long ago carted off to the market and canning factory, it'd be unusual for anyone to be motoring in or out of Rusholme at night. No one but Teddy Bishop had much reason to leave Rusholme after dark.

In the back of her mind, Addy wondered if her father might have sent the constabulary from Chatham after her. Her father held her responsible for the tragedies, as did most of the town, and Addy feared being sent to prison for the murder of her brother and Chester and Zach Heron too. Best, she thought, not to be seen.

The Pastor's wool coat was much too large for her and all the warmer because of it. The black hat fell over her eyes and she cursed it until she tore it off and the bitter wind filled her ears. The sack of food was still too heavy so she reached inside and found a big potato. She ate it like an apple and thought it tasted good. She could not have known when she dressed yesterday morning that life would set her on this path, but if she had she would have chosen her field boots and not the thin-soled lace-up shoes that she wore inside the house. Her feet were already sore and swollen and she knew she'd be walking until the sun rose and then some.

The night was so black that Addy could not see her hand an inch from her face. She had to walk slowly and was cross at that because she only had so many steps in her legs, and small ones were nothing but wasteful. She coaxed her feet toward the edge of the gravel so she could feel she was on the road and counted her wasteful little steps to distract her mind from pain.

She tried to hum but she had no song. She tried to dream but couldn't think what to dream of. In her other life, she dreamt of Chester and their wedding day, and her friendship with Birdie Brown, and Leam, and how they'd all grow old together and watch their grandbabies splash in the lake. Addy forced herself to think of her future and what might become of her after she reached Windsor. She would birth Zach Heron's baby, that was certain, but where and how would she raise her child to grown? And where and how would she live out her days? Would she be loved again? Would she be hiding always?

She reckoned there must be a few colored people in Windsor. She thought she might try to find the colored church and appeal to the Pastor. Or maybe a kind old colored woman, a widow, who might be glad for the company and help in the kitchen. Addy wasn't sure what gave her faith, but she did have faith that someone would help her and her baby to be born. Her faith grew even stronger when she stuck her cold hand in the black coat pocket and found what she knew was a thick roll of money. She suspected the Pastor took the money from the church coffer and couldn't know how right she was. But she was eager to see it and count it and would when there was daylight. For the moment, she felt saved.

She'd been thinking all those thoughts, feeling her burden lighten, when a twig snapped in the ditch ahead of her and her heart went thud in her ears. She stopped, looking into the darkness of the ditch, but could not see any animal. She whispered, "Who's there?"

The thing that answered was not human. Another twig snapped and she knew whatever it was, it wasn't afraid of her, but just hungry and wild. Addy imagined it was a huge black dog ready to attack. Or maybe it was a smaller animal, a raccoon or badger or fox, whose bite she could die from. The animal started up from the ditch and even in the blackness Addy could see the white streak. She stood paralyzed. If she frightened the skunk it would spray, and to be sprayed by a skunk was a terrible thing.

The white streak approached. Addy watched until the animal was within a foot of her own foot, then with a short scream she began to run. Almost right away she tripped and tumbled back into the muddy ditch. She cursed, for she'd hurt her hip and lost a few potatoes from her sack. She rose, letting the mud drip from her hands and her big black coat. Another twig snapped behind her and she turned to find the curious skunk approaching once again. She ran as fast as she could run carrying the weight of her baby and her sack of food, and it was another half mile before she felt safe enough to stop and catch her breath.

She silently thanked Leam for his help escaping the skunk, for he'd become Godly to her in his death. When her heart slowed down some, she started to walk again. Still taking the small steps forward, she realized there were two words beating with her heart, rush, home, rush, home, rush, home. But Addy would not look back.

After hours and hours of walking, Addy realized the sun had begun its ascent behind the gray clouds and she could see her hands in front of her face and her black coat covered in mud. The woods had given way to farmland and Addy knew she must be close to Windsor. She kept walking, wondering with each step if she could take another.

There was a farm truck heading her way but she had not the strength to hide in the ditch. If the white men in the truck knew about her and wanted to take her to prison that's just how it was going to be. Although the men in the truck did look at her sideways, they did not stop. Addy wondered if Windsor was such an unusual place that muddy girls in men's clothes were often seen staggering by the side of the road.

Another truck passed by and then a fancy auto carrying a white-haired old woman and a man in a dark suit. They did stare, but also drove on without stopping. Addy could still see only farms in the distance and wondered when, if ever, she would arrive in Windsor. She knew that Rusholme was a rare place in that it had once been, and still was, mostly colored. She didn't know how life was for colored people outside of her town, how many there were, and where they might all live. It occurred to her that maybe there was no colored church here and no colored widow lady who'd want to take her in.

It was then that Addy glanced to the left and saw the tiny brown boy watching her from inside a big barn door. She felt it was a miracle and waved her black hat, shouting, "You there!"

The small boy disappeared into the barn and left her wondering if she'd seen him at all. After a moment, a tall, broad-shouldered woman Addy judged to be the boy's mother appeared. She had a stern look on her face as she set her hands on her wide round hips. Addy was standing on the stone lane leading up to the barn and did not know what to do. The big woman did not smile or wave but called out crossly, "What you want, Girl?"

Addy opened her mouth to speak, but something touched her forehead and she was sure it was the cool finger of the Lord. She felt another touch and another and she realized it was snowflakes, the first of the season. She looked up into the close sky where the snowflakes seemed big and heavy as maple leaves. They fell into her eyes and her wide-open mouth. She dropped her sack of food and closed her eyes. She meant to open her eyes again but they must have been stuck, for the blackness stayed and there was a sharp white pain, then nothing.

W hen Addy opened her eyes again, she was laying in a small bed, covered by a damp urine-smelling blanket. There was a pint-sized white man with sunburned skin and orange hair standing over her. She had never seen such a man in her life and thought he looked like an orange-haired devil. The man said nothing but watched her with his see-through blue eyes, shook his head, and disappeared. Addy closed her eyes again and longed to return to wherever she'd just been. She felt an icy palm on her forehead and forced herself to open her eyes again.

The icy hand belonged to the big woman she'd seen in the barn. The woman did not smile and was not tender, but drew the blanket up around Addy's chin and left the room once more. Addy shivered and looked at herself under the covers. Her black coat and hat and even her shoes were somewhere else but she was glad to see she was still dressed. Addy looked around the room. It was so small that if she stood, she could touch both walls at once. When she noticed a small wardrobe open in the corner and inside it some children's clothes, she wondered if this was the room of the little brown boy.

Addy's hip ached from her tumble in the ditch. She could not have moved her legs to rise even if she had a mind to. She shut her eyes again when she heard movement outside the door. The big woman's voice was heavy and her manner curt. "Time to open them eyes now, Girl."

Addy did as she was told and watched the woman carry a steamy bowl of something toward her. The woman rested her bulk on a chair by the bed, telling Addy, "Sit up. Sit up now and get this broth down you."

Addy's arms moved on command but she could not use them to pull the rest of her to sitting. Annoyed, the woman set down the bowl and hefted the girl up to lean against the headboard. The woman smelled like a man. She had arms and hands as big as a man, wiry gray whiskers on her chin and curly dark ones jutting out her nostrils. She picked up the bowl of soup again, ordering, "Get some of this broth down you."

Addy couldn't see a spoon in the woman's hand and wondered how she meant for her to drink the broth, until the woman set the chipped bowl to Addy's lip and tilted it up. Addy let the hot liquid into her mouth. It was salty and beef tasting and there was nothing solid in it to worry she couldn't keep down.

Images rained on Addy's head until they collected in a puddle and she remembered what all had happened to her. As if the woman knew her thoughts, she said, "You near passed right here on Mr. MacLeod's laneway."

Addy nodded slightly and let the woman tilt the bowl to her lips once more. She thought to ask, "Am I in Windsor?"

The woman shook her head. "Windsor a few miles down the road yet. We're closer to Sandwich. This here is Mr. MacLeod's farm. It's one of the biggest in the county."

Addy looked around the tiny room. The woman said, "This the house out back. This where my husband, Morris, and my children live."

Addy nodded, feeling stronger from the broth. She took the bowl in her own hands now and drank it in gulps. The plump woman stopped her, saying, "Slow. Drink it slow." Then she looked at the door and whispered, "I saved a slice of kidney pie from the Mister's supper. You can have that later if you think you can keep it down."

Addy smiled and thanked the woman with her eyes. The woman watched her drink and asked, "What's your name?"

Addy thought to lie but couldn't. "Adelaide Shadd."

"Adelaide Shadd. So you *are* the girl from Rusholme."

Addy could not have been more shocked if the woman had slapped her across the face.

"I says to my husband, I says that girl is Wallace Shadd's daughter from Rusholme and don't tell me it ain't." She was pleased with herself and smiled for the first time. "When I seen you up close, I knew right off because of them big ears of yours.

You know you look just like your Daddy. I come from Rusholme too, but I left when I got married and I do curse the day."

Addy didn't know what it meant that this woman knew her father, but felt compelled to be truthful. "My Daddy turned me out."

"I know. All the colored folks around these parts know everything about what happened. It was reported in *The Border City Star*, the deaths at the river and all, and wasn't Mr. MacLeod asking some questions about *you*. I knew your Daddy when he was just a boy. Heard he was working over to Chatham."

"Yes, Ma'am."

"Doing well for hisself."

"Yes, Ma'am."

"He was sweet on me, your Daddy. Suppose you didn't know that."

"No, Ma'am."

"I'm Leona Davies. You call me Lenny like everybody else."

"Yes, Lenny."

"Quite a thing. Three people dead in one day. That gonna be hard for you to live with, all them people dead on account of you."

"Yes," Addy whispered. She choked back some more soup, thinking of Leam and Chester, and was relieved when she felt her baby kick and had not a moment to think of Zach Heron. In the short time she'd been awake and sipping broth, she'd nearly forgotten there was a child inside her and was only happy the baby was kicking and reminding her it lived. Her hand flew to her stomach but she did not make a circle, unsure if Lenny knew about her condition and what all she'd think about it.

Lenny gestured at the swell under the old blanket. "I felt moving when I first brung you in and I been checking every day. That baby fine. Better off dead though, that's my opinion."

Addy set the bowl by the side of the bed, suddenly hot and confused. "How many days I been here?"

"Three."

"Three?"

"Mr. MacLeod said one more day and he'd wake you up himself and you don't wanna know about that. Ain't nobody happy to see you."

Addy thought about the law. "My Daddy know I'm here?"

"Just my man Morris and Mr. MacLeod. And the children of course. This Lincoln's room you're in. My oldest boy. He been wondering when you gonna wake up."

"I have to thank Lincoln then. And I have to thank you, Lenny. I wonder what might have become of me if you hadn't taken me in."

"Oh no, Girl. I ain't taking you in. I can't take you in. Mr. MacLeod won't have it and I got enough to do with my own children. Just I couldn't leave you on the lane like that is all. No. I did my deed nursing you back and you got to find some other place to go tomorrow or the next day when you up to walking again."

Addy looked up at the woman. "Where you think I can go?"

Lenny Davies shrugged and thought. "I been asking myself that same thing but I truly do not know. You got no other kin in these parts?"

Addy shook her head.

"Well, ladies at the church won't have nothing to do with you, you must know that."

Addy nodded, even though she had thought the church the first place to go.

"You know you brung this on yourself."

A part of Addy believed she had. She answered truthfully, "Yes, Ma'am."

"You reap what you sow. Shouldn't have been messing with that young boy."

"Yes, Ma'am," Addy said, knowing the woman thought the baby was Chester's.

"I judge that baby come out by winter's end. That right?"

Addy made a circle on her stomach. "I wonder how it's gonna be."

"It hurt good, but not as much as it hurt your whole life to look at it and recall what happened to make it. You gonna hate that child. You not gonna love it like you think. You gonna wish it dead."

Addy could not make her chin stop quivering.

"I'm just telling you the truth is all."

"Yes, Ma'am."

"Don't you cry now."

"I won't."

"Well don't, because after all the trouble you caused you don't got the right to be feeling sorry for yourself. You understand?"

Addy nodded and swallowed and closed her eyes.

Leona Davies surprised Addy when she spoke again and there was an undertone of tenderness in her mannish voice. "I got a cousin over to Detroit City. His wife been sick and good for nothing for years. His children grown but he's like a baby hisself and needs some looking after. Used to be a preacher but he got sent out of the church for thinking he's better than the rest. Truth is I don't care for him one bit and haven't seen his face in years. But I heard his woman near gone and if it weren't for that child to be born, I believe he would be very pleased to see you. I don't know. I have to do some more thinking about that. You want that kidney pie now?"

Addy shuddered and did not want the pie. She shook her head and slid back down into the little bed. "All right if I stay here till morning?"

Lenny heaved herself to standing and played with the whiskers on her chin. "You help me get the supper tonight though, just so Mr. MacLeod feel like you paying him back a little."

"I make a nice crust. I could bake a pie."

"*I* bake the pies, Adelaide. You can pluck the chickens and get the dishes cleaned up after. But don't let Mr. MacLeod see you in the dining room. He's already worried you be stealing things."

Lenny left the room and Addy whispered to her baby, "Don't mind what she said. I won't hate you. I will love you. I will be your good mother and I will nurse you from my breast and I will hold you when you cry and I will never wish you die."

Tiger Tail

Sharla and her Mum Addy settled into a pattern of easy living, feeling as if they'd always been together somehow. Sharla woke first in the mornings and would creep down the skinny hall, open the bedroom door, and wait quietly until the old woman opened her eyes. Addy would always smile at her, glad the child loved and needed her in such a way.

Some nights Sharla would dream of Collette and whatever boyfriend and pee the bed. She'd wake to find herself soaked and call out, "Mum Addy? Mu-um?" After the first time, they'd taken a taxicab to the Kmart and bought a plastic sheet to protect the mattress. Sharla'd pouted and said plastic sheets were for a baby, and Mum'd said, "For grown people too, Honey. Sometimes older people can't hold their pee neither and that's nothing to be ashamed of."

They cooked good suppers together, and Sharla got used to eating the vegetables and fruits Mum Addy said were healthy. She also got used to drinking the skim milk Mum'd make out of powder because it was cheaper and lasted longer in the fridge. Sharla thinned out fast without the potato chips and canned food she'd eaten at Collette's, and after a month she didn't look like the same child who came stinking and saucy on that hot June night.

Addy took out her old sewing basket and sat with Sharla at the kitchen table. She moistened the thread with her tongue and guided it through the needle's eye. She helped Sharla's sausage fingers sew cross-stitches and knots, never making her rip them out or saying they weren't good enough. She taught the little girl how to wash the dishes, not to leave damp things to get moldy and to nod to the neighbors and say, "Fine day," no matter how they looked at her.

They took walks up and down the mud lane for exercise. Addy's old legs started to feel stronger and the cherry cane gathered dust in the closet. They made bride bouquets from the little white flowers out front of the trailer and sang songs that Mum Addy said Billie Holiday made up a long time ago. She had to explain that Billie was a girl, not a boy, and had a short hard life with men.

It was late July. The blistering sun had forced them outside where Sharla could play under the hose. Sharla'd seen it first, and pointed when the big golden Cadillac snaked down the mud lane and stopped in front of their trailer. The Caddy had blue Michigan plates, and the closed darkened windows meant air-conditioning. Neither Addy nor Sharla'd ever seen a car quite so grand before. They watched the old man climb out with his fine clothes and clean white hat and fat cigar hanging off his lip. Addy felt her heart tug, for the old man was big and could have been Chester Monk, except that he was long dead.

The old man nodded to Addy and said, "Good morning, Ma'am." Addy felt shy like she was a young girl again. She wondered where the big man's wife was and why he didn't bring her along.

The old man strode toward her, tipping his hat in a fancy way and saying, "How do? I'm Earl Bolton."

"Adelaide Shadd," she said.

"This here your granddaughter?" he asked, smiling at Sharla.

No one had yet inquired as to her relationship with the child, and though she felt wicked for lying, she let herself nod and changed the subject quickly. "You up from Michigan?"

The old man mopped the sweat on his chin with the silky cloth from his suit pocket. "Detroit. I'm up to see my daughter and my grandbaby. You know Bonita Berry?"

Addy pointed at the trailer a few doors down. The old man looked at the trailer and shook his head. She knew what he was thinking. There were no flowers in front of Bonita Berry's trailer, just the broken lawn chair and some dirty children's toys in the knee-high weeds. The vinyl siding was cracked and soiled, and for all of Bonita's talk of pride, she didn't keep her home very tidy or clean. Her young husband was only seen from time to time, and Addy hoped it was because he had a good job that kept him out of town. Addy shuddered, thinking of the squalor inside the place.

Sharla was a different child, not afraid the way she used to be. She looked up at the big old man and said, "You Nedda's Granddaddy?"

Earl Bolton nodded. "Yes I am, Young Miss. What is your name?"

"My name is Sharla Cody."

Earl Bolton winked at Addy, liking the look of the little mixed girl in her clean summer shorts set and pink canvas sneakers. "You like ice cream, Sharla?"

Sharla glanced up to see if she should say yes, but Mum Addy was lost in the man's eyes so she had to decide for herself. "Mmm-hmmm."

The old man reached into his pocket and extracted a thick brown wallet. He took out a crisp bill, the likes of which Sharla'd never seen before, and handed it to her, saying, "You buy yourself some ice cream with this here and maybe your Grandma like some too."

Sharla squinted at the paper money and glanced up at Mum Addy again like she didn't know what she was supposed to do. Addy decided quickly. "Thank you, Sir," she said, "but the child can't take this from you."

She'd passed the bill back to the stranger, but he would not take it. He pressed it into her hand and held it there a moment longer than he had to. "It would please an old man very much to treat a sweet child to some ice cream. Say it's fine, won't you?"

Addy nodded, though she felt strange and confused by his generosity, and passed the money back to Sharla. Earl turned to look at his daughter's trailer. Addy hoped he didn't rush off. She couldn't remember when last she passed time with a gentleman. She reckoned he was about her age and wondered if he called himself black or colored or even Negro. She wondered about his life and where he'd come from and how it'd been. She cleared her throat and found her voice. "You born and raised in Detroit?"

The old man shook his head. "Born in Carolina, but my Daddy brought us up to Detroit when he got work at the Ford plant. Thirteen children. Imagine my Mama caring for thirteen children in the back of a dusty old wagon."

Addy *could* imagine that. She wanted to bring the man inside her trailer, pour some cold lemonade from her fridge and ask him to tell her the whole long tale of his life. She wanted to tell this man her tale too, for lately she'd been thinking if she didn't tell someone, she would die and her story be lost on the worms and on the Lord, who already knew.

Earl Bolton leaned against his car, smiling easily, like he and Addy'd always been friends. "You born and raised in Chatham?"

Addy shook her head and almost said "Rusholme." But she was suddenly anxious. Most colored people, even across the border, knew about Rusholme and its history, and Dresden and Chatham too. She was afraid that not only would he know about Rusholme, but that he'd have also heard the story about the girl who ran away after causing the deaths of three people. She didn't have to worry what to say next though, because Nedda Berry came running up behind them and jumped into her Granddaddy's arms. "Got some money for me, Poppy?"

Earl laughed, but Addy knew he was ashamed to have his granddaughter acting impolitely in front of her. He shook his head. Nedda pouted. Sharla tucked the bill into her shorts pocket so Nedda wouldn't see. Bonita Berry looked out from her trailer door. She'd just woken up and was unprepared for the visit. She called, "Daddy. Come on!" then disappeared inside the trailer.

Addy smiled and said, "Thank you very kindly, Mr. Bolton. We'll let you be getting on to your family now."

Earl Bolton returned her smile, feeling the tug of duty. He climbed into his shiny gold car, letting Nedda sit on his lap so she could pretend to steer the few yards over to Bonita's trailer. When he got out of the car Addy was still watching, recalling when she was fifteen years old and standing in the hot, buggy fields, wishing Chester Monk would glance her way. It was not just his bigness but the soft intimate way Earl Bolton had spoken to her that put her in mind of Chester. She could hardly believe that, after all these years and her whole lifetime of people and changes, thinking of Chester Monk could still make her sad.

Addy thought to take a walk now. She didn't want Sharla to see her face and know she was holding tears. Hand in hand they started down the mud lane, Sharla singing the old song Addy taught her the last time they cleaned the tub.

Addy smiled, for Sharla's voice was sweet and right on key. She wanted her to keep on singing and was sorry when the child stopped and took the money Earl Bolton gave her from her pocket. Sharla waved the bill, asking, "Mum?"

"Yes, Sharla, Honey?"

"This real money?"

"Course it is. That's American money."

"It's not colored."

"Americans only use green money, Sharla."

"Can we walk to Sweet Freeze and buy ice cream with it?"

The ice cream shop was nearly a mile past the trailer park entrance. It was the place families stopped for cones and sundaes on the way to or from a day's swimming at the lake. The Sweet Freeze had been there since Addy could remember. She marked time by it and knew that winter was really here when the owner locked the doors and hung his old hand-painted sign:

CLOSED FOR THE SEASON. REASON? FREEZIN'!

The sun wasn't brilliant and the sky wasn't blue but a suffocating blanket of gray yellow haze. Dogs and cats hid under porches and trees. The trailers conducted the heat and cooked the flesh inside well-done. Though Addy was dizzy and vaguely sick to her stomach, she thought she could walk the long mile to the Sweet Freeze and wanted to do it for Sharla. She was even cheered at the notion she could sip a cup of coffee in the air-conditioning and not have to look at the golden Cadillac and think of Earl Bolton, who made her think of Chester Monk.

"Why, Mum?"

"Why what, Sharla?"

"Why they use green money?"

"Why? Because America's a different country."

"It is?"

"Course it is. Our country's called Canada. Don't you know that?"

"Mmm-hmm." Sharla'd taken to saying "Mmm-hmm" just as she'd taken to imitating Mum Addy in other ways.

"We call ourselfs Canadians and they call theirself Americans."

"Americans."

"We got a different way about us." Addy couldn't think how to explain further. "We're Canadian."

Sharla squinted into the sun. "They all like you in America?"

"Like me?"

Sharla used the word deliberately, remembering what Mum Addy had told her. "They all *black?*"

Addy laughed and snorted and coughed. "No, Child. They are not all black." She laughed some more at the thought of it. "They are all kinds of races and colors, just like in Canada."

"They got different animals?"

"No. Well, yes, some. Down south they got alligators and armadillos. Won't see them here but in the zoo."

"They got different words?"

"Different language you mean?"

Sharla nodded. "Like the Chinkies?"

"Don't say Chinkies, Sharla. That's an ignorant word."

Sharla didn't know it was ignorant. She waved her American bill in the soupy air and ventured, "Say just *Chinks?*"

"No. No, Sharla." Addy tried not to blame Sharla for her ignorance. "You don't say Chink, Honey. You say . . ." But the name escaped her, as so many names and phrases escaped her these days, and she found only empty spaces when she reached for familiar things. "You say," she cleared her throat, "China person."

Sharla nodded. "China person. I'm getting Tiger Tail. Can I get two scoops?"

Addy nodded and shivered when a gentle breeze snuck up and pushed the fishy odor of Lake Erie into her nostrils. She loved the lake and was glad she could smell it, if not view it, from the trailer park. Rusholme was a good forty miles west of the Lakeview, and the lake smell had been different there, sweeter and richer, like something from the oven. Today the breeze came from the west and with it the stink of Mr. Kenny's barn and Laisa's hot corn bread and Chester Monk's sweat. She wanted the memories and the smells to leave her as much as she longed for them to stay, and she felt her dead brother whisper in her ear, "Rush home, Addy Shadd. Rush home."

Leam had come around a good deal in the past few months and Addy could not say why. Mostly she was glad for his company, but he vexed her too. She'd been planting tomatoes behind the trailer when he'd tapped her on the back, saying, "Dig a little deeper, Sister, else the roots won't take right."

She'd planted tomatoes successfully all her life and didn't much care for his advice. She thought to ignore him, as she did sometimes, but he continued, "Your hip giving you trouble again?"

"Mmm-hmm."

"You coughing a lot too. Best to give up them cigarettes."

"I'm fine."

"No, you're old and dying, Adelaide. Give up them cigarettes."

"I will."

"Make a promise."

"I will!"

"Don't get sharp."

"I'm tired is all."

"I know."

"Tired of missing my dead people."

"I know."

"And tired of being alone and only myself to talk with."

"And me."

"You trouble me though, Leam, and tell me things I like not to hear."

"Don't be a child."

"You think I'm dying?"

"Yes, Sister. You think it too."

"Go away now, Leam. I got my work to do."

"Put them cigarettes in the trash though, won't you, Addy? Do like Dr. Zimmer said 'cause you got to keep yourself well for a while. You got one more thing to do."

Addy didn't know what the *one thing* might be since she hadn't yet met Sharla Cody. Addy argued with her brother's ghost as she never had in life. "Why you always telling me how it is?" He hadn't answered and she wasn't sorry she drove him off. He'd be back and she knew it.

Walking with Sharla now, Addy felt her lungs squeeze, and she stopped a moment at the side of the road. She reached into her purse, drew out her package of cigarettes, and hurled them into the ditch. Cars whizzed past, spraying grit in their eyes and choking them with dust. Addy took a long look at Sharla beside her and wondered what would happen to the child if she passed right here and now.

"Honey?"

"Mmm-hmm?"

"You know who your Daddy is? You know his name? Or where he lives even?"

For as long as she could remember Sharla had asked Collette the same questions. She'd wait till her mother was in a good mood, then wonder out loud why her Daddy never comes to see her. What's his name? Does he have a nice house? Does he have other children? Collette would only roll her eyes and say, "I do not have a clue. Anyways, lots of kids don't got Daddies living with them."

Sharla longed to lick a cold Tiger Tail cone and taste the mix of sweet orange and black licorice. She let Addy lean on her, afraid the wheezing old woman wouldn't make it all the way to the Sweet Freeze. She wondered if she ought to stick her thumb out like Collette used to do so one of the whizzing cars would stop and give them a ride. She hadn't answered Mum Addy's question about her father. She couldn't.

Addy asked again, "You ever see your Daddy before? You know what he looks like?"

Sharla shrugged and didn't want to talk about the Daddy she didn't know.

"You know his name?"

"Cody."

"I guess that."

"Not Depuis."

"What's not Depuis?"

Sharla giggled because Mum Addy didn't know. "My Mum. Collette Depuis."

Of course, thought Addy, surprised she hadn't thought it before. Collette had not married Sharla's daddy and was not a Cody. Most likely she'd never been married at all before. Addy remembered a family of Depuis living on the north side of Chatham in a big house in the new subdivision. The father, Reggie Depuis, was a church-going man who owned the Family Time Restaurant on Highway 2. She remembered delivering his bread order the first time and how he'd told her kindly to come in the back door, not because she was colored, just deliveries had to come in the back. She remembered he had a pretty baby daughter and his wife, Arla, was sickly and later died. Addy'd heard how Reggie cut off two fingers slicing cold cuts after the funeral and nearly died from that himself.

Addy could see the face of the fat baby girl. Could that pretty baby have been Collette? Addy doubted it, thinking Reggie Depuis was a good man and it didn't seem likely that Collette was his. But hadn't she said something about her mother dying that day she came to ask if Addy'd take Sharla? Addy stopped again and was racked by a cough and the voice of her brother saying, "Addy. You got to find the child a home. You got to find the child a home because you won't be on earth much longer and you know it."

Sharla looked up, worried. Mum Addy looked gray and like she couldn't walk another step. Sharla'd thought so much about the two scoops of Tiger Tail, she felt she'd already licked it done and chewed the cone and didn't need the real thing after all. "Wanna go back home, Mum Addy?"

Addy smiled and shook her head, not wanting Sharla to see the thoughts on her face. She'd get the child her ice cream, look up Reggie Depuis in the phone book and see if she had the courage to make the call. She didn't want to give Sharla up, like she didn't want to believe she was dying, but Leam was right, any way you looked at it, she could not raise the little girl to grown.

The Sweet Freeze was busy but they found stools at the counter. Sharla got her Tiger Tail scoops and was happy. Addy felt better in the cool air and thought she wouldn't make that telephone call after all. But Leam nudged her so she took a dime from her purse and found the telephone near the rest rooms.

Reggie was the only Depuis in the county directory and that made it simple, but when a thick smoky voice answered, "Hello?" Addy's first thought was to hang up. Instead she said, "Hello. Mr. Depuis?"

"Yes?" came the voice, chilly and suspicious.

"This is Adelaide Shadd, Mr. Depuis. Maybe you remember me? I used to deliver for Mr. Folo? Over to The Oakwood Bakery?"

There was no voice on the other end of the phone.

"Mr. Depuis?"

"Yes?" came the voice again, as if he hadn't heard the last.

"I used to deliver crusty buns and rye breads out to your family restaurant way back when? I remember your good wife, Arla."

"Arla died years ago. My wife's name is Delia." He was impatient.

Addy took a quick look to make sure Sharla was fine by herself at the counter, and she was. She cleared her throat. "Yes, well,

Sir, I don't know exactly how to ask except to ask, do you have a daughter by the name of Collette?"

There was no voice again and Addy thought the man hung up. "Mr. Depuis?"

"Who the hell is this?"

"It's Adelaide Shadd, Mr. Depuis. I thought you might remember me from making bread deliveries to your restaurant?"

"I sold the Family Time. Owner's called Telfer. Call him if you want to sell bread."

"Yes, Sir. It's not . . . Mr. Depuis, the reason that I'm calling you is that I live out at the Lakeview trailer park and I'm wondering if the girl from there, Collette Depuis, is she your daughter, Sir?"

There was a pause, as if he were deciding. After a moment, the voice came, "No."

Adelaide knew the man was lying. "It's just, Sir, Collette, well, she run off a while back, and she asked me to look after her daughter. You sure that's not your —"

The receiver went dead in her hands and Addy Shadd could only guess at what happened. She thought of her own father and how easy it had been for him to reject her and not to think of her except in a mean way. She thought Reggie Depuis must feel the same, though she couldn't know why. She felt a rush of tenderness toward Collette and was sorry she'd judged her so harshly.

Addy flipped the phone book pages until she found the Cs. But there was not one single Cody in the book. She limped back to the counter, her hip paining her. Sharla had Tiger Tail dripping down her chin, onto her top and shorts, and a sticky cloud around her mouth. Addy didn't care. She wrapped her arms around Sharla's stiff little body and squeezed her eyes shut.

The families at the Sweet Freeze watched Addy hug the messy little girl to her caved-in chest. Everyone knew something sad must have happened and wished they knew what. Sharla didn't know what to think, and even though her hands were ice-creamy and it was an unfamiliar thing to do, she wrapped her little arms around the old woman's back and patted like she'd seen good mothers do on TV. Sharla whispered, "Don't cry, Mum Addy. Shh. Don't cry."

The bearded man behind the counter brought Addy a cool glass of water. She blew her nose into a napkin from the greasy dispenser, looking away, when a white lady with a baby on her hip took the stool beside her and asked, "You okay, Dear?"

Addy felt foolish for all the fuss she was causing. It wasn't just the phone call with Reggie Depuis that got her upset, it was Collette and Sharla and herself and all the other souls who got left and cursed by those that should have loved and cared. Addy shook her head at the lady and was grateful when she offered a soft tissue from her purse because the scratchy napkin was hurting her nose.

The lady rocked her baby, squeezed Addy's brown arm, and almost had her crying again when she asked in her gentle voice, "Anything I can do?"

"No. Thank you for asking though."

Addy thought the woman would leave now, but she stayed. "My name is Rita Whiffen." She gestured at the cranky baby. "This is little Roger."

"Adelaide Shadd. Very pleased to meet you. This here's Sharla."

Rita Whiffen smiled at Sharla and reached into her purse for another tissue. She dipped the tissue into Addy's water glass and deftly wiped the Tiger Tail from Sharla's mouth. "Your grand-daughter?" she asked.

Addy didn't want to lie to this kind woman so she didn't say anything except that her baby was sweet and thank you again for troubling. The woman continued, "I don't mean to be nosy, but I think my husband and I saw you walking on the road before. You need a ride back to wherever you're going? Awful hot out there."

It was Leam again, and Addy was sure of it, coaxing this woman to her goodness, for most people, especially strangers, didn't care to wonder or trouble. Addy said yes and was thankful to take the ride. Looking at Rita Whiffen's smiling face, Addy thought to ask did she have enough room in her heart to love another child, but just then Rita's husband came up and asked his wife, "They need a ride, Hon?"

Three small sunburned children toddled like ducklings behind Rita's husband, and Addy laughed at what she'd been thinking because the Whiffens already had their hands full. They were led out to a big station wagon, where Rita and her husband insisted Addy take the front seat.

Feeling a little unsure, Sharla climbed into the backseat with the other children and the kind woman. Before the car even started up, the two-year-old, Peter, put his arms around Sharla's neck and pressed his drooling lips to her cheek. Sharla wasn't sure she liked that, until Rita Whiffen said, "He does like the pretty girls." Sharla'd stopped hiding her smiles a few weeks back and now she even laughed and said Peter could sit on her lap.

On the short drive back to Lakeview, the adults complained of the heat and humidity, but then, like most people from these parts, reminded each other that winter'd be along soon enough. They'd all be wishing they were hot and sweaty and down at the lake instead of stuck in the house due to high-drifting snow. Although she'd already thanked the couple several times, Addy thought to say it again. "It's not many people think to offer a ride and it's really much appreciated."

Rita nodded and said, "Well, we think the best way to be is color-blind and we'd like to teach that to our children."

Addy was surprised by what Rita said. She hadn't meant *offer a ride to a colored lady,* but she didn't think ill of her for misunderstanding. Rita combed Sharla's hair with her fingers like she was her own little girl and said, "How old are you, Sweetness?"

Sharla smiled, hoping the hand would not leave her scalp. "Five."

"When do you turn six?" Rita asked as her fingers moved through the tangle of curls.

"On my birthday."

Rita Whiffen laughed. "When's your birthday?"

Sharla considered this for a moment. She knew it wasn't normal not to know when your birthday was. She had only a vague memory of a birthday cake from a long time ago and no presents she could think of or point to. "I think it used to be in winter."

Rita Whiffen tried to hide her alarm. "Used to be? Well, birthdays don't change, Hon. They're always on the same day. Don't you know when your birthday is?"

"Maybe in summer?"

"Well when in summer?"

Addy realized that it was likely Collette had forgotten Sharla's last birthday and maybe even the one before that. Addy suddenly knew that Sharla'd never had a birthday party and was already six years old and just didn't know it. She took a deep breath and turned to Rita in the backseat. "August. Sharla'll be six years old August fifteen," she said, because that was what came to her head.

Sharla thought Addy must be magic. They'd never spoken of her birthday. How could Mum Addy know?

It was shortly after the Whiffens dropped them off at the trailer and wished them well that Addy decided to give Sharla a birthday party. She'd told Sharla about the party then and there and wished she hadn't for she'd have no peace now until it was over.

"Can we have balloons?"

"Yes."

"Can Lionel and Nedda come?"

"Yes."

"Can we have firecrackers?"

"No."

"Can we have cake?"

"Yes."

"Candles?"

"Six candles."

"Can I be the one blows them out?"

"You have to blow them out, Sharla. You're the birthday girl."

Apple Cake

*I*t *was Lenny Davies' husband, Morris,* who came to wake Addy some time in the night with a small lantern and a hard look. She hadn't laid eyes on Morris yet, having spent most of the evening working in the kitchen, but Addy couldn't shake the feeling she knew him. She quickly realized what was familiar about the man was that he was wearing the Pastor's black wool coat. She suddenly remembered the fat roll of money in the coat pocket and was sorry she hadn't thought to take it out and hide it somewhere near her skin. But she was in no position to ask for either the coat or the money back.

Morris handed Addy a small pile of Lenny's old clothes and a thin cloth coat with worn elbows. "Get yourself together, Girl. We're going to Detroit City."

Addy found her food sack empty and supposed the smoked meat and potatoes had been taken, along with the black coat and money roll, to pay Morris and Lenny back for their generosity. She pulled the thin coat on and stuffed the rest of the clothes into the sack. She'd eaten chicken legs and biscuits in the kitchen with Lenny earlier, but never did hear about that kidney pie again. She wished she could have it now, for she was very hungry and it appeared she was to leave without breakfast.

It was a horse-drawn wagon, and as old a wagon as Addy'd ever seen, that Morris Davies led her to. She moved forward, thinking she'd sit with him on the bench, but Morris shook his head and gestured behind. Addy climbed into the wagon with some effort and settled down in the dust. As the horse began a trot, she wondered about the two fishing rods and wicker bait basket in the wagon beside her. She tried not to think what Lenny Davies' cousin must be like because that's where she was headed, and that's just what was. The swayback old horse snorted when Morris snapped a leather cord across his flanks and drew the wagon down the lane. The jostling hurt Addy's still-sore body and shook the child in her womb.

The streets were quiet but for the rhythm of the horse's hooves. Addy called out to Morris up front, "This here Windsor?"

Morris shook his head and said simply, "Sandwich."

The sun rose as they drove. Addy watched the town move past her — modest frame houses crowded together and set close to the road, short and square brick buildings on the main street, a shabby clapboard structure she was shocked to see was a church. No people anywhere, black or white. Sandwich was not at all what she'd imagined. She wondered what Windsor might look like. She'd find out about Detroit soon enough.

Morris had made it clear he did not want to exchange words or pleasantries, and she was relieved for she'd none to offer. She held onto the side of the wagon as it rocked over the broken road, wincing when she got a long splinter of wood stuck in her palm. The splinter went in so deep she was sure she'd never get it out.

Addy knew that Detroit City was in America and that America was a different country. She knew there was a border and that Teddy Bishop crossed back and forth on it to run his rum. But when she saw the wide river in the first light of day she was afraid and wondered how they would get from here to there. Morris Davies stopped the wagon and tied up his old horse. He said, "Bring the fishing rods," then went to exchange a few words with a frightening-looking white man who peered out from a shanty near the water's edge.

Morris disappeared inside the shanty a moment then returned carrying a wooden crate, which Addy knew was liquor. She thought of Chester and could hardly believe that he'd been here, had a life as a bootlegger, and that he and Leam lost their lives in that thick swampy water. She wondered if Chester was still here, floating dead on the surface of the water, and hoped not to see if he were.

Morris pointed to a sad little rowboat with only one plank seat, the other plank broken and wet on the floor. He climbed inside the boat with the liquor and held out his hand. Addy thought he meant to help her down but he gestured at the fishing rods and basket so she passed the things over. Morris did hold out his hand to help her into the boat, but only when it was clear she couldn't make it on her own. He balanced the broken plank seat on top of the liquor case and gestured for Addy to sit herself down on it. Then he reached over and pulled the skirt of Addy's dress this way and that until the crate was completely hidden. Addy bent her head, ashamed.

As they pushed off from the dock, Addy reckoned Morris'd likely give her the oars and make her row herself. But he took them instead, keeping the fishing rods by his side. It was only when they were midway across the river and a small motorized boat puttered toward them carrying two young white men dressed like the law that Addy began to understand.

As the boat approached, Morris brought the oars inside and took up the fishing rods. He passed one to Addy and quickly opened the basket. He hitched a worm to his hook and reached for another as one of the lawmen called out, "Getting an early start?"

Morris looked up, acting like he hadn't seen the men coming. He broke out into a huge grin and called back, "Oh yes, yes Sir. Good morning to you."

The lawmen drew closer, cutting the motor on their boat. Addy could see they were trying to peer into the rowboat and were suspicious. "Brought your wife along, did you?"

"Yes," Morris said. "Likely wasting my time though. She squeamy about the worms."

The white men chuckled. They could see there was nothing inside the boat but the fishing basket. Still they didn't seem satisfied.

"What you out for today?"

"Pickerel if they biting. Or whatever my hook like to catch."

One of the white men was looking at the swell under Addy's dress. He tipped his cap at her and said, "Don't care for fishing, Ma'am?"

Addy glanced at Morris, shook her head, and cast her eyes.

"Funny thing you're out here on the river then, wouldn't you say?" The other man set his foot on the side of his own boat and leaned over. "You wouldn't have come along for any purpose other than fishing, would you, Ma'am?"

Addy looked at the white man squarely and thought his eyes strange and weak. She shook her head and said in a small voice, "I got growing children at home and only thought with two of us catching we might have a fine supper this evening and some left over for fish cakes at breakfast."

The man watching her seemed satisfied, but the other did not. He pointed at her stomach and said, "You wouldn't have a few bottles of liquor hidden in that pillow under your dress, would you, Ma'am?"

Addy was shocked by the question even as she knew she was sitting on the crate. Morris laughed much too hard, and the first lawman said, "You mind lifting up your skirt, Ma'am, just so we're sure you're not toting illegal liquor across the river?"

Addy's voice wasn't small this time. "I never heard so indecent a question in all my days."

The lawmen looked a little sheepish but would not let it go. "Mind standing up then, just so we can have a good look at you?"

Morris looked grim but Addy was fearless. "I do mind. I can't barely stand right on dry land with this load I got on me and I ain't gonna stand up in no rowboat." She opened her cloth coat and pulled the fabric of her dress across her stomach and the nub of her big belly button. "You see that? If you think that there's a bottle of liquor then you need to go ask your Mama how a lady gets a baby."

The first lawman tapped the other on the shoulder. They started the motor back up and left without saying sorry to have troubled. Morris waited until the Patrol boat disappeared around the bend, then he took up the oars and drove them into the water, not stopping to catch his breath until they hit the shore on the other side.

There was a man waiting in the bushes nearby to collect the crate from Morris and to pay him for the liquor and a little for his trouble. Addy knew he'd done the deed before, for the man who paid him knew him well. She wondered what all Lenny Davies'd think about her husband being a bootlegger.

They made their way up the riverbank, through some bush, and finally to a road. Morris pressed a piece of paper, on which there was an address and crude map, into her hand. He pointed at a street with tiny clapboard houses and skinny dogs and a few colored children, who were kicking a ball and making clouds with their breath. Morris gestured at the map and said, "Go down this street a ways, turn at the end, then turn again here and here again. You're looking for Chestnut Street. Lenny's cousin live at the first corner house on the third block and he don't know you're coming so you'll have to think how to explain it all."

Addy had a hundred more questions, but Morris didn't say another word and just started back the way they'd come. Addy wondered what he'd say if he got stopped by the Patrol again and had no wife in the boat and just the broken plank seat. She hoped he would get stopped, for she didn't like the man and thought he might have at least said she'd done well with the lawmen and offered her a dollar from the money they gave him, or more from the roll he surely found in the Pastor's black coat.

She wished she had some money to give to Lenny's cousin, whose name she realized she didn't even know, and continued to think on that as she walked. The streets, with their recently built clapboard houses and older two-story brick homes with gray slate roofs, were quiet. The yards were tended, the road was paved, and it appeared many of the people owned automobiles. It didn't look to Addy like a big-city neighborhood though, not the way she'd imagined. At the end of each block, Addy looked up to read the street signs and grew increasingly anxious as many of the names were unfamiliar and unpronounceable.

Her muscles ached and her stomach churned and her legs wondered if they would ever rest again. Finally she found Chestnut Street and stood in front of the house of Lenny's cousin. It was small, but red brick and tidy, with white lacy curtains in the windows on either side of the door. There were two high-back chairs on the porch out front, and even though it was cold, she wondered if she might sit a while before she knocked. But the door opened, and a skinny, sickly looking man-child with a look-away eye and a too-big black suit came through it. Addy thought he was too young to be Lenny's cousin and must be one of the grown children. The boy looked at her strangely, for she just stood there staring at the house. After a moment, he said, "You come to pay your respects?"

Addy quickly realized that the boy's dying Mama must be recent gone and was altogether sorry she'd come. She nodded all the same, and the boy opened the door wide to let her into the house. There were three people in the sitting room, two men and one woman, all of them older than her father. They were quiet, sipping tea and smoking hand-rolled cigarettes. They looked up and said nothing, taking note of her shabby clothing and swelling middle. No one in the room resembled Lenny Davies, and Addy did not know who to look at or what to do next.

The boy with the look-away eye stepped up behind her, saying, "She came to pay her respects, Poppa."

Though he did not rise, the smallest and oldest of the men set his cigarette in a glass saucer and held out his hand. Addy took the hand and whispered, "I'm sorry for your loss, Sir."

The man nodded and gestured at a chair. "Sit down, Miss. Riley get you some tea."

Addy took the chair, wishing her legs would stop trembling. The woman stood and smiled at Addy in a genuine way, then turned to the other man and said, "Best be getting on now."

The man rose and Lenny's cousin too and the three shuffled over to the door. The boy came back into the room, handed her a cup of tea, and sat down in the chair beside. He reached for a tobacco pouch, deftly rolled a cigarette, and offered it to Addy.

She shook her head, so he lit the thing himself and blew out his words with the smoke, "I never want to live these last three days over, no thank you, Ma'am."

Addy nodded and thought how the boy and all the people outside of Rusholme had a different way with their words. The boy turned on her with his look-away eye and must have seen her clearly because he said, "You don't look atall familiar to me."

Addy shook her head, still wondering how to explain all she had to, but she was saved because Lenny's cousin came back in the room and asked, "Would you like a slice of apple cake, young Miss?"

It was wrong, she knew, to drink tea and eat apple cake and not say why and how she'd come to be here, but Addy wanted the cake badly. "I would, Sir. Very much, Sir. Thank you kindly, Sir."

The old man laughed and said, "I believe this young lady would like *two* slices of apple cake."

Riley didn't huff at having to rise again but plugged his cigarette into his mouth and went back down the hall. Lenny's cousin rubbed his eyes, sat back down, and said, "You must be a friend of Verilynn's. She's gone back to school, you know. I said, Child, I said, stay until we got your mother buried, then go back and get on with your life. Riley and I be fine. She left yesterday. She'll be sorry she missed you though. What's your name?"

Addy found her voice just as Riley walked back into the room and passed her a delicate china plate with two fat cake slices and what looked like a fork for a baby. "My name's Adelaide Shadd, Sir."

The boy's good eye found her. He asked, "You a friend of Verilynn's, Adelaide?"

Addy shook her head and Lenny's cousin looked surprised. "You must have known Rosalie then? You knew my wife?"

Addy shook her head again. The fork began to clatter on the cake plate. Her chin quivered and tears squeezed out her eyes. She knew it had to be told, but was sorry as she was telling it that the ears that heard had deep troubles of their own. Once she began though, she could not stop the rush of words. By the end, after she'd explained about Lenny taking the Pastor's money roll and how Morris rowed her across the river and pointed the way, she felt like she'd lived it all over again and she could scarcely breathe. Wallace and Laisa, Chester Monk and L'il Leam, and especially Zach Heron had filled up the room and stolen all the air.

The faces of the man and the young man had said many things as they listened to her story, but she could not tell if the anger she saw was toward her or Zach Heron or Wallace or who. Finally, after a long moment filled by the distant sound of children and barking dogs, Lenny's cousin rose and said, "Adelaide Shadd, I do not believe you."

Riley looked up from his teacup, his face drained. "I believe her, Poppa. Who could make up such a story as that?"

But the older man just shook his head and said, "No Sir, I do not believe it was cousin Lenny who sent you to us."

Addy waited and didn't know what to think when he bent down and took her hand in his. "I believe it was the Lord, Miss Shadd. For who else could know your trouble and ours and bring us together in this right way?"

Riley smiled and liked his father for what he said. His Poppa'd been a preacher years ago and still had a preacher way about him even though he questioned the Bible and said it could not all be right. The old man had decided there was only one thing in that whole big book he could fully believe and that was *love one another*. Simply, love one another.

Riley nodded. "That's right, Adelaide. What with Mama passing and Verilynn gone off to her school, we been saying how we're gonna need a woman in the house. We're both lonely and sick and you look like medicine to us, isn't that right, Poppa?"

Addy was puzzled and sure they hadn't heard her correctly. "But I got a baby coming, Sir, and I ain't married. I'm ruined and that's the only truth."

The man shook his head slowly and said, "This is what I believe, Young Adelaide, I believe that you are a good child and a grievous wrong has been done unto you. I believe that the Lord sent you to us like a gift, and I would be honored if you lived in my home and allowed me to know the power of the Holy Spirit through you."

Addy thought there must be rum in the house but couldn't smell any on this rare man's breath. She let him collect her tears in his soft white handkerchief and said, "Sir. I be most grateful if you and your son here take me into this house. I won't never let myself be seen with you or shame you in any way. I am a fine baker and a good sewer and I could do for you and earn my keep."

"Call me Poppa, Adelaide, like my other children do. And I'll be a Poppa to you, and not like your own Daddy, who needs not our hatred but our forgiveness. And I'll be a Poppa to your child too, for the only thing left to do is love."

Addy felt the sting of rising tears again, but her eye caught the apple cake still untouched on her lap. Poppa saw the way she looked at it and said, "Riley, let's get Adelaide fed proper with good meat and some of the other victuals our friends have brought to us."

Riley nodded and went back down the hall. When he returned, Addy thought she might be dreaming, for he brought a pretty china plate so full of good food it was like the best church supper. She ate that plateful and more, until Poppa said she might get sick and best to lay down in Verilynn's room now.

When Addy woke the next morning, Riley was sitting on a chair near the bed, his eyes watching the rise and fall of her growing stomach. He smiled shyly and said, "I thought you might sleep all day, Adelaide." She smiled just as shyly at Riley and wondered why she hadn't seen before that this young man was so much like L'il Leam in nature and stature he might have been her own dear brother himself. She said, "Thank you for me being here."

Riley shrugged and said, "Well, Poppa knows the Lord like no man living and if he thinks it's the best thing, I think it is too. Verilynn won't agree. Very's not the agreeable type. Poppa made some tea and I thought you might like an apple turnover for your breakfast."

Addy nodded and smiled and didn't tell Riley that whoever made the turnovers had worked the dough too long. She watched him leave the room, feeling Heaven's grace just as Poppa had said.

Glancing around, Addy saw there was a writing desk in the corner, a shelf filled with books, and a certificate of merit on the wall on which she could read "Verilynn Rippey." *Rippey,* she thought, and how strange it was she was only now learning Poppa and Riley's last name.

Verilynn's bedroom was unlike the rest of the house. There was a dark blue curtain without trim or ribbon, and the quilt was not like the delicate patchwork one she saw when she looked into Poppa's room. Her bed had a thick brown blanket that was warm enough, but not pretty. Addy wondered about Verilynn, remembering what Poppa told her last night about his daughter being away at school learning how to be a nurse. She'd been envious and impressed and wondered if the woman would be wearing a starchy white apron and nurse cap when she came home. She also wondered what all Riley meant about Very not being agreeable.

When Riley returned with the sweet milky tea and two heavy turnovers, Addy could see that he was changed. He'd become distant and sullen and hardly responded when she inquired about the neighborhood. "Black Bottom," was all he said, and she had no idea what it meant. She reckoned he was tired and still sad at losing his Mama. She understood. She was still sad at losing her own.

Red Licorice

Addy was loathe to do it because she did not like to beg favors, but she knocked on the screen door to Bonita Berry's trailer all the same. Bonita came to the door wearing just a T-shirt and her underpants, coughing and swallowing her snot. "Thought you was one of the kids."

Addy wondered how that explained her answering the door in just her underwear. "Could I trouble you to keep an eye out for Sharla? I'll just be gone ten minutes or so. She's over there building a twig tower with your Nedda."

Sharla and Nedda Berry had become friends of sorts. Sharla said they were *best* friends and was devoted to the older child. But Addy thought Nedda was bossy and mean and knew the child liked to go through her cupboards and sneak things. Just moments ago she'd overheard Sharla say to Nedda, "Put them back. Don't."

"She won't know! There's a whole package here!"

"That's stealing though. Same as if you put something in your pocket and don't pay for it."

"You're a suck, Sharla."

Addy stepped out from the hall and caught Nedda with her fingers in the cookie tin, a coconut log already stuffed in her chocolate-smeared mouth. Addy narrowed her eyes at Nedda and said, "How many of my cookies you eat already, Young Miss?"

Nedda closed the tin and stepped down from the chair, chewing, stalling. Finally she swallowed. "None."

"Sharla knows how I feel about thieving and I'll tell you right now if you ask me for something, chances are I'll give it to you. But if you think you are gonna sneak from me, then lie about it, you won't be welcome here."

Nedda didn't like to be scolded and got sassy right away. "You ain't my mother. You can't hit me. Only my mother can hit me."

Suddenly understanding why Nedda was Nedda, Addy sat down in a hardback chair and said, "Come here, Nedda Berry." Nedda shook her head. Addy reached out, taking Nedda's hand, and pulled her firmly, till the child stood in front of her. Addy asked softly, "Now, would you two girls like a coconut log?"

Sharla clapped her hands. Nedda nodded, confused. Addy gave each of the girls a cookie and sent them outside lest they get their sticky chocolate fingers all over her clean walls. She called after them, "Do not go near them cows!"

Bonita Berry squinted and scanned the field behind the trailers until she could see the children. Addy knew this woman was not a reliable guardian but reckoned she'd only be gone a short time and felt sure that Sharla'd be all right until she returned. "Just ten minutes. Just going up to Warren's office."

"I'm not feeding her lunch," Bonita warned, and Addy felt cross at that because she often fed Nedda lunch. In fact, Sharla begged her to make peanut butter and banana sandwiches just because they were Nedda's favorite.

"Won't have to. I'll be back long before."

"Good, 'cause I got nothing in my fridge."

"You remember it's Sharla's birthday party tomorrow?"

"Shit."

"Beg pardon?"

"I forgot about her birthday."

Addy tried to sound calm. "That little girl be heartbroken if Nedda can't come."

"Well, I don't have a present and I don't have the money to buy one now."

"That's all right. That's all right. Just wrap up any old thing and say it's a present. Just please let her come. Around eleven. We'll feed her lunch and have her home by three."

Bonita yawned. "All right."

Addy had a final look at the girls and a flash of worry. "They shouldn't be going near the pasture, though."

"Uh-huh." Bonita left the door and plodded back into her trailer without another word.

Addy sighed and started off down the road, hoping Sharla wouldn't see her leave. The air was heavy and dusty, and there was no hint of cool like sometimes happened in mid-August. Addy's garden had been miserable without rain. The children were suffering and the mangy dogs and cats too. Originally Addy thought to make a party for Sharla at the lake and take her and Lionel and Nedda and a picnic basket full of goodies out there in a taxicab. But she knew it would be too hard for her and too much responsibility to look after three children who she knew couldn't swim.

In the end, she decided on hot dogs and ice cream, a few games, and a run under the big waving sprinkler that she was going to borrow from Warren and Peggy Souchuck's office now.

Addy imagined what Sharla's face would be like when she opened her presents. There were three presents in all: a beautiful fairy-tale book with a three-dimensional mermaid picture on the cover that Sharla'd been eyeing at the Kmart, a fancy cartoon lunch box for school, and — Addy smiled thinking of it — Chick's doll.

Chick's doll, her sixth birthday present, had been slumbering in a shoebox, saved along with the white cotton dress and hidden in Addy's closet all through the years. She was a baby doll with porcelain arms and feet and a porcelain face. Her watery blue eyes looked out from beneath a head of delicate blond curls, and her white cotton dress was carefully sewn. It didn't hurt Addy to look at the doll again as much as she thought it would. In fact it pleased her to think of giving it to Sharla. She wouldn't tell Sharla it was a doll to be looked at and not played with the way she'd done with Chick. If the doll was played with and ruined, so be it, Addy thought.

By the time Addy reached Warren and Peggy's office her hip was aching and she was well out of breath. Warren's big German shepherd greeted her at the door with a wag and a bark. She patted his head but said, "Go on, Chipper. I don't trust you one bit."

Addy sat for a moment in the musty chair by Warren's desk and was glad when he offered a cigarette. Then she remembered the promise to Leam and shook her head. Warren didn't mind loaning the sprinkler to Addy Shadd but wondered if her hose was long enough to reach the field. She said it was, and he remembered, "I got a call from Frank Kuiper yesterday. That's his cow pasture out back."

"Mmm-hmm?"

"He says trailer kids been climbing the fence again and someone's gonna get hurt. You think a cow's a gentle animal, eh, but that ain't always the case."

"I'll talk to Sharla again and make sure she won't go climbing. I think she's got more sense but she does get led astray."

"Don't we all." Warren laughed.

Addy took the heavy sprinkler and rose to go. Warren checked to make sure his wife hadn't entered through the back office door and stopped Addy, asking quietly, "You heard from Collette?"

The question took Addy by surprise. She shook her head.

"Let me know if you do, will you, Mizz Shadd?"

"Mmm-hmm. Course I will. Course I will, Warren." She knew she was being nosy but couldn't help it. "You got business with Collette?"

"She owes me a few hundred, but Christ, don't say nothing to Peg, eh?"

Addy nodded.

Warren looked serious. "You thought about calling the police?"

"Police?" Addy's heart thumped.

"Well, yeah, I mean, Collette just up and left the kid. Never said where she was going or when she'd be back or *if* she'd be back. I mean, yeah, I'd think about calling the police."

"If I called the police they'd take that child to foster care."

"Likely. Peg and I were saying that might be the best thing though."

Addy couldn't tell anymore if Warren was friend or foe. Did he mean to have Sharla taken away? She cleared her throat and asked quietly, "You think it's so bad the child's living with me, Warren?"

"No. I just, Christ, Mizz Shadd, you don't *want* her, do you? I mean, you're getting up there, no offense. Peg and I looked after the kid for Collette a couple of times. Not an easy child to like."

"I like her fine."

"I just figure you don't need some brat eating up your pension."

"Well, Warren, truth is, Sharla ain't no brat. She's a sweet thing, really, and gives me comfort. But I am getting old, like you say, and seeing it don't look like Collette's coming back, I did have a mind to find her a more permanent place to live. I called Collette's father."

Warren whistled and shook his head. "He's quite the bastard, eh? 'Scuse my French, but . . ."

"You know him?"

Warren nodded. "We were neighbors. I've known Collette since, oh, way before her mother died. When I got my job here I helped her out, you know, like you do. Guess we were going steady for a while. But Collette isn't exactly a one-man woman." He checked the back door again and gestured with a hand to his throat. "Peggy's the jealous type though, so."

"Why you think so lowly of Reggie Depuis? What'd he do to her?"

"You know Collette's Mum died of cancer?"

"Mmm-hmm. Arla. I knew them a little way back when."

"Then you know Reggie married that Delia woman right away."

"Yes. Yes. I knew about that."

"Well, Delia moves into the house and first thing she does is get rid of the family dog. Said she was allergic but no one believed her. He was an old dog, sure, but . . . Collette never did get over that."

"I imagine she didn't."

"Reggie and Delia were always going out for dinners and card parties and whatever. Pretty much left Collette to fend for herself, so."

"You know Sharla's Daddy, Warren?"

Warren shrugged. "Saw him once or twice at roller-skating. Collette told me his name was Cody. I don't know. He's a colored fella. Sorry, Mizz Shadd. I should say black, eh?"

Addy laughed. "I'm too old to know the right word, Warren. I think you say what you say with your intention and that's good enough for me."

"Well, anyway, Cody was a big fella, kinda fat. Not exactly good-looking. Not exactly somebody you'd expect Collette to go for."

Addy nodded. "Don't know nothing about where he lived?"

"Far as I know she only went out with him the one time. My Mom wouldn't let my little sister go roller-skating on account of what happened to Collette. She's pretty racial, eh, so."

Addy nodded, knowing what Warren meant and how his mother thought. Colored boys went roller-skating and colored boys made white girls pregnant.

"Well, I best be getting on, Warren. I can get the sprinkler back by tomorrow."

"Sure, leave it with Peggy, and don't say nothing about Collette, eh, or my ass is grass."

"I understand, Son."

Addy left the office with a queasy feeling and it wasn't the heat. Leam was walking beside her now and offered his arm for support when she stumbled.

"You think Warren's gonna call the police about Sharla, Leam?"

"No. You heard him. He's a good fella."

"I don't feel well."

"I know, Addy. Been a long hot summer already. You feel better when the north wind blows again."

"What if I die before then, Leam? What's gonna happen to that little girl?"

"Nothing good, Addy."

"If I could just find her Daddy. If I could just find her Daddy."

"Who you talking to?" The voice Addy heard was not Leam's but a squeaky little girl's voice and for a second Addy's heart stopped, thinking it might be Chick. She looked up ahead of her on the road and saw a familiar child swinging her arms and staring. Addy looked at the white-haired child, searching for her name and the context of their knowing each other.

"Hello, Child."

Fawn Trochaud smalled her eyes and asked again, "Who were you talking to?"

Addy shrugged. "Oh, just my own self. Old ladies do that, you know."

Fawn fell into step beside her. "Aunt Krystal buried Trixie out back the trailer."

"Trixie?"

"It stunk like poo too."

"Trixie?"

"She said you should have stayed to help. She was mad."

Addy remembered. "Oh! You're Sharla's little friend. Dear. Dear? That your name? Dear?"

"Try Fawn," she sassed.

"Fawn. Well, what a lucky thing to see you, Fawn. Let's go on over to your Aunt's place a minute. Which one is it again?"

Fawn pointed to a shabby trailer a few yards away where Krystal Trochaud lay stretched out on a cat hair blanket, stuffed into a too-small bikini, letting the sun at her greasy pink flesh.

Addy called out, "Hello there!"

Krystal glanced up and closed her eyes again, calling, "Whatever you come to ask the answer's no."

Addy reached the edge of the blanket. "Beg pardon?"

"Whatever you're asking me to do, I can't do it. I can't take Sharla. I won't take Sharla. Not for a day. Not for an hour."

"Well, actually, I came to ask if Fawn here wants to come to Sharla's birthday party tomorrow."

"Oh." Krystal sat up, imagining a day all to herself.

Fawn shook her head. "I don't want to go."

Addy laughed, thinking the little girl was just being sassy again. "Course you do. Sharla's your friend. And it's gonna be fun. We'll have hot dogs and whatnot. Games and all, and I'm running this big sprinkler here so bring your swimsuit too."

Fawn crossed her arms over her chest. "I hate Sharla's guts."

Krystal lit a Kool and told Fawn evenly, "Too bad, brat. You're going."

Addy told Krystal the time and reminded her to send Fawn with her swimsuit. She walked away from the charbroiled woman and the sassy child and knew she'd just made a big mistake.

In bed that night, after Addy'd finished reading Sharla a favorite book from the Chatham library, she wondered should she tell Sharla now about Fawn coming or leave it till tomorrow. She decided to leave it. Sharla nestled against Addy's shoulder and put her hand on Addy's thigh. She yawned, "Mu–um . . . ?"

"Yes, Honey?"

"Is it really my birthday tomorrow or just pretend?"

"Well, what do you think?"

"Just pretend?"

"Why you think that?"

"Nedda says you're just a pretend Mum and not a real Mum."

"Never mind what Nedda says, Honey. I don't think she's getting much good mothering herself, but don't repeat that and make her feel bad the way she done to you."

"You do good mothering."

Addy smiled and brushed her lips against Sharla's forehead. "I love you like you are my own little girl. Do you love me like I'm your own Mum?"

Sharla nodded.

"Well," Addy continued, "that's good enough."

"Collette's my *real* real Mum."

"That's right."

"But I want to live here with you."

"We just have to see what happens, Honey. Ain't really in our hands."

"Whose hands it in?"

"Well, the Lord's hands, I guess."

"Does the Lord like us?"

Addy laughed. "Course he likes us."

"Much as people who live in Chatham?"

"Yes, Sharla. He likes us all the same."

"'Cept for when you do a bad thing though."

"Even when you do a bad thing."

"I wish we had red licorice for my birthday."

"Did you go sneaking through my cupboards?"

"No." Sharla looked away, guilty.

"Well, you might get your wish."

Sharla grinned about the licorice, then paused before she asked, "Are you a *real* real Mum too?"

"What do you mean?"

"Did you have your own little girl when you weren't old?"

Addy was still. "Yes I did, Sharla."

Sharla looked surprised. "What's her name?"

"Well, I had two babies, Honey," Addy whispered.

"What's their names?"

Addy couldn't remember the last time she spoke her children's names to anyone living and wondered if she could, till she did. "I had a little girl called Beatrice, but we all called her Chick."

Sharla giggled. "Chick. That's like chicken."

"Mmm-hmm. That's short for Chicken and that's what we called her."

"And what's the other baby?"

"Well, the other baby was, he was named after my brother, Leam."

"Leam."

"Mmm-hmm."

"Chick and Leam."

"Mmm-hmm."

"Do you miss them?"

Addy nodded.

"Does Collette miss me?"

"She sure does."

They were quiet for a moment and let the sounds of the crickets and the rustling trees and the lowing cows in the distance fill the room. Addy broke the silence. "Suppose I could sleep here with you on your bed tonight, Honey?"

Sharla breathed deeply and nodded, half-asleep. "Mmm–hmm."

Apple Snow

*B*y *December the ice had not yet frozen solid* on the river, but rose to the surface in ragged chunks that tore at the fragile wooden boats and cost the bootleggers their fortunes. Addy could stroll down to the river's edge to watch the ice chunks float past and allow her heartstrings to be tugged by quiet thoughts of Chester and Leam. She wondered if Chester's body'd ever been found, or if it was just loose bones now, making broth out of the river. She tried to talk to Chester's ghost the way she did Leam's, but she was answered by silence when she called, "Chester? You there, Chester?"

Adelaide had found a home with Poppa and Riley on Chestnut Street, but Detroit City was not Rusholme and it would take some adjusting and educating to understand and accept the difference. It was Poppa who Addy turned to when she had questions, for after that first morning when she woke to find Riley Rippey sitting by her bedside, she'd seen little of the boy and exchanged only a few words each day. He was polite, even pleasant, but Addy feared he'd changed his mind and didn't want her there after all.

A week or so after her arrival, Poppa took a gray wool coat from Verilynn's closet and, though it looked hardly worn, said, "Very got herself a fancy new coat this year so this old one is yours now and just big enough, I think, not to tell the world of your misfortune."

Addy was sorry that Poppa said *misfortune*. "I won't hate this baby, Poppa. Even though I hate how it came to be."

Poppa said, "Of course not, Adelaide. Forgive me."

"I understand you feel ashamed of me. I feel ashamed of myself. But I don't, and I won't, feel ashamed of my baby." She paused, making a circle on her stomach. She'd been worried about something and thought there was no right time to ask. "When this baby is born, Poppa, do you know any lady who can come and be with me?"

Poppa reckoned he could call on Emeline Fraser, reminding Addy she'd met her that first day she came to the house. Addy recalled the kind older woman and was relieved to learn she lived just around the corner.

Poppa helped Addy into Verilynn's coat, saying, "Let me take you outside now, Adelaide, and show you this place we call Black Bottom." He wanted Addy to know he was not ashamed to walk with her down Chestnut Street and took her arm to prove it. They strolled through the neighborhood, Poppa teaching her how to pronounce the hard French street names: *St. Antoine, St. Aubin, Beaubien, Joseph Campau,* and pointing out the fish market and the butcher and the grocer. Finally, when her soles were tender and aching, Poppa brought her to the chili parlor on Hastings Street.

Never having been to a chili parlor, and never having tasted chili, Addy was not sure she was pleased to make the stop. She was even less sure when Poppa said, "We'll be eating *in* today, thank you," to the man behind the counter who'd started to pack their order in a brown paper bag. The man looked directly at Addy's big baby stomach and arched a brow before he took the crackers out of the bag and ladled the spicy chili into large china bowls. Sitting in the uncomfortable iron chairs, Poppa shrugged and told Addy, "Folks judge. If you can say you've never done so yourself, be righteous. If you can't, forgive them, Adelaide, and let's enjoy our chili and some pleasant conversation."

A tall, thin young man, a friend of Riley's, stopped by the table and told Poppa excitedly that he'd left his job at the mine and was going to work on the assembly line at Henry Ford's Rouge plant.

The young man looked Addy directly in the eye and said it was a pleasure to make her acquaintance, then surprised her by adding, "Riley told me about you. He said you were pretty and you are."

It was cruel, Addy thought, for the thin man to mock her like that, and she wondered why Poppa didn't scold him. After he left Addy said, "I didn't know there was a coal mine near Detroit."

Poppa said, "Not a coal mine, Adelaide. That fellow was working for the Detroit Rock Salt Company. Don't you know about the salt mines? Right here." He stomped on the floor with his boot. "A thousand feet below us, right under the city, is the country's largest salt mine. I went down there once. Quite a sight. Bright and clean. Won't make you cough. Salt mining won't ever make a man sick."

No matter how she tried, Addy could not picture the salt mine and could not believe it was there under the very earth they trod upon. She wondered out loud, "Everything's salt? The walls and floors and ceilings? Why don't it crumble? What if it gets wet?"

Poppa tried to explain about the hardness and density of the rock salt, but Addy'd been distracted by the end of her chili and crackers and the hope that she could have another bowl. She recited the street names Poppa'd taught her: *St. Antoine, St. Aubin, Beaubien, Joseph Campau, Fort, Woodward, Gratiot.*

Poppa ordered a second bowl of chili even though Addy hadn't asked and wished silently that Riley could get work in the salt mines, or better still at the Ford Motor Company with his tall, thin friend. Riley worked in the warehouse at the *Detroit Free Press,* putting the big newspaper together, tying it in bundles to ready for the deliverymen. It was good work for a sickly, walleyed fellow and paid the bills on Chestnut Street well enough, but Poppa worried about Riley's future.

Poppa himself didn't work and had never been ashamed to accept charity in one form or another since long before he became a preacher. It was charity sending Verilynn to school in Cleveland. An old friend of Poppa's, "Rich Enos" was what Riley called him, insisted on paying for Verilynn's education and would not be dissuaded. Rich Enos had offered to send Riley to school too, but

Riley couldn't leave his father alone with his dying mother and had never understood what made Verilynn so different that she could.

Riley came home each night with inky fingers and the smell of newsprint burned into his black-smudged clothes. Addy thought to herself that just scrubbing such ink stains was enough to send a woman to her grave and wondered how exactly Poppa's wife Rosalie did die. She was concerned the same disease would be taking Poppa soon, for he never looked too well or rose too quickly from a chair.

A few days after their visit to the chili parlor, when Addy felt she had her strength back and wanted to be useful, Poppa'd agreed she could venture out on her own. "You go on to the grocery and get yourself some things for your pantry, why don't you, Adelaide?"

Addy had been thrilled with the way Poppa described the pantry as hers. And the way he called Verilynn's bedroom *your* room. And the way both he and Riley called her Adelaide and never Addy, because it made her feel different and not at all like the girl from Rusholme. Poppa reached into his trouser pockets and found several dollar bills, which he passed to her and said with a wink, "Won't hurt to get a piece of peppermint candy, Adelaide. I got a sweet tooth for it and I bet you do too."

Addy hardly heard what he said, though, because she was distracted by the strange look of the money and thought it must not be real. Poppa laughed and said, "I forget you come from Canada, Child. Your dollars look like playing cards with your King and Queen faces on them, and all colors like you don't mean business too."

Addy read the name on the American dollar bill. "George Washington."

Poppa said, "He was the president of these here United States a long time ago, Adelaide. Our president today is Calvin Coolidge. We admire our presidents here in America, some better than others, true, and we think they're important enough to put their face on a dollar."

"Oh."

"Can't say I ever did see a dollar with a picture of your Canadian president. Don't even know who your president is. Do you?"

Heat rose in Addy's face and she shook her head, ashamed. "I know the prime minister is William Lyon Mackenzie King but I never did know the name of our president. I never even knew there was a president to learn his name."

Poppa said it was all right because Canadians were just naturally more ignorant than Americans. But, he reminded Addy, she should always be proud that Canada was not a nation of slavery while America had to have a shameful bloody war over it. So many things were different in America, and though Addy never said so to Poppa, she thought it was the Americans who were the ignorant ones. Poppa had warned her, when she went out on her errands, to be cautious, to know where she could go but more importantly where she couldn't. Addy'd been surprised to learn there were places where colored people were not welcome. In Rusholme, she could go anywhere.

She'd found comfort in the simple task of caring for Poppa and Riley. She mended their shirts and trousers, stitching buttons where they hung by a thread, and made all the good things to eat that she could remember Laisa teaching her those long hours together in the kitchen on Fowell Street. There was no venison to be found at the grocer, and Addy felt smug that such a big-city store would be so lacking in essentials. She used beef for her stew recipe instead and was relieved when Poppa pronounced it delicious. She made a nice light batter for her fish fry and because she wanted to mark her first week in her new home, she made a special dessert called Apple Snow. Poppa said he could eat Apple Snow every night of the week. With only five or six teeth left in his whole wide mouth, he preferred a dinner that didn't need much chewing.

Addy was dismayed there was never food to turn over for the next day, but proud how the men liked her cooking. It'd be some time, though, before she'd fix Apple Snow again. The memory of her mother and the day Laisa taught her how to make the sweet fluff brought a choke to Addy's throat as she cooked, cored, peeled, and mashed the tart apples and as she whipped the egg whites with sugar, then folded the mixture together to set. She could not have been more than five or six years old and it was November, the apples well off the trees but still fresh and crisp in the cool root cellar. Leam was recovering from illness and Laisa thought to buy extra eggs for Apple Snow, hoping he'd have an appetite for it, knowing it would give him strength. Laisa had been happy that day and her voice softer than usual. "No, Addy. Like this, Child. You make sure you got all the peel off, every little bit else it only look like snow with red apple skin bits."

"Like this, Mama?"

"That's right. You're doing a fine job. We'll tell your Daddy how you made this all yourself and you should know this is his very favorite sweet dish."

Addy glanced down the hallway to see that her brother's bedroom door was shut. "Mama?"

"Yes, Addy?"

"Leam gonna stay alive now?"

"Yes he is. His fever passed and his eyes bright and the Lord did hear my prayers and them of the whole congregation at church on Sunday."

"He gonna play in the yard with me again?"

"Sure he is. You're his little sister. That's a special thing to be."

"I don't have no sister."

"Your Mama got sick having you, Little Girl. Heaven said no more children for that woman. She's blessed enough." She'd guided Addy's small hand around the big bowl. "Like this, Daughter, faster, because you need to get air inside and that's what make it fluff up so nice and look like real snow."

"Apples kinda brown though."

"Mmm–hmm."

"Like dirty snow."

Laisa laughed at that and said, "I always thought that myself but don't say so to your Daddy. I don't think he's gonna like to eat something called Dirty Apple Snow."

Addy smiled at the silhouette of her mother in the kitchen window and pointed. "Look!"

It was the first snowfall of the season and as magical a thing as nature could produce. Though the snow meant hardship and struggle for Rusholme, it also meant the Christmas celebration and sledding and snowballs and watching the men drag massive ice chunks from the lake to the icehouse. Finally, it meant the anticipation of the glory of spring, for even the children knew that without winter's wither there would be no bud or blossom in which to rejoice.

Laisa and Addy had stood at the window and watched the snowflakes drift from Heaven and settle on the bare branches and on the ground, then melt away like they were never there at all. Laisa put her two working hands on little Addy's narrow shoulders and said, "I do feel a blessed woman today. I do have joy in my heart. May all our days be happy as this one and our family safe in God's embrace."

Addy shook the memory away now, for it would be some time before she was ready to think of her mother in a soft way and not be angry anymore. She also had enough to concern herself with and that was the challenge of getting the black ink stains out of Riley Rippey's shirt cuffs.

It was two weeks before Christmas and there was no snow in Detroit City, neither on the ground nor in the air. Poppa said just wait, and he was right. For one day the cold blue sky turned gray and nearly fell as low as the rooftops, then let go a storm of white like Addy knew winter to be. Poppa and a friend had driven off in a slow-moving auto to see people over to Port Huron, east of the city, before the sun even rose. He'd have reached his destination before the storm stopped him, but not be able to return that evening.

Riley would not go to work, it being a Sunday, and the two would pass a strange and strained morning together. Addy fixed a good breakfast of fried ham and hotcakes and Riley was grateful and said thank you and she didn't have to trouble. He had intended to visit a friend himself today and Addy wondered was that a female friend but didn't dare ask. The snow prevented him from leaving, though, for it was foolish to start out on a journey when the sky warned stay home. He rolled himself a cigarette and settled back on the sofa to smoke it. Addy came into the room with some crochet work, not only because of the good light, but also because she meant to ask Riley some questions, most importantly, did he want her to leave.

Riley exhaled a cloud of smoke and never glanced Addy's way. Addy's fingers flew, looping delicate white thread from the skein beside her into a round lacy pattern with her crochet hook. "Riley?"

"Yes, Adelaide?"

She held up her work. "You think Verilynn like this for Christmas?"

Riley looked at the lacy circle. "What is it?"

"It's a decoration doily. To put on a table. Or the back of a chair. I thought Verilynn have some place to put it in her room at school."

"Adelaide, I'll tell you true, nothing pleases my sister Very so don't try too hard or wish too well."

"You think she doesn't want me here?"

"I wrote to her at Oberlin College and told her about you. I know Poppa did too. Didn't neither of us get a letter back, but then we never do."

"She coming back for Christmas though?"

Riley shrugged and picked up his cigarette.

"She gonna want her room back?"

Riley laughed at that. "Oh, yes."

"I'll give it back. I can sleep right where you are now. I slept in some surprising places before."

"You'll sleep in my room, Adelaide. I'll sleep here on the sofa and that's the last word."

"You mind?"

"I don't mind."

"I mean, you mind me being here?"

Riley cleared his throat and took a long puff. "I like you being here." With that, Riley crushed his cigarette in the dish on the table and stood. "Well, I think I'll go have a rest."

"Riley?"

Riley left the room and Adelaide felt more confused than ever. Of course Riley was lying. How could he *like* her being there? He could not have friends visit him without explaining her presence and the circumstances of her swollen belly. He'd have to vacate his room when his sister came home, and his own father doted so on her, he could not be blamed if he felt envious and displaced.

Addy set her crochet work on the table, drew in her breath, and squared her shoulders. She was prepared to leave Chestnut Street and find some other place to live, but first she'd talk to Riley and she quietly asked Leam for help.

She knocked on the door to Riley's bedroom and did not wait before she turned the doorknob. Riley was stretched out on his bed but sat up quickly, angry. "Can't a man get a little privacy in his own house?"

Addy was about to speak when a wave of dizziness overtook her and she could do nothing but ease herself to the bed and let her head sink into her palms.

"Adelaide?"

"I'm fine. Just dizzy. Happens all the time."

"That bad?"

Addy couldn't look up yet. She swallowed. "I seen ladies in my condition getting dizzy before, Riley. Don't think it means nothing but that the baby wants you to sit yourself down."

Riley swung his legs over the side of the bed and set a pillow against his stomach. Addy didn't know the pillow was to hide the fact that his trouser buttons were undone.

The dizzy feeling left her and Addy glanced up. Riley's face had never been so close and she had not seen before the soft wispy hairs under his nose, nor the tiny black freckles sprayed on his cheeks, nor the dense black pools of his eyes that could never look straight on together. She smiled at him and said, "You remind me of my brother, Riley. You make me think of Leam."

"That make you sad?"

"No. It makes me happy. Especially when you smile."

Riley did smile at that and looked at her close face too. "You make me feel like a boy, Adelaide. And here I am eighteen years old."

"So truly you don't want me to leave?"

"Truly I don't."

Addy nodded and made a circle on her belly. As she did, the baby inside of her moved and twisted and the flesh on her stomach rippled and stopped and rippled again. Riley could see the moving under her dress and was alarmed by it. "You see that? You see that?!"

Addy laughed and reached for his hand. She gently placed his inky palm on her moving stomach, but he was frightened and pulled it away. "S'all right, Riley. It's just the baby needs a little stretch like any person."

She took his hand again, placed it near her stick-out belly button, and held it there. This time Riley left his hand and let the baby push against his palm. He looked into Addy's eyes and said, "That's a blessed thing to feel."

Addy nodded and released Riley's hand, but he did not pull away and instead began to move his palm tenderly over the swell of her belly all the way down and back up again. Addy felt vaguely ashamed to let him do it, but did not want him to stop. Her congested pelvis had been vexing her lately and she'd more than once taken Verilynn's pillow from under her head and thrust it between her legs, moving against it until she felt an explosion of relief. She felt the building tension between her legs now and a smooth wet feeling too.

Riley moved his palm crossways from hip to hip, then in a circle like Addy liked to do herself. Neither of them felt powerless over their actions, but rather anxious to continue, prepared to deny the implications. Riley unhooked the buttons of her dress and pulled up her thin undergarments, exposing the whole of her brown baby stomach. He traced with his finger the straight black line from her pubis to her belly button and back again, tickling the coarse hair near her lady part, making Addy feel dizzy again.

She had not known she would do such a thing, nor even that she wanted such a thing done, so Addy surprised herself when she reached for Riley's hand and guided it toward her heavy breasts. Riley moaned and pinched her hard nipple with one hand as he worked the rest of the buttons on her dress with the other. He pulled at her undergarments, not roughly, but eager to free her from the fabric and to touch her smooth burning skin.

Riley guided Addy back onto his mattress and did not look into her eyes lest the spell be broken. He leaned over top of her, careful not to rest his weight on her stomach, pressing his mouth against hers and thinking instantly that he'd never tasted any candy so sweet as Adelaide Shadd's lips. Addy, having never been kissed, for what Zach Heron had done was no kiss, thought at first that Riley's mouth was strange and wormlike, his teeth slippery, his tongue a weapon. But after she relaxed and let her own lips and tongue explore, the feeling was no longer wormy and strange, but hot and good.

She was sorry when he pulled his lips away and glad when he pressed them again to her neck, and then to her collarbone, and then even further, searching her heaving breasts and finally latching onto her big dark nipples. Addy peered from under her eyelids and was glad that Riley's own eyes were closed, for she wanted to watch as he worked his fist up and down the slender shaft sprouting rigid from his trousers. She wanted to see his tongue lick the tip of her nipple and flick its way over the mound of her belly, and to her surprise, explore further down yet. She watched as Riley moved his mouth back and forth and up and down until Addy knew she would explode as she'd done against Verilynn's pillow. Riley groaned and fell against her, his breath still quick, his eyes still closed.

They slept like that, Riley's cheek on Addy's thigh, until the snow stopped falling and they woke hungry, in darkness. They had not feared Poppa might come home and find them, for even the main roads would not be passable tonight, but they did fear something when they woke half-clothed and steeped in each other's scent, and that was what would come next.

They said not a word as they pulled on their clothing and rose from the bed. Addy waded into the kitchen and Riley into the sitting room to roll himself a cigarette. Addy came into the room a little later and said, "Supper's ready."

Riley ate his salt beef hash like a starving man and said yes when Addy asked did he want a slice of pear pie. Addy served him the pie but could not stand another moment's silence. "Riley?"

"Yes, Adelaide?"

"I feel so ashamed." Her chin quivered and she sat down in her chair.

"I feel the same way. It's my fault, Adelaide."

"But I done it too." She wrung her hands a little. "Will you tell Poppa?"

"No. Never."

"Will he know?"

"He can't know." Riley'd been playing with his fork and put it down now, looking at Addy squarely for the first time. "Poppa . . . ," he said, but he didn't finish his thought and she couldn't imagine how it might end.

Addy rose from her chair and went to Riley now, lowering her bulk into the small man's lap. She wrapped her arms around his neck and rested her head on his shoulder, whispering, "I love you, Riley. I love you."

They stayed together that night in Riley's narrow bed, his bony arms enclosing Addy's big breathing stomach. They did not make love but kissed and caressed in a sweet gentle way until dreams stole them off and it was another day.

Poppa arrived late the following morning, long after they'd risen and eaten a hearty breakfast. He was beaten from his difficult journey back on the snow-covered roads and took to his bed. He suspected nothing. Poppa loved Riley deeply but wouldn't believe a woman might find his son appealing with his stick limbs and look-away eye. He was certain Riley would never disobey or betray him, just as he was certain his daughter, Verilynn, would.

The next day, the sun rose high in the cloudless sky, but Poppa did not rise from his bed. He was still tired from his journey and still without appetite. Adelaide sat on the bed beside him and forced some broth down his throat. When he smiled at her, a big yellow tooth dropped from his black gums and fell on the clean bed linen. Poppa laughed at the tooth and blew out a cloud of putrid air. Adelaide shuddered. But Poppa was a good man, and decent too, so she felt nothing but tenderness toward him and tried to breathe from her mouth whenever he was near.

The snow didn't melt but stayed on the ground and Addy thought it was like seeing an old friend. The blizzard made a thick fleece blanket for the ugly brown grass and clothed the naked trees and capped the rooftops in a thousand sparkling stars. She and Riley tossed snowballs at each other in the yard and laughed to sore stomachs, until Poppa came to the porch coughing and called hoarsely, "Riley! Riley! You got no sense at all? You forget about that girl's condition?!" Riley hung his head and said he was sorry, then fired a bull's-eye at Addy's behind the second Poppa closed the door.

It was more outside the house on Chestnut Street than inside that Addy felt the approach of Christmas. The shops were bustling, the streets crowded with boot-clad families juggling gift parcels and food sacks. There was a nativity scene on the lawn of the Polish church down the road and a choir practicing inside. Addy had not been to church since she left Rusholme, and she longed to inhale the wood and candle scent and hear the rise and fall of singing voices. She looked at the porcelain baby Jesus in the crèche and prayed silently, "Dear Jesus, please make my baby strong. And please make her come out easy." Then she corrected herself lest she sound too demanding. "Easy as you see fit."

The Rippeys had precious few Christmas traditions aside from exchanging gifts, and even that was thought tedious and done begrudgingly. It was not because the family didn't love, but mostly because Poppa said the true meaning of Christmas was to remember the birth of the Lord Jesus Christ and the rest of it was claptrap. Nevertheless, Addy wanted to make the house feel festive so she popped corn kernels on the stove and strung the puffy white clouds with dry cranberries, hanging the garlands all over the house. She baked sugar cookies and did her best without a proper cutter to shape them into stars. And she kept her fingers busy making presents for Poppa and Riley and Verilynn.

It was not as difficult as Addy thought it might be to steal time alone with Riley, for Poppa had been ill since his trip to Port Huron. He spent a good deal of time asleep or coughing in his bed, and in his waking hours visited with the many friends who came to wish him well. When Poppa was asleep or distracted by guests, Riley'd join Addy in the kitchen to talk and help with the recipes and cleaning-up just like L'il Leam'd done back in Rusholme. Sometimes they would steal into one bedroom or the other and kiss and hold each other, but they would not do what they'd done before. Both of them longed to, of course, but could not bear the shame if they were found.

It was on one such night, when Poppa was propped up in bed and involved in a passionate discussion with a few male friends, that Addy and Riley stole away to the bedroom and set upon each other's mouths. They had been whispering to each other between kisses. "You gonna stink like ink your whole long life?" Addy teased.

"You stink too, Adelaide. Don't think you don't."

"I do? What do I stink like, Riley?"

"Like cake and pie and anything sweet a person could eat."

"Mmmm."

"I wish I could lay down with you."

"Shh."

"I wish I could —"

"Shh." Addy covered his mouth now and it was not because she didn't want Riley to continue. It was because she thought she'd heard the doorknob turn. And she had. For in the next moment the bedroom door opened and the silhouette of a striking young woman was revealed. Riley and Addy pulled apart but not quickly enough. Verilynn had seen them and they knew it.

"Well," Verilynn said. "This must be young Adelaide Shadd. Haven't you two become good friends?"

Riley neither laughed nor smiled but said, "You might have let us know when you were coming, Very."

"Why?"

"We could have met you at the station."

"I didn't ride the train. In fact, I had a drive from a very nice gentleman who teaches at the school and whose family happens to live not far from here."

"Poppa won't like that."

"You won't tell Poppa then, will you Riley?"

The first thing Addy noticed, since she couldn't see Very's face yet, was that her voice was rich and smooth and she had a fancier way about her words than any person she'd ever heard talk before.

Riley pulled Addy out of the room and into the light, and Verilynn stepped out behind them. Addy nearly lost her knees at the sight of the woman. Verilynn was tall as Poppa and not like Riley at all. Her limbs were long and strong, her waist narrow, her hips and bust full. Her face was beautiful, with sharp almond eyes and a long sloping nose, perfect white teeth, and full, wide, berry-stained lips. The breathtaking young woman held her hand out and smiled with her red, red mouth.

Addy just looked at the hand, unaccustomed as she was to such a greeting, and said, "I'd have washed your sheets if I'd knowed you was coming tonight."

Verilynn opened her mouth and dazzled with her laughter as the three moved into the sitting room. "Charming," she said. She set her leather suitcase down on the floor and looked around the room at the popcorn and cranberry garlands and the plate of oddly shaped cookies on the table. "Well, Merry Christmas, as they say."

The beautiful woman arranged herself on the sofa and pulled a silver case from her handbag. She opened the case and extracted a long, slim, perfectly shaped cigarette, then passed the case to Riley. He took one of the cigarettes, examined it, and nodded, impressed. Riley passed his sister a red candle they'd left burning, then lit his own cigarette with it too. They inhaled and exhaled and said not a word.

There was something different in the room and it was not just Verilynn. Riley was different too, and not the young man Addy knew. She watched brother and sister smoke their cigarettes as she made circles on her stomach. Verilynn narrowed her eyes and blew out a ring of smoke in Addy's direction. "When is your baby due, Adelaide?"

Addy swallowed and searched for her voice. She couldn't find it though, and turned to Riley for help.

Riley cleared his throat. "Baby's due in March, Very."

Verilynn nodded and took a long look at Addy's protrusion. "Looks bigger than just six months. Poppa's been feeding her well." She plucked a strand of tobacco from her soft pink tongue. "Now, just so I have my information correct, this is not your baby, Riley. Is that right?"

A breeze stole through the room though the windows were all shut tight. Riley smiled at his sister for the first time, though it was a dark smile, and Addy didn't like to see it. "Did you come back home just to make trouble, Very?"

"How can you say that?" She pretended to be hurt.

"I wrote to you about Adelaide. Three letters. And didn't Enos tell you about her circumstances when he visited you at the college?"

"Well, it's all a little complicated, Riley. You'll just have to be patient if I forget some of the details." She turned to Addy again. "You come from Rusholme, Adelaide? Have I got that part of the story right?"

"You know Rusholme?" Addy asked, surprised.

Very yawned deliberately. "Some little Canadian town settled by slaves."

Addy sat up. "Rusholme's a rare place. One of the last stops on the Underground Railroad. Some important Negroes settled that town."

"Really? Someone ought to write a book about it. Can you read?"

"Yes," Addy answered, insulted.

"I recently read a book called *Uncle Tom's Cabin*. It's an old book. Have you ever heard of it, Adelaide?'"

Addy didn't like being talked down to. "I read that book when I was twelve years old."

"Have you ever heard the name Josiah Henson? He was a preacher somewhere in Canada. He's the man Harriet Beecher Stowe interviewed for her story. A man I know gave me the book and told me all about him."

Riley blew his smoke at the ceiling. "I thought *Uncle Tom* was a made-up story. I never heard of a preacher called Henson. Have you, Adelaide?"

Addy could not hide her pride. "My Daddy sat on Reverend Henson's knee when he was a boy. His Daddy played trumpet in the band that saw the Reverend to his grave."

Verilynn laughed at the outrageousness of Adelaide's claim. "Well I doubt that, seeing as Reverend Henson lived in a place called *Dawn*. And it was a long, long time ago." She tried to share a look with her brother but Riley kept his eyes on Addy.

Addy drew herself up, not caring that Verilynn was watching her make circles on her stomach. "Reverend Henson lived to be ninety-some years old. *Dawn* is called Dresden now and it ain't too far from Rusholme. Reverend Henson had not just a church in Dresden, but he and a Quaker man built a school there called the British American Institute for Fugitive Slaves. Most people think Harriet Beecher Stowe interviewed him, but the truth is they didn't meet till years after she wrote her book. Did *you* know *that,* Verilynn?"

A round of laughter rose from the back of the house and saved Verilynn from further embarrassment. Riley waited to see if Poppa's door would open and his visitors come out. He turned to his sister. "Poppa know you're here?"

Verilynn shook her head. Addy felt suddenly ashamed for her show of pride. She leaned toward the woman, speaking softly. "I should have said earlier — my condolences to you on your mother's passing."

Verilynn wagged her finger. "No. No. Save your condolences. Rosalie was Riley's mother. Not *my* mother. *My* mother died in childbirth many years ago. Though I suppose I shouldn't tell you that, Adelaide. Sure you're frightened enough about giving birth to that baby."

Addy nodded and could not stop her chin from quivering. Riley ground his half-smoked cigarette in the dish and called, "Poppa! Poppa! Very's home! VERY'S HOME!"

The door to Poppa's bedroom opened. He shuffled out wearing a toothless smile and an old robe, which he had not belted carefully. He was followed by two old men, one of them being Rich Enos himself. There was a good deal of laughter and embracing, for all the men wanted to embrace Very, and Rich Enos more than once.

Riley and Addy slipped off to his bedroom. When they were alone, Addy sunk to the bed. "She hates me, Riley. She hates me."

"I don't mind. I hate her."

"I do mind. You shouldn't hate your sister, Riley. You should love your sister." Addy blinked back tears.

"Shhh. It's just the baby getting you teary, Adelaide." He kissed her wet lips and whispered, "You have a good sleep in my bed and I can't tell you how I wish I could stay. Very's only here for a few days. Stay out of her way and everything'll be fine."

Addy nodded but pulled Riley back when he made a move to go. "Riley?"

"Shh."

"Am I gonna die having this baby?"

"No. Shh. Everything's gonna be fine."

"I'm afraid."

Riley stroked Addy's cheek and smiled and whispered, "I'll be right beside you, Adelaide. Don't be afraid."

Riley left Addy in the darkness. She curled up in his narrow bed and wondered how she'd ever fall asleep, only to find daylight streaming in through the window and the smell of strong coffee coming from the kitchen.

The two days before Christmas while Verilynn was home passed smoothly and without incident. As Riley had instructed, Addy stayed out of his sister's way even while she sought to please. Verilynn preferred coffee to tea and so they would have coffee. And Verilynn did not care for beef or fowl, so they ate fish for supper and listened patiently to her prattle at the table. Poppa adored his daughter, but feared her too and would only smile and listen quietly. Riley fixed a scowl on his face and didn't pass up an opportunity to argue. Addy was quiet and tried to be invisible. She thought Verilynn was like a scared skunk and prayed she would not get sprayed.

It was the evening before Christmas. The air was filled with promise and the scent of Verilynn's perfume. Addy hurried out the door late in the afternoon, just before darkness settled. She was hoping for a good price on whatever she might buy, seeing as the shops would be closed down tomorrow and the merchants not wanting anything unsold and spoiled on Christmas day. She raced past the butcher on her way to buy fish and was all the sudden spitting mad at Verilynn and at herself for not speaking up.

She hadn't thought a mess of pickerel, what the Americans called walleye, would be a proper Christmas supper, but Verilynn had cornered her in the kitchen and mentioned she had a particular fancy for the fish. Addy had intended to buy the walleye like Very wanted, until the moment she stopped herself on the street and headed back for the butcher. She chose a large and costly pork loin and didn't get a good price on it, seeing as the place was full of shoppers with the same idea. Addy was pleased nonetheless. They'd have pork roast and gravy for Christmas supper and if Verilynn wanted fish she could just take herself down to the river and catch one.

The evening passed without a song or hymn or prayer, as Poppa was feeling poorly and retired to his room just after supper saying, "Don't worry, children. I'll be fine by morning." Addy stood at the window, trying not to wonder what her own mother and father were doing this Christmas Eve in Rusholme. She thought of the food and the traditions and the joy of Christmas on Fowell Street and called silently, "Merry Christmas, Mama and Daddy." She couldn't know her mother was sitting alone, staring into the fire, or that her father had crossed over in his sleep nearly two weeks before.

Riley and Addy shared a quick kiss and embrace before she climbed into bed for the night, but she could not sleep for the noise and the cigarette smoke sneaking under her door. Riley and Verilynn were in the sitting room, and by the tone of their conversation and the trill of their laughter, Addy reckoned one of them had brought a bottle of spirits into the house. She was surprised to hear Verilynn and Riley carrying on like old friends, and though she didn't like to think Riley hated his sister, she wasn't sure she liked to know he was fond of her either.

In the morning, Addy fixed a breakfast of pork sausage and eggs and biscuits with strawberry preserves, which she knew the rest of them would enjoy but she could not eat herself. Poppa ate heartily and did seem better and was full of good cheer when he said it was time to open the gifts. Addy had crocheted long scarves and soft wool caps for Riley and Poppa, and they put the hats on their heads, saying beautiful work and thank you, Adelaide. Verilynn pursed her lips at the crocheted white doily and set it upon her head like she mistook it for a hat. Riley laughed at that and Addy felt cross with them both.

Riley gave Addy a wicker basket filled with needles and different-colored thread and soft wool and a new large-size crochet hook and Addy loved it all and didn't mind that Emeline Fraser helped pick it out. Verilynn said, "I didn't know you could read, so," and passed Addy a picture book, which came from the Cleveland library and said so in ink printing on the very first page. Addy thought Verilynn not so intelligent after all to make a gift of a stolen book, but she reminded herself the woman'd be leaving tomorrow and life on Chestnut Street would return to normal.

Poppa presented Riley with a gift of dollars, and judging by his son's face, it was just what he'd hoped for. Riley knew the money came from Rich Enos and his bootlegging, even if Poppa would never admit that was how his old friend made his fortune. Poppa reached into his pocket and pulled out two small velvet boxes wrapped in pretty lace handkerchiefs, saying, "The handkerchief's part of the present. That was Emeline's idea."

Verilynn raised a brow at seeing the package, not only because hers was identical to Adelaide's but because she'd hoped for a gift of dollars too and already felt disappointed. She tore at the handkerchief on the package and didn't care when she ripped the lace. She opened the small velvet box and smiled tightly. Inside was a gold broach that had belonged to Rosalie Rippey. The broach was circular, with a delicate pearl and ruby-chip setting, not modern or chic in Verilynn's eyes. She'd never wear the thing and doubted she'd even be able to sell it. She said, "Thank you, Poppa," and didn't even try to act pleased.

Addy was next. She thought the handkerchief beautiful and the lace edging excellent workmanship. She smoothed her palm over the fabric, admiring it, until finally Poppa laughed and said, "Open the box, Child. Open the box."

Addy opened the box and looked at the thing inside. She looked back up at Poppa and was so overwhelmed she could not do or say anything.

Verilynn could stand the suspense no longer and moved from her place on the sofa to see what it was that made Addy's face go blank. Her own face was not to be believed when she saw it was a white-gold ring with a beautiful marquis diamond flanked by two green emeralds. Even Riley winced when Verilynn looked at her father and choked, "Mama's ring?"

Poppa nodded and forced a smile. He had not anticipated Verilynn's feelings about the ring and it was too late to address them now. "Yes, Very. I'm giving Adelaide that ring. It's a wedding ring and wouldn't be proper to go to you anyway. But I want to say now, in front of Riley and you and the Good Lord, who I know is with us too, that I would like to take this girl for my wife. And to give that child of hers my name." He looked up shyly. "If Adelaide will have such a old man as me, that is."

Addy trembled and set the velvet box on the table, sure she had not heard right. Very couldn't decide between laughing or crying so her face stayed fixed. Riley just hung his head and didn't look at anyone. He already knew about Poppa's intentions because he'd been told that very first morning when he went to get Adelaide's tea. Riley had wanted to tell her himself, but kept hoping his father would have a change of heart.

Poppa waited. Addy did not know what gave her the courage to speak or the sense to say just the right thing. "Poppa, I think of you as my father and never thought of loving you as my husband. I wonder if you might give me some time to think on that?"

Riley had been studying the smoke rising from his cigarette, marveling at how quickly the present could collapse the future. He looked up now and thought Adelaide Shadd the wisest woman he ever knew.

Poppa nodded and said, "Yes, Child. I do understand such a confusing thing as love. I only want you to say yes if you think you might be happy to share my bed. I already know the answer to that myself."

Addy nodded and sat paralyzed in the chair. Verilynn snatched the diamond ring from the box. She smiled darkly and looked back and forth from Addy to Riley before turning on her father. "Poppa, she'll never take this ring. You ought to know that now and save yourself the wondering."

Poppa didn't want to hear it. "Sit down, Very. I'm sorry if this takes you by surprise, but you left this home and family and hardly even bother with a letter. You can't expect to understand the things that have happened in your absence."

The smooth voice was gone, and an angry, quivering one suffered Verilynn's throat now as she held the ring between her finger and thumb and shook it at Poppa. "I understand that this ring belonged to *my mother* and should be *mine*. I understand that it's Riley who owns this ignorant country girl's heart and not you. It's you who doesn't know what happens in your absence, Poppa. It's *you*."

Addy could not feel her legs to rise and could not glance at Riley nor he at her. Poppa shook his fist and opened his mouth and said, "Cherry bridge middle up." They all stopped and knew they weren't imagining that Poppa's words made no sense.

Poppa's eyes moved from Addy to Riley to Verilynn. He looked like he didn't know them and was wondering what business they had in his house. He laughed strangely, then grasped his head as a sharp knife pain drove into his right eyeball. He opened his mouth again, but no words came out. He opened wider, thinking the words were clogged and he needed a bigger spout, but still there was nothing. Poppa made a choking sound and fell to the floor before any of them could stop him. He sunk to his knees, then tipped over on his head and lay there unconscious, wheezing.

There was only the tick of the clock on the wall and the chime of the church bells in the distance, as Poppa's three fearful children carried him down the hallway to his soft bed. Riley seethed at his sister over the slack body of their father. "If he dies, Very, it's on your hands."

Addy scolded Riley, "Shh. He can hear you, Riley. Don't say such things."

Verilynn said nothing, but Addy could tell she felt sorry and loved her father and couldn't help that she was a spoiled child. Later, Addy was bringing a cloth and basin of cool water into Poppa's room when she saw Verilynn kiss his fetid mouth and whisper, "I'm sorry, Poppa. I'm so sorry." Addy wanted to tell the woman she understood what it was to be sorry, but Verilynn turned to find her watching, muttered a curse word, and left the room.

Rich Enos came with the doctor, and Emeline arrived still wearing her apron and smelling of roast goose from her own Christmas supper. They applied cool cloths to Poppa's head and knew it was bad when the doctor spoke of oxygen not reaching his brain. Even if he survived, they were warned, he might never walk again.

The pork roast was dry and the gravy burned, the potatoes too salty and the butternut squash bland. Riley had insisted they eat the Christmas supper, and though neither Adelaide nor Verilynn had much appetite, he reminded Addy that her baby was hungry even if she was not. Addy'd made Apple Snow for dessert, knowing Poppa'd be pleased, but he didn't open his eyes that whole long night. Later, alone and cold in Riley's bed, Addy wept, for she knew it wasn't Verilynn who'd caused Poppa's attack, but the silent power of her own horror at his unexpected proposal.

Poppa opened his eyes the next morning when Addy went in to draw the curtains, or rather, he opened his right eye. The left stayed all the way shut. He could not separate his jaw to speak and only managed to part his lips enough to make a small cave on the right side of his mouth. His words didn't sound like words at all, but Addy pretended she understood him perfectly. "I know you feel confused," she said. "You had a heart spasm, Poppa. Doctor said something happened to your brain too and that's why you're having trouble with your talking and your moving. He said you're gonna be fine though. Just take a little time to heal is all."

Poppa tried to shake his head. He knew the truth and hated to be lied to. But his head would not shake and his lips not speak and though he didn't mean to pity himself, a single fat tear betrayed him. Addy sat down on the bed and wiped the tear, trying not to mind about his breath. "Don't worry, Poppa. Riley and me gonna take care of you."

Verilynn was already gone. She'd risen before the sun, packed her things, and left without a word. Riley reckoned she must have walked to the gentleman's house, the one who gave her the drive to Chestnut Street, but he didn't really care how she got where she was going and was only relieved she was gone. He was filled with dark thoughts and did not have enough room in his conscience for hating Very too. He knew his Poppa was dying, but as deeply as he loved his father, he loved Adelaide Shadd too, and could not convince himself to hope the old man would recover.

The diamond and emerald ring was gone. His sister had claimed her mother's ring and Riley knew it would never be mentioned again. He'd inherited his own mother's ring anyway and meant to give it to Adelaide when Poppa passed. And each day it seemed that Poppa would pass. He was not able to rise from his bed, nor drink a cup of tea, nor read a book, nor even visit with his friends. When Rich Enos and Emeline Fraser came by, Poppa made such a noise out of his mouth cave that Riley had to send them away. Addy knew it was because Poppa didn't want to be seen the way he was and understood he felt ashamed.

One week spread to two, and Riley was glad to return to the *Free Press* and joke with his friends and smell the inky smell of the newsprint and not the dying smell of Poppa. And he was glad to head to the rum joint they called "Jerome's Place" after work and never be scolded like his married friends. He wished he had courage like Adelaide, to offer his father care and comfort him, instead of just wishing him gone. He did not help Adelaide position his father over the porcelain pot, nor offer to scrub the soiled sheets when she didn't get there in time. He didn't offer to heft his father up against the headboard so he could drink a little broth, and he found himself another chore when he saw Addy filling a washbasin with kettle water and soap for his father's bath.

Things had changed between them. Addy could not have been more consumed with Poppa's care if she had been his loyal loving wife. Riley was resentful and lonely and jealous and guilty all at the same time. He ate his suppers alone at the table while Adelaide fussed over Poppa. In the evenings, she was so weary from her work and from the weight of her growing child that she could not even manage an inquiry about his day, the weather, or how he'd enjoyed his food. Addy'd taken over Verilynn's room again, and though it occurred to her that she and Riley could be together now without being secretive, she knew, they both knew, they could not and would not until Poppa was gone.

Poppa was aware that he was dying. He lost weight steadily and hardly recognized his own body when Adelaide pulled back the covers. He understood Riley's revulsion and was relieved his son hardly entered his room. But watching Adelaide hover and smile and scour and nourish, he was reminded that he'd often thought *how right and good is woman*. In his early days at the pulpit, Poppa'd even mused that the Lord himself might be a woman. His congregation had been outraged, of course, and now he knew he'd been wrong, for no she-God would punish him in this exceptional way without leaving him the voice to say, "Let me die."

If he had his voice, Poppa thought, he'd ask Riley to carry him outside and set him down in the deep, deep snow, as he'd heard freezing was a sleepy and gentle death. If Riley wouldn't do it, Adelaide would, and Poppa loved her for knowing she could be relied upon. He realized he'd been deceiving himself, thinking the child could feel more than a paternal love for him. More likely, he thought, Verilynn was right, Adelaide and Riley had eyes for each other and he was merely an old fool, and a regretful fool now, for he could not even offer them his blessing.

There was no thaw in January, and by the middle of February the ice was frozen solid on the river, some said two feet, some said ten. The ice skaters had to compete with the jalopy-driving boot-leggers, and the fishermen couldn't drill far enough to reach water. Poppa was like a cadaver and Adelaide prayed each night for the Lord to call him home. Rich Enos came by from time to time and gave her rolls of dollar bills, which he'd have to press back when Addy said no thank you. Addy was confused by the man's generosity and didn't know that Poppa saved Rich Enos from drowning when they were boys. Riley didn't know about Poppa's bravery either, but took the dollars anyway. Addy suspected they went to whiskey, but she didn't mind much. Whiskey brought a shine to his eyes and a smile to his lips, and Addy only wanted to see Riley happy.

The sitting room was warm from the fire she'd made earlier in the day and Addy thought to rest her head a moment. She was surprised when she woke to darkness and the sound of Riley coming home from work. There was no supper on the stove and Addy realized she hadn't even been to the grocer yet. She sat up on the sofa but had not the strength to rise. Riley pulled off his heavy coat and winter boots, came into the room, and sat down beside her. He put his cool hand to her hot forehead. "You have a fever?"

"No. I don't think so, Riley. Just a little tired is all."

"You feel warm."

"You feel cold." She smiled and closed her eyes. "Cold feels good."

Riley watched her closed eyes a moment, then pressed his icy mouth against hers. He moaned, for he had not kissed her since Christmas and had longed to do so every day. Addy opened her

mouth to his tongue, tasting the sweet rum on his breath, knowing he'd stopped off at Jerome's Place. Finally she pulled away, sat
up on the sofa, and wondered if she did have a fever after all.
"What's got into you all the sudden, Riley?"

Riley drew his finger over her lip and whispered, "I'm hungry. What's for my supper, Young Adelaide?"

Addy shook her head. "I never got out today. I suppose we
have to make do with potatoes and biscuits." She rose and made
her way to the kitchen. She set the potatoes on the counter and
settled in to peel. Riley came up behind her, his slender hands
reaching around her stomach. "How big's this baby gonna get by
March?"

"Not too big, I hope. The bigger the baby the more trouble
I'm likely to have getting her out."

"You won't have trouble."

"I might. Ladies do. Verilynn's mother *died*."

"Verilynn's mother was sick to begin with. You're healthy,
Addy. There's nothing to worry about."

Addy stopped, for something struck her. "What did you call
me?"

Riley shrugged. "Addy?"

"You never called me that before."

"Don't you like it?"

"I was never called anything else my whole life."

"Why didn't you say so? Why didn't you say call me Addy
when you came here?"

Addy shrugged. "Adelaide sounded different. Suppose I liked
to feel a little different."

"And now?"

"Suppose I like to feel a little same."

Riley stayed behind her, holding her close and swaying a little
as he hummed a song. Addy closed her eyes, and except that
Poppa was dying in the room down the hall, she felt like her life
was sweet.

"I've missed you, Addy. You got so busy taking care of Poppa,
seemed like you forgot all about me."

"When Poppa took ill, I guess I felt pretty bad. I guess I felt like maybe it happened because of what we done."

"It happened because of my sister. It happened because of what Very done."

Addy set the peeler down and turned to face him. "No, Riley. It happened because Poppa's old and sick. It could have happened just as easy when he was eating a piece of pie or having a laugh with old Rich Enos. Just happened because of life. Let's not blame ourselfs."

"Fine."

"And let's not blame Verilynn."

"Don't go soft on that sister of mine. She's got the devil in her. I believe that."

Riley found a chair nearby and watched Addy set the potatoes in a pot of water on the hot stove. "What are you gonna name that baby, Addy? Have you thought about it?"

Addy sucked her lip, considering. "If it comes out a boy, I like to name him Leam after my brother."

"Leam's a good name. Leam Rippey." Riley smiled at the look on Addy's face. "You know I want to give him my name. You know I want to be his Daddy."

Addy nodded, relieved it had finally been said. "You'll be a good Daddy, Riley."

"What if he comes out a girl? Will you name her after your mother?"

"No. I couldn't name her after Mama because the reminding would be too painful."

"Did you have an Auntie or a best friend? Somebody you thought highly of?"

Addy thought about that and grinned. "Yes. I had a good friend, a best friend. And she was the nicest and prettiest girl."

"What was her name?"

"Beatrice."

Riley made a face. "Don't care for that name much. Have to shorten it or give her a nickname."

"We called Beatrice *Birdie*. Her Mama hated that."

"Maybe you could name her Emeline since Emeline'll be the one bringing her into the world."

"I think I like Beatrice. Maybe Beatrice Emeline. That be a nice way to honor them both. Emeline's good to say she'd help me."

"She'd do anything for Poppa. And you're lucky too because she's got eight grandbabies of her own she helped birth. She'll know what to do when the time comes."

Addy nodded. "I'm still afraid though."

"I know."

"For such a natural thing, it seems unnatural."

Riley squinted at her stomach. "Beatrice or Leam. Mmm. Well, just have to hope it's a boy."

Addy giggled and fired a piece of potato skin at him. It landed in the middle of his forehead and stuck there. He peeled it off and threw it back. "I'm going to smoke a cigarette. Call me when supper's ready."

Addy stopped him, saying, "Check on Poppa though, will you? I haven't seen to him all afternoon. I'd like to try to get a sip of water down him. It's on the table by the bed." She added, "And talk to him, Riley. He gets lonesome."

Riley hung his head. For the second time tonight Riley wished he'd had the money for a third glass of rum at Jerome's Place. He didn't like having to see his Poppa and would have preferred to be glowing a little brighter, so he could take things more in stride.

Addy shook her peeler. "That man spent his whole life caring for you and doing for you. You get in there and give him a drink of water and tell him how was your workday. Wake him up if he's sleeping. He hasn't had but a sip since he woke this morning."

Riley knew he could not decline, but first he stopped in the sitting room to roll a cigarette. He lit the cigarette before he made his way down the hall and didn't put it out when Addy called, "Don't be smoking a cigarette in Poppa's room, Riley."

He shuddered before he pulled the door open and did not glance at Poppa. He didn't think of the frail dying man as his father, and never knew what to do or say to the stranger in his bed. He was relieved Poppa's good eye was shut and thought to leave the room as quickly as he came, but Addy'd be cross if he didn't wake Poppa and lift his head for some water and say a few words to his unknowing body. He reckoned he'd just sit down in the chair by the bed and smoke his cigarette until it seemed long enough for him to have done what she asked.

Cigarette smoke filled the room and Riley was glad he'd brought it along, for it masked the smell of Poppa's breath and Poppa's piss and the dusty smell of Poppa's scalp. Riley strummed on his thigh and hung his head back over the chair, making clicking sounds with his tongue. Then he sang a verse from a song that'd been playing on the phonograph at Jerome's. Finally, he picked up the glass of water from the table by the bed. He sniffed it and thought it smelled odd. He looked for a place to spill it so it'd appear he'd given Poppa a big long drink. He tried to open the window, but it was frozen shut. He leaned over the bed and tilted the glass over the bedpan on the other side. As he did, he felt a strange stiffness beneath him and slowly realized it was Poppa. He jerked back and stumbled. He'd been waiting for his father to die since Christmas, but now he felt shocked and afraid. He called out, "Adelaide!"

In seconds Addy appeared, drying her hands on a dishtowel. She could see right away that Poppa was gone. Neither of them called his name, nor touched him, nor tried to shake him back. Addy sank to the mattress, her hands encircling her stomach, and said a silent prayer. Riley looked at the ceiling and wondered if Poppa's ghost had been watching and knew he'd meant to deceive Addy about the water.

It was only out on the cold street, on his way to fetch Rich Enos, that Riley began to feel the full loss of his father. *Poppa,* he thought, *Oh Poppa.* He'd grieved him since Christmas when he first took ill and cursed him for hanging on so long, but it was here now, an empty place where once had been Poppa. A quietness to replace Poppa's good voice. A gust of wind that said he was there, not on earth, but in the air. Riley knew he would not be the same man again, for Riley had been Poppa's son and was now only his survivor.

With his grief came relief. Poppa was dead and the suffering was done for them all. He and Adelaide could wed and make their own home of the house on Chestnut Street. Their life could begin. He thought of his friends at the newspaper and at Jerome's and what they would think when he told them he got hitched. He'd already planned how he'd tell them the baby was his and he was just now getting around to doing the right thing. He'd let them visit, he thought: play cards, admire his child, drink a little whiskey. Addy wouldn't mind and would never be the kind of wife he heard of from others. Riley liked the thought of his new life and quietly thanked Poppa for making it come true.

Rich Enos took care of the arrangements and no one questioned when he said there'd be no church service. Poppa did not want to be buried in the church graveyard either. Enos said he wanted to be burned and his ashes rained over the Detroit River. Addy thought the idea most unholy but said nothing to anyone. She merely stood next to Riley on the riverbank to watch Poppa's gray ashes settle on the clean white ice, then get whipped by the wind toward some children skating nearby. In the end, she thought, they ought to have waited until spring, for the ashes went not to the river but into the weave of the children's coats, to be shaken out in backyards by mothers, wondering from where the gray dust had come.

The supper at the house was grand and there would be food for weeks after, which pleased Addy greatly, for she was heavy and sad and mostly just wanted to sit. It seemed hundreds of people came by to pay their respects, Negro people and white people and even a Chinaman Riley wondered if he should let in the door. One of the men, Dr. Shepherd, came all the way from Toronto. He told Riley and Addy about his practice and his education at Knox College and how it was Poppa he thanked for his very life. "Your father clothed and housed me when I was a youth. But more than that he gave me confidence and courage. If you ever want to come north to Toronto, there'll be a place for you in my home. Consider it, Children. Life is different in Canada."

Poppa'd been loved and that was sure. None of the mourners questioned Addy's presence, nor appeared to wonder or judge. Rich Enos said Poppa was the best man he knew. He blew his nose into a handkerchief and gave Riley a roll of dollars, saying he'd always be there to help.

The house was quiet when they were all gone and there was much to do preparing the leftover food for the icebox and pantry. Riley smoked cigarettes and gazed at the ceiling. Addy knew he was deeply grievous and guilty too. She felt the same way and wished they might say it out loud, but they retreated to their separate rooms that night and didn't speak of Poppa.

Addy did not sleep. The baby was astir all night long and moving in a way she hadn't felt before. Toward morning, she turned her face into her pillow and cried, for the baby had not let her rest and was reminding her with a mean punch, every quarter hour or so, that Zach Heron's blood was in its veins. She felt moments of relief, and whispered, "Go to sleep now, Child. I got enough to do today. Don't make me cross, now. Shh. Go to sleep."

Addy glanced at the clock in Verilynn's room and realized that Riley was late for work. She rose and hurried into his room and was relieved to find him gone, though she hadn't heard him nor smelled the coffee he'd surely made for breakfast. But then she smelled cigarettes and went to the sitting room to find him stretched out on the sofa, gazing at the ceiling. She whispered, "Riley?"

"I just been laying here dreaming up some plans."

"You're not going to work?" Addy sat down in the chair across from Riley, watching as he puffed his cigarette and shook his head. "But, don't you think they gonna miss you?"

"Look," he said and held out a fat roll of dollars.

"From Enos?"

"And other people too. Just everyone wanted to give a little something to make things easier. It was like I was the church collection plate."

"But it won't last forever."

"Last a while."

"But if you don't go to work, they'll give your job to someone else, won't they?"

"Don't care if they do." He sat up. "I'm thinking about buying us an automobile, Addy. You were just saying last week how you'd like to learn to drive."

Addy doubled over, suddenly overcome by the baby pain again. She grasped the arms of the chair.

"What's wrong?"

She waited until the pain passed. "I'm all right. Just the baby's moving is all. Doing handstands I think. You want some breakfast?"

Riley nodded absently as Addy rose and started for the kitchen. She stopped when she saw a figure shifting on the front porch. She knew they'd have visitors for weeks to come and was not surprised, only sorry she hadn't fixed herself up. She opened the door.

Verilynn stood in the shadows, her eyes cast, her lips pale. She didn't look up at Addy and barely murmured, "I didn't find out until . . ."

Verilynn had no suitcase and her clothes looked strangely shabby. She entered the sitting room and sat down in the chair without taking off her coat or boots. She didn't look at Riley as she passed him her silver cigarette case.

"Sent word to the school, Very."

Verilynn nodded.

"I telephoned there. Tried to leave a message. Fella on the telephone said he never heard your name before."

Verilynn looked up but said nothing.

"You never went to Oberlin, did you?"

Addy was shocked by the accusation and more shocked when Verilynn shook her head.

"Have you even been in Cleveland?"

"Yes, Riley. I've been in Cleveland."

"Doing what?"

"I work in a nightclub. I work in a nightclub and I did not want Poppa to know."

"What about Rich Enos? What about the money he gave you for nurse school?"

Verilynn laughed. "Who do you think got me the nightclub job?"

"Where you been then? Didn't he tell you about Poppa?"

"Course he did."

"Then why didn't you come home?"

"I couldn't face all those people, Riley. I just couldn't."

"Then why you home now?"

Verilynn looked at her brother for a long moment, then rose from her chair. Addy thought she meant to strike him or spit on him or anything but what she did. Verilynn sat down beside Riley. She reached up, hooked her arms around his neck, buried her pretty face in his chest, and sobbed. Riley said, "Shh. I got you, Very. I got you." He kissed her head and sailed his ink-stained palm over her long smooth back.

Addy moved out of the room and wasn't sure why she felt disturbed. She told herself not to be jealous, for it was only natural for a brother and sister to grieve together for their father. Then she told her baby to settle down, for the child kicked her so violently she felt ill.

Pies and cakes and every manner of food covered every flat surface in the kitchen. Addy took two pretty china plates from the cupboard, filled them, and brought them out to the sitting room. She stood at the entrance a moment, hesitant and embarrassed, for Very had laid her head in Riley's lap and was weeping with abandon. Addy cleared her throat and held out the plates. "Would you like — ?"

The plates crashed to the floor. Verilynn stopped weeping and Riley looked up. Addy was gripping the wall with one hand and holding her abdomen with the other. She could scarcely catch her breath. "Something's wrong," she said.

Verilynn and Riley were too surprised to move. It was Riley who saw the moisture soak through Addy's skirt. He pointed. "Adelaide. Have you lost your bladder?"

Addy looked down and began to cry. She thought the fluid was pee and was ashamed to have peed on the rug, especially in front of Riley and Verilynn. But more than shame she was in pain and afraid she was going to die from it. She knew little about the events of childbirth and it was weeks too early for anything normal to be happening. She could barely croak out the words, "Get Emeline."

Riley rose first. "I'll go."

"No. NO!" Verilynn shouted. "Don't leave me here, Riley. Don't do it!"

Addy could not move to ease herself into a chair so she stood with her hand on the wall, begging, "Please, please one of you go get Emeline."

Riley narrowed his eyes. "You're nearly a month away, Addy. You think it might just be all the work of putting Poppa to rest? You sure — ?"

"I'm *sure*, Riley," Addy said, trying to keep her tone even. "I know enough that a lady gets bad pains, a whole lot of them, and that tells her it's time. It's *time*, Riley. Please, please get Emeline."

Verilynn stood and because she had not yet removed her coat and boots she raced out the door so fast that, except for her handbag on the floor at Riley's feet, it was like she'd never been there at all.

Riley was afraid. Addy could see that, and his fear made her own less important. She smiled at him, for her pain had retreated somewhat, and she said, "Might just be nothing, Riley. Best to have Emeline come along though, don't you think?"

Riley nodded dumbly and still did not move.

Addy said, "How about you help me down the hall and I'll get off my feet and see doesn't that make it go away."

Riley nodded and felt better. He put his hand around her waist and let Addy lean on him. "You do still have a month to go."

"Yes. Well, few weeks at least. Likely just Leam doing some extra hard kicking and punching today."

"Maybe he's gonna be a boxer." Riley smiled. "Maybe he's gonna be another Jack Johnson."

"Or maybe *he's* gonna be a *Beatrice* and *she's* just giving her Mama a little taste of what's to come. Mamas and daughters do have their struggles."

Riley nodded. "Let's take you to Poppa's room, Addy. That's the biggest bed."

Addy had washed the walls and the linen and hacked at the ice inside and out to get the window open in the days since Poppa's passing. She was glad she hadn't put off the chore even though she'd been tired and hadn't wanted to spend time in the room. Now the air was fresh and wintry and didn't smell like death at all. The mattress was caved in the middle and she found it comforting to think of Poppa lying there. She imagined she could still feel his warmth in the bedding. She was about to tell Riley just that when another stabbing pain made her cry out.

Riley put his palm on her forehead and did not know what to do. When the pain passed, Addy said, "There's some clean linen in the cupboard. Bring that, Riley. Emeline's gonna need it. And a piece of yarn from my basket for tying the cord. And a glass of cool water for me."

"You think the baby's coming?"

"I think it is."

"What if she's not here in time?"

"She will be. Takes a long time to have a baby. Sometimes it takes days."

She thought of her Rusholme neighbor, Claire Williams, and her two-day labor with her oldest son, Isaac. It was the only birth Addy'd witnessed, and even then she hadn't seen the whole thing for all the clucking women in the room. Still, she could recall the shouting and the pushing and the blood and the tying off of the cord and finally the cry of the baby and how the whole room was instantly filled with joy.

Addy was about to tell Riley about Isaac Williams' birth, but the pain came again and then quickly again, and each time it came it grew worse and stayed longer. Addy had the sudden feeling she might be giving birth to Mr. Kenny's Ford truck and not a child at all.

Riley left the room and did not run back when he heard Addy cry out with another wave of pain. He wanted to cry himself, for he'd never expected to be present at the child's birth and certainly not the only other person in the house. He ran to the front door and opened it to see if Emeline and Verilynn were near, but there was no sign of them or anyone on the snowy streets. Addy yowled in the back bedroom and Riley was suddenly cross with her and disappointed, for she'd seemed such a brave girl and not one that would cry out like she was doing now. He wished she could be stronger, at least until Emeline and Very got back and he could leave the house.

Addy wanted Riley to return, for she felt panic at being alone in the room. She pulled up her heavy, wet dress, thankful she didn't have to struggle with bloomers. She hadn't fit into them in the last few weeks and, though she felt immodest, simply wore nothing at all. Another pain struck her and she felt the baby move within. She felt her own body bear down and push as if only her womb had a will. With some effort, Addy reached down to feel her lady part. She found the hole big as an apple and felt the greasy hair on the head of her baby coming through.

"RILEY!" she screamed and he came running, frightened when he saw there was blood streaming out from the hairy moon between Addy's legs.

"There's blood, Addy! There's blood!" Riley cried.

Addy could not catch her breath to say the baby was coming. Her muscles contracted and her pelvis tilted. She could do nothing but give over to her urge and bear down with all the strength she had. Riley did not catch the baby as it fell onto the bed and only watched as the fluids gushed out after.

Addy didn't know how much time had passed. She struggled to sit up to see if what she thought happened really had, but she did not have the strength to rise. "Is it out?" she asked. "Is it out, Riley?"

Riley could barely nod as he watched the quiet blue thing and the pulsing purple cord pendulant between Addy's legs.

"Why ain't it crying? Pick it up, Riley," she said. "You gotta shake it or slap its bottom and get some air in its lungs."

The seconds turned to a minute and Addy struggled to stay conscious. "Pick it up, Riley," she begged, and again, "You got to pick it up, Riley."

But Riley could not pick up the child and could hardly bear to look at it, for he knew that something was very wrong indeed. Its head was shaped like a butternut squash and not like a head at all. Its ears and nose were flat, its mouth gaping like a fish. There was long dark animal hair matted down on its back and chest and *Zach Heron* was all Riley could think, recalling what Adelaide told them about the devil and what he'd done to her. And now, lying there on the bed in a pool of filth, a baby version of the same devil, hairy and blue and covered in white clotted cream.

Addy was saying something, but Riley couldn't hear her. He hardly even noticed that she was reaching over her still-round stomach, searching for the baby. She found the child and dragged it by its slippery leg, over the hill of her belly and onto her breast.

When Addy saw the child, she called, "Tie the cord, Riley. Tie the cord." But Riley could not find the piece of yarn and left the room to get another.

Addy shook the baby. "Come on. Come on," she urged in a sweet breathless voice. "Give a little cry now. Give a little cry." She could see the child was not breathing and growing bluer by the second. "Come on, Baby. Come on, Baby." She held the baby in one hand and pulled at the cord still attached to herself. She leaned forward as far as she could, bit down on the cord, and severed it. Riley entered the room just as she did this. He saw the blood on her mouth and the slick blue baby in her arms and nearly turned and left again.

"Riley," Addy whispered. "Help me, Riley."

The baby was still not breathing. Addy held it in the air and slapped its bottom and shook it. "Come on, Baby," she cried. She shook it and cried and shook it and cried and shook it and cried. "Riley?"

Neither of them had heard the front door open and was surprised when Emeline Fraser appeared in the room. She'd heard the crying from outside the house and along with Verilynn had sprinted up the walk and down the hall. Emeline knew things had not gone well and told Verilynn stay out of the room.

When Addy saw her, she looked relieved and held up the baby. "Can you help us?" Emeline took the blue baby but knew it was already too late. "Oh, Child," she said. "Oh, Child."

Addy wiped her blood-smeared mouth. "Can you get him breathing, Emeline? Can you get him breathing?"

Emeline settled the baby into the cradle of her arm and sat down on the bed. She could not speak at first, for the hope on Addy's face was not to be borne. She looked up at Riley but he was drained and speechless and could not take his eyes from the devil child. She asked quietly, "What happened?"

Riley couldn't answer. Addy caught her breath between words. "He, wouldn't, pick, him, up. He, came, out, but, Riley, wouldn't, pick, him, up."

Emeline waited but Riley didn't explain. Babies were born a little blue sometimes. It was necessary to suck the mucus from the nose or jolt the baby to cry and get oxygen into the small lungs. For how long the baby lay there before being picked up, Emeline would not ask.

Emeline had delivered all of her grandchildren. Some went hard and long, some went fast and easy, but she'd been spared the task of telling a mother the baby she'd nourished in her body would not take breath in this world. She gestured for Riley to leave. He did so quickly, closing the door behind him. She set the baby on the clean linen beside Addy Shadd, wanting her to see how beautiful he was.

Addy studied the little being and said, "He don't look right, Emeline." She didn't know her baby was already gone. "Why don't he look right?"

"This baby boy," Emeline said, then had to catch her breath, for she was needed to comfort Addy and could not cry herself. "This baby boy is already gone to Heaven."

Addy could not believe it even though she knew it was true. She reached out and stroked the underside of his tiny curled-up foot, drawing a line from his toe, up his plush leg, over his soft belly to his still, closed eyes. She whispered, as if she was afraid she'd wake him, "Why's he have hair here and here?" She pointed to his tiny shoulders and sunken chest.

Emeline cleared her throat. "Well, babies got hair like that to keep them warm in the womb. Like a coat. Usually falls out by week or two later."

"Will this hair fall out?" Addy asked.

Emeline couldn't imagine why Addy wanted to know. Had she not understood the child was dead? "He's a beautiful boy, Adelaide. A big boy too, considering you're early."

Addy nodded and said, "His Daddy was biggest man in Rusholme." She held out her arms. "Could I hold him a minute?"

Emeline picked up the infant and carefully passed him to his Mama. "What's his name, Honey? What you gonna name this baby boy?"

"Do I still get to name him?" Addy asked, confused.

"Course you name him. That's your boy. And you always remember you gave birth to that boy. And you always love him and think about him."

Addy nodded. "He never saw me."

"No. But he knew you. Don't think he didn't. Babies know their Mamas from the inside out." Emeline reached into her pocket and drew out a handkerchief. She blew her nose and dabbed her eyes as she watched the young mother cuddle her newborn son.

"Did he know I loved him?"

"Yes he did, Child."

Addy looked into the older woman's eyes. "Looks like he's just sleeping. You sure he's gone?"

Emeline nodded.

Addy looked back at the quiet baby in her arms. "Does he have to get buried right away?"

"Child, you hold your boy just as long as you care to. You tell him all the sweet things you been thinking about him and then you say good-bye when you're ready. All right?"

Addy nodded and kissed the baby's parted lips. "Leam," she whispered. "I love you, Leam."

Emeline left the room, shutting the door behind her. She blew her nose again before she made her way down the hall. In the sitting room she fell into a chair, heaving, wiping her eyes and cheeks. She had not been surprised that Addy was dry-eyed. The child was in shock, likely, and exhausted from the efforts of her labor. But the look on Verilynn's face surprised her. And the look on Riley's even more.

Verilynn was herself sobbing and red-eyed. Emeline had never thought her a compassionate young woman and was glad to know she felt Adelaide's pain. The child was going to need some comfort and the understanding of this, her only family.

It was Riley who worried Emeline, for he was reclining on the sofa smoking a cigarette and did not seem devastated or even very upset. She looked at him squarely and, as always, felt displaced by his look-away eye and the feeling that he was not the man he appeared to be. "Riley. Don't blame yourself too much. You couldn't know what to do."

Riley sat up, surprised. "Blame myself? I don't blame myself, Emeline. You saw that thing. There was no measure for me to take to save it."

"What do you mean, Son?"

"I know I did the right thing in letting it die. Addy'd be worse off if it had lived."

Emeline was profoundly confused. "Are you saying you did that on purpose? Do you mean you didn't pick that baby up because you *wanted* him to die?"

Verilynn shot a look at Emeline. "Why would Riley want to save the baby if it was deformed and looked like a devil?"

Emeline still did not understand.

Verilynn went on, "He said it came out a monster, with a big horny head and puss all over his body and hair on his chest like a grown-up man."

Emeline's heart fluttered and she grew sick as she began to understand what had happened. She turned back to Riley. "That's a perfectly healthy baby boy, Riley. Babies born early sometimes got a little hair and that white creamy fluid just something covers the baby in the womb. That was a healthy baby boy, Riley." She felt she had to say it again. "That was a healthy baby boy."

Verilynn's face went slack. Riley cleared his throat several times before he could speak again. "What about his head? His head was all, all pointed and long and looked like the picture of the devil."

"That's the head bones squeezing together to come out is all. They drift apart and round up after a few days. Most babies look like that, Riley. Most babies look just like that baby in there, except they're breathing and suckling right now, and not waiting to be laid in the ground." Emeline could hardly control her rage even as she sensed Riley's horror at what he'd done.

Riley rose from the sofa, put his feet into his boots, took his coat from a hook by the door, and left the house. Emeline and Verilynn looked at each other.

"I need to get on back to my family, Verilynn. Nothing more I can do here."

Verilynn nodded.

"I'm sorry about your father. You know he was like a brother to me."

Verilynn nodded again.

"This house has seen too much sadness. Much too much." She shivered. "You have to help her, Verilynn. Doesn't look like Riley's gonna take this too well and she's gonna need someone strong to help her through. There's some cleaning up and washing to do. You'll have to get that baby buried too."

Verilynn nodded.

"Ground's frozen hard. Likely have to dig close to the house."

Verilynn nodded once more, then asked, "Did she give him a name?"

Emeline blew her nose. "She calls him Leam."

Verilynn repeated, "Leam."

Verilynn waited until some time after Emeline left to venture down the hall toward Poppa's room. She opened the door slowly and stood very still. Addy was gazing into the face of her son and did not seem to see Verilynn there.

Soft afternoon light filtered through the window and fell upon Addy's calm, gentle face, and since the child was hidden in the cradle of her arm and might have been alive for the way Addy looked at him, Verilynn thought it a most beautiful picture.

"Adelaide?" Verilynn ventured.

Addy looked up, said nothing, then looked back down at her child.

Verilynn crept forward and wondered why she had hated this big-eared, sweet-faced girl so much. She stood next to the bed and peered into Addy's arms. She herself had seen just one newborn baby and thought only that this one was uglier than that. She reached down to touch the baby's toe, startled by the coolness of his flesh.

Addy looked up into her face. "He's a big boy, Very. Especially considering he come early."

"Leam," she said quietly and Addy smiled at that, and at her.

Addy tried to peer down the hall. "Where's Riley?"

Very didn't want to say she suspected he went to Jerome's Place.

Addy held the baby up. "Want to hold him?" she asked.

Very reached for the child, remembering to support his wobbly neck as her stepmother, Rosalie, had shown her when Riley was an infant. She stroked the baby's cheek with the back of her hand. "Soft," she said.

Addy glanced out the window. "Pretty like that, with the sun on the snow."

Verilynn squeezed her eyes and whispered, "I'm sorry, Adelaide."

"Call me Addy." Addy touched Verilynn's arm. "I know, Very. I am too. I feel so sad I can't even cry."

Very handed the baby back and left the room without a word. In a moment she returned holding something in her palm. She reached for Addy's free hand and placed the thing in it. Her mother's marquis diamond and emerald ring.

Addy shook her head. "No, Very. I can't. You were right. This is your mother's ring. You should have it."

Very shook her head and could not speak. She left the room again, shutting the door behind her. She moved into the living room and settled on the sofa and grieved for Addy and Riley and Poppa and Rosalie and her own long-dead Mama, whom she longed to be held by now.

In the quiet of Poppa's room, Addy Shadd looked upon the face of her child and thought of her own mother, Laisa. She whispered, "He come out pretty, Mama. You should see him. Even if he was Zach Heron's son, he came out looking like an angel."

Addy turned her attention to the blinding white snow out the window and called quietly, "Leam? L'il Leam?" But L'il Leam did not come and she could only hope it was because he was too busy welcoming his namesake to Heaven. Addy kissed her baby's mouth, telling herself not to think of Riley or worry over what she'd do next. She quietly sang the lullaby Laisa had sung to her:

> *Sleep Child, deep Child, Mama holds you near.*
> *Sleep Child, keep Child, nothing need you fear.*
> *May all your dreams be sweet,*
> *And all your days be bright,*
> *Sleep until the sunrise,*
> *My little one, good night.*

Coconut Logs

*A*ddy woke first the morning of Sharla's birthday party and was
stiff and sore but not sorry she'd slept in the small bed with
Sharla. She eased herself up, trying to be quiet, then realized she
was too excited to be quiet and felt like she was a child herself
and that this was her birthday. She kissed Sharla's sleeping cheek and
got batted away like some annoying fly. Addy laughed at that and
whispered, "Happy birthday, Little Miss Six Years Old."

Sharla opened her eyes and smiled though she was a little
grouchy. Addy moved into the kitchen, announcing, "Pancakes
and maple syrup for breakfast then pretty soon Lionel and Nedda
and Fawn'll be here."

Sharla pulled herself up in her bed, wondering if she heard
right. "Fawn?"

"That's right, Honey. Fawn's coming to your birthday party
too. What do you think of that?"

Sharla clapped her hands and grinned like that was a present
itself and Addy thought it was a blessing how a child could not
know she was hated.

Sharla ate her pancakes quickly. Addy wondered if she should
correct the child's habit of holding her fork in her fist like a baby,
but decided not to. There were two bags of colored balloons and
Addy made a stab at blowing up a pink balloon, only she had not
enough breath to finish. Sharla blew up four balloons and felt a

little dizzy too, so she said four was enough and they'd likely just get popped anyway.

They hadn't discussed it, but they both knew Sharla would wear the pretty white cotton dress with the lace collar and pink ribbon trim and she'd already chosen that dress to wear the first day of school too. Mum Addy got her registered at a different school from the one where Claude was janitor and said it wasn't a religion school but sometimes that was just as well. She'd told the secretary at the desk that she was the grandmother looking after Sharla and the lady didn't blink or ask was that a lie.

When Sharla pulled on the white dress, Addy was pleased to see that it was no longer tight at the waist and surprised that it grazed her knee and didn't hang below. She thought it was a miracle that a child's body could grow and change so much in only weeks. She thought it was an even greater miracle to feel an abiding love for a little girl who she had never laid eyes on till after the lilacs bloomed.

Lionel Chase's mother knocked on the door just after Sharla had slipped into her white T-strap sandals, saying that Lionel was being punished for some misdeed and would not be coming to Sharla's party. Addy nodded politely and said she understood but really she was thinking it was more a punishment against Sharla and wondered if that was the woman's real intention after all. She'd noticed the way Lionel's mother hated the half-and-half look of Sharla and thought her just as racial as the worst of them. She was sorry though, because Lionel was a gentle boy and Sharla was truly fond of him.

Fawn was the next to show up. Addy imagined Krystal pushing the child out the door and telling her she could play over at Sharla's all day if the old colored lady said it was fine. Fawn was dressed in her bathing suit top and a pair of soiled, much-too-big plaid shorts. Krystal had pulled her hair into a ponytail but hadn't bothered to wash her face after breakfast, which was fried eggs, judging by the yellow yolk flakes on her cheek. Sharla clapped at seeing Fawn, letting her in the house and showing her everything:

the sofa bed and blue blanket, the salt'n'pepper shakers, the tidy kitchen, and even the gleaming white tub. But Fawn didn't look at any of the things in the trailer, for her eyes could not leave the beautiful white dress on Sharla Cody's different body. They sat down on the bed in Addy's bedroom and Addy stood in the hall and listened to their words.

"Ain't this a nice bedspread, Fawn? See, it's a match to the curtains too. Mum got it out of the catalogue."

"This supposed to be a birthday party? Where's the treats?"

"Nedda's coming too though."

"Who's Nedda?"

Fawn hadn't ventured down the mud lane much and didn't know the children there. When a moment later Nedda knocked on the door, Sharla and Fawn shot out of the room to go see. The way Fawn and Nedda looked at each other told Addy it was going to be a long day. She had the three girls sit at the kitchen table and gave each of them a birthday grab bag with a bubble blower, some marbles, and several licorice whips tied in a bow. Addy noted that neither Fawn nor Nedda had brought a gift for Sharla, and though it wasn't good manners, she understood it was not their fault.

"Well," Addy said, "time to open presents."

Sharla clapped her hands. Nedda and Fawn looked at their grab bags and Addy knew they felt ashamed they'd come empty-handed.

Addy reached into a hiding space above the refrigerator and took down the three presents wrapped in pretty pink paper and decorated with the stinky white flowers from her garden. Sharla grinned and counted, "One, two, three!"

"Yes," Addy said. "You're a very lucky girl to get three presents."

Nedda let her chin sink to the table and didn't care she was spoiling things. "I never got but one present on my berfday and that was a Sally Server I never even wanted."

Fawn smalled her eyes. "My Aunt Krystal give me twenty dollars and I got a pink wagon for pulling my dolls."

Sharla explained to Mum Addy, "Fawn put the kittens in but they didn't like the wagon and one of them jumped out and died on the grass."

Nedda let her head roll on the table. "I got a twenty dollars from my Poppy one time."

Addy ground her teeth. "Well, girls, why don't we see what all Sharla got for her birthday."

Sharla glanced at Mum Addy and could not have surprised the old woman more when she said, "Three girls. Three presents. Can one present be for each girl?"

"But Sharla, Honey, these here are *your* presents because it's *your* birthday."

"But we could *pretend* it's everybody's birthday."

Addy did not know if she felt like scolding the child or kissing her. She had not intended for these presents to go to the snotty girls who sat at her kitchen table. She did not feel the generosity toward them that Sharla did. Addy wanted to make sure that Sharla was not just afraid of them, or of having her day spoiled by their petulance. "You don't have to give your presents away, Honey."

"I know."

Nedda said, "It's her berfday ain't it? She could give us a present if she wants."

Addy squeezed Sharla's shoulder and decided on the book for Nedda and the cartoon lunch box for Fawn. They tore the pink paper off before Addy had a chance to say wait. They loved their presents, and though neither girl remembered to say thank you, you could tell they were very glad to have come to Sharla Cody's party.

Finally, Addy handed the last present to Sharla. The girls watched silently as she took her time unwrapping it. When at last the paper was set aside and the porcelain baby doll revealed, there was a collective gasp around the kitchen table. Sharla looked up from the doll to Mum Addy, then back again because she couldn't believe it. "This is *mine?*"

"She's yours, Honey."

"Could I see her, Sharla?" Fawn begged, and reached for the doll.

Sharla shook her head. "She wants to stay with me for a minute."

Nedda touched the porcelain toe. "That's a Chinky-doll. My cousin in Detroit got one of them."

Sharla corrected her. "That's a China-*person*-doll, right Mum Addy?"

Addy hid a grin and nodded. "What you gonna call her?"

Sharla didn't hesitate. "Chick."

Addy thought that was a fine name.

"Could I see her now, Sharla? Please?" Fawn begged again.

Sharla shook her head. Generous as she had been, she could not let Fawn or Nedda touch this precious gift yet.

"You're just hoggin' her," Nedda complained.

"Yeah. You're hoggin' her," Fawn chimed.

"That's Sharla's doll." Addy tried to keep her voice smooth. "And that's fine if she wants to hold onto her for a while. You girls got two nice presents there to be thankful for."

"Not nice as that doll though," Nedda whined and made Addy sorry she'd allowed Sharla to give up the gifts at all. She decided that now was a good time to get the girls into their bathing suits and under the sprinkler, then they'd have hot dogs and a few games and she'd be relieved when it was time to send Fawn and Nedda home.

The sprinkler was set in the little green patch they called a field, which separated the trailers on the mud lane from Frank Kuiper's cow pasture, and Addy's hose just barely reached. It was a large sprinkler and shot into the air for what seemed like a thousand feet. The girls jumped over it and around it and screamed and ran away from the pelting, follow-you-everywhere spray. Addy had a hard time getting them inside for lunch and was glad, when they finally came in wet and grinning, that they all seemed to be getting along. Sharla told Mum Addy, "Chipper come and played with us too. He was biting at the water like this."

Addy shook her head. "I don't trust that animal, Sharla. Don't get too close to him."

The girls stuffed themselves with hot dogs and potato chips but no one touched the coleslaw Addy'd scraped her knuckles making the day before. Addy didn't care. She loved to see Sharla damp and giggling and she even felt her heart tug for the smiling little girls beside her, who only needed good mothers much as any child does. Addy had a few games planned, pin the tail on the donkey and hot potato, but after lunch the girls decided they'd rather just take a blanket out to the field and read from Nedda's storybook, then maybe play a game of tag. That was fine with Addy. The girls wouldn't need much supervision if they were just sitting in the field, and she had a mind to put her feet up and close her eyes a moment or two till they came back inside for cake.

Sharla wanted to put her white dress back on and though Addy knew it'd come back dirty and possibly even stained, she did not have the heart to say no. She watched the girls carry a blanket out to the field and settle down on it to hear Nedda read. Almost at once Fawn pulled the book out of Nedda's hands, but Sharla persuaded her to give it back and the crisis was averted. Addy went into the trailer, taking the china doll in her arms. "Chick." She smiled and hugged the twice-loved doll. Then she closed her eyes and drifted off to sleep.

Addy's eyes were still closed a short time later when Nedda crept into the trailer. She had come to touch the doll, but seeing it there in Addy Shadd's sleeping arms she knew she could get no piece of it. Instead, she remembered the coconut log cookies she'd snuck before and carefully, quietly, pulled a chair over to the cupboard. She opened the door and found the tin, opened it, and took out the package.

Nedda joined the girls on the blanket and showed them the cookies, saying, "She said we could," as she passed the package from Fawn to Sharla. Sharla was careful not to let a crumb fall on the pretty white dress. Fawn took a bite and looked around. "This is boring."

"Wanna play tag?" Sharla asked.

"Tag's for babies."

"No it ain't," Nedda said.

"Yes it is."

"We can play Red Rover," Sharla offered.

"Not with only three people, Dumb Dumb."

"Don't call her Dumb Dumb on her berfday."

"I'll call her what I wanna call her."

"Then I'll call you something too."

"Oh yeah," Fawn said, leaning over on the blanket, "what?"

Sharla warned, "Don't say names though. We'll get in trouble."

"Like *what?*" Fawn repeated, glaring at Nedda.

"I'm not telling." Nedda grabbed her storybook and pretended to read.

Fawn wouldn't let it go. "You know the name I can call you and it starts with a N and you can't call me such a bad name as that because alls I am is white."

Sharla shook her cookie like a pointer. "Don't Fawn. Don't say names!"

Fawn used her backhand to knock the cookie out of Sharla's fingers. It landed with a melty plop on the white cotton dress.

"Look what you done!"

"*You* done that, Sharla. *You* dropped it." Fawn stood and looked around. "Let's go bug the cows."

"Mum Addy said don't be climbing that fence."

"Don't have to climb it, Stoop. Alls you have to do is pull the wires a little and go through at the bottom. I done it a million times before."

Nedda and Sharla shared a look, impressed. Nedda brought the package of cookies along as they followed Fawn out to the barbwire fence. They all had a quick look around to make sure no one was watching before Fawn lowered herself to her knees and, carefully, avoiding the barbs, pulled the wires apart and put her head through the fence.

Nedda clucked her tongue and said, "She's gonna get stuck." Nedda was right. Fawn had never gone through the fence before and she had not the strength to pull the wires further. They sprang back against her neck, locking her in place with the barbs. All of Fawn's struggling did not release her head but did cause her too-big shorts and bathing suit bottom to slip farther down on her hips, exposing the cleave of her butt. She could not turn her head to see the girls standing behind her and could only say, "I'm stuck. Help me."

Nedda chewed a coconut cookie. "Thought you done this a million times."

Sharla knew it was wrong to enjoy seeing Fawn's head caught in the fence, but looking at the chocolate stain on her pretty dress made her feel spiteful. "Yeah, Fawn, thought you done it a million times."

"I have done it a million times, but just not in this spot. Help me. Come and help me."

Nedda and Sharla chewed their cookies and watched Fawn struggle and twist and pull at the wires, her shorts and bathing suit bottom sliding farther and farther down on her hips. The more she struggled, the more Nedda and Sharla thought it was the best thing they'd ever seen.

Fawn's little white body was quickly exhausted. There were red smears of blood on her neck and hands from the sharp edges of the barbs. She was mad now. "Help me or you're gonna get it," she seethed.

Nedda laughed and pointed at Fawn's bottom. "Look. You can see her whole butt!"

Sharla laughed too and reached through the crinkly cellophane for another cookie. Fawn let out a howl but they were far enough away, and it such a breezy enough day, that no one in the trailers could hear. "GET ME OUT!"

Nedda sneered, "Get yourself out!"

Fawn began to cry a little. "My Aunt Krystal's gonna kill you."

Sharla had a sudden sickening thought that Fawn's Aunt Krystal looked like a woman who *could* kill, but still she made no move to help.

The next thing that happened was Nedda's idea but Sharla knew she'd pay for it in some way or other. Nedda was ready to take a bite of another coconut log when she stopped and announced to Sharla, "I got a good idea."

Sharla giggled and waited to see Nedda's good idea. Fawn cried, "HELP ME. HEEELLLPPP MEEEEEEeeeee."

Nedda lunged forward. Sharla was surprised she'd decided to help Fawn out of the fence after all. But when Nedda stepped back, Fawn was still stuck, and there was a coconut log cookie jammed into the crack of her butt. Sharla laughed in a way she had never laughed before. Fawn cried, "What is that? Get it out! Get it out! I'll kill you! I'll kill you, Nedda!"

Fawn wagged her bottom this way and that trying to shake the cookie free, but that only made Sharla and Nedda laugh harder.

It wasn't until Chipper showed up that Sharla and Nedda stopped laughing. Chipper stopped a few yards from Fawn, licking his black and pink lips and baring his teeth. The big shepherd was unpredictable and all the trailer kids had been warned by Warren and Peggy he was a dog to guard and not to play with. Nedda clapped her hands and squealed, "Uh-oh, Fawn. Chipper's coming. Chipper's coming!"

Fawn screamed as Chipper began to creep forward, sniffing the air and stalking the cookie. Sharla thought how much she would like to see Chipper eat the cookie out of Fawn's white butt, then it occurred to her the big dog might not know enough to stop at the cookie. Sharla charged forward, pulled the melting cookie out, and threw it as far as she could behind her. Chipper chased the cookie, swallowing it without a chew.

Sharla pulled apart the wires holding down Fawn's head and helped her to her feet. Fawn's face, which they hadn't been able to see till now, was wet with tears and apple red. She said not a word but ran out of the field and disappeared down the mud lane.

Everything was quiet. Chipper trotted off sneezing. Sharla and Nedda returned to the blanket. Nedda laughed and said, "That was funny." Sharla nodded but she felt ashamed. She didn't say good-bye Nedda or thanks for coming to my birthday but rose from the blanket and ran all the way to the trailer and into the comfort of Mum Addy's just-waking arms.

After she had tearfully confessed everything to Mum Addy, Sharla felt better, then quickly worse when Mum said, "Well, you know what you have to do now?" Sharla shook her head because she'd been sure confessing would be the end of it.

"We are gonna take a little walk over to Fawn's trailer and you are gonna tell her how very, very sorry you are for what you done."

Sharla folded her arms. "No I'm not."

"I beg your pardon, Miss Sassafrass? You go get Fawn's lunch box, Sharla. We'll bring that over too."

"No. I don't wanna give her my lunch box."

"Make no mistake, Child. That's *her* lunch box and you *will* bring it."

They said not a word to each other on the long walk to Fawn's trailer. Addy allowed Sharla to take her hand but did not call her Honey or offer any other words of comfort. She wanted Sharla to feel bad, very bad, for what she'd done. She knew Fawn was a bully, but she also knew that Sharla would not grow up to be a good person if she believed people should get what they deserved.

Addy made Sharla knock on the door and was glad when Fawn answered and not Krystal. Fawn's face was puffy and blotched and there was crusty snot caked around her nostrils. She looked at Sharla standing on the other side of the screen and said nothing. Addy backed away a little to give the girls their privacy, but wanted to be within earshot.

"Where's Krystal?"

"None of your beeswax."

"You tell her?"

"She's sleeping, but I'm gonna."

"Sorry, Fawn."

"I got cuts here and here you know," she said, pointing out the wounds on her neck and hands.

"Hurt?"

"Yup."

"Sorry, Fawn."

"Chipper coulda bit me, y'know."

"I know."

"I coulda got the rabies, y'know."

"I know."

"Krystal's gonna kill you when she finds out."

"Sorry, Fawn."

"What you got there?"

"Mum Addy said I had to give you your lunch box."

Fawn opened the screen door, grabbed the lunch box, and closed the door again.

"I wish Nedda never put a cookie in your butt."

"Well she did."

"But if she didn't it was fun before that."

"It was all right."

"It was fun going in the sprinkler."

"Yeah."

"Sorry, Fawn."

Fawn shrugged and Sharla knew her apology had finally been accepted.

"I better go now."

Fawn scratched the screen with her dirty fingernails. "Okay."

Sharla turned and started down the steps. Fawn stopped her. "Wait."

Fawn disappeared from the door and returned after a moment with something in her hand. She opened the screen door and passed a folded-up white envelope to Sharla, saying, "Aunt Krystal took the money 'cause of your Mom scoffing her leather coat and records and that. Don't tell her I give you this though."

Sharla nodded, took the white envelope, and hopped off the last step. Fawn disappeared inside the trailer. Sharla held up the white envelope to Addy.

Addy's heart was thudding, for she knew there was a letter from Collette in the envelope and she could not imagine what it might say. She couldn't tell if she was more worried that Collette was coming back or that she never would. She smiled at Sharla, took the envelope, and said, "That was a very nice apology. You feel better, Honey?"

Sharla glanced up. "You love me again?"

"I never don't love you, Sharla. But I sure don't like what you did."

"I won't do it no more."

"No you won't."

Sharla gestured at the envelope. "That a letter from Collette?"

"I believe it is."

"You gonna read it?"

Addy could not wait. She stood in the middle of the hot dusty road, opened the envelope, and unfolded the four crisp white pages. She was relieved to see the big looping script, for if Collette had written smaller she'd have had to wait till she got home and found her eyeglasses.

She read to herself:

Dear Mizz Shadd,

I bet you thought you'll never see it but here's the hunnerd dollars like we agreed on for taking care of Sharla. Me and Emilios had a change in plans and stead of staying here in Lakeview we are gonna go for trip down to the States and won't be able to see Sharla on them Sundays like we said. We likely won't be back in time for when school starts and if you want you can get her registered at St. Theresa's because that's where my ex Claude works and she really likes Claude. If you dont get her registered that's okay because its just Grade one and not like they do alot. Me and Emilio might even end up getting a place in California because he got a cousin there and thinks he can get work. This has all come up pretty sudden so don't blame me for not telling you when I didn't know myself. We will likely want to get settled in before we send for Sharla to come and I guess I'd mail you some money and get her on a train but we haven't go that far in figuring things out yet. If your finding Sharla to much I don't blame you if you send her to foster care because I myself found her to much on many days and that's my own daughter. Maybe she might be better off

*in foster care anyway because she needs some disiplin. There is
really no place else for her because I don't know her Daddy and he
doesn't know she was even born. My own father hates me and
because Sharla's half colored she don't count as a granddaughter
and his wife Delia is a bitch so don't even think of that.*

She signed the letter: *"Love, Collette."*

Addy finished and read it quickly once more, for she couldn't
understand what Collette was really saying. It seemed to Addy she
meant never to come back and that she didn't much care what became of Sharla. She thought to burn the letter to make sure Sharla
could never read it, but realized she ought to keep it as proof that
the child had been abandoned.

Sharla was waiting to hear what the letter said. Addy folded
the pages and stuffed them back in the envelope. "Well, your
Mama gonna stay away for a long while I think. But she says in
there that she loves you a lot and she thinks about you every day."

They held each other's hands much tighter than usual on the
way home. Addy took a deep breath and Sharla did too. Sharla
suddenly remembered, "We never had cake and ice cream."

When they returned to the trailer Addy cut each of them a
huge slice of chocolate cake. She watched Sharla eat but could not
eat herself. She had a picky feeling in her lungs and stomach that
made her afraid if she closed her eyes tonight she would not wake
again. She wondered who would love this child as their own when
she was gone, and she would spend a long sleepless night thinking
of Sharla Cody and all the other children lost in the world.

Diamonds

*R*iley Rippey *never did come home.* Not the night baby Leam died. Not the next day to help Addy and Verilynn shovel the frozen earth for the little grave near the house. And not even the next day, when Addy filled Poppa's old suitcase with the few things she called hers and left Chestnut Street, knowing she'd never fulfill her promise to Verilynn to return someday.

Addy Shadd didn't know where she was going. Her heart urged, "Rush home. Rush home," but much as Addy longed to, she could not return to Rusholme. She doubted her father would take her back into his house and even if he would, she could not go, for he would say her baby's death was for the best, and that was something Addy could not bear. She would never think her son's death was anything but tragic, and her only grace was to know that he was an angel in heaven, keeping company with his Uncle Leam and her sweet Chester Monk.

Verilynn had begged her not to leave. "You could come to Cleveland with me, Addy. I could get you a job at the club."

"I ain't pretty like you," Addy'd whispered. "Who'd want to see me working in a nightclub?"

"We'll get you work in the back. In the kitchen."

"No. But thank you, Very. You're good to think of me."

"Then stay here, Addy." Verilynn's chin puckered. "Stay till Riley comes home. It'll kill him if you're gone. It will."

"I believe he's staying away now just till he's *sure* I'm gone. He feels guilty and ashamed in a way we can't hardly imagine. My face will only remind him what happened. He don't want to see me, Verilynn. I know that to be true."

After a long and frustrating search, they collected only a few dollars from here and there around the house. Verilynn couldn't understand why there wasn't more, seeing as her brother'd told her about the money from Enos and the others, but Addy knew it was because Riley liked to carry the whole fat roll around in his pocket and pretend like he was a rich, rich man.

"Least you got Mama's ring, Addy. You can sell that. But don't take less than it's worth."

"What's it worth?"

Verilynn shrugged, unsure. "A lot. More than fifty dollars."

"Who can I sell it to?"

"Anyone who'll pay your price."

Addy nodded and thought of the little blue box in the side pocket of the old leather suitcase. The greatest treasure in the box was not the ring though. It was the black curl of her baby boy's hair, which she'd carefully snipped from his angel head and placed beneath the velvet square on which the sparkling marquis sat.

It was as cold and dark a day as Detroit would see that year. The wind shook the windowpanes and the house on Chestnut Street groaned at the loss of yet another soul. Addy was still weak from the efforts of her labor, and still sore and bleeding, but she knew she had to leave and she had to leave today. Late in the afternoon she boiled a dozen potatoes and fried the chicken legs Verilynn bought at the butcher. She ate heartily, without appetite, Verilynn's portion too, for she remembered only a few months ago being hungry and alone and unsure when she would eat again.

Verilynn insisted Addy take her gray coat and she was grateful, for all she had besides was the threadbare cloth coat Lenny Davies had given her back at that farm in Sandwich.

Addy was glad too that Verilynn loaned her warm gloves and her much-too-big boots, though Addy'd protested at the time, knowing she'd never return them. And she was further glad she'd spent all that time crocheting, for Poppa's wool hat and scarf would fight the wind and chase the chill from her cheeks and chin on her journey back to Canada.

The nights had been long and sleepless in the days since she bore her silent son, and Addy had walked the floor of Poppa's bedroom, frantic to come up with some plan for her future. She'd seen in Riley's face, the instant he looked down upon her just-pushed-out baby, her dream of life on Chestnut Street fade away. Finally, after hours and days of thinking on it, she decided to make her way to far-off Toronto and find that friend of Poppa's, Dr. Shepherd, who'd said, "Life is different in Canada." Addy reckoned that a kind man such as he, especially one called *Shepherd,* would show her how to make her way in the world.

The sky was icy black by the time Addy dried the last dish from supper, and though frightened, she was eager to leave. Verilynn was concerned about Addy traveling in the darkness but understood she couldn't cross the river by day and risk being stopped or questioned and sent back. "But where you gonna go when you get to the other side?"

"I'll go to one of the bootleggers and ask which direction to Toronto and how can I get there on the dollars I got," Addy said as she filled her pockets with fat Spy apples.

She worried what would become of Verilynn Rippey and tried not to think of Riley at all. The two women embraced but Verilynn would not let go when Addy pulled away. She whispered in her ear, "You're so brave, Addy Shadd. I'll never be as brave as you are this moment."

The remark, and the sincerity in Verilynn's eyes, made Addy want to laugh because she didn't feel brave at all. How could she explain to Verilynn or anyone that to do what a person *must* do requires no bravery? She called upon bravery not to do what she *did,* but rather *not* do what she *wished* to do, and that was throw herself under the tires of a fast-moving truck. And when midway across the black frozen river she felt the ice heave and crack, she did laugh, and cry a little too, for her terror was complete and she wished Verilynn or anyone was there to see it.

There were no bootleggers on the other side of the river, and as Addy scaled the bank toward the mostly deserted street, she wondered if they'd all been caught and jailed. She could hear the rumble of the trolley cars in the distance and wondered if the drivers could be trusted to point out the way to Toronto. She limped forth and cursed the ache between her legs as she watched a pale, stout man in a rich wool overcoat lock the doors to a darkened shoe shop.

The stout man pulled his hat down on his head, stuffed his bare hands in his pockets, and started down the street. Addy was frightened by the man and the strange way he looked at her, then she realized how oddly she must be walking with her sore lady parts and Verilynn's much-too-big boots. She called with some difficulty, her jaw being all but frozen shut. "Excuse me, Sir."

The man stopped, annoyed but polite. "Yes?"

"I was wanting to get to Toronto and wonder could you point me the way?"

The man regarded her suspiciously and answered with a crisp English accent. "One cannot *walk* to Toronto, Young Lady. Toronto is a great distance."

"Yes, Sir. I know. Just, I don't even know where to point myself is all."

He raised one brow. "Are you traveling alone?"

"Yes I am," she answered, thinking it a foolish question.

"Why do you want to go all the way to Toronto?" the stout man asked. "Are you in some sort of *trouble?*"

Addy shook her head. Trouble was not the word for what she was in. "I'm going to see a friend of mine there. A doctor."

"Are you ill?" The man glanced at her pigeon-toed feet.

"No," Addy said, then changed her mind. "Yes. In a manner, I suppose I am."

"Polio?" the man asked in a sad quiet voice, and Addy realized her awkward gait had misled him. Before she had a chance to correct the man, he set his large white hand on her shoulder and confided, "My son has polio. What doctor is it you're seeing in Toronto?"

"Dr. Shepherd."

"I don't know him. Is he good?"

"I hope he's good, Sir."

"Do you mean to ride the train then, my dear? To Toronto?"

Addy brightened, for she hadn't thought of the train. "Yes. I'll ride the train. I only have eleven dollars though. You suppose that get me all the way there?"

"Eleven dollars isn't what it was."

"I'll just have to see. Which way is it, Sir, to the train station?"

"You don't intend to *walk* there?"

"Well. Yes. I don't know another way."

"Come. That's my automobile," he said, pointing to a snow-dusted Ford parked nearby. "I'll drive you to the train station. I live not far from there."

"Thank you, Sir. Thank you very much."

Addy was shocked by the stranger's kindness and thanked her brother and her son in Heaven for guiding the man's good deed. She thanked them again when she climbed into the fancy automobile with the smooth velvety cushion seats, for Addy felt like a fairy-tale queen in her carriage as they followed the winding river road to the station.

It was her first glimpse of the city of Windsor and her first real view of Detroit on the other side of the river. It seemed to her impossible now, that only hours ago, her feet had walked on American soil. The neighborhood she'd lived in east of downtown did not compare with the impressive cluster of tall brick buildings she could see now. Addy never imagined that the city was so large and tall and shone each evening in this magical and mysterious way. She swung her head back and forth from glittering Detroit to the wide river road on the Canadian side, where the houses were grander than any she'd seen in life. How could it be, she thought, that only one family should live in a house thrice the size of the church back in Rusholme?

She wanted to ask the stout man, whose name she didn't know, if one of those mansions was home to the president of Canada, but she loved the silence in the plush auto and didn't want the man to think her ignorant. For a moment, she imagined she was alone and driving the car herself. She imagined she could press her foot down on the gas pedal and drive all the way to Toronto and beyond. She closed her eyes and thought of her hands on the steering wheel.

They arrived at the train station all too quickly, and though the man did not accompany Addy inside, he did another surprising thing. He reached into his pocket, withdrew his wallet, pulled out two five-dollar bills, and pressed them into Addy's hands. "Godspeed, Young Lady."

Addy was moved by the man's compassion and generosity and thanked him in a whisper, glad the lump only rose up in her throat after he'd waved and driven off. She'd been wrong to allow the kind man to think she had polio, though, and quickly asked God's forgiveness before she sent up a prayer for his poor stricken son. After the prayer, she felt a little lighter and ready to resume her journey.

She entered the busy station with a thudding chest. Her spirits fell quickly when the weasely fellow behind the counter told her, in a manner suggesting she should have known, that the train for Toronto left a quarter hour ago and another would not be departing until the following morning. There were a dozen people like her in the station, sore at missing the last train and wondering what to do next.

Addy hoped she'd be able to pass the night there in the warm safe building but dared not ask the weasely clerk. She looked around. It was clear, though there were no signs, that there were separate seating areas for white people and colored. Addy knew from her education in the little schoolhouse on King Street that separation signs existed all over the southern United States, but she also knew that signs didn't need to be printed and posted, but could be read simply enough in a man's eyes.

She hefted her suitcase and hobbled toward a small group of people near the rest rooms at the back of the station. Though she smiled before she took a seat on the bench, she felt no warmth nor kinship from anyone. Big-city people, she reckoned, and worried what the Negro people in Toronto would be like.

When it became clear that travelers would not be asked to leave the station, Addy relaxed. She ate two apples, made a pillow of Poppa's old suitcase, and rested her head for the night. She did not sleep, though, not a wink, for not only did the babies in the station wail into the wee hours, but the doors to the rest rooms swung open and shut the whole night long and the odor of waste wafted up her nostrils each time they did. By morning the station was crowded and close and Addy felt queasy and miserable. When a shabby old country woman sat down beside her, Addy showed her no warmth nor kinship and felt some satisfaction in the sophistication of misery.

The station clerk brightly announced that the train would be an hour late arriving, hence departing, and the travelers groaned loudly. The old woman beside Addy shook her head, sucked her teeth, and said, "Well, they'll blame me for this and that's sure."

Though Addy'd ignored her, the old woman sucked her teeth again and answered like she'd been asked, "Going up to Chatham to see my granddaughter Olivia get married today." The woman gazed out the big station windows. "Gonna be a blizzard though. Sky looks fit to storm." The old woman sighed loudly and a few people nearby glanced over. "Dragging your guests from four corners through the snow. Why would not the child wait till June when there's flowers for the picking and barbecue supper and strawberries for shortcake?" She shifted in her seat. "Well, I suppose everyone knows why a girl can't wait to get married. Like they say, she either done the deed and got the seed, or she just can't wait to part the gate. Shameful either way. But I don't like to judge. You married?"

Addy shook her head and pretended to be interested in the clasp on her suitcase.

"Olivia's husband-to-be, Darryl, he's nineteen years of age and never worked a day in his life. Never thought I'd see the day. He's going to school up to Toronto, says he wants to be a lawyer, though I don't see such respectability in that as others do. And don't his folks think he's too good for Olivia. Lord. His Daddy owns a restaurant and that's quite a thing for a colored man. Olivia's Daddy, Hamond, that's my son, he's a farmer. Olivia feels ashamed her Daddy not a educated man." She huffed, "Blames *me* I didn't let him stay in school."

Addy pulled an apple from her pocket and bit into it noisily, hoping to offend the woman and discourage any further conversation.

"That look like a nice apple. Spy, ain't it? Don't this county turn out the nicest Spys?"

Addy turned on the old woman coolly. "Apple comes from Detroit, Ma'am."

"Oh. Well. Close enough. Close enough. Same soil really. Looks juicy like the Spys from around here. And don't that apple know how to hold on its flesh in a hot oven too. Make my fingers itch to roll a pie crust when I smell that apple smell."

Addy felt a faint rush of tenderness toward the woman, thinking that was just the kind of thing her own mother might have told a stranger. She reached into her pocket and pulled another Spy and shined it on her coat before she gave it as a gift.

"Why thank you. Thank you very kindly. I didn't have time to eat much more than some bread and honey before I left this morning. I get dizzy now, being old as I am and heavier than in my youth."

Addy turned to look at the woman more closely. She was heavy and coarse, her fingernails dirty, her gray hair oiled and pulled back from her face. Her dress looked dusty and slept in and Addy wondered vaguely what Olivia and Darryl would think when she stepped off the train.

As if the woman could read Addy's thoughts, she said, "Olivia's Mama, that's Mary Alice, sewed me a pink dress matches with the wedding decorations at the church basement. I never did care for pink decorations and I'm too old to wear a pink dress, but I'm not one to complain. Where you headed to?"

"Toronto," Addy said, smiling. "I'm going to Toronto."

The old woman sucked her teeth again. "You won't like it."

Addy was startled. "I believe I will."

"It's muddy and crowded and cold. 'Whites Only' signs in all the windows."

Addy looked at the woman, not comprehending. Surely this could not be true in Toronto, for what had Dr. Shepherd meant then, when he'd said life in Canada was different?

The woman continued, "Don't know where you'll be living but I can tell you white people won't rent you an apartment." She chewed off a hangnail and spat it on the floor. "The Jews'll rent to you though. Most of them real good, real kind. They ain't Christian, but you wouldn't know it from their actions. Jesus musta forgive them too because at least a few of them got houses of their own. Not one house in that whole big city owned by a Negro though, no matter if he a lawyer or not."

"That can't be true." Addy was shocked.

"That's what I'm told. That's what I told Olivia, but don't nobody listen to me. I'm just a old woman. You got kin in Toronto?"

"No, Ma'am. I'm going to see a doctor there."

"Colored doctor? You sick?"

"Yes, Ma'am. No, Ma'am."

"You rich?"

"Beg your pardon, Ma'am?"

"'Cause if you gonna live in Toronto you wanna be rich and that's a fine wool coat you're wearing, but I don't think you're rich."

Addy set her jaw and answered carefully. "Well, Ma'am, I do have a valuable ring my Poppa left me and I intend to sell it for quite a sum of money."

The old woman narrowed her eyes. "What kind of ring?"

"Diamond."

"Diamond ring?"

"Yes, Ma'am."

"Well maybe you are rich then. Maybe you are."

Addy was annoyed to see that the old woman did not believe her so she reached into the side pocket of Poppa's old suitcase and pulled out the little velvet box. She opened the box slowly and presented it with a flourish.

The old woman flared her nostrils. "That's a diamond ring all right."

Addy glanced up to notice an attractive, white, mustachioed gentleman dressed in a fine black coat and beautiful, though not warm or practical, blue silk scarf pause on his way to the men's room and steal a look inside the velvet box. He stopped a moment to admire the exquisite diamond before the old woman closed the lid and handed it back to Addy. As Addy'd caught the gentleman's eye, she nodded politely and he did the same before he went through the men's room door. There was no question the man was interested in the ring and no doubt he was a man of means. Addy felt relieved at the prospect of a buyer for the diamond and hoped she might be seated near him on the train.

The train announced its arrival before it appeared. The station shook tremulously as the smoke smell blew in through the window cracks and the gap beneath the doors. Addy picked up her suitcase, intending to wait by the rest rooms to speak to the gentleman with the mustache, but she was swept along with the rest of the crowd, out the doors and onto the steam-fogged platform.

As late as the train had been, there was a surliness in the conductor's manner and an impatience in the locomotive itself that seemed to blame the travelers for the delay. There was much shuffling and shouting and cries of "Step up! Step lively!" Negro porters in stiff white jackets hefted suitcases with astounding speed. People pushed and shoved and were anything but civil in their desire to be first aboard the train and to get the choicest of seats.

Addy craned above the throng, searching for the fancy gentleman, and finally caught a glimpse. She started toward him through the crowd but was stopped by a firm hand tugging her arm. She turned, incensed to find it was the shabby old woman. The woman laughed and shouted over the train, "Colored people back here! Where you think you're going?!"

It had not occurred to Addy that there would be a separate coach for Negro travelers and she could not know yet how often in the years to come she would be shocked and wounded by such things that had not occurred to her. At this moment, she was also vexed to have to share the same space with the irritating old woman and promised herself to sit as far away from her as possible.

The train was not all that Addy had imagined. It was cold and drafty, and being so tender as she was from her recent birth trauma, the hard uncomfortable seats would make the long trip to Toronto difficult. She was only glad she could smell food being cooked somewhere and relieved she had a few dollars left to buy something to eat. Addy waited until the old woman had settled herself at the back of the car and took her own seat near the front. She could see through the glass door into the overcrowded coach ahead and wondered if the man she sought was there or in the coach in front of that.

As they pulled away from the station, Addy looked out across the river, bidding a quiet farewell to Verilynn and Riley Rippey. The train rocked from side to side, playing a heartbeat rhythm on the rails. As it gathered speed and the icy river blurred into frosty fields, she clung to the armrest, a little afraid. She drew back when they entered dense bush and giant branches attacked her window and hardly glanced at the uniformed man who stopped to collect her ticket. "Destination?" he asked in a smooth voice.

Addy turned away from the window. The ticket taker was young, though not young as she, and tall and thin. His skin was unusually pale, stretched taut over a web of blue veins. His eyes were deep and green like the Rusholme crick in summer. The white man smiled at Addy. "All alone, Miss?"

She nodded as he read her ticket.

"Toronto?"

"Yes. Toronto." Addy cleared her throat.

"Long way."

She nodded again and waited for the fellow to move along.

"Mean to stare out the window the whole way there?" he asked seriously.

"I don't think so," she said. "I'm dizzy from it already."

He nodded. "Just gets worse when you get up past London and the land's not so flat. Sometimes we go over a trestle and you're looking a hundred feet down into a river. Don't you like to read?"

Addy liked the way the thin man assumed she *could* read and only wondered if she *liked* to. "Yes," she said. "But I never thought to bring a book."

The young man didn't hear her answer, for just then he glanced ahead into the next car and was distracted by what he saw. His voice dropped. "Only eleven people back here and so crowded up there, mothers got children on their laps and two men standing." He shook his head and laughed darkly.

Addy looked at the car ahead and ventured, "Guess they don't want to sit back here in the colored coach?"

The tall man shook his head slowly. "Guess they don't. Maybe I don't need to care anymore." He pulled at a thread on the button of his cuff and announced casually, "I been promoted up to porter on the sleeping car line. Be starting that job next week."

"Oh," Addy said, and couldn't imagine why he was telling her.

"Bet you never saw the Rocky Mountains."

Addy shook her head.

"Didn't think so. A few weeks from now I'll be looking out a window just like that one and there they'll be. And it's not just the Rocky Mountains, but I'm gonna see the wheat fields of the prairies and the Pacific Ocean too."

Addy nodded absently and turned to look out the window, thinking the white man boastful and boring.

He said, "See, a trip across the country takes about four days there and four days back. I board the train at 4 A.M. I make the beds and get things ready. Passengers board at 9 A.M. and if you want to know something, I'll tell you, *that's* when the payday starts. That ain't right, but there's a Brotherhood now, just like in America." He glanced around to make sure he couldn't be overheard. "We're getting organized. Things are gonna change."

Addy nodded again and wished he would leave now so she could think her own thoughts and not hear any more about Rocky Mountains or Brotherhoods.

"Costs a good deal of money to buy a berth on the sleeping car. I'm told I won't see such a thing as a Negro passenger on that line."

Addy reckoned his point in telling her was to say he was *glad* he wouldn't be seeing any more Negro passengers. She pursed her lips to show she was insulted.

He went on, "Pay's better than working these short runs and I'll be able to live at home on my off days too."

Addy looked into the man's swampy green eyes and yawned deliberately. She was glad when he blushed and moved along and didn't care if he was hurt or annoyed by her disinterest. She looked ahead at the crowded car again, wondering if she'd be allowed to look for the fancy man she thought might buy her ring. She hoped it was not the pale ticket taker she had to ask for permission.

Five minutes could not have passed before the ticket taker returned. Addy wondered if the fellow was a simpleton, for he just stood there, still blushing deeply, but saying nothing.

"You already took my ticket."

"I know."

"I'm going to Toronto," Addy reminded him, in case he'd forgotten.

"I know." The young man cast his eyes. "I'm sorry if I was disturbing you before. It's just, I forget sometimes, that not everyone likes to talk as much as I do. My mother used to tell me I shouldn't act so familiar with people."

Addy just looked at the man.

"She said remember that just because I get excited about a thing doesn't mean the rest of the world will. I remember that most times, but I guess my mouth forgets."

Addy smiled accidentally and wished she hadn't, for the young man grinned broadly and thought he was forgiven. He leaned a little closer. "May I ask your name?"

"Why?" Addy shivered and wondered if his inquiry had something to do with the incidents in Rusholme.

"I have something to give you, but it's special and not something I'd give to a stranger. If I know your name you won't be a stranger."

Addy considered lying about her name but when she opened her mouth the truth was on her tongue. "My name is Adelaide Shadd. Mostly I'm called Addy."

"Pleasure to make your acquaintance, Addy. My name is Gradison Mosely. They call me George here on the train," he said, squinting into the crowded car ahead, "but my friends back home call me Mose."

"Why they call you George if your name is Mose?"

"All the porters are called George. After George Pullman. He's the rich fella who started the Pullman Palace Car Company. Sleeping car, that is. This train doesn't have a sleeping car but the passengers call us George anyway."

Addy nodded, sorry she'd asked.

"Me and the other fellas are trying to get name tags put on our uniforms. I won't turn around anymore when people call me George." With that, Gradison Mosely reached into his uniform pocket and pulled out a small book. He passed her the book, saying, "I don't like to see my passengers getting dizzy from the view so I thought, well, this is one of the finest books ever written."

Addy read the cover out loud. "*Walden Pond.*"

"By Henry David Thoreau. American fella, but don't hold that against him."

Addy surprised herself and giggled. "I won't."

"Read it slow as you can. It's like a fine meal. You don't want to gulp it, but savor it so you can taste it in your memory when you're long done."

Addy's skin bubbled, for she'd never heard a person talk in such a way. "If I read it slow, how can I finish it before Toronto?"

Gradison Mosely shrugged. "All right if you don't."

Addy did not know what young Mr. Mosely's intentions were and thought it strange that this white man would just give her a book and ask nothing in return. She figured the young man's Mama likely have something to say about that too, but she accepted the book gratefully. When Gradison Mosely asked where she'd be living in Toronto she told him with slight hesitation. "I'm not sure exactly. I know a man there, a doctor friend of my Poppa's. He's going to help me find a place to live."

The strange young man nodded and left her once again.

There was just enough time to open the book and read the first line before a shadow crossed the page and made her look up. She had no doubt it was Gradison Mosely returning and was shocked to see another, older conductor standing there beside the fancy gentleman with the blue silk scarf. She smiled, though she was unsure why the man had come. Although he'd seen the diamond ring at the station, he couldn't know yet she meant to sell it. She closed her book and nodded politely. "Hello."

The fancy gentleman did not nod politely as he'd done before and the conductor's face looked severe. "This gentleman here claims you have something that belongs to him."

Addy had no idea what the conductor could be referring to. She only thought to say, "I do?"

Gradison Mosely appeared then and asked his superior, "Can I help with anything, Sir?"

Whatever the matter was, the conductor was cross and wanted it to be over quickly. "This gentleman," he said, gesturing at the mustachioed man, "claims this colored girl stole a diamond ring from him back at the station."

Addy did not gasp in horror or cry or plead innocence. She merely looked at the man's face and thought how clever the devil's disguise. "Well, Sir," she said to the conductor, "I do have a ring. But it was given me by my Poppa back in Detroit and most surely does not belong to this man here."

Mose watched young Addy Shadd's face, wishing he could know from the timbre of her voice if she was telling the truth. The conductor glanced at the man, then turned back to Addy. "Do you have any identification papers?"

"No."

"What's your citizenship?"

"I'm Canadian."

"But your father lives in Detroit?"

"My *Poppa* lives in Detroit," Addy corrected.

"What's his name?"

Addy shivered, for she could see this would not go well and decided she could not even begin to explain. She felt tears spring to her eyes and blinked them back angrily. "The ring is mine," she said, looking at Gradison Mosely.

The devil sneered at Addy, then turned back to the conductor. "I had the ring before I went to the lavatory and it was gone when I came out. This girl bumped into me and I believe she lifted it from my pocket. It's in a little midnight-blue velvet box."

"Where is it?" the conductor asked.

Addy reached into the side pocket of the leather suitcase and withdrew the little blue box with trembling hands. She felt defeated and was prepared to hand the thing over when she caught sight of the chatty old country woman snoozing in her seat at the back. "That old woman." Addy pointed. "That woman was with me and I showed her the ring and it was when she was looking at it that this man here caught a glimpse."

Gradison turned to see where Addy pointed and said, "That's Willow Ferguson. I know her well. She's been riding this train for years."

The conductor snorted, disgusted by Addy's vain attempt, and gestured for Gradison Mosely to wake the woman and bring her over. Willow Ferguson looked groggy and confused as the tall white ticket taker led her to where Addy sat trembling and clasping the little velvet box.

"Ma'am," the conductor began, "this girl says she showed you a diamond ring?"

"Yes," the woman answered, looking at Adelaide strangely.

Gradison Mosely spoke up, ignoring the stare from his superior. "She say where she got the ring from, Mizz Ferguson?"

"Yes. She said her Poppa give her the ring."

The conductor glanced at the man with the mustache, hoping he was not being made a fool of. He turned back to the old woman. "And when exactly was it she showed it to you?"

"Oh I don't know. Guess it was just before the train come in. We were talking about my granddaughter Olivia's wedding and she said she had this ring she was wanting to sell."

"Uh-huh!" the devil shouted. "You see! That proves she stole it! What kind of person would sell an *heirloom* from her *Poppa?*"

Addy hated the way the man said Poppa's name and hated the way he seemed so certain he'd emerge victorious in this fraud.

"Did she say where she came from?" the conductor asked the old woman.

"Well she said something about Detroit, didn't you, Child?"

Addy nodded and smiled gratefully. The man with the mustache was outraged. "Well anyone can see they're in cahoots!"

The conductor looked at the man squarely. "Can you describe the ring, Sir?"

"Of course I can," the devil said plainly. "It's a marquis diamond set with two green emeralds and a white-gold band. I purchased it from a private dealer in Windsor and meant to propose with it to my intended on my return to Montreal."

It was the old woman who noticed and clucked her tongue. "Looks to me like you married enough, Sir. What with that gold band already on your wedding finger."

The man paled and hid his hand, fumbling for an explanation. "I do wear a wedding ring, yes, you see, because, because I'm sorry to say I find modern women terribly solicitous around unmarried men and I wish to avoid the embarrassment of — well, that's neither here nor there. This girl stole my ring. How dare you question me!"

The conductor cleared his throat. If the man's description matched the ring, he'd put the girl off at the next station stop and have the local police take over. He'd already decided she was guilty. "You best show us the ring, Girl."

Addy passed over the box. The conductor opened it. He had no idea what a marquis diamond looked like but he recognized the two other gems as green and the band as white gold and that was good enough. Gradison peered inside the box, disconcerted to find the description matched. They all looked at Addy.

She could not guess how the strength came to her legs, but Addy rose to standing and looked squarely into the devil's blue eyes. "Well," she said, because she'd suddenly remembered. "Can you tell these people what other valuable thing lay beneath the square in that velvet box? *Sir?*"

The man returned Addy's contempt but he was afraid too, not only to be caught out in his deception, but because if there was another jewel hidden in the box it could be even more valuable than the ring. He cleared his throat. "Yes, as a matter of fact." He stalled as his mind reeled. The box was small and it was not likely it held another ring or anything as large as a broach. He cleared his throat once more and ventured, "Yes. There's also a small diamond pendant on a delicate gold chain."

Gradison knew the man was lying. "And you bought the necklace from the same private dealer?"

"Yes," the man answered coolly. "But if it's not in the box that's hardly proof. She may have sold the necklace already." The man grinned and thought himself terribly clever. "Or she may have stolen a different jewel from another passenger and put it there in its place."

Even the conductor was becoming suspicious. Gradison turned to Addy and asked softly, "What else is in the box?"

Addy was too angry for tears. "There's a lock of my baby son's hair. He died three days ago and I don't care if you take my ring or my suitcase or all the clothes off my back, I want that little curl of my baby boy's hair 'cause it's all I got to remember him."

The conductor opened the velvet box once more and pulled the little square on which the diamond ring sat. There, as Addy told, was a tiny curl of soft black hair.

"That proves nothing!" the man with the mustache squawked. "It's a ridiculous story. She's a charlatan! There's no baby! She's a child herself! She put that lock of hair there just to fool us all!"

The conductor closed the velvet box, sure now it was the man who was the charlatan and not the sad young colored girl. He passed the velvet box back to Addy. But the devil continued to protest, desperate for some kind of victory. "Put her off the train!

I demand that you put that THIEF off the train! I promise you that I will not move from this spot and I will shout loud enough for all of the passengers to hear, that this nigger girl has stolen my ring and justice has been undone!"

Addy crumpled into the seat by the window and though she had the ring back in her possession she could not feel relieved or vindicated. She only felt sad and guilty that she'd forgotten about the lock of her son's hair, even for an instant. She barely noticed when the mustachioed man stopped yelling and the conductor told her quietly and with regret that he'd have to put her off the train at Chatham. She'd nodded, hardly caring, and looked out the window, wondering if what happened meant that God was watching over her or had abandoned her once again.

When the old woman eased into the seat beside her, Addy was grateful. And when she took Addy's trembling hand in her own calloused, steady one, Addy was certain the Lord was watching. "Thank you, Ma'am, Mizz Ferguson," she said.

"You call me Willow. And your name is Addy? Addy what?"

"Addy Shadd."

"Shadd? I believe my son used to know some Shadds. They don't come from Detroit though."

"Thank you for your kindness, Ma'am."

"Just returning your own, Child. I don't forget you give me that nice apple to slake my hunger. And I know you was telling the truth about that diamond ring."

Addy was further grateful that Willow Ferguson didn't ask any nosy questions about her dead son. The two women just sat quietly, hand in hand, looking out at the flat snowy landscape.

Gradison Mosely waited until his superior was busy in the overcrowded coach ahead before he returned. His green eyes were filled with concern and his cheeks flushed pink against his pale white skin. He whispered, "What'll you do about getting to Toronto?"

Addy shrugged, unable to think beyond the moment. The old woman squeezed Addy's hand and answered for her, "I think this young lady need a day or two rest before she decides where she's going and what she'll do. You come to my son's house in Chatham. It ain't fancy, maybe it ain't what you're used to, but my son and his wife are good people and with Olivia moving out there's an extra bed for long as you need."

Shame filled Addy, for she'd hated this old woman and her country manners and chattiness and couldn't have guessed how she'd reveal herself a savior. Addy didn't look Gradison Mosely in the eye as she held up his book and said, "Suppose you should take this back, Sir."

The young man shook his head. "I'm not *Sir,* I'm *Mose,* and I already told you, you can keep it." With that, he tipped his cap and left.

The old woman chuckled. "Mose got eyes for you."

Addy looked at Willow, shocked and speechless.

"But don't put much faith in it. I seen him working his flirtations on many a pretty young passenger."

"But he's *white,*" Addy whispered, trying not to sound horrified.

"You're young, but I know you lived some lives already. Do you think a white man couldn't be sweet on a Negro girl or even the other way around? It happens, Addy. But see, Mose ain't exactly white anyway."

"He ain't?"

Willow shook her head. "His Mama's Negro and his Daddy's white."

"How'd you know?"

"Oh, I been riding this train for years. I was here when he started when he was all of seventeen years old. I figured what I figured and I just asked him was I right."

"Oh."

"He comes from Africville out East. You heard of that place?"

"No."

"You never heard of Africville?"

"No."

"And you never knew anyone who was half colored and half white?"

"No, I never did."

The old woman shook her head and sucked her teeth. "What world you been living in, Child?"

Addy paused a moment, looking into Willow Ferguson's eyes, then she took a deep breath and told the old woman about the world she'd been living in. About Chestnut Street and Poppa and Verilynn and Riley and Enos and Emeline and how it was just days ago but seemed liked years when she felt the pains and knew her baby was coming. Willow listened to the story and just nodded. Addy left out the earlier parts about Rusholme and Zach Heron so Willow just assumed Riley was the father of her baby and was glad Addy hadn't stayed there in Detroit to forgive him.

"I myself had two babies die and there's no word a person can offer as comfort."

Addy thought she was right.

"Just don't punish yourself is all. And don't be sad all your life now. Let go some grief, a little every day, else you won't never feel much of anything, happy or sad, again."

Addy closed her eyes and found some peace in slumber. She'd slept for what seemed only seconds before Willow shook her gently and whispered, "Chatham, Addy. We're nearly at Chatham."

The train slowed for miles and finally came to a full stop. Willow and Addy made their way to the exit door, but there was no conductor to help them off and the distance to the ground was too great to chance a jump. Addy saw that the passengers in the cars ahead were being helped off the train first, some already rushing into the arms of their loved ones on the foggy platform. She sighed and reckoned they'd just have to wait, but Willow Ferguson was impatient. She heaved open the steel door like a professional and craned out for a look, smiling when she saw her grown son striding toward the train looking crisp and clean in his best church suit. She waved and called out, "Hamond! Over here!"

Hamond, who was in his early forties but looked much older with his weathered farmer skin and his graying hair, reached up with both arms and found his mother's waist through the folds of her shabby coat. He lifted her to the ground in one swing and tried not to let on how his back hurt when she protested she was too heavy.

Addy stood at the train door and shuddered when a blast of cold damp air hit her face. Something frightened her but she couldn't tell what it was. She couldn't tell if she was afraid of being in Chatham where she knew her father worked, so near to Rusholme and all her ghosts. She couldn't tell if it was a leftover fear of the man who'd accused her of stealing, who she could see now grinning and watching from his seat in the coach ahead. And she couldn't help but wonder if it was Willow's son Hamond causing this fresh crop of fear, for he'd looked disturbed when Willow explained she'd be coming along. When he reached up and lifted her down, he looked at her strangely, and Addy thought she heard him whisper, "I know you. I know all about you."

Salt

*M*rs. *Pigot, the first-grade teacher,* was standing over Sharla, flicking her red fingernails like she did when she wanted a fight. Sharla was silent, in the thrall of the fat yellow boogers riding hairs in Mrs. Pigot's nostrils. The teacher opened her mouth and Sharla winced at the spoiled-turkey smell of her breath.

"I asked you a question, Sharla Cody," the teacher said in her slow, slurry voice, as the other children watched and waited, fearing and hoping for the worst.

Sharla didn't know how to explain why she hadn't handed in her work page or why it was still in her lift-up desk or why she hadn't brought it home at all since it *was* called *home*work.

Mrs. Pigot pointed around the room, saying, "Cindy turned in her page. And Terry turned in his. Prasora's mother helped," she said, pointing to the Portuguese girl in the back row, "and she hardly speaks English!"

Sharla looked at Prasora and wished she could get ear holes and hang swingy gold hoops from her lobes too.

"Sharla! Sharla Cody! I'm waiting for an answer!"

Sharla had no answer so she looked down at her shoes. This wasn't the first time Mrs. Pigot had stood over her and hated her in this way. The first time was on her very first day at Princess Street Public School. Sharla'd been looking out the window, watching Mum Addy hobble toward her waiting taxi, noticing how she was slower now than at the beginning of summer. Sharla wished she could go back to the little trailer with her porcelain doll and her soap-smell Mum Addy, instead of sitting in the grade-one classroom with Mrs. Pigot and her mothball fall clothes. Mrs. Pigot was calling out attendance. "Sharla Cody? Is Sharla Cody present? Sharla Cody?"

Sharla didn't hear, or wasn't listening, and when her ears finally caught the pattern of her name, she'd swiveled in her chair and shouted without meaning to, "What?"

The other children laughed, thinking Sharla was a sassy brat. Mrs. Pigot strode down the aisle to Sharla's desk, grabbed her by the fabric of her pretty white dress, and dragged her up to the front of the class. She stood there, clutching the eyelet collar in a way that made Sharla worry it'd rip. Her eyes were bulging and her face was red as she said, "Children, do you all know what the word *example* means?"

The children sat in silence, for even the ones who knew thought better than to call attention to themselves just now.

Mrs. Pigot shook Sharla like she was a bad cat or a just-killed rabbit. "I'm going to make an *example* out of Sharla Cody, so you will know, class, what the *consequences* are for misbehaving." With that, Mrs. Pigot dragged her big oak chair out from behind her desk so that all the children could see. She sat down on the chair and pulled Sharla over her lap. She lifted up the white dress to show Sharla's new-for-school pink underwear and yanked down the underwear to show Sharla's soft brown bum. She drew back her hand and brought it down until the brown bum was red and quivering and she was sure Sharla looked ashamed enough for the other children to be scared.

Sharla'd returned to her seat, hot and humiliated, with not a single tear on her cheek or waiting to fall from her eye. *I hate you I hate you I hate you* was all Sharla could think for the rest of the morning. She didn't hear the storybook Mrs. Pigot read to the class and she didn't see the puppet show some sixth graders came to perform. She sat straight in her chair, dreaming of a day when she was big, big as Krystal Trochaud, and could come back and hit

Mrs. Pigot and pull her pants down and stick something sharp in the hole of her bum.

Mum Addy came back in a taxi that afternoon with a big smile and wide-open arms, asking, "How was your first day of school, Honey?" Sharla fell against her sunken chest and whispered, "Good." But Addy could tell by her blotchy face that school had not been good and she felt guilty and responsible.

Addy'd been fretting for weeks about Sharla's school and worrying did she make the right choice. She'd chosen the school in the east end of Chatham, the very school she'd sent her own daughter to, figuring there were still a lot of Negroes in the neighborhood and hoping Sharla wouldn't be singled out, at least not for the color of her skin. She'd been relieved when she dropped Sharla off in the playground and saw that there were not only colored children but also Chinese and Italian and one little boy who might have come from India. Addy thought how Chatham, and the whole world, had changed.

In the taxi back to Lakeview, Addy'd been eager to know how school was. "Well, what all happened in school?"

"Nothing."

"Nothing? Nothing happened that whole long morning?"

"No."

"Did you do some coloring?"

"No."

"Did you do some other art?"

"No."

"Did you sing some songs?"

"No."

"Not even the good morning song?"

"No."

"Don't children sing the good morning song anymore?"

"I don't know."

"Did you make some little friends?"

"No."

"No little girls or boys you like to talk to or play with?"

"No."

"No recess?"

"No."

"Don't children have recess anymore?"

"No." What Sharla didn't tell Mum Addy was that she'd stayed in during recess and cleaned the chalkboard as part of her punishment.

It was clear to Addy that something was wrong. "Did one of the children say something to you, Honey? Something that made you feel bad?"

"No." And that was the truth, for the other children hadn't been allowed to talk to Sharla. That was part of her punishment too.

"Well. Things'll be better tomorrow. They always are."

"Do I have to go back though?" Sharla looked at Addy for the first time since she climbed into the taxi.

"Yes. Yes you do, Sharla. And tomorrow I can't bring you too. You're gonna start taking the bus tomorrow and that's gonna be so much fun."

"I don't wanna take the bus."

"I can't bring you and pick you up in a taxi every day, Honey. Today's special 'cause it's the first. But we paying the week's grocery money to this taxi company and we'd go broke if we did that every day."

"But I don't wanna take the bus."

"Sure you do. There's all kinds of kids on the bus and that's always fun when you get a bunch of children together."

"No it ain't."

"Now you're in school, Honey, say 'No it's *not*' 'stead of *ain't*. All right?"

"No it's *not*."

"Pretty soon you'll have so many little friends you'll be looking forward to going to school and you'll be sorry when the weekend comes around and you get stuck with your old Mum Addy. You know that?"

Sharla replied by burrowing into Addy's chest and taking her hand.

As they drove out of Chatham, Addy watched the farms roll by and marveled at the sunburned maples and the saffron elms and the lemony top leaves on the catalpas. Oak leaves went last, she recalled, so stubborn and disbelieving they might cling till spring, when buds advised of their demise and pushed them to the earth. She thought, with some anxiety, that it was early to see the turning, but no matter what September day the trees showed their preview, it always seemed too early. She squeezed Sharla's hand and said quietly, "Anyone says something hurtful, you tell me and I'll take care of it, all right?"

Sharla looked up, worried. "What they gonna say?"

"I don't know. Just if they do, you tell me."

"They gonna be mean?"

Addy patted the little girl's leg. "We are all of us a little mean when we're children. Just part of how we learn right from wrong."

"Not you though," Sharla stated, and was shocked when Mum Addy nodded.

"Oh yes, Sharla. I was mean just like all the children were." She remembered and smiled. "All except my brother. He never said a mean thing to anyone."

"Mean to who? Who were you mean to?"

"Well, the one I remember being mean to most was a boy called Jonas."

"Why?"

Addy didn't want to say it was because Jonas was fat. "He was different, I suppose, and sometimes children feel a little confused by someone different. Like maybe if they're different from you, they must not be right, because what does that make you, if different is right. You understand?"

Sharla nodded, but didn't. "You laugh at him?"

"At Jonas? Oh, yes. Children laughed at him and teased him and guess it made us all feel better. Long as we were laughing at Jonas no one was laughing at us."

"Kids laugh at you?"

"Mmm-hmm. Sometimes."

"Why?"

Addy turned to Sharla, raised her hands, and pulled at the tips of her big stick-out ears. Sharla laughed. "Because of your ears?"

"Mmm-hmm."

"Did you take the bus?"

"I walked to school. My school was close to my house. Not far away like yours."

"Wish I didn't have to take the bus."

"I know, Honey. I know."

"Wish there was a television here."

The weeks passed and the leaves fell and it was time to take out the extra blankets and close the storm windows for good. Addy grew more and more concerned as it seemed every afternoon Sharla climbed off the bus, she was just sadder than the day before. "What did you do today, Sharla?"

"Nothing."

"Nothing?"

Sharla didn't want to tell Mum Addy about Mrs. Pigot. Sharla didn't want to tell her how the teacher hated the look of her and how she spent most of the time feeling she deserved it. The teacher hated the look of Prasora Dacosta too, and she especially didn't like the little Portuguese girl's swingy hoop earrings and said so that first week when Prasora's left ear got a green puss infection and she had to be sent to the nurse. Sharla wasn't sure what *barbaric* meant, but knew it wasn't good.

Sharla didn't want to tell Mum Addy about Lee-Ann either. Lee-Ann was the little girl with curly hair and a bloody rash on her hands and cheeks who sat beside her. Mrs. Pigot told the class, "Do *not* hold Lee-Ann's hand in music circle, *please*. Just in case her disease is catchy." Lee-Ann told the teacher it was excema and even the doctor said no one could *catch* it. But Mrs. Pigot took another look at the child's cracked and bleeding palms and said better safe than sorry. Sharla could see how Mrs. Pigot hated Lee-Ann for crying and breaking the chain of hands when they went around in the circle.

Most of all Sharla didn't want to tell Mum Addy about the homework. It was the sixth week of school when Mrs. Pigot passed out a page with a picture of a tree and some waiting-to-be-colored-in leaves and said, "Class. Does everyone know what a tree is?"

Every hand shot up at once, for of course they all knew the answer to that. Mrs. Pigot held up the page and went on. "Well, this is a *family* tree. You, each one of you, represent the tree's trunk, and each of these leaves represents a person in your family. These leaves," she said, pointing, "are your mothers and fathers, and these your aunts and uncles, and these ones are your grandmothers and grandfathers, and so on and so on. Each and every one of us has a family tree and some people can trace their trees all the way back to the time of Jesus."

The children raised their brows at that, for they all knew Jesus lived a long time ago. One of the children's hands shot up.

"Yes, Michelle?" said Mrs. Pigot.

"My Nanna has a pear tree."

"That's fine, but that's not the kind of tree we're talking about. We're talking about our families."

Another hand shot up. "Yes, Robbie?"

"I got a uncle what's in jail."

Mrs. Pigot made a mental note and continued, "Yes, well, any of you children with older brothers and sisters will know what the term *homework* means. Hands?"

Prasora Dacosta had six older brothers, and even though hers was the only hand that rose, Mrs. Pigot did not call on her for the answer. The teacher started down the aisle and tripped on a foot, stumbling for several steps before she caught her balance again. All of the children laughed, except Sharla Cody, for it was her foot.

Mrs. Pigot turned around, steaming. "Sharla Cody?"

"Yes, Mrs. Pigot?"

"Did you do that on purpose?"

"No."

"Excuse me?"

"No."

"*Excuse me?*" Her face was so close Sharla could see the pig's tail hair curling out from the mole above her left eye.

"I didn't do it on purpose. I was just sitting." Sharla's chin quivered, for she fully expected another bare bum spank and that would make the second this week. But Mrs. Pigot did not yank her from her seat or tell her to leave the class or pinch the fat on the back of her arm. She just returned to the front of the room, held up the leaf page, and went on. "What I want you to do, class, is to take this page home for the weekend. Sit down with your mothers and fathers and ask them to help you fill the names in your leaves, then color each a different fall color. That is your *homework*."

The bell for recess rang and Sharla was not surprised when Mrs. Pigot said without even looking up, "Not you, Sharla." Sharla stayed at her desk and laid her head on her hands as she was instructed. She waited until Mrs. Pigot left the room to go smoke in the teacher's lounge, then she hurried to the front of the room and snatched a piece of long white chalk from the ledge. She snuck back to her desk and ate the chalk in small bites, pushing it against the roof of her mouth and letting it melt like chocolate. She felt better after she ate the chalk and remembered to wipe the white powder from her lips when the recess bell rang and the children filed back into the class.

Mrs. Pigot entered the room trailed by the odor of cigarette smoke. She went to the blackboard to get her chalk. She looked and looked and scratched her head like she had bugs before she got another stick from the box in the locked-up supply drawer. Sharla thought it was funny that Mrs. Pigot didn't suspect she was the chalk thief, even though a piece was missing each time she was punished at recess.

Sharla knew when she was climbing the bus that Friday afternoon that she'd left the work page in her lift-up desk. She also knew that though she'd enjoy coloring the leaves, she could not fill in any names except Collette's and that only reminded her Mum Addy wasn't her real Mum and made her feel sad and mad at once. She could only hope that her missing page would go unnoticed when the homework was turned in on Monday morning.

It hadn't occurred to Addy that it'd be anyone other than another child causing Sharla's unhappiness, and when she got a call from Mrs. Pigot that Monday evening saying she'd like a word, Addy assumed it was to discuss what they might do about the other children's teasing.

Addy felt anxious about her visit to the teacher and hoped she wouldn't be asked too many questions like where was Sharla's mother. Sharla was anxious too. Though she was pleased Mum Addy'd be taking her home in the taxicab and she could avoid the bus ride and the bumpy, sick-making, never-ending country roads back to Lakeview, she knew Mrs. Pigot would tell about the misbehaving and the recesses inside at her desk. Maybe she even knew about the stolen chalk and Mum Addy wouldn't like that one bit.

Sharla was waiting alone in the classroom when Addy arrived, and the old woman felt proud seeing Sharla sit up so straight in her chair with her hands clasped together and her feet crossed at the ankles. She smiled and called, "My, my, Mizz Cody! Look at you! Aren't you the young lady! I thought you'd be out playing with the other children."

Fear flashed on Sharla's face and she shook her head slightly.

Addy didn't understand. "What's wrong, Sharla?"

Sharla glanced at the door before she whispered, "I'm not allowed to talk."

"Why?"

"I'll get another spank."

"Spank?" Addy was shocked, for it was the first she'd heard of a spank. "Why would you get a spank?"

Sharla glanced at the door and shook her head.

"Sharla Cody you tell me right now, why would the teacher *spank* you? What's going on here?"

Sharla whispered, "Nothing."

Addy shuddered. "Something. Something, and you're gonna tell me what it is."

Sharla glanced at the door again. "What it is, is I get in trouble. I get a bare bum spank. Mrs. Pigot says when a little girl gets *unruly* she needs a punishment to learn. She says unruly comes from my colored side."

Addy was horrified. She never imagined it had been the *teacher* causing Sharla's pain. "Why are you sitting like that? Did she make you stay after school?"

Sharla nodded. "I was singing too loud."

"Singing too loud?" Addy's heart squeezed.

"Mrs. Pigot said —"

"Mrs. Pigot said she's had enough of your tomfoolery," the teacher bellowed as she strode into the room. "You may wait outside, Sharla."

Sharla rose from her desk and marched up the aisle like a soldier, staring straight ahead and not glancing back at Mum Addy before she left the room.

Addy did her best to be civil and thrust out her hand, saying, "I'm sorry we didn't get a chance to meet each other on the first day of school, Mrs. Pigot. I'm told you were busy getting some things together. I had a taxicab waiting."

The teacher shook Addy's hand limply and with barely concealed disdain. "Yes well, what was your name again? It's not Cody, is it?"

"Adelaide Shadd."

"And you're the grandmother, Adelaide, is that right?"

"Yes. I'm Sharla's guardian," Addy answered.

"And is it Sharla's mother or her father that's a relation to you?"

"Excuse me?"

Mrs. Pigot smiled. "I was just wondering, seeing as she's so clearly *mulatto,* which parent is it that's, well, is it your son or daughter?"

"Not that I see it matters, but it's my son," Adelaide lied outright.

Mrs. Pigot sighed and blew a gust of something familiar Addy's way. "I suspected as much."

"I beg your pardon?" Addy cringed, thinking she could not be right about what she thought she could smell or what Mrs. Pigot meant by the remark.

"It's just more typical for — oh never mind, Adelaide."

Adelaide cleared her throat. "Mizz Shadd, if you don't mind. Now, Mrs. Pigot, maybe you could tell me just what alls been going on here with my Sharla."

Mrs. Pigot could see now where Sharla got her ways and was sorry she'd asked for the meeting. She only cared to have parent-child discussions if the parent was afraid of her.

"Well, Mizz Shadd, if you're the guardian, I'm sure I don't have to tell you about Sharla's behavioral problems."

"In fact you do. Because I don't have any problems atall with the child at home but I've certainly noticed she's none too happy being here at school."

Mrs. Pigot did not offer Addy a chair but sat down herself and leaned back, scratching her head. "Sharla has *many* problems here at school."

"Mmm-hmm."

"Are there a lot of slow learners in the family? Discipline problems?"

"No." Addy ground her teeth. "Sharla is quite a bright little girl and she minds me very well."

"Yes, well, all parents think their children are bright. I'm sure Sharla told you about the homework she didn't hand in? The last straw, as it were?"

"You giving six-year-olds homework?"

"It was a simple task, a little project for the children to work on with their parents."

"Mmm-hmm."

"Sharla was the only child in the class who didn't hand in her page. All of the other parents found time to help." Mrs. Pigot gestured around the room, where the artwork was hung over the blackboards.

Addy looked at the pages and the colored-in leaves of the family trees and the names of grandparents and aunts and uncles and cousins and understood at once. Sharla had no family. How could a six-year-old explain such a thing? She smiled at the teacher and tried not to sound angry. "Sharla's family situation is a little more complicated than some."

"Well, if the girl's ashamed of her family perhaps that's something you should be addressing. It would certainly explain her behavior."

At that moment, there was a knock at the classroom door. A smiling, young woman peered inside, saying, "Excuse me, Mrs. Pigot. I didn't know you had a guest. You have a telephone call. Shall I take a message?"

"No. No. I'll . . ." The teacher rose and bolted for the door, barely remembering to say, "I'll be back in a moment."

Addy nodded and watched the woman go. She was sure she was right in her suspicion now, for as the woman walked away she detected the faint, though familiar, smell of gin. Addy went toward the hallway, looking up and down to make sure it was vacant. Then she crept back into the room, sat down in the chair behind the big oak desk, and carefully pulled open the first desk drawer. There, at the bottom, barely concealed, was a pint-sized bottle of liquor.

Addy closed the drawer and went to the window, wondering what to do next. She could see Sharla outside, alone, balancing on the bike racks, looking up from time to time to watch a group of children playing dodgeball nearby. The sight made Addy want to cry. But that's life, she thought, some people have love, friendship, and good fortune come easy, some have to work for it, and some never get it at all. Still she wanted to give Sharla a fighting chance. Something had to be done.

It was a full fifteen minutes before Mrs. Pigot returned. The teacher breezed back into the room and deposited herself in the chair, looking distracted and disturbed. "Where were we?"

Addy drew a breath and surprised herself when she said, "We were just about to talk about the fact, Mrs. Pigot, that you are not fit to be within one hundred feet of a precious child let alone teacher to a whole class of them."

Now it was Mrs. Pigot's turn to be shocked. "How dare you?!"

Addy squared her shoulders. Her fury made her feel young and strong. "How dare *you?!* How dare you spank my child's bare bottom! How dare you punish her for singing loud! And how dare you suggest that her being part Negro has anything to do with what you call her 'behavior' problems!"

The teacher's jaw dropped, for she had hardly expected this. She shifted in her chair and cleared her throat, a little less sure of herself. "Sharla does have a problem with unruly behavior, Mizz Shadd."

"It's you who has the problem, Teacher. It's you."

"I beg your pardon?" Mrs. Pigot had grown smaller, such as happens when the bully becomes the coward.

Addy was trembling, emboldened by her rage. "Yes. Beg my pardon and beg my patience because if I ever, ever hear again that you were anything but kind and helpful and fair with Sharla, I will have my son and his gang of big, *unruly* Negro friends pay you a visit and make sure it don't happen again."

Mrs. Pigot was speechless. Addy leaned in a little closer. "And if I ever come into this room and smell liquor on your breath while you are teaching these children I will march into your principal's office and tell him about that bottle of gin in your desk and I'll make sure you're never hired by this school board or any other. You understand? Mrs. Pigot?"

Mrs. Pigot nodded twice and squeezed her eyes to dam a flood of tears. Addy felt cold. "I ask you if you understand me?"

"Yes," the teacher whispered without opening her eyes.

Addy nodded and left the room, pausing for a moment in the hall. After she'd calmed herself a little, she went outside and found Sharla still balancing on the bike racks. "I got a surprise, Honey."

"What?" Sharla blinked against the sun.

"We're going to have our supper in a restaurant tonight."

"We are?" Sharla said and clapped her hands. Living out at Lakeview without a car, they had not the opportunity to eat out and no extra money anyway. But Addy thought Sharla deserved a treat today and maybe she did too. She had twenty-four dollars in her vinyl purse, which would buy them the fish-dinner special at The Satellite Restaurant downtown and leave enough for the taxi ride home. She knew Sharla'd have a hard time choosing between pudding and Jell-O for dessert, and she smiled to herself, thinking how she'd order whatever Sharla didn't and give it to her as an extra surprise.

The restaurant was crowded but there was room for two by the window with a view of the Thames River. The pretty young waitress took great pleasure in showing them to their table, laying Sharla's linen napkin across her lap and saying, "What would you like to drink this evening, Miss?"

"Coke, Miss," Sharla answered.

"Milk," Addy corrected and winked at the young girl. "*Please.*"

"*Please,*" Sharla repeated in the exact tone and timbre.

The girl winked back and smiled at Sharla, saying, "You ladies should know you have the best table in the house."

Sharla waited until the waitress had taken their order and walked away before she whispered, "We got the best table, Mum Addy."

"Mmm-hmm," Addy said, looking out at the river.

"Ain't we in a restaurant though?"

"Of course we are."

"But she said best in the *house.*"

"Sometimes we call a restaurant a house."

"And sometimes we call a house a restaurant?"

"No, Honey. Doesn't work the other way around."

"Why?"

"Just doesn't."

Addy had glanced around the room when they came in and noticed an older Negro couple dining on the other side of the room. She'd given them a second look and then a third. There was something familiar about the couple, though she was certain she didn't know them. She couldn't help staring though, and wondering. It was the man, his nose, and the profile of his chin. She'd seen him somewhere maybe. She turned around again when Sharla's voice rose above a polite octave.

"Mu-um?!" Sharla said for the fourteenth time.

"Let's mind our manners, Young Lady. We don't raise our voices in public. Remember what we said about yelling?"

Sharla nodded solemnly. "Yelling's only for emergencies." She held up two fingers and counted down. "If the trailer's on fire or if you're cut'n'bleedin'."

"That's right. Now what was it you wanted to ask me?"

"*Why* doesn't it work the other way around?"

"What, Honey?"

Addy was distracted again and could not bring herself to look away from the profile of the man on the other side of the room. He was around her age, she guessed, maybe a few years younger. Maybe she'd delivered bread to him when she was working for The Oakwood. Maybe he'd even worked at the bakery. He hadn't been on the bread ovens. No. That man was shorter and rounder. But something. Something.

Sharla was frustrated, trying to whisper and still get Addy's attention. "Mu-um?"

Addy turned back and laughed and squeezed Sharla's arm with affection and said, "I'm sorry, Honey. I'm not being very good company, am I?"

"No," Sharla answered shortly, "you're just looking over there and you're not talking to me too."

Addy and Sharla ate their fish dinner and pronounced it the best they'd ever had. Addy broached the subject of Mrs. Pigot gingerly, and when she saw Sharla still didn't want to talk about her, she promised, "Don't worry, Sharla. Mrs. Pigot's not gonna be spanking you anymore. She's gonna be nice to you from now on."

"She is?"

"Mmm-hmm. You tell me if she isn't because she and I, we made a kind of agreement."

"To be nice to me?"

"Mmm-hmm."

"And Prasora too?"

"I think she's gonna be nicer to all the children from now on."

The waitress set the desserts before them and surprised Addy by bringing both Jell-O and pudding for Sharla. Sharla clapped and took a spoonful of each, letting them melt together in her mouth as she watched the waitress walk away. "That waitress is *really* nice to me."

"Yes she is, Honey."

Sharla licked her spoon clean of pudding, then announced casually, "Collette used to be a waitress."

Addy bristled because Collette's name had not come up in weeks. "Did she?"

Sharla nodded and said no more. Addy didn't ask questions. She knew Collette was never coming home and thought it might be easier for Sharla if they didn't talk about her at all. She was about to ask Sharla how her pudding was when she felt eyes on the back of her head and turned around to see whose. The couple she'd been watching were at the coat stand, the man helping the woman into her jacket. He was looking at Addy with the same curious expression she'd trained on him. So they *did* know each other. But the man also seemed unsure of the nature of their acquaintance. He nodded to Addy and she nodded back. The woman said something to her husband and he just shook his head.

When the couple was gone, Addy felt relieved and couldn't say why. The nice waitress called them a taxicab. Addy left the girl a larger-than-usual tip, squeezed her arm, and whispered, "Thank you for being so nice to the child." The waitress squeezed back and said, "No problem, Ma'am. She's a sweetie."

Addy took Sharla's hand and thought, *yes she is,* as they climbed into the taxi. The driver was one Addy knew and she didn't even have to say where she wanted to go. He asked, "Nice dinner at The Satellite, Mizz Shadd?"

"Very nice, thank you, Calvin. We had the fish," she answered, smiling.

"We had the best table in the house," Sharla added.

Addy leaned forward. "Why aren't you taking Wellington Street, Calvin?"

"Accident, Ma'am. It's all blocked off."

"Accident? Oh, my."

"Driver slammed into that big oak near Gilbert's gas station on Harvey. Car's a wreck."

"Oh no. But that oak's way off the road." Addy glanced beside her, glad that Sharla was looking out the window and not paying attention to the conversation. She leaned a little closer and lowered her voice. "He must have been driving some speed. Was he hurt?"

"She. Teacher over at the school there on Princess Street."

Addy's heart seized. She struggled for breath before she asked in a whisper, "Mrs. Pigot?"

Calvin took his eyes from the road to look at her. "How'd you know?"

"I didn't. Oh, Lord."

Calvin glanced into the rearview to make sure Sharla wasn't listening and added through the side of his mouth, "Drunk as a skunk too. And it wasn't five o'clock when it happened so they figure she must have been tippin' 'er back at school."

Addy could barely whisper. "Was she killed?"

"Hardly a scratch. Isn't that the way?"

Addy paused to take it in, then nodded. That was the way. "She'll lose her job though, won't she?"

Calvin nodded. Addy felt relieved, but ashamed too. Why hadn't she gone straight to the principal and told him about the bottle of gin? What if the drunken teacher had run into some innocent person instead of an oak tree? Why had Addy threatened and frightened the woman instead of trying to reason with her? In the end, was she just a bully too?

The wind was strong that night. It howled through the trees and tore down branches and knocked over garbage cans and kicked them around the mud lane. Addy slept not a wink. She couldn't help but think that old as she was she still had so many lessons to learn. And she knew that she'd die before she learned them all. She thought of Mrs. Pigot and how the woman's worst sin was likely just ignorance.

In the morning Addy made sausage and eggs. She was drying the dishes when Sharla asked, "Who's gonna be my new teacher?"

"New teacher?"

"'Cause of Mrs. Pigot hitting that oak."

"I didn't know you were listening to me and Calvin, Sharla. I didn't want you to hear all about that."

"Why?"

"Because that's a distressing thing when a person's in a car accident."

"Because she's drunk as a skunk?"

"Don't you *ever* be repeating a thing like that, Sharla," Addy said sharply. "You understand me? Ever."

"Yes, Ma'am."

"That woman must have a tortured soul to do the things she does."

"I hate her."

"No, Sharla. You don't hate anyone."

"Yes I do."

"Look at me." Addy sat down next to Sharla and took her soft face in her old hands. "I know Mrs. Pigot was mean to you, but you gotta find it in your heart to forgive her."

"Why?"

"Because if you don't, you carry those bad feelings around with you all your life and hate's like salt in water, Sharla. Once it gets in there it's a hard thing to get out. You forgive Mrs. Pigot. All right?"

"All right. But can I be glad there's gonna be a new teacher?"

Addy ignored the question, hurrying Sharla out the door with her school snack and warm hat. It was not unusual to hear voices from the other side and it rarely frightened her, but Addy shuddered, when she sat down at the table and everything was still, to hear a low voice whisper, "What about me, Adelaide?"

The voice did not belong to Leam or the few others Addy spoke with from time to time. It was her father, and he asked again, "What about me? Do you forgive *me*, Addy?"

Addy couldn't answer. She rose and left the room, hoping that her father's voice wouldn't follow. Hoping she wouldn't hear it again. She would *never* forgive *him*.

Tea

amond Ferguson had taken Addy's suitcase and his mother's, of course, and begun to walk away from the train station in Chatham without a word or second glance. He kept his eyes on his boots and swung his head from side to side as Willow peppered him with questions about Olivia's wedding. "Have to ask Mary Alice about that," he said seven times before Willow caught on she was talking to the wrong person.

Addy'd expected Hamond to be driving a truck, seeing as Willow'd said he was a farmer, but they walked past the Chatham station and crossed two busy streets and there appeared to be no truck or wagon or any other method of transport waiting for them. Addy wondered if they were going straight to the wedding and if the roof would cave in if she dared to enter the church. She was sore and still not accustomed to the weight of Verilynn's big boots but didn't mind that she lagged behind. She wanted to give Hamond and Willow a little privacy in case he had a protest.

She looked around the busy streets and marveled at how one town could look so much like another. The little neighborhood they were heading for now looked not unlike the one where she'd lived in Detroit, nor the one Morris Davies drove her through in Sandwich. She wondered if when she got to Toronto, she'd be disappointed by the sameness of it too.

They walked down a street called Degge Street, past modest clapboard houses with tiny front yards and backyards that were small patches of grass with wood sheds and not much else. Hamond turned when they reached the end of the street and started up the walkway of the smaller-than-the-rest corner house. Willow turned to look at Addy, as if she suddenly remembered her presence. "Hamond says it's fine for you to stay."

Given the man's expression when he first laid eyes on her, Addy was surprised by Hamond's generosity. "He said it's fine?"

Willow nodded. "He said you can stay as long as you need. This is his and Mary Alice's house. You coming inside or not?"

Addy looked up at the little house, confused. "I thought he was a farmer."

Willow laughed. "He is a farmer, but he don't *own* the land he farms, Child. Not many Negro landowners around here. Unless you count Rusholme, but that's a whole different story."

Addy shivered at the mention of Rusholme and thought of her father. She looked down Degge Street, wondering if Wallace's feet had trod upon this very sidewalk. She felt a rush of panic when she realized she didn't know where the canning factory was. She'd find out though and be sure to avoid that part of town during her short stay. She reckoned Hamond Ferguson'd be able to direct her to a jeweler who'd give her a good price on her diamond and emerald ring. Then she could get back on the train and go. She was determined to go to Toronto, or anywhere that wasn't here.

Before Hamond even pulled open the front door, Addy could hear the commotion inside. There were easily a dozen women, young and old, quiet and bold, all crammed into the little sitting room. Addy could see Olivia Ferguson in her long buttery gown, her headpiece askew, a sheer veil falling over her tear-streaked face. The bride exhaled a sob and the women's voices rose above in wails of comfort. Addy watched Willow fold into the crowd and make her way to Olivia, glad she herself had become invisible.

A few more women flowed out from the kitchen fussing with pastry trays and pies and crocks of beans and pans of scalloped potatoes. It took three of them to carry a huge covered roasting pan and the look and smell of the food reminded Addy she'd eaten only a few apples since her chicken leg supper the night before. She was perspiring from hunger and heat but she dared not doff her coat or boots before she was invited to do so by her host, and as yet she didn't know which one of the women was Mary Alice. She pressed herself against the wall, watching, waiting, and wondering what to do next.

The women, whatever they were saying to Olivia, seemed to be making the girl more miserable. Addy's heart thumped as Olivia's sobs grew louder. She could only imagine the horror that must have befallen the young bride. *Oh Lord,* Addy thought, *the groom has fled town. Or worse, it's been discovered he was already married. Or maybe his parents forbade the union at the last moment, reckoning a restaurant owner's son could do better than to wed a farmhand's daughter.* Poor Olivia's wails had reached a crescendo and finally she blurted, "They don't match. They *don't match!*"

Addy stood on her tiptoes to see into the crowd of women. What didn't match, she wondered, that would make Olivia sound so desperate? And then she saw, in Olivia's hands, a pair of beautiful silky white slippers. It was Willow who'd pointed out, and caused a fresh flood of tears, "Only time folks is gonna see your shoes is when you're dancing, Livvy. If you really care so much, why, just slip them off and go barefoot!"

"They're white!" Olivia wailed. "They're white and they're wrong and they spoil this gown! They *do!*" She held the slippers against the bodice of her dress and cried in horror, "*Look!*"

Olivia was right. The slippers were too sharp and too white and didn't favor the less dazzling, soft, creamy tone of the dress. Addy knew right away what to do, for she remembered Laisa fretting over her new white curtains for the bedrooms, which she very much wanted to match with her old faded curtains in the front room "so it looks just right from the street." It wasn't until the whole room went silent and one by one they turned to look at her that Addy realized she'd spoken her thoughts out loud.

A stern older woman wearing a blue dress and smart hat stepped forward and eyed her coolly. "The wedding starts in exactly six minutes and Darryl's already at the church. How exactly do you think you can take the white out these slippers in six minutes, Young Lady?"

Olivia watched Addy in her too-big coat and boots and didn't think to wonder who she was or why she was there. She brushed back her veil and wiped the tears from her cheeks and said, "Can you do it? Can you? It ruins *everything* if they don't match."

Addy moved through the crowd, taking the slippers and turning back to the woman in the blue dress to ask, "Is there tea? And an old handkerchief?"

There were murmurs all around, especially among the older women, for it was common to use tea as stain. The woman in blue returned at once with a cup of tea and a torn handkerchief, which Addy quickly dipped and wiped over the silky surface of the slippers. In less than seconds the tea soaked the satin and the white disappeared, and though the tone was not so soft and creamy as the gown, it was better and closer and Olivia started to cry all over again. "Thank you. Oh thank you," she said. She eased her feet into the tea-damp slippers and sailed out the door with the rest of the crowd in tow.

Addy stood alone in the room, which seemed much larger now, though the energy of the women and the smell of the food on its way to the church basement still clung to the air. She'd been forgotten and was severely relieved, for she didn't see how she could go into a church, any church, and she'd feel foolish pretending to celebrate the wedding of a spoiled young woman whose acquaintance she'd just made. Besides, she was still feeling sorry enough for herself over her soured love with Riley Rippey and the too-recent tragedy of her baby's death.

Though she felt a little strange, Addy slipped out of her coat and boots, settled into one of the high-back chairs by the window, and closed her eyes. It was almost dark when she awoke but she didn't feel afraid and remembered right off she was at the Ferguson house in Chatham. On the table in front of her, which she smelled before she saw, was a plate of wedding food that someone fixed and brought over and went to the trouble of covering with a pot lid to keep it warm. There was also a glass of milk and a slice of butter pie and three different kinds of fruit squares. Addy smiled when she saw the food and looked around, even as she knew she was alone and there was no one to thank but the Lord. She reckoned it must have been Willow who remembered her and she felt ashamed once more at how she'd hated the old woman when first they met. She ate every last morsel much too quickly, then closed her eyes and fell instantly back to sleep.

When Addy woke again, it was morning, and this time she was confused and felt like she might be dreaming. She was not upright in the chair by the window, but supine on the sofa, a soft pillow beneath her head and a warm blanket covering her body. She could smell coffee, and after her eyes adjusted to the light, she could see a woman sitting across from her. The woman was tall and sat queenly in her chair. Her head was perched on a neck so long and slight it seemed in the process of being swallowed by her collar. She was in silhouette against the window and her details were lost in shadow, but Addy guessed the woman young rather than old, and pretty, if not outright beautiful. The woman turned to look out the window and Addy glimpsed her feline eyes.

Addy sat up, feeling caught and guilty. "Ma'am," she said.

The woman turned, took a slow deliberate sip of coffee, and gestured at the cup she'd set on the table for Addy. "Mary Alice. You call me Mary Alice."

Addy rubbed her eyes and thought it strange she couldn't remember the woman's face from the crowded room yesterday. "Thank you for your hospitality, Ma'am. I know it musta been a surprise to have Willow bringing me here on your daughter's day and I just hope I wasn't too much trouble."

"No trouble, Child. In fact, we was all talking later about how surprising it was none of us thought to take them slippers down with tea. Suppose it needs a person looking in from the outside to see things clear sometimes."

"Your daughter looked very beautiful. Was it a lovely wedding, Mary Alice Ma'am?"

"Yes it was. And she did look beautiful, didn't she?" Mary Alice coughed so she would not cry. "Can't believe she's gone.

Can't believe how fast the years passed. I look at my hands and I see them wiping carrot mash off my baby girl's face. I can't believe she's married now. Can't believe it won't be long before she has a child of her own and she looks down at her hands, and sees mine. Wish she was small for just one more day, so I could hold her like I used to, so she'd need me like she used to."

Addy sipped some of the steaming coffee and said nothing, for all she wanted herself was to hold her own baby and to be held by her own Mama. She wondered if Willow had told her daughter-in-law her story, or at least what Willow knew of her story, but dared not ask.

"You can't stay here, Child," Mary Alice said evenly.

Addy looked at her, thinking she had not heard right. "Ma'am?"

"Not even for one night."

Addy nodded and did not know what to do except rise and look for her coat.

"Sit down, Adelaide. That's your name, Adelaide?"

She nodded. "Addy."

"Sit down, Addy. I want to explain it, because I'm surely grateful for what you did yesterday. No telling where Olivia's drama might have ended. I believe you changed the course of the whole wedding."

"I only took the white out her slippers."

Mary Alice took another sip of coffee and did not look at Addy directly. "Willow told me about your recent troubles. I feel sorry for you. I really do. I came to see you yesterday but you were fast asleep."

Addy could see now that Mary Alice was older than she first appeared. Closer to her own mother's age than hers, but still much younger looking than Hamond. It suddenly occurred to Addy. "*You* brought the food?"

"My mother-in-law is a good person but she does get to telling folks how it is. In the meantime she misplaces how it *really* is and what she ought to be doing about it. I asked her who you were and she told me about the man on the train, and I asked her where you were and she said she thought she'd seen you helping some of the ladies in the church kitchen. I knew by watching you yesterday you wouldn't be comfortable just coming along to the church and I guessed you were still back here. I guessed right you hadn't had much to eat."

Addy shook her head. "Thank you, Ma'am. It was one of the best suppers I ever took in my life."

Mary Alice nodded and cleared her throat. "I'm sorry for what I'm about to tell you, but let me just say it plain. See, Addy, my husband, Hamond, is a good man. But he walks in his Daddy's shoes and Willow knows all about that. It's in his nature and I knew it when we wed. I don't mind so much, long as he tells me who she was and who else knows, so I don't seem a fool if it ever comes up outside the home."

The coffee was strong and Addy was awake, but she still could not believe she was hearing right. Was Mary Alice saying that Hamond was unfaithful? Addy looked away. "I'm sorry to know, Ma'am."

"Like I say, I really don't mind so much. Not a blessed thing I could do if I did. It's just that Hamond's father went away with one of his women and never was seen again. I still got two small boys to grow here and I'm not about to have my man run off with a girl younger than my daughter."

"No, Ma'am." Addy couldn't believe what she was hearing and had no idea how to respond.

"I overheard my Hamond last night, talking with some of his men friends, saying how you was gonna be staying with us all and about how you was giving him eyes all the way back from the train station."

"Ma'am?" Addy was too stunned to protest.

"I didn't believe him. Fact is though, if Hamond thinks you like to be with him, he'll just work you till you do. And he has a way about him that ain't so evident on first glance."

Addy shook her head and felt nauseated by the thought of Hamond and the way he'd looked at her when he helped her off the train.

Mary Alice looked out the window again. "Hamond knew your father."

Addy shuddered. "My father?"

"Wallace Shadd?"

Addy nodded slowly.

"Hamond used to talk with him at the factory when he brung the harvest in on the truck. He said he knew who you were the very second he laid eyes because you happen to be the image of your Daddy."

Addy swallowed the bile in her throat and waited. She sensed there was more and worse to come.

"You don't have to look at me like that. I got a good idea about what happened to you in Rusholme. Same thing happened to me when I was a girl, only it was my own father's brother. I never told a soul. I knew I wouldn't be believed. And even then, I remembered thinking, if this happened to me, how many other girls have the same secret?"

Tears appeared at the corners of Mary Alice's cat eyes. She blinked them back and sighed. "I know Hamond. Hamond thinks if you done it before you must be ripe for it again. Don't matter what the truth *is*. Just matters what he *thinks* is true. That's why I can't have you here. Not even for one night. I got to protect my own, and that means Hamond too. From himself, though it is."

Addy nodded and rose again to leave.

"Sit down, Adelaide."

This time Addy did not want to sit or to hear any more. She was ashamed, even though she knew Mary Alice didn't hold her responsible. She watched her reflection in the black coffee on the table and asked quietly, "He gonna tell my Daddy about seeing me?"

Mary Alice stared at her blankly.

Addy looked up. "Will you ask Hamond to tell my Daddy he seen me, and to say I'm fine? My Mama must worry so."

Mary Alice rose herself now, crossed the room and sat down beside Addy on the sofa. She took Addy's hand and furrowed her brow and said, "I thought you knew. Your father passed. Just before Christmas. It was talked about some at Libby's, as you can imagine, after what all happened with his children."

Addy nodded and wondered why she was neither shocked nor aggrieved. She didn't ask for any more details and it occurred to her that she knew all along her father would not last, could not live after what happened, or what he believed happened. "What about my Mama? Do you know?"

Mary Alice shook her head. "Heard she went south. Has a sister in Georgia was it?"

"South Carolina." Addy drew her hand away from Mary Alice, set to rise once more. Mary Alice pulled her back and smiled tenderly. "I got one more thing to tell you and this time it ain't bad news. See, I talked things over with my mother last night. She don't know nothing about you except you come from Detroit and had that trouble on the train and need to stay a few days before you start back up to Toronto. She lives just a few streets over on Murray Ave. She says you can stay as long as you like. She keeps a nice home and has an extra room too. You met her yesterday. She was wearing the blue dress. Her name's Nora, but you best call her Mrs. Lemoine."

Mary Alice handed Addy a slip of paper with her mother's address. Addy read it and asked, "Should I go now?"

"Yes, yes. Go on now and my mother's sure to feed you a nice breakfast."

"You'll tell Willow thanks, and good-bye?"

"I'll tell her."

"Mary Alice?"

"Yes, Addy?"

Addy wanted to tell the woman how relieved she was to be believed about what happened in Rusholme, and how grateful she was Mrs. Lemoine had a room, and how she knew that even as Mary Alice said she was protecting her own, she was protecting Addy too. Instead she said, "Olivia still needs you."

Mary Alice nodded. Addy found her coat and Verilynn's big boots and without another word she opened the door and stepped out into the wintry air. Addy didn't need to avoid the canning factory after all, and she'd ask Mrs. Lemoine about a jeweler before night fell. She reckoned she'd only be a few days in Chatham. She reckoned she could endure a few days.

Cream Cake

*I*t *was not a few days but five years* Addy Shadd endured in
Chatham. Addy had saved the train fare and more by the end of
her first month there but had not even considered heading for
Toronto. Mrs. Lemoine had given her a room of her own and
three meals a day and paid her well for the work she did: cooking,
cleaning, laundry, and gardening. For the first time in some time,
Addy felt safe and believed if she stayed put, she could pretend
her life was what it ought to be. Afraid as she'd been when
she first set down, Chatham felt enough like home now not to
bother looking someplace else. She never again thought of selling
Poppa's ring.

Addy had a good friend in Mary Alice and was like a second
mother to the two little Ferguson boys, Simon and Samuel. As
long as she avoided being alone with Hamond there was harmony
to the collusion of their lives. Mrs. Lemoine was not a gentle
woman, but she was fair and rarely cross. The only conflict between
the older and younger woman was over Addy's baking. Mrs.
Lemoine had grown fat on Addy's pies and cakes and butter tarts
and cursed Addy for her temptations. Even so she fussed like a
child when there was nothing to satisfy her sweet tooth after a
roast supper and demanded to know if it was because she was too
fat. Addy could easily convince her, though, that her girth was
likely caused by her headache medicine and not those second and
third helpings of cream cake.

It was Mary Alice's belief that it was time Addy settled down with a husband, an idea she shared with her mother, but not Addy herself. If Mary Alice had said what she thought, Addy'd have told her kindly but forcefully that she was not interested in a love affair. The fact was that Addy *was* interested, very interested, in a young man named Gabriel Green who lived on Degge Street, three doors down from Mary Alice.

Gabriel was, at twenty, a year younger than Addy. There was something in the young man's face, maybe it was the line of his jaw or the fluttery lashes over his black eyes, whatever it was it reminded her of that someone from Rusholme whose name was too painful to say. When he came into her thoughts, she told herself she'd imagined the whole romance, that no matter his size he was just a boy, and she just a girl. He couldn't have loved her the way she thought, nor she him, for in the end she could write down all the words they'd exchanged on a single piece of paper and still have room left for the Lord's Prayer.

Addy admitted to herself, but never to anyone else, that at least some of her visits to the Ferguson house were an attempt to cross paths with Gabriel Green and to feel her heart race when his eyes roamed her body in the bold way they did.

It was summer in Chatham, a steaming, stinking hot July day, when Addy first laid eyes on Gabriel Green. She'd been in town five months and, while living at Mrs. Lemoine's, was fixed in the Fergusons' life on Degge Street. Addy was sixteen years old and Gabriel Green was fifteen, but he looked and acted like a man. He'd come to the back door at Mary Alice's house, head bowed and handsome, professing to see if Mrs. Ferguson needed any yard work done. When Mary Alice expressed surprise at his thoughtfulness, he'd shrugged and said, "Well, I know Mr. Ferguson into his long days at the farm. Your boys still too young to be much good with heavy work. I just thought to offer my services."

He'd acted surprised to see Addy there and his act was a good one. He made a show of not wanting to intrude and it took some convincing to get the boy to sit down at the kitchen table and enjoy a cool glass of lemonade. Addy had shivered watching his big hands stroke the slippery glass, and when his lips met the rim and his tongue lifted a lemon slice into his mouth, she'd had to turn away. Mary Alice acted flustered and chatty and apologized later, saying she didn't know what got into her.

Addy looked serious. "Don't be thinking about hitching me up with that boy, Mary Alice."

"Why? But why? He's an angel. He's an outright angel. He never lets his Mama lift a finger in the yard and you saw yourself he has the nicest manners. And he's more than a boy, Addy. He may only be fifteen but his Granddaddy's getting him a place at the jute factory come September. He's got plans to buy a house out on the river road and he will too. You just don't know him."

"Sounds like you know him well enough for both of us."

Mary Alice looked away. "Well, I done a little inquiring."

"You tell him to come by and say that about wanting to help you in the yard?"

"No I did not." Mary Alice was indignant.

"He done that before? Come over to offer his help?"

"No."

"Just happened he came by today?"

"Well." Mary Alice swallowed and held her breath in a way Addy'd seen her do before when she got skitty. "I guess he must have seen you here and wanted to make your acquaintance."

"Mmm-hmm." Addy had no doubt Mary Alice was lying. "Well, I think you told him come by and I think you're trying to hitch us up."

"I won't if you don't want me to."

Addy sighed and rose to leave. "I got to get on home and start supper for your Mama."

Mary Alice shrugged and scratched at a mosquito bite under her sleeve. It was then Addy saw the four purple bruises on her soft upper arm. The bruises were distinct and made by a man's strong hand. "Hamond do that?" Addy asked, already knowing the answer.

Mary Alice looked at the bruises like she'd never seen them before. "No," was all she said before she changed the subject.

"You could do worse than Gabriel, Addy. He's got a strong back and good looks and a good heart too."

Addy wondered how her friend seemed so sure about the boy's good heart but didn't ask. "He's not for me, Mary Alice. No girl wants a boy prettier than she is. And that boy'll just grow bigger and prettier and his shoulders wider and his jaw squarer. I won't give him a second thought. And I bet he won't give me one neither. Seemed interested in the cold drink was about all."

The women were lying to each other and both knew it. Mary Alice *had* asked the boy to come by that day. And Addy *would* give Gabriel Green a second thought and a third and a fourth and over the next five years she would look for him on Degge Street and scan the crowds at the market and make it to all the Ferguson boys' baseball games just because Gabriel Green helped coach. But Addy didn't believe she deserved romance and simply dreaded the inevitable. For how could she love a man and be loved by a man who didn't know her story? How could she be touched by a man who didn't know she'd been touched before? And how could she bear a child and not say there was a baby brother who was loved, but never lived? Addy often imagined Gabriel in her bed, but never in her life.

In the afternoons Mary Alice and Addy went to the Farmer's Market in the center of town. Afterward, if the weather was fine and their food sacks not too heavy, they'd take a stroll by the Thames River to watch the children swim and the men fish and the boats sail off to points unknown.

It was early in June and the kind of perfect day Addy thought of as a God day. She'd long ago stopped thinking of Sunday as a day of the Lord and found just any day and any time the right time to give thanks and praise. Mary Alice brought a pint of strawberries to her face and let her nose do the tasting. She set the berries down and picked them up again, fretting. "Hamond's fussy about his berries. Have to put these in a jam or a pie I suppose. They ain't quite right to eat just simple yet."

Addy nodded absently and moved away, for while the berries smelled sweet and delicious, she felt her stomach roil at the memory of the church supper and Zach Heron and in fact hadn't tasted a strawberry since that day six years ago. She selected a bunch of rhubarb and a basket of sweet green peas, thinking how Mrs. Lemoine would complain if she forgot to buy butter again. She was hardly listening to Mary Alice say how hurt she was Olivia wouldn't return to Chatham to celebrate her birthday again this year. Mary Alice's question surprised Addy, as much as anything because she couldn't remember the last time she'd been asked. "When's your birthday, Addy?"

Mary Alice made parties for her sons and her husband, though she ignored her own birthday, and it had just suddenly occurred to her that she didn't know the date of Adelaide's birth. "When, Addy?"

Addy nibbled a stalk of tart rhubarb and shrugged. "Winter."

"When in winter?"

"January."

"When in January?"

"Twenty-fifth."

"Why didn't I know that?"

Addy shrugged again and moved along to another stall. The old farmer behind the counter glanced up. Addy's heart began to thud. She knew the farmer, a man from Rusholme, the father of one of the older boys that used to work the fields at Mr. Kenny's. She could not take her eyes from his. In his face she saw Rusholme and in the reflection of his pupils she saw her father. For it was true she was the image of her father, and it was only when she wore her hat and hid her ears that she could convince herself otherwise. Addy was mildly shocked when the man didn't look at her sideways. How strange, she thought, not to be recognized.

Mary Alice startled her, coming up from behind. "Addy. Don't ignore me. Why didn't you never tell me when was your birthday?"

"I don't know, Mary Alice. I haven't made a celebration out of it since, well, since a long time."

"Since Rusholme?" Mary Alice inquired, louder than she meant to.

Addy steered away from the market stalls and started for home, begging herself not to look back at the Rusholme farmer but doing so anyway.

"Well," Mary Alice began, "see, a woman's only supposed to stop celebrating her birthday when she has a husband and children of her own. I think you're still fine to have a celebration. It's been all that long?"

Addy nodded and wished Mary Alice had never asked the question, for now her mind was flooded with pictures and even the happy ones made her sad. She remembered the year she was with Riley and Poppa in Detroit. She remembered waking on her birthday and feeling sorry for herself and ashamed of her sorrow. She remembered being heavy with her baby and walking down the hallway with a glass of water and a bowl of corn she'd cooked in milk. She remembered how Poppa had not opened his mouth to let the spoon pass and how she'd convinced herself he couldn't, not wouldn't. She'd used her fingers to pry his jaw open and dragged the spoon against his loose teeth, trying not to be angry when he pushed the yellow mush back out with his tongue. Addy'd said, "Please take it. Please swallow. It's my sixteenth birthday today and that's the best present my good Poppa could give me." Poppa had found her eyes and been held by her gaze and he did open his mouth then and take in and swallow the creamed corn. Addy smiled at the memory of Poppa.

She walked beside Mary Alice, feeling the beat of their feet on the road and thinking of her mother and her childhood and her birthdays in Rusholme. January twenty-fifth meant berry preserves for breakfast, whether it was the last of the jars or not, and special suppers and walnut squares or Apple Snow, much as she cared to eat, no matter what her father's face said. There would be walks through the snowy woods or skating on the crick or if it was cold enough, down at the lake. Addy's face would go numb and L'il Leam's too and they would laugh with their eyes because their jaws were frozen shut. Later, by the fire, they'd sing songs with Laisa, breathing the steam from a scalding cup of tea, feeling the prickly sensation of life returning to their flesh. And at night,

Laisa would come to her bedroom and tell her the same story, year after year. "You was covered in blood and wailing like you been done wrong, but I was so happy to see you, Addy. I never told another soul case the Lord overheard, and I certainly never told your Daddy 'cause he would've been angry with my wish. But I did wish my second child was a baby girl. And all the time I carried you I dreamed how you'd be and never even cared when you looked more like your Daddy than a girl should. I thought of all the things I'd teach you and all the talks we'd have. And I knew, and I was right, that you'd be a good and loyal sister."

Addy would close her eyes in the darkness and listen to the sound of her mother's voice and fall asleep feeling loved and cherished. As she walked beside Mary Alice, she thought about how she would never see Laisa again. And never tend the grave or even know when her mother died or where she was buried. When she heard a voice, she forgot where she was a moment and asked, "I beg your pardon, Mama?"

"Mama?" Mary Alice said. "You just called me Mama."

Addy blinked. "I'm sorry, Mary Alice. I was thinking of my mother. Wondering about her health. She never was too fond of her sister. I suppose she doesn't do much but work the house and make herself scarce. Least she don't have to live a hard winter anymore. She used to complain about the snow."

"Everyone complains about the snow."

"Mmm-hmm."

"Addy?"

"Yes, Mary Alice?"

"I'm sorry I didn't know your birthday."

"Truly, it don't hurt me one bit. I just as soon let it pass quiet."

Mary Alice nodded but didn't believe her. She thought of Addy as a friend *and* a daughter and felt guilty and sorry she hadn't asked about her birthday sooner. It was then she had the idea. A gathering, she thought, a birthday party of sorts, or at least a party to make up for all the birthdays lost. A surprise, she thought, so Addy couldn't say no. A mixer with a few young men, grandsons of her mother's friends and Gabriel Green with the soft eyes and big hands. Gabriel's Mama was pushing him to marry a second cousin who stood to gain some land out near the lake. But Mary Alice was determined, and felt sure she'd have what she wanted. And what she wanted, more than she had a right to want, was for Addy Shadd to marry Gabriel and stay in Chatham, right there on Degge Street, just three doors down.

June slid into July and the air turned swampy and sick. The sun fired the earth all the long day and left the ground to smolder when it set. On such nights Addy couldn't sleep. She'd rise and slip out into the darkness to go sit by the river, or just stroll the quiet, empty streets and wonder at the stars. The first night, years ago, when Mrs. Lemoine'd found Addy gone from her bed, the woman assumed she'd run off to Toronto, or that the boy from Detroit had come and claimed her back. She'd been surprised to find her in the kitchen the next morning and wasn't sure she believed her when Addy explained she'd gone to the park near the river for some air and a few winks of sleep.

Addy woke in her bed, slimy with perspiration, her heart racing from a bad dream. She felt too tired to head for the river, so she took to the porch to try to catch a breeze. The air was lazy, but the mosquitoes were lively and enjoyed a feast of her blood that left her with welts on her arms and face. Mrs. Lemoine was normally unconcerned about the welts, for it was the same with Addy every year. She could never persuade the girl to come inside on those heat-wave summer nights. This morning, however, she was vexed. "Adelaide Shadd," she said, "you look like you been stung by fifty bees!"

"Like to take a wire brush to myself," Addy said and brought her fingernails to her cheeks. She was shocked when Mrs. Lemoine slapped her hands from her face and fairly screeched, "Don't scratch!"

Addy shrugged. "They'll go away in a few days, Mrs. Lemoine. They always do."

Mrs. Lemoine kept a special homemade ointment she called a "potion" in her bedside drawer. She insisted it would ease inflammation and ward off infection. She used the same ointment for toothaches and pinkeye and seemed not to notice it stunk of rotten cabbage. She brought the jar into the kitchen and though Addy protested loudly, smeared the greasy stuff over her face and neck and arms, announcing, "That'll take it down by tonight, don't you worry, Addy."

Addy hadn't been worried and except for the itching, didn't care much about the appearance of the welts. As it was, she was merely annoyed that with the awful odor up her nose, she could no longer eat her breakfast.

"Don't forget," Mrs. Lemoine called out before Addy left with a batch of blueberry tarts for the Ferguson boys, "I'll be over to Mrs. Alexander's house this afternoon and evening."

"I know."

"So don't come back here thinking you have to cook my dinner."

"I won't."

"You could do anything you like today, Addy."

"Mmm-hmm. I appreciate that, Mrs. Lemoine." Addy grinned tightly and wondered if Mrs. Lemoine was losing her mind. She'd come to her Monday and said it was high time she take a day off and Friday'd be a good one seeing as how she'd be spending it with her sick friend, Mrs. Butler.

"Just no reason whatever to come back here. You could go do whatever you like and no reason to come back here until after supper time."

"All right, Mrs. Lemoine."

"Won't be able to get inside anyway, Adelaide. I'm locking this house up and I have the only key."

"All right, Mrs. Lemoine." Addy'd flown out the door wondering why on earth Mrs. Lemoine would lock her house when there was nothing to steal and stealing hardly a common thing in the neighborhood anyway.

As was her habit, Addy entered the Ferguson home without a knock at the door or any other formality. She was not surprised to look down the hall and see Gabriel Green sitting at the kitchen table, for he often lent a hand, especially in the summer when

Hamond was on the farm. But she was surprised by the strange look on his face and by the tone in Mary Alice's voice when she called out, "That you, Addy? Just wait. Just wait there. I'll be right out!"

Addy stood in the front room, staring down the hall at Gabriel. She waited, thinking it most annoying to have been told to do so. She minded less when Gabriel rose and came down the hall to join her. His face took on an even stranger look and he asked with grave concern, "You sick, Addy?"

"Sick? No." Addy shrugged, then remembered the welts and touched her face. "This? These? Just mosquito bites is all."

"I get skeeter bites too, but they don't . . . well, they don't look like *that*."

"I know."

"Sure you're not sick?"

"I'm not sick, Gabriel." Addy smiled and leaned in to squeeze his big arm. "But I do appreciate your concern."

The odor of the ointment hit Gabriel Green like a fist. "WHOA!" he cried, stepping back.

Addy cringed, for she'd grown accustomed to the stench. "It's ointment. That's all. A smelly one. Mrs. Lemoine put it on the bites."

Gabriel used some restraint not to gag. He called out to Mary Alice in a voice that said he was holding his breath, "I'll come by later if you need."

"That's all right, Gabriel," Mary Alice trilled. "Thanks for your help and don't let me keep you now."

Addy silently cursed Mrs. Lemoine as she scratched the itchiest of the welts on the left side of her nose. "Mary Alice?" she called.

"Just wait one minute, Addy." The way Mary Alice spoke was more like singing than talking and that meant she was hiding something. Addy strode down the hall and came upon her friend in the small kitchen, her back toward the door, her face buried in the icebox. Mary Alice shut the door quickly and turned around, damp and glistening. Addy looked at her. "What are you hiding?"

Mary Alice would be spared telling Addy that her icebox was filled with food for tonight's party and that she'd just put the finishing touches on a tray of canapés, because at that moment she noticed the welts on Addy's face and shrieked, "No!"

"It's all right. It's all right. It's just the mosquitoes again."

"You look terrible! You're swollen and puffy and . . ." Mary Alice drew closer to have a better look. "You stink!"

"Your Mama's ointment."

"Oh, Addy." Mary Alice looked like she might cry. "You think they'll go down by tonight?"

"They'll go down when they go down. I don't care, long as they stop itching me." Addy settled into a kitchen chair and fanned herself. "Have a cold drink, Mary Alice?" She passed her the plate of blueberry tarts. "These want to go into the icebox too."

Mary Alice hesitated, opened the icebox a crack, and drew out a pitcher of fresh lemonade. She set the plate of tarts on the counter, hoping Addy wouldn't notice. She poured the lemonade and asked casually, "Don't you have any nice summer dress to put on yourself?"

"Looking nice ain't in my mind now, Mary Alice. I'm just so hot and scratchy. Wish it was winter and the river half frozen. Wouldn't that be nice? To float down the river on a chunk of ice?"

Mary Alice wasn't listening. She left the room and returned after a moment with a new dress, cotton, pink-hued, not too fancy, but pretty and cool. "Try this on. It was a present for Olivia, but if she doesn't want to come home for her birthday, I guess she doesn't get a present."

Addy liked the look of the dress and didn't care that it had been meant for Olivia. She slipped out of the old dress and slid into the new one. Caressed by the soft cotton, she felt better and cooler than she had in days. Mary Alice pronounced the fit perfect and said she looked pretty as a picture, "Except for the skeeter welts."

Addy looked out into the backyard. "What'd he help you with?"

"Mmm?"

"Gabriel? What'd he help you with?"

"Oh, some things in the yard is all." Mary Alice looked away like she always did when she was lying. "How long's that smell gonna last, anyway?"

Addy shrugged and sniffed the back of her hand. "Your mother was in a strange humor."

"She was?"

"Mmm-hmm. She told me do whatever I like today. I don't even have to cook dinner tonight."

"That's good, isn't it?"

"Suppose. I just hardly know what to do with myself though." Addy sniffed her hand again. "Think it truly does ward off infection?"

Mary Alice lowered her voice. "I *know* it truly ward off a hus-band. I put a little under my arms from time to time just so Hamond be sure to give me a night off."

Addy was shocked at first, then began to laugh. Mary Alice began to laugh and soon they were both laughing so hard they sounded like mad women. They'd been laughing that same crazy laugh on another occasion when Hamond had unexpectedly come home. He'd known that they were laughing about him and he'd sneered at his wife and warned quietly, "Neighbors think you lost your mind again, woman." Addy had wondered briefly what Hamond meant by again.

Addy asked Mary Alice if she and the boys wanted to take a stroll down by the river or through the path in the woods by the edge of town. Mary Alice pretended to consider her invitation, then decided she had too much work to do. She was telling the truth too, for there was still more food to prepare and decorations to be hung around her mother's house. It was Hamond who'd suggested the ruse. He'd said, "Tell Addy old Nora's got to tend to a sick friend. Just get her out the house for the day is all you really have to do. Have her come back after the dinner hour and make sure you got the party guests all in by then."

Hamond wouldn't attend the party of course, and that was fine with Mary Alice. He'd promised to take the boys out to the pond for a swim in the evening and she thought that was the best help he could give. She didn't need the boys getting in the way or making a mess of her mother's house the way they did. They'd be happy to go swimming with their father and wouldn't even have to know there was a party they were missing.

Alone as she was, and unsure what to do with her time, Addy walked down to the park to sit in the shade, watch the river ripple, and think her thoughts. But today her thoughts were cluttered and confused, and though it was not to say things would make *sense* to her by the end of the day, at least some of the things she was wondering would be availed of a reason. Like why Mrs. Lemoine and Mary Alice had been so concerned about the welts on her face. And why she'd been told to take the day off and not come back till after supper, and why Gabriel Green had looked the way he did when she came in the front door on Degge Street.

The bark on the maple behind her was sharp and informed her of a few bites on her shoulder blades she didn't even know she had. She squirmed and scratched her back against the tree, thinking she must look like an animal and maybe that's just what she was. She closed her eyes and as often happened when she came here, L'il Leam whispered in her ear, "Hey, Sister. Why you think Mary Alice and her Mama acting so peculiar today?"

"I don't know. At first I thought I was just imagining. But Mary Alice *was* telling some lies."

"Why though?"

"Must have something to do with Gabriel and me. He sure had a look on his face."

"She'd like to match the two of you up, that's sure. Been trying for years."

"He make a good husband do you think, Leam?"

"Maybe. Maybe not. Best husband be one that loves his wife."

"He could love me." Addy was indignant at what Leam was implying. "I know he had that look on his face when he got close and smelled my ointment, but he's had other looks on his face too. I see him glance my way. I see him think his thoughts."

"Maybe. Maybe not."

Addy sighed and scratched her face and thought it was lovely when the wind blew a gentle gust her way. "Leam? You think it's fine I'm here in Chatham looking out for Mrs. Lemoine or you think I should be somewhere else?"

"Where else you like to be, Addy?"

"I don't know exactly. I suppose I just worry sometimes that I might get to the end of my life and think I should have done something I never did."

"Done what?"

"I don't know. Something special, I guess."

"Special? Good thing Daddy's not around to hear you talk like that. You know how he feels about people thinking they're special."

"I know, but to live a life and never do anything *important?* Don't it seem like that's a life wasted?"

"I never did one important thing in my life, Addy. Not one. I don't like to think my life was wasted."

"You're wrong, Leam. What you did important was you were good beyond measure and you made people happy and never complained when you was sick and never was cruel to any person and best of all, you loved Birdie Brown in a way that made her feel like she won a prize."

"That's all just simple living though, Addy. Simple living."

"Think simple living is special living?"

"I do."

If her feet had seen her fate, they might have hastened to take Addy past the train station months or even years earlier. As it was, she'd fallen asleep under the tree by the river and awoken feeling groggy and thick. She thought she'd walk for a while, then head on over to Degge Street to catch a glimpse of Gabriel Green and see what Mary Alice was fixing for supper. She'd seen him then, sitting on the old wooden bench with his legs propped up on a luggage trolley, a newspaper opened in his hands. He wasn't wearing his uniform, but she'd recognized him, even a hundred feet away as he was. She'd hardly thought of that train ride from Windsor all those years ago, and only remembered him when she poked through her undergarment drawer and found the book he gave her, the one she never read.

It was as though her flush and rush of blood called to him, for he looked up just then, folded his newspaper, and laid it down on his knee. He never took his eyes off her as she walked up the path to the bench where he sat. They neither of them smiled too broadly but were familiar with each other in a way that surprised them both. Addy had never forgotten his name. "Mose," she said simply.

"Addy," he returned, and tipped his absent cap.

She did smile then and was flattered by his recollection. "Shouldn't you be dipping your feet in the Pacific Ocean right now? Or looking out the window at them big Rocky Mountains?"

Gradison Mosely laughed and stood. Addy was surprised, being a tall young woman as she was, how far she had to look up, past his white neck and chin and cheeks, to see those grinning eyes.

She looked at the newspaper in his hand and saw it was not the *Chatham Daily News* but something else. Mose followed her gaze. "It's the Brotherhood paper."

"The Brotherhood. I remember you talking about that."

Mose laughed. "I haven't stopped talking about it either. And never will. It's the reason I'm here today. Brotherhood meeting at the hall in the East End."

"Quite a thing to see you here in Chatham, Mose."

"Quite a thing to see you, Addy. I thought you were heading to Toronto."

"I never made it."

"I figured. I asked — whenever I was at the Union Station — I asked did a pretty young lady ever come by to return a book and if so did she leave an address where I might reach her?"

Addy cast her eyes. "I'm sorry."

"Don't be sorry. I only gave the book to you so I'd have a chance at seeing you again."

Addy looked at him, remembering what Willow Ferguson had said about his making flirtations. She grinned. "You likely keep a box of those old books and hand them out to every girl alone on the train. I know fellas like you. You're a time maker."

Mose laughed and shook his head. "Whatever a time maker is, I swear I'm not one. I never in my life gave a book to one girl but you."

Addy didn't believe him and didn't care. "Well, Mose, whatever you are, I suppose you ought to be getting to your meeting and I ought to be getting on too."

Mose nodded and hesitated before deciding to venture, "Suppose you're married off now?"

Addy shook her head. She glanced at his ring finger but couldn't see behind his paper.

"You're free to marry me then," Mose didn't so much ask as state.

Addy giggled like a schoolgirl, turned, and began to walk away. Mose loped up behind her and linked his arm through hers. She wasn't offended and knew Mose only meant to be charming, but she yanked her arm back anyway.

Mose hung his head and sighed. "What sort of fiancée won't let her intended escort her down the street?"

Though her heart was fluttering, Addy smoothed the folds of her dress and tried to act bored. "Don't you have to go?"

"Not for an hour or so. Could I . . . in seriousness, Adelaide, could I stroll with you a little? I have thought of you over these years and I, well, I admired how you handled what happened on the train and I truly would like to know how you've been. May I? Stroll with you?"

Addy looked up, and in the way a flash of lightning could reveal the secrets of the dark, she thought in that second she could see her future in Mose's crick green eyes. She didn't smile at him, but nodded and put her arm through his. Their strides matched perfectly as they headed toward the sidewalk. Though they'd never touched before, it seemed to Addy they'd always been like this, elbows linked, shoulder brushing arm, a breath apart.

Neither of them noticed, or if Mose did he made no indication, the eyes of the people they passed. Some glanced with disapproval, some pierced with outright contempt, and some just widened in such surprise you might have thought they were watching Jesus and Mary Magdalene arm in arm on the sidewalk instead of just a tall, white-looking man and a pretty black girl in a pink cotton dress.

They'd walked and talked, or rather Mose had talked, for more than an hour before he realized he'd missed his meeting. Addy hardly spoke a word, so charmed was she by the man she'd found boastful and boring on the train all those years ago. There seemed to be nothing that Mose didn't know and his passion for what he called *the cause* was a thing she'd never encountered, a thing that stirred her.

"My fellow porter was fired last week. You know what for, Addy? He shined a passenger's shoes and left them outside the wrong berth. We were at the end of a cross-country run, been sleeping maybe three hours a night, on call the rest of the time. The man was tired. He was tired and for that he lost his job."

"Can the Brotherhood get his job back?"

Mose shook his head. "But we're fighting for rights, Addy. We want to be paid for the hours we work and we don't want to work no more twenty-hour shifts. We want a decent place to sleep and eat. And we want the chance to be promoted. And we don't want demerit points just because a passenger says we been rude. I myself once left a pair of shoes outside the wrong berth but caught my mistake before the inspector did. I have also been accused of rudeness, if you can believe that." Mose stopped. "I have been going on, Addy. I'm sorry."

"I don't mind, Mose," Addy told him. "Though it do look like that vein in your temple might bust wide open."

Mose laughed and took her hand and walked on in silence. They weren't walking anywhere in particular when they found themselves east on King Street. Addy stopped, gesturing at the First Baptist Church to their left. "See this church, Mose? A famous thing happened here at this church. Did you know that?"

He'd only seen Chatham from the train window until today, but Mose was familiar with the town's history. He knew it had been a terminus on the Underground Railroad. He knew the abolitionist newspaper *The Provincial Freeman* had been published

here by a famous Negro woman. And he was aware of the historical significance of the ordinary-looking church Addy Shadd was
pointing to now. He shrugged and shook his head though,
because he wanted to hear her tell it.

Addy grinned, pleased to know something that Gradison
Mosely did not. "This here," she said, "is the church where John
Brown — do you know who John Brown was?"

"He was an American abolitionist. A white abolitionist,"
Mose said.

"Yes he was. He came to Chatham in I forget exactly what
year, eighteen fifty-nine I think, it was just before the Civil War."
She pointed. "Right here at this church is where him and his men
planned the raid on the U.S. Arsenal at Harpers Ferry in West
Virginia. John Brown was gonna lead the slaves in a revolt but it
didn't work out. He was caught at Harpers Ferry and hung for
what he done. People say that raid is what started the whole Civil
War, but you likely already knew that."

In spite of the fact that she had strange bumps on her face and
body, some of them bloody from scratching, and in spite of the
fact that he detected the odor of spoiled food when he'd taken
her arm, Mose thought Addy Shadd was the most beautiful girl
he'd ever known and he desired her beyond what he thought was
imaginable. He looked at the church, then back at her smiling
face. "You're quite a historical expert, Mizz Shadd."

Addy shook her head. "I wouldn't say expert. Just I learned
about it in school is all. Most of the colored folks around these
parts know our own history." She took his arm and started walking again. "Guess your meeting's almost over now. Sorry I took
you away from it."

She wasn't really sorry. Mose wasn't either, but as they walked
back toward the river and found a quiet spot under a tree, he
promised himself that he would not let down the Brotherhood
again. For tonight though, he found it unthinkable to leave Addy
Shadd's side.

Darkness crept up on them as they lounged beneath the tree,
holding hands at first, then daring to share a first kiss. Addy, for

her part, could hardly bear her own pumping blood. It was impossible to hide from Mose the craving of her mouth and the interest of her tongue. She pushed him off though she wanted to pull him in. She scratched a welt on her forehead and watched Mose lick the film of perspiration from his upper lip. "Mose," she said, "remember what happened, back on the train, that man accusing me of stealing? And how it was that lock of baby hair proved the ring was mine?"

Mose nodded and pressed his finger to her lips. "It doesn't matter, Addy. It doesn't matter."

She kissed the finger and said softly, but insistently, "It does matter. It matters because I need to tell you."

Mose leaned back against the tree and closed his eyes. Addy was grateful it was dark and his eyes were closed, for she didn't want to see what they said. He made only two sounds throughout her whole tale. The first came when she told about smelling a smell and waking in her bed that Strawberry Sunday, the second when she told about baby Leam's birth and death. By the end, though he kept his eyes closed, Mose had reached for Addy and was rocking her like she was a baby herself. He stroked her cheek and said, "It's gonna be fine, Addy. It's gonna be fine." Addy knew it was.

*M*rs. Lemoine *checked the clock on the wall.* There were some two dozen folks in her home and not one of them was Adelaide Shadd. She sought solace at the food table, filling her plate a full three times before the evening's end. There were four young men to every woman in the room but only one of the women, Mary Alice, did not have liver spots. All the young men knew they'd been brought there to mix with Addy Shadd and they came willingly, for even those who'd not yet made her acquaintance had been told she was an excellent homemaker, lively and lovely, except for her ears. All the men had been cautioned about her ears.

Mary Alice exchanged a few glances with her mother. They were not worried, just annoyed. Addy had disappeared on several occasions and it only meant she went out walking and got lost in her thoughts or was sitting at the river or out on the path in the woods. Mrs. Lemoine herself stomped down to the river to have a look, long before night fell. She'd seen the couple reclining under the tree, but hadn't known it was Addy, having never seen the pink dress before. And she wouldn't have expected to find Addy Shadd sitting under a tree with a white boy anyway. Mary Alice blamed her mother for not coming up with a good reason to bring Addy back to the house in the evening. Mrs. Lemoine blamed Mary Alice for the rest.

One after another the folks left, bewildered by the absence of the guest of honor. Mrs. Lemoine and Mary Alice cleaned up the considerable mess and did not exchange a word. When the last glass was washed and dried and Addy still not home, Mary Alice left, slamming the door behind her. She stepped out into the evening, relieved to find a breeze. She checked the street to make sure there were no eyes upon her and lifted the fabric of her skirt to fan the flesh of her thighs. She thought of Addy on the short walk home and how she likely lost her chance forever with Gabriel Green. Gabriel'd be leaving in a few weeks, presumably to go work with his cousin, but mostly to see if he and the man's daughter would get along well enough to make it permanent. Mary Alice wondered idly if Hamond was home, and if so had he yet laid down his head. She hoped he had, for Hamond slept like the dead.

As it was, Hamond had come home and set the two tired, swum-out little boys in their beds, then gone to his mother-in-law's to see how the matchmaking party was going. It wasn't a likely thing, but he and his wife had just missed each other, like a thread slipping to one side of the needle's eye when by rights it should have slid through. Hamond had agreed with Mary Alice that Addy Shadd ought to get on with things and start a life of her own. He didn't care for his wife's friendship with the girl. Seemed to him, since Addy'd come to town, Mary Alice had been slipping away again. Not so anyone else might notice. Just little things, here and there. The way she'd sing a song when she thought he couldn't hear. The way she wouldn't mind him. And the way she'd taken to putting creams on her skin and scents on her neck. She was trying to be young, he knew, and there was no telling where that might lead.

Mrs. Lemoine was still awake and with the clock reading well past ten she was worried now, not terribly, but enough to ask Hamond to go have a look. Hamond set off on foot and went first to the park by the river. As always on steamy summer nights, there were a few dozen folks scattered around the lawn. The evening was bright with moonlight, and it was simple enough to see the families and lovers and single people out to get some air. Hamond's attention was caught by a familiar figure sitting alone under a tree near the water. He knew her by the curve of her neck, the way she wore her hair. He moved forward, quietly calling her name so she would turn and see him. It was a young girl who tended the house on the farm where he worked. He approached slowly, not wanting to frighten her.

Mose was staying with a retired porter near the tannery at the far end of town and though she insisted she'd be fine, he wouldn't consider letting Addy walk home alone. They'd left the park just moments before Hamond arrived, Addy remarking on the stew-thick air, and Mose remarking on the sharp white moon and how well it lit their way. The only sound, save for the murmuring of the other nightwalkers, was the symphony of crickets courting in the grass. The sound put Addy in mind of Rusholme and the year she and Leam had started off for the lake one August morning. They thought they must be still asleep and dreaming for what they saw: a blanket of crickets inching across the road, coming up from the ditch on one side, struggling toward the ditch on the other, like they hoped the water'd be different there and save them. Addy had laughed, stomping on the crickets and squealing at the sound of their crunchy skeletons, excited by the sheer number she could kill with just one foot. But Leam had been afraid. He'd reminded her of the locust in the Bible, and how any time insects swarmed it meant there was a bad thing coming.

Addy had shivered, realizing the crickets might indeed be an omen of destruction. If Leam was right, the fact she was amusing herself by killing them might bring the doom directly down upon *her* head. They stood still, she and her brother, watching the insects inch past them, hearing for the first time the whispery sound their bellies made as they stroked the dusty road. L'il Leam had said, "Shh. Listen. Sounds like they're saying, 'Watch out. Watch out. Watch out.'"

Addy began to cry. Leam had been sorry then because scaring Addy had not been his intention. He'd simply said what he believed. And he believed in warnings.

They decided not to go to the lake after all and didn't venture into the ditch to raid the errant stalks of sweet corn as they usually did. "What about the monarchs, Leam?" Addy asked hopefully as they headed back to Fowell Street. "Why ain't there no destruction from the monarchs?"

"Well, Little Sister," he considered, knowing she meant the yearly migration of monarch butterflies to the lake. It was a tradition in Rusholme, much like Christmas and Thanksgiving, to go see the monarchs. The whole town would set off on some certain fall day with old horse blankets and picnic baskets and spectacles if they needed them. The butterflies would have beat them to the place. They'd have been arriving for days and by the end the sky'd be full of them, thick as raindrops. They'd settle on the near-bare branches, fluttering their magnificent black and orange wings, making the trees look alive and like they'd take off flying too, if not for their stubborn roots. "The monarchs don't count, seeing as they ain't *crawling* insects, Addy," L'il Leam had concluded. "It's just the crawling and hopping ones, like crickets and grasshoppers, what bring the doom."

They couldn't bear for the evening to end so Mose and Addy took the long way home, quiet, unaware that they were leaning against each other for support. Addy would tell Mose about the monarchs some day, and about the crickets and her mother and father and brother and all the things about Rusholme she'd kept to herself since the day she left. They passed the Ferguson house on Degge Street and Addy saw there was a light in the sitting room. She was sure it would be Mary Alice and not Hamond still awake.

"This is Mary Alice's house," she said. "Too hot for her to sleep, I suppose. I think I'll go on in and see does she want some company."

Mose didn't like the sound of that but couldn't say exactly why. "It's late, Addy. Awful late to be calling on a person."

"Mary Alice is more than a person though, more than a friend or a mother. She won't mind. Besides, don't you know I'll burst if I don't tell her about seeing you again?"

Even in the moonlight Addy saw that Mose was blushing. "I can, can't I, Mose? Tell her about seeing you?"

He set his hands lightly upon her arms in a way that made her shiver. Then he leaned down and pressed his mouth to hers. When his tongue politely begged to explore, she parted her lips and allowed. She breathed the air he exhaled and tasted his mouth. Addy might have gone on kissing Mose right there on Degge Street, but all at once she felt him grow hard and press against her stomach and suddenly she wondered if she'd been wrong. Was he a gentleman after all? For that matter, was she a lady? She pushed him off and wiped her lips with the back of her hand.

"I'm sorry, Addy," Mose whispered and wished she hadn't looked away. "After what you told me tonight, I don't want you to think I think . . ." He struggled with the right phrasing. "I just want you to know I'm a gentleman and wouldn't, couldn't . . ."

"I know," Addy said, turning to meet his gaze, and now she truly did know. "I'm going inside, Mose."

"To tell Mary Alice about me?"

"Yes."

"You gonna tell her we're getting married?"

Addy giggled. "I'm not sure I believe that myself."

Mose reached down, took her hand, and lifted it to his lips. Addy squeezed his fingers and turned around, telling herself not to run like a child or squeal with delight as she made her way up the walkway to the Ferguson home. She turned when she reached the door, knowing he'd still be there. She held her breath as she gave a little wave and watched him walk down the street, thinking how beautiful and mysterious a simple life could be.

The house was quiet. Addy knew not to call out. Hamond was a sound enough sleeper but she wouldn't want to wake Simon and Samuel. If she did they'd want a glass of water, then a pee, then it'd be another hour before they'd be back down. She crept through the sitting room and down the hall and like a storm that appears suddenly overhead, she felt some ill wind blow in from the back door and she knew something terrible, something she couldn't stop, was just about to happen. She realized she could hear the crickets again, so many and so loud it was like to pop her ear. She took a deep breath and opened the back door.

There was someone in the yard and though she couldn't see in the darkness or hear any person's voice, she could sense a presence. Addy had not the will to turn back so she crept down the stairs, squinting at the bushes and the fence beyond. It was then she heard whispering in the woodshed. There were two voices, and though she couldn't identify them precisely, she had a flash in her mind of what Mary Alice had told her of Hamond's infidelity. He's there, Addy thought, he's in there with one of his women. There was a trill of laughter followed by a hard slap, and then silence. The door to the shed never had shut right and even now was half-open. Through it came another sound, a moaning sound, like someone was hurt. Addy swallowed hard and moved forward, knowing if she reached the pear tree she'd get a clear view inside the shed.

Years later, Addy would think on that night and wonder if the moon had ever shone so bright. She'd taken the steps toward the pear tree, hidden behind its trunk, and seen clearly a thing she had never seen before. A thing she could not believe. Gabriel Green was buck-naked, his skin silvery with sweat, his chest heaving, his long body rippling and shivering in pain. His back was pressed against the wall of the shed, his arms stretched out and strung with rope tied to hooks. His head hung to one side, and with his arms like they were, he looked just like Jesus on the cross. It was from Gabriel's lips the moans escaped and Addy could see now, though it was another thing she could not believe, that there was pleasure in his pain. Mary Alice stood in front of Gabriel, naked too, glistening too, making circles with her round behind, back and forth and in and out, barely brushing his thick erection. Gabriel leaned forward, opening his mouth and finding Mary Alice's soft shoulder. He bit her hard and she brought up her hand to slap his face. He let his head hang again and moaned a little more as Mary Alice scraped his nipples with her fingernails.

Addy could scarcely breathe and much as she knew it was a thing not to be seen, she could not look away and could not fathom the depth of her own arousal. She would not tell a soul what she saw, not Mose or anyone, for if she told there would be judgment, and feeling as she did, any judgment would then also be against her. What she saw she'd keep quietly and wonder over and be confused by, until she concluded that humans were only creatures, and creatures as unpredictable, noble and base, brutal and benevolent as any animal, or the weather, or the Lord.

She watched Gabriel start to move again, struggling against the ropes, thrusting, his eyes small and searing. Mary Alice stepped back, teasing. Gabriel lifted his right leg and hooked it around her narrow waist, drawing her in, seizing and squeezing until she was pressed against him. Mary Alice was the one to struggle now, as he tightened his leg hold and began to buck against her. Suddenly she stopped struggling. She lifted her leg, set her foot against the wall, reached for Gabriel, and guided him inside her. They both moaned quietly in their pleasure and pain. Addy might have spoken then, or walked directly inside the shed, for Gabriel Green and Mary Alice were so lost in the desperate love they were making, she was sure she would have stayed invisible.

*A*ddy *arrived home shortly after midnight* to find Mrs. Lemoine sitting up, more tired and worried than angry. After a long talk about the surprise party, and an even longer apology for going off the way she did, Addy retreated to her room. Her mind tore through the events of the day. She'd been stunned to learn Mary Alice had thrown her a matchmaking party, even if she wasn't sorry she missed it. It certainly explained the peculiar way she and

Mrs. Lemoine had been acting that morning. But how could she make sense of what happened in the woodshed? Or, moreover, how she felt watching it?

Mose, she thought, and felt a surge of what she imagined was true love. Although she would think of Mose and be with Mose for many hours and weeks and years, she thought no more of her future husband that night. She waited with a galloping heart until she heard the door to Mrs. Lemoine's bedroom close shut, then she stripped off her clothes and stretched naked on the bed, not minding, even liking, that her skin was hot and damp. As she listened to the crickets Addy slowly guided her finger toward her nipple. She moved the finger back and forth, pinching a little, sensing the heat in her groin. With one hand still attending her nipple, she directed the other down her concave belly to burrow in the slick coarse hair between her legs. Almost at once she felt the same sensation she'd felt those years ago, and not since, the white-hot tingle provoked by Riley Rippey's tongue. As she probed and caressed herself, a thing she'd never done before, she thought of Mary Alice and Gabriel Green in the woodshed. Until this night she would never have allowed that such a thing could be. It was savage, Addy knew, but it was also love.

Hamond slept through it all. He'd spoken briefly with the girl at the park by the river, then headed back to Degge Street to see if Addy had shown up there. He found his wife sitting on the steps in the backyard and had asked, "Think I ought to go looking some more?"

Mary Alice had been impatient. "Oh go on to bed, Hamond. She'll get home. She always does. If anyone can take care of her own self it's Addy Shadd."

Hamond lingered a moment, listening to the crickets. "Hot."

"Well it's summer, isn't it?"

"Why don't you come on to bed?"

"I'm not tired."

"Why don't you come on anyway?" Hamond said in a way that left no doubt what he meant.

"Good night, Hamond," she said simply, and he knew that meant go away.

It wasn't a thing he'd admit to, but Hamond was hurt by his wife's rejection. He didn't understand why Mary Alice held him in such contempt. He was, after all, a good father and a good provider and he never once laid a hand on her. And he never once, though the Lord knew he'd been tempted, shared himself with another woman. Even in those long years after Olivia was born and Mary Alice would not be touched. And even when the pretty young whore at the tavern told him he looked so sad she'd love him for free.

Hamond didn't know exactly why Mary Alice'd gone off like she did that first time. She'd sat day after day in the chair by the window, drinking coffee till she got the jitters, her baby daughter screaming in the crib, diaper full, stomach empty. He didn't talk to anyone about his wife's condition, of course. Anyone who knew her knew something was wrong, and anyone who didn't, well, it was none of their business. She had come back to herself eventually. She would come back again, Hamond thought. The bed was hot and lonely, but he fell right off that night, and as he always did, slept like the dead.

Addy understood now that Mary Alice had lied about Hamond. She stopped being cool to him after that night, and though Hamond had never quite noticed her coolness to begin with, he did notice Addy stopped coming by the house so often now. Simon and Samuel missed her sorely, and he realized he did too. When he asked Mary Alice if they had a quarrel, she just shrugged and looked out the window.

If Hamond had known the truth he'd have noticed it was the very day Gabriel Green left for his cousin's place at the lake that Mary Alice stopped caring about her appearance and wasting money on creams and perfumes. As he didn't know anything at all, Hamond was pleased with his wife's new prudence, until she also stopped bathing or fixing her hair or changing her clothes altogether.

Mrs. Lemoine would sit with Mary Alice in the chairs by the window, sip hot coffee, and gossip about the neighbors, trying to get her daughter's mind off the thing that was troubling her. But it was Addy alone who knew what the thing was. Willow Ferguson even came down on the train and stayed for a week to see if she could help set her daughter-in-law right, but they all feared by the glassy look of her feline eyes that Mary Alice would never be right again.

The winter came fast and furious that year. The Ferguson boys would remember, among other things, that there'd been skating on the river a full week before Christmas. Addy and Mose were wed on his four days off in late October and Addy would learn quickly why porter's wives were called porter's widows. Even so, she loved him, and she loved the little apartment they kept on the third floor of the big old house on William Street, and the shabby wine-colored sofa Hamond'd brought over from the farm when the owner'd told him burn it out back. And she loved the way Mose brought her a present, a pair of salt'n'pepper shakers, each time he came home. His homecomings were always a celebration, except the one that February. That February he got special leave and he didn't bring salt'n'pepper shakers.

It had been Nora Lemoine who'd planned and hosted Addy's wedding and Nora Lemoine who stood at her side when the Justice of the Peace pronounced Mose and her man and wife. And Nora who said, "Wear my good pearl earrings as your 'something old,' Child." Mose was ashamed he had not the money to buy a ring for his bride but Addy wanted her wedding ring to be the diamond and emerald from Poppa, sure it would bring them luck, as it had brought them together in the first place. Hamond was there in that same suit he'd pulled on years earlier for Olivia's wedding and no one minded he wore his work boots, seeing as the wedding wasn't in a church anyway.

Mose hadn't cared about the church part. His mother would have, though, and he'd agreed with Addy that just this once they could lie in their letter to Nova Scotia, and say how it was a lovely church service and how they wished she wasn't feeling poorly and could have stood the long trip.

Mary Alice had not attended the wedding. Mary Alice had not set foot outside the house in weeks. The doctor had used the word *catatonic,* which made Addy think of Mary Alice's cat eyes and wonder if the secret of her illness lay in their shape. It was a windy fall day and it seemed that all the leaves took up and fell whirling and swirling to the earth at once. Hamond had come home with a bushel of fresh apples and found his wife at the kitchen table where he left her that morning. The smell in the room made him gag. He thought his mother-in-law must have smothered Mary Alice in liniment or that maybe an animal had died in the wall, until he realized the smell was his wife and that she had evacuated right there in her dress. He'd cleaned her up before the boys could see their mother that way, and carried her to her bed and called for the doctor.

Addy could not bring herself to feel sympathy for her friend and was ashamed of that. She could only think of Mary Alice as a glutton, one starving and sinister and retaliating against a world that would dare deprive her of her cream cake. On that cold February day, when Gabriel Green married his cousin by the lake, Mary Alice shook herself out of her stupor, went to the woodshed, and hung herself with the ropes she'd once used to tie the arms of her young lover.

After the funeral, back at home in their apartment on William Street, Addy and Mose made a fire in their little sitting room and slept there on the thin red rug as they always would in winter. With music drifting up from the phonograph in the apartment below, they'd made slow, sweet love. Addy begged Mose as she kissed his mouth, "Give me a baby, Mose. Give me a baby."

Seeds

The song Sharla'd been singing was beautiful but Addy wondered if it was an appropriate song to teach to a grade-one class. Sharla's new teacher, Mr. Toohey, brought his guitar for music circle on Thursdays and Sharla always came home singing folk songs. But how, Addy thought, could a six-year-old understand lyrics about *answers blowing in the wind?*

Sharla was drying the supper dishes and Addy smiled, thinking what a good girl she was and how she never had to be asked to help with chores. Sharla's little pink tongue lolled against her lower lip as it liked to when she was concentrating. She dried the top and bottom of the plate in her hand, folded the plaid dishcloth, and started toward the towel rack beside the stove. She began to sing again, in her high sweet voice.

The old woman leaned against the sink. It had suddenly occurred to Addy that she'd already walked down her many roads and that if there was an answer in the wind, it had long since blown past her. She listened to Sharla's pretty voice grow dimmer and dimmer until she knew the little girl had left the room. She looked out the trailer window and watched the moonlight make stars on the snow. She knew her brother Leam was behind her but didn't turn to look when she whispered, "Leam?"

"Yes, Addy?"

"I can't seem to get my head outta the past."

"I know."

"Was it the same for you?"

"I had just a little time before the river choked me, but I did think of the past, Addy. I thought of you and Mama and Daddy and Birdie and of the things that happened to me and to everyone I knew."

"You think of the crickets on the road? Remember how we thought it was a omen of doom? I was thinking about the crickets and remembering that day like it was this morning."

"I remember the crickets. And I remember that time you got lost too."

"I don't remember getting lost, Leam."

"You got lost. You were somewhere near six years old. You were living out at Teddy Bishop's for a while."

"I don't remember being lost. And I don't remember living out at Teddy Bishop's. If I was six years old I'd surely remember that."

"It was a hot summer day. I was sickly."

"I remember you being sickly."

"You were chasing a little gray kitten."

"A gray kitten. I do remember a little gray kitten."

"Whose kitten was it?"

Addy tried to picture the kitten, annoyed when Leam asked again, "Whose kitten was it?" She shook her head and looked out the trailer window, craving a cold bottle of beer. She turned around from the sink, startled to see Sharla standing there holding the neatly folded dishcloth.

Sharla asked for the third time, "Whose kitten was it though, Mum Addy?"

Addy blinked and smiled calmly. She reached for the handle on the refrigerator door, frightened to think she'd been talking out loud and that the child had heard it all. She found the cold brown beer bottle and further stalled as she searched the drawer for the opener. She took a long drink of the crisp pilsner, sat down in the hardback chair, and lifted her arms, bidding Sharla to come. She gathered the little girl in an embrace, kissed her cheek, and said, "I do love you, Sharla Cody."

Sharla nuzzled Mum Addy's old neck. "Was it your kitten?"

Addy held Sharla back a little so she could look into her eyes. "What kitten, Honey?"

"The one you was chasing when you got lost."

Addy cleared her throat but didn't know what to say.

"Maybe it was a stray."

"Mmm?"

"Musta been a stray," Sharla concluded, drawing her finger around the edge of Addy's ear. It was a thing Sharla did that irritated Addy, but she'd never say so and risk hurting the child's feelings. She pulled the little hand away and kissed the chubby brown fingers, saying, "I sure like that song you were singing. You want to sing for me some more?"

Sharla shook her head.

"You want to sing something else?"

Sharla shook her head again. "You're coming on our field trip tomorrow. Mr. Toohey said me and Prasora can sit with you on the bus."

"Well, good."

"Mr. Toohey said old people are a gift."

Addy laughed at that. "Wait till he's old. He'll be saying old people are old."

"Christmas is soon."

"Mmm-hmm."

"Mr. Toohey likes that candy-cane ice cream what they make at Blenheim Dairy. Bet I do too."

"Think so?"

"They bringing Santa to my school. Mr. Toohey says don't ask for a toy but just ask for a good thing to happen to your neighbor and that's two gifts for the price of one."

Several weeks ago, just after Mrs. Pigot's accident, Addy'd come down with a fever and felt sure it was the end. She feared that Sharla'd wake one morning and find her dead in her bed.

When she didn't die after a few days, Addy knew it was just the flu. She'd been eager to meet Sharla's Mr. Toohey, but until now hadn't had the strength to leave the trailer. She liked the changes she saw in the child since the new teacher's arrival. Sharla couldn't wait to get on the school bus each morning and at the end of the day she had a thousand stories to tell. Most of the stories began with "Mr. Toohey says. . . ." When the letter was sent home Monday asking for chaperones for Friday's museum field trip, Addy'd agreed right away. The truth was Addy didn't even know Chatham had a museum and thought the trip would be educational for her too. She just hoped there wouldn't be too much walking.

The brown bottle was empty and Addy hesitated a moment before she reached for the refrigerator again. She was thirsty. Lately the water tasted briny, juice gave her heartburn, and she liked to save the milk for Sharla. Sharla watched as Mum Addy opened a second beer and brought the cold bottle to her lips.

"Mr. Toohey said past means *old*. Past means it happened before."

"That's right."

"Mr. Toohey said Chatham Museum is our past."

"That's right."

"Is yesterday our past?"

"Mmm–hmm."

"Is me saying *Chatham Museum* our past?"

"If it happened before, it's the past. If it's yet to happen, it's the future."

"Mr. Toohey says you learn who you are from the past."

"Mr. Toohey say anything about little girls needing a bath before bedtime?"

"My bedtime is the future."

"That's right, Honey. Go run the tub."

A little later, Mum Addy pulled the covers up to Sharla's clean soft chin and made sure that her doll, Chick, was tucked in too. Sharla hugged Chick to her cheek and said it again. "Christmas is coming soon."

"Few days off yet." Addy tried to act casual but she was excited about Christmas this year and had an order in to Krazy Kyle's Electronics for a used color TV that Kyle himself had assured her over the phone he could deliver on Christmas Eve day. Addy knew a young child would get bored silly with an old woman like herself. The winter was upon them and it was a struggle to get outdoors. The flu had laid her up half the fall and her hip was giving her grief. Addy realized she was spending most of her hours now just sitting in that hardback chair at the kitchen table, sifting through unseen photographs and talking to the dead. Least a television would connect the child with the outside world.

Addy adjusted the covers, when Sharla complained Chick's nose was covered up and she couldn't breathe. She stroked Sharla's head. "Wonder if you been good enough this year, Santa bring you something special?"

"There's no Santa though."

Addy looked at her child, for in every way Sharla was *her* child, and asked quietly, "Why do you say that, Honey? Why do you think there's no Santa?"

"He don't come to the trailer park. Not to my house and not to Fawn's house too."

"No?"

"Krystal just gets her a new pajamas."

Addy wondered for a moment if it was the right thing to do before she said, "Well, I happen to know for a fact there *is* a Santa Claus and he *is* coming to the trailer park this year."

Sharla wrestled free of her blanket cocoon and sat up in the bed. She looked into Mum Addy's eyes, vaguely suspicious. "How do you know?"

"I know because I know."

"You talk to him?"

"Well, yes."

"You can talk to Santa?"

"Yes I can."

"You can talk to anybody."

"Mmm-hmm."

"Even if they're dead."

Addy held her breath. "What do you mean?"

"Like your brother. He's dead but you can talk to him."

Addy smoothed the covers over Sharla's little legs so she had a reason to look away. How many times had it happened? How often had she talked to Leam and been overheard by Sharla? Or anyone else? Had she done it in public? Why couldn't she remember?

"Santa isn't dead, Honey. But I'll tell you what. You been such a good, good girl this year and I happen to know Santa's coming here and I happen to know he's bringing something special."

"Something special?"

"Mmm-hmm."

"I think I know what," she said, grinning.

"You think you know but you're only guessing. Now you get back under and go to sleep now. We got a big day tomorrow."

Sharla nodded and eased herself back under the covers.

Addy kissed Sharla's cheek, shut out the light, and started down the hall toward her own room.

"Mu-um . . . ?" Sharla called.

"What, Honey?"

"Did you find him?"

"Who? Did I find who?"

"That little kitten you was chasing?"

Addy couldn't remember. "Of course I did, Sharla. Now go to sleep."

The smoke-choked little school bus pulled up in front of the Chatham Museum, but Addy's eyes were squeezed shut and she wasn't aware they'd arrived. She loved the children and the looks on their six-year-old faces but their joy was deafening. Her temples were throbbing and she felt sure a vessel would burst if the bus doors didn't open to let the screeching creatures out. Mr. Toohey, who with his cropped blond hair looked more like an all-American army boy than a folksinger, had turned and caught the expression on Addy's face. She hoped the teacher would suggest she get in a taxi and go on back to the Lakeview before her head exploded into a million pieces. Instead, he moved to the seat in front of her, opened his fist, and whispered in his deep, smooth voice, "A chaperone's best friend." There were three aspirins in the man's white palm. Addy took the aspirins gratefully and felt twice blessed when he passed her a thermos of sweet milky tea.

She was responsible for four children: Sharla, Prasora, Otto Todino, and the little girl with the rash, Lee-Ann. At first, climbing off the bus and heading past the cedar hedges that flanked the cobblestone walkway to the museum, Addy could see nothing but the heads of her charges and feel nothing but terror at her responsibility. She feared one of them might break free and dart out into the traffic. Or one might fall on the slippery cobblestone and crack open her head. "Stick close to me, children," she shouted over the din, and wondered if the other chaperones, four young mothers, were as anxious as she was. Once inside the place, though, once the big oak doors closed behind her, Addy saw the children were safely confined and she relaxed enough to look around.

The place smelled familiar but she couldn't say why. She reckoned it was just the musty smell of old age she couldn't help but know intimately. She was relieved when the museum's curator, a plump, pink young woman who introduced herself as Miss Beth, gathered the children into a circle near a display of military uniforms and she could settle herself on a bench near the back and just watch and listen.

Miss Beth pointed at a handsome red serge jacket in a glass display case, asking, "Does anyone know what this is?"

Three hands shot up, all of them boys. They shouted without waiting to be called on. "That's a uniform!" "That's from the army!" "That's a soldier coat!"

"Very good!" Miss Beth clapped her hands and went on. "It is a soldier's uniform. And does anyone know when this uniform was worn?"

The boys looked at each other. The smallest of them ventured, "In the war?"

"In the war, yes, but what war? No one? Well, this coat was worn by a British officer in the War of Eighteen Twelve. That's such a long time ago that your grandfathers were not born yet and their fathers were not born yet and *their* fathers were not even born yet."

The children watched Miss Beth, stone-eyed. They had little grasp of time and none at all of time before them. Addy glanced around the room at the other artifacts, most of them from the 1800s. There were a few muskets and rifles and bayonets in a display case near the big roaring fireplace, and Addy could see some of the boys' big eyes drifting toward the weapons. She laughed to herself, thinking how boyish the boys were and how Miss Beth could really get their attention if she just opened up the case and let them touch the guns.

In another corner of the room there was a display of cooking utensils, an old kettle, a muffin tin shaped like ears of corn, a rusty rotary beater, and a cast-iron frying pan like the one Addy still used for chicken and potatoes. She thought how common they looked and not like things that belonged in a museum at all. Hanging on the wall nearby was a patchwork quilt. Addy clucked her tongue at the sloppy stitching and crooked seams, thinking she'd done better when she was barely thirteen. She even took exception to the fabric and color choices, which she thought garish and wrong. The young mother sitting beside her mistook Addy's clucking tongue for admiration and whispered of the careless quilt, "It's really beautiful, eh?"

Miss Beth was waving her arms, still discussing the significance of the red serge uniform in the case. "And though it's a historical fact you'll find in few *American* history books, the British and the Canadian forces distinguished themselves in the War of Eighteen Twelve when they defeated our neighbors to the south and . . ."

There was a butter churn and a butter mold, a rusty pitchfork, an old wheelchair, a washboard, and a loom. Addy remembered her mother coveting a similar-style loom, even though she'd never seen her weave an inch of cloth and Laisa regularly bought fabric from the dry-goods store in Rusholme, or clothes ready-made from the catalog. Addy thought how her mother would laugh at the museum's collection and say, "They think these things old? These things ain't old!"

Mr. Toohey found a path through the restless children and whispered something to Miss Beth. Addy reckoned he was telling her what Addy herself was thinking. That the children were far too young for any history lesson on the War of 1812 and why doesn't she just let them loose to wander and wonder? Miss Beth looked huffy, then announced, "Children, you may take a moment to browse. But do not touch anything. I repeat — do not touch *anything.*"

Sharla appeared at Addy's knee with Prasora, Otto, and Lee-Ann in tow. They were smiling and pleased not to be sitting cross-legged on the floor. Otto noticed a tall oak chair nearby. He laughed and pointed. "Got a big hole."

Addy looked at the chair and nodded. "Mmm-hmm. You know why that hole's there, don't you, Otto?"

The boy shook his head. A few other children gathered around. Addy went on, "Well, when you was growing and ready to get yourself out of diapers your Mama put you on a chair with a hole, didn't she?"

"A potty chair?" Lee-Ann asked, scratching her face.

"Mmm-hmm."

The rest of the children had joined in looking at the big oak chair.

"That's too big for a potty chair though," Sharla said.

"That's for big folks, Honey. That's a kind of chair folks used before they got flushing toilets in their house."

The children squeezed in closer, curious and giggly.

"Used to be when there wasn't plumbing you had to get into your coat and boots and go all the way out back to the outhouse. That was sure some thing to do in winter."

"What about summer?"

"In summer, well, you mostly just had to hold your nose. Sometimes, 'specially at night, you used this here kind of chair instead of making the trip all the way out back."

"But . . . ?" The children looked at the chair, bewildered.

Addy saw a ceramic chamber pot nearby and put it under the hole and the children all at once understood.

"Number one *and* number two?" a boy asked. "Then what you do with the pot?"

"What do you think you do?" Addy asked with a raised brow.

"Clean it out?!" the children chimed.

"Well of course you clean it out!" Addy laughed.

Miss Beth had been standing nearby, watching enviously, for it was her mission to teach through history and it annoyed her greatly that the children were more interested in the oak commode than the brilliant lesson she'd prepared on the American invasion. She cleared her throat and addressed Mr. Toohey. "Is this discussion really valuable, Mr. Toohey?"

Mr. Toohey grinned at the woman but said nothing. A little boy with red hair pointed at a strange instrument hanging on a peg on the wall alongside some kitchen utensils. "What's that?"

Miss Beth stepped up. "That, Young Man, is what we call *bellows*. A person would open those two ends there and fan the flames of the fire in a wood stove or a fireplace."

Addy couldn't help but correct the woman. "Looks like bellows, Ma'am, but it's not."

"Oh really?" Miss Beth huffed. "Then what is it?"

"It's a seed planter." The children watched as Addy took the thing down to demonstrate. "See, here, you put your seeds in this sack part here, then look inside. Look right there, there's a tiny hole just the size of a seed. You set down like this. The sharp part goes in the earth right up to the end of the metal. See? That way all the seeds get planted at the same depth. Then you open these ends and just the one seed gets let out and down in the dirt she goes."

The children fully understood the mechanics of the seed planter and now they each wanted a turn trying it out for themselves. Mr. Toohey sidled up to Addy and whispered, "Can you come on all my field trips?"

Addy grinned but had not a moment to answer as suddenly Miss Beth clapped her hands and cried out, "Who wants to see the mummy?!"

The children shrieked and raised their hands. No one had told them there was a mummy at the Chatham Museum.

Miss Beth threw Addy a look of triumph, then shouted over the clamor, "The mummy is in his *sarcophagus* on the third floor, but do not run. I repeat — do not run! Children!" Miss Beth was huffing and red before she reached the stairs.

Addy watched the grade-one class and the other chaperones disappear up the stairs. She was relieved Mr. Toohey had been as eager to see the mummy as the children were, and grateful to have a few moments alone. That flu had taken more life out of her than she'd imagined and she was feeling profoundly fatigued. She recalled there was a comfortable-looking sofa near the big oak doors at the front. She held the wall for support as she made her way to the entrance hall. She eased herself down on the sofa and closed her eyes.

Not a moment's rest did Addy enjoy though, before the front door opened and there stood the silhouette of a tall, thin man. Even though his face was in shadow Addy could see it was her husband, Gradison Mosely. She did not pause to wonder where she was or what Mose was doing here, for she knew full well she was in the entrance hall of the house where she lived and that she'd fallen asleep waiting for Mose. Waiting for Mose. She was always waiting for Mose.

She smiled at him as he burst through the door and put her fingers to her lips to shush him. "Mrs. Yardley's just got her baby down," she whispered and pointed to the closed door of the first-floor apartment.

Mose nodded and closed the big oak door gently behind him, making a comical show of tiptoeing down the hall to where Addy sat. He set his luggage on the sofa beside her and drew from his back a small box wrapped in red foil. The box was not a surprise, for there was always a present when Mose came home and it was always a pair of salt'n'pepper shakers. The last pair had been ceramic lobsters from Nova Scotia, made to look like a bride and groom. Addy had laughed and laughed when she saw them.

This time though, she'd wait to open her present. She smiled into her husband's green eyes and rose, reaching her arms around his neck. She kissed him deeply, feeling him swell, then whispered a thing into his ear that she knew would have him bounding up the stairs to their shabby, cold, wonderful little home.

It was two years to the month since the wedding. Addy was twenty-three years old and still there was no child. Addy knew how desperately Mose wanted a family and she feared God was punishing her, making her barren as retribution for her sins. She felt ashamed for herself and hurt on behalf of Mose, who, far as she knew, never did much of anything wrong. Addy hadn't seen Mose in a number of weeks and in that time she'd gone to Nora Lemoine, with whom she'd grown especially close since the death of Mary Alice, and confessed tearfully. The old woman had stroked her back and said, "Nonsense, Adelaide. God isn't punishing you."

She blew her nose noisily. "What am I gonna do, Nora?"

"Well, you don't see your husband every night like most women do. And you don't get yourself *close* to him as often as most either. Mind you some women wouldn't mind that arrangement but if you're looking to have a child you need to get . . . close . . . just as often as you can."

Addy shook her head. "You don't understand. Every time he comes home. The whole time he's home. It's not just once, it's not just at night. It's twice in the morning and again at night and sometimes if we brush up against each other in the afternoon. . . ." She started weeping again. "I just don't understand."

After she heard that, Nora Lemoine didn't understand either, for she'd always just assumed Mose was too tired on his days off to be much good, or that Adelaide rejected his amorous advances because she resented his being gone. She raised the issue carefully, knowing that Addy would resist. "Maybe you want to see the doctor, Honey."

Addy did resist the idea of talking with the doctor but only because she knew Mose would not approve. Early on in their marriage, she'd suggested the doctor and Mose'd gone pale, stomping and declaring, "I forbid it," which caused another round of stomping but this time from Addy, who would not be *forbid* anything. Later in bed, Mose had quietly apologized, a thing she could always expect from her good man. He'd said, "I'm sorry, Addy. Don't know what good *you* seeing a doctor's gonna do though."

"Why?"

He'd been grateful for the darkness. "Can't help but figure if it's not working it's because there's something wrong with *me*."

"Doesn't have to be you, Mose," Addy'd assured, kissing his neck.

"But you already . . ."

"Don't believe it works like that, Mose. Just because I had the one baby doesn't mean something hasn't gone wrong with me."

He waited a moment, loving her lips on his throat, then asked, "If you did see the doctor, Addy, what would he do?"

"I don't know."

"Think he'd give you some medicine?"

Addy kissed the hill of her husband's chest. "Don't know."

"Think he have to . . ." Mose swallowed and pulled her to his mouth. "Think he ask you to take off your clothes? Think he do that? Think he have to touch you here? Addy? Or here? Or here?"

"Mmm-hmm." Addy moved against his finger.

When Mose bit Addy's lip she knew it had been deliberate. She opened her bloody mouth and pushed her salty wet tongue against his. Mose drew blood, and Addy knew why. Mose didn't want her to see the doctor, to be looked over by the doctor, to be touched by the doctor, because it both horrified and aroused him in equal measure.

In the end, after talking with Nora, feeling desperate as she did, Addy decided she would make the appointment and much as she hated to, she'd have to deceive Mose. When she finally did see the doctor she wished she'd gone two years earlier, for what he told her was surprising, something she'd never have guessed. After her visit, she'd walked all the way home wondering, "Only two or three days in a whole long month a woman can get herself with a child. Mose and me never once hit on them days but Zach Heron, one time, one terrible time . . ."

The doctor had told her some other things too, signs to look for on her body and days to count on a calendar so she could know better when she was ready. That's why today she'd open her present later. Near as she could tell, with the information the doctor'd given her, Addy was ripe and Mose was here. If ever they were gonna make a baby it was gonna be now.

After Addy whispered into Mose's ear, he flew up the stairs as she'd known he would, and had to come back down to collect his bag. Addy giggled and went up the stairs in front of him, wagging her behind in his face as he clasped his big hands to her breasts. When they reached the third floor Mose opened the door. Though the fire'd gone out and the furniture looked more ragged than he remembered, he wanted to cry at his joy to be home.

There was music playing in the apartment of Martin and Kay Baldwin on the second floor and Addy could not have chosen a finer selection. It was Billie Holiday's voice rising up through the floorboards and Billie made the blues sound so sweet Addy hoped the singer'd never get over her grief. Addy didn't mind that the Baldwins liked to play their music loud, for Mose did make some passionate noises and the bedsprings were broken in three places.

The first time, their wedding night, Mose had been tentative and it was over nearly before it began. He told his new bride he knew, or at least he reckoned, because of what happened in Rusholme, that part of their marriage — he'd cleared his throat and said, "the loving part" — would be difficult for her. He told her he thought it best to get it over and done with, and said he'd always understand if she'd just like her back scratched instead. Addy knew that Mose had never been with a woman and that he was unsure and afraid himself. She'd lain awake for some time listening to his kitteny snore, then moved her hand to his hard stomach and caressed him with her fingernails until she felt him wake and swell once more. Then she stroked him with a firmer touch, and when she thought he might burst she stopped and asked, "Feel good, Mose?"

He murmured something that sounded like yes and held his breath when she climbed atop him and brought him inside her. Mose would never have to know the extent of her experience, as witness or participant, but Addy would make sure he understood that her desire, and his own, could tether them to each other. She wanted him to know that the loving part was an important part of their marriage. She knew Mose would learn what to do soon enough.

Mose did learn what to do, and not just what to do but exactly when to do it, and that part of their marriage, Addy thought often, was the only part she had faith in. For Mose was home so seldom that, except for the intimate way in which she recognized his body, he was like a stranger each time he returned. Addy knew none of his fellow porters, had no faces for the names and no imagination for his stories. And though she tried, she could not feel so indignant as he about the working conditions of his fellows, nor fully understand his passion for the Brotherhood. But when they moved into each other's arms, sharing mouth and skin and scent and fluid, he was Mose, her good husband, and she was so glad he was finally home.

The pillows had been the doctor's suggestion but of course Addy could not tell Mose. Soon as he'd risen from the bed she pulled the pillows from near the headboard and crammed them under her behind. Mose had laughed and waited for an explanation.

"My back aches from hefting that sack of potatoes from the market," she said, and that was that. Addy lay still with her hindquarters raised up, letting gravity do its chore as the doctor advised, listening to Billie downstairs, weeping with the willow and all the men who'd done her wrong.

It was the next morning, over fresh eggs and biscuits, with the accompaniment of Louis Armstrong on jazz trumpet, that Mose told Addy he'd be leaving a day early this trip. He was heading up to a meeting in Toronto, then off to Vancouver, back to Montreal, out East, then home again in four weeks. Addy was beyond hurt and angry, for this wasn't the first time he'd left early. "Why can't you miss a meeting? Why can't you miss just one precious meeting?"

"Because I can't. Because I won't. Because my job is impor-tant. Because the Brotherhood is important. Asa Randolph, that American labor activist I told you about, he's coming to Canada to meet with Arthur Blanchette and a few other men and I'm proud to be a part of that."

"I hate the Brotherhood."

"How many times have I told you, with a union representing us we're all gonna make a lot more money. My job'll be safe. You're acting like a baby, Adelaide."

"I don't care. I hate it. And I hate that train."

"Don't let anyone else hear you talk like that. You have any idea how lucky I am to have work? Do you ever read the newspaper, Woman? Do you understand there's a depression?"

Addy didn't tell Mose that her true reason for being troubled was she feared if he left a day early this time, it would be *the* day she was the ripest, *the* day they were most likely to make a child. "I know there's a depression, Mose. I *do* read the newspaper. I just don't understand why this one time you can't stay home with me and miss your meeting and say *I'm* the important one."

"And I don't understand why we can't move to Montreal like we talked about so I can see you more."

"On your way from here to there? A few hours? A day?"

"That's what you're crossing me over now, isn't it, Adelaide? A day?"

"I don't want to live in Montreal all by myself, Mose. Chatham is my home. I got Nora Lemoine here, and Hamond and the boys, and Mrs. Yardley and the Baldwins. I don't know what I'd do without all them. That's my family."

"I'm your husband."

"And you expect I'm just gonna sit there in Montreal where I can't even understand the language, waiting and waiting for my husband?"

"I'm tired of arguing, Addy."

"And what about driving, Mose? You promised you'd teach me how to drive. How am I ever gonna learn when you're never home?"

The music had been turned off downstairs and Addy knew it was because Mrs. Baldwin liked to listen in. She lowered her voice. "Just this once, Mose?"

Mose shook his head as he reached for another biscuit. Addy knew, as she'd always known, that she could not fight her husband's conscience. Addy also knew that at least some of Mose's passion came from his denial of the obvious. His skin was white, his hair was fair, his eyes were green, and few people might have guessed his mother was Negro. And few people might have guessed he thought of himself as Negro. Addy knew Mose felt betrayed by his pale skin and all the more driven to fight the cause of social injustice. Addy knew all of this because Addy knew Mose. They never talked about such things though, for Addy understood how deeply it would wound her husband if she ever let on she thought he was different.

The red foil–wrapped present sat untouched on the dresser. Even though Addy was annoyed, she found the will to pull Mose back to her bed not once but twice that day, and three times the next. By the following evening, as Mose was preparing his things for his departure, he'd looked at his wife with deep concern and said, "Your back hurt again?"

"It'll be fine, Mose," Addy'd said, her hips hoisted up on the pillows.

"But except for cooking, eating, and loving, you been laying like that since I came home."

"Be fine, Mose. Just I shouldn't be so ambitious in carrying home my groceries is all. You sure you have to go?"

After Mose left Addy remembered the present on the dresser and went to open it. The salt'n'pepper shakers were in the shape of two entwined dolphins. If you were to use the thing for its practical purpose, just the one shake would give you all the seasoning you needed. She set it on a nearby shelf with the others and thought, *Mose.*

Addy had marked the days on a calendar with a soft pencil. When it was time for her moon to come on she'd woken breathless two mornings in a row, having dreamt she was choking on apple seeds. She prayed not to feel the dull ache in her pelvis that said there'd be blood. Be a baby, she begged. Be a baby. But the ache came, and the blood came, and the tears as they always did now. Dutifully, she counted the days again and watched for the signs again and she waited, waited for Mose.

There was knocking at the door, or rather pounding, and the sound of it chilled Addy, for something was wrong. It was Mrs. Yardley standing there on the landing, her fat baby boy on her hip, her eyes bulging and bloodshot from the effort of dragging her own weight and his up the two flights of stairs.

"There's a telephone call for you, Addy," she said, looking worried. "I couldn't tell who. A man. Line's not very clear."

Addy flew down the stairs, rushed through Mrs. Yardley's open door, and set the telephone to her ear. She was expecting to hear her husband's voice and was surprised to find an old man at the other end of the line. She held her breath, waiting to hear the worst, for it was only a death, or near death, that would have necessitated a telephone call. She heard her name. "Addy?"

"Yes."

"It's Mama."

For a moment Addy had no picture in her mind and could only wonder, *Whose Mama? My Mama?*

"Addy?"

"Yes."

"I have to go."

"Yes," Addy said, but she was thinking, *Go where?*

"I'm in Montreal now but I'll get to Halifax sometime tomorrow and I guess best I can hope for is she can hang on till I . . ."

"Mose?"

There was no answer. Addy thought the line had gone dead until she heard a short breath and a sniff. "Oh Mose."

"I wish you got a chance to meet her. She would have liked you."

"Oh Mose, I wish that too. Tell her so, won't you?"

"I'll tell her."

"And say how I love you and how I'll be looking out for you so."

"She knows. Addy? Are you still there, Addy?"

"I'm here."

"I won't have time to get to Chatham at all."

Addy had wanted to say "You have to" but said instead, "I know, Mose. I know."

Though she couldn't remember bending her knees or shifting her weight or when the tears came to her eyes, Addy realized she was sitting on Mrs. Yardley's velveteen chaise, crying soundlessly. Mrs. Yardley was sitting beside her, grasping her hand. Addy put the receiver down and fell against her friend, sharing the woman's ample chest with her big baby boy.

"Poor Mose," Mrs. Yardley said, sniffing. "And his poor, poor mother." Addy wasn't crying for Mose's mother though, and she wasn't even crying for Mose. She was crying for her baby yet to be conceived and because it would be another whole month before Mose could even try to sow his seed.

As when the sky turns black and a storm is certain but passes with nary a drop, Mose's mother did not die that day or the next day or even the next week. Her son by her side, she clung to her sickly life and would elude death for years to come. Mose would tell Addy later that the doctor'd been shocked by her sudden recovery. An hour after her son's arrival she had been able to choke down some hot soup and by the third day of his stay she'd been pleased to save his dear young wife the trouble of darning his socks. She'd even insisted on getting out of her bed before Mose was to leave, to make him his favorite meal. The woman nearly danced the jitterbug when Mose confided that although Addy was a wonderful cook she never could get rice so soft and fluffy as his Mama did.

Someone was at her door and it was the second time in a day there'd been pounding. Addy prepared herself to run down the stairs and hear Mose's old man's voice on the telephone again but it wasn't Mrs. Yardley at the door. It was Simon Ferguson standing there on the third-floor landing, looking like he'd just run to the lake and back. He was holding in tears, Addy could see, and since it wasn't the first time he'd shown up at her door this way, Addy reckoned he'd had another argument with his young sweetheart.

She thought the time was right to advise Simon, who was like a son, that he ought to bid that never-satisfied young lady farewell.

"Simon Ferguson, did you and that silly girl have another spat?"

Simon didn't have the breath to speak.

"What is it? What's wrong? Come on, tell Addy."

Simon swallowed and said, "It's Nana."

Addy grabbed her coat and together they raced down the stairs, out the door, up William Street and down Murray, racing toward Nora's old house. On the lawn, a huge black crow dug for treasure under the soggy autumn leaves. The crow didn't flap and fly away when Simon and Addy approached, but looked up and gawked at them, like the way people stare when they see another in despair.

Hamond was on the sofa in the sitting room with his head in his hands. Samuel was turned toward the window, sobbing shamelessly. Simon needed courage to speak. He reached for Addy's hand and squeezed before he asked his father, "What the doctor say?"

Hamond looked up from his hands. Addy would wonder later about balance, the question of balance, the balance of life, for Mose's mother did not die that night, but Nora Lemoine did.

The crow outside cawed just then, more a scream than a caw, and Addy knew that although the sound was coming from the bird's throat, it had originated in her own. Nora could not be gone. Nora, who was never sick. Nora, who she'd seen just that morning. Nora? Addy'd hear some of the details of what happened from Hamond. Later, Simon would tearfully confess the truth.

Nora'd come home from a visit to a friend's and decided to bake a few pumpkin pies for Hamond and the boys. She asked Simon, who'd been living with her for the past year, to heft the pumpkin from the counter to the table and clean it out but save the seeds for roasting. She'd been annoyed with Simon, the way he handled the carving knife, and felt sure he'd slice off a finger in his carelessness and haste. She'd taken the knife back, finished the job herself, and was separating the seeds from the thick sticky pulp when she stopped, feeling strange. She grasped the edge of the table. The pumpkin fell on its side, spilling juice, pulp, and seeds onto the floor. Truly cross now, she told Simon get out of her kitchen, which he did and was glad to. Nora got a soapy rag and eased herself down onto the floor.

While she was there on her hands and knees, Nora thought to give the rest of the floor a once-over too and scrubbed what looked like a black tar stain for a full four minutes before a kicked-in-the-chest pain took her breath. She called for her grandson then, and in a decision that would alter the rest of his life, Simon did not come.

Simon had gone to his room and shut the door. *It would be easy enough,* he thought, *to say he hadn't heard his Grandmother if she barged in and confronted him. Otherwise,* he thought, *she can do whatever it is she wants done herself.* Nora called again and again and after a few moments she called once more, but Simon truly couldn't hear the last time, for her voice was so weak it was barely a whisper.

At some point Simon had wondered absently why the kitchen was so quiet. Then he wondered why he couldn't smell pumpkin seeds, for his Grandmother always put the seeds to roast before she started rolling the dough and fixing the filling. He admired himself in his dresser mirror for a time, then decided to go see if the seeds'd gone in the oven yet as he had a hankering for a salty snack and was worried the old woman forgot. He found her then, on her side, curled in a ball, one hand clutching her left breast, the other clutching the soapy rag. Simon bent and tried to lift the old woman but she was much too heavy for just one man. She couldn't speak but she reached out with her soapy rag and clung to her grandson like he was life itself. Simon could think of nothing to do or say except, "Oh no." Finally Nora's strength left her altogether and she fell back quiet on the just-cleaned floor.

He'd taken off running then, first to the doctor, which he was grateful was only two blocks away, then to his father's, then finally to his Aunt Addy's. Here they all were now and not one of them could quite believe Nora was gone.

Since the death of Mary Alice, the Yuletide season had not been a happy one for Addy and the Ferguson family. This year they would all have liked to let it pass without the pretense of celebration. But Mose was to be home for three days and he insisted they have Christmas, as they always did, on Degge Street. He thought it would be the best thing, just to be together for the day, and he reminded Addy how lucky they were to have each other, for he thought of the Ferguson men as brothers.

Somehow the puddings got made and the gifts knitted or baked, the fowl slaughtered and dragged home and the decorations hung. Snow came on Christmas morning, along with a bitter northeasterly wind. Mose and Addy arrived at the little house on Degge Street, their arms filled with food and brightly wrapped packages. Addy fired up the stove and Samuel, without being asked, came in to help with supper. After they'd eaten too much and all the men had a few glasses of rum, they sang a few hymns, though not a single one of them was a churchgoer, then Mose started on about the Brotherhood with Hamond.

It wasn't that Hamond didn't care, it's just that he had troubles of his own. His back was so sore now at the end of the day he could hardly straighten up to lay down in his bed. His knuckles had grown gnarled and thick. He couldn't grip the way he used to and was ashamed to see how the younger men shook their heads when he dropped things. He was hopeful the matter of Nora's estate would be settled up sooner rather than later so he could sell her old house and quit the farm, maybe even buy himself a truck. He'd shrugged and explained, when Mose accused him of indifference, "Maybe you're right. Guess I'm just getting old."

Mose's speech was slurred from the rum. Addy wanted to go home, but her husband was just getting started. "Imagine, Hamond, imagine if our forefathers felt like you. Just shrugging their shoulders like that? Imagine where we'd be today. We'd still be in bondage, don't you see? Your sons would never have learned to read. You wouldn't own your own house. You can't just shrug your shoulders, Ham. We got a long row to hoe yet."

Hamond nodded, careful to keep his thoughts from his face. He loved Mose like family, but it was impossible to look at him and not see a white man. It was all he could do not to chuckle when Mose spoke of the black man's struggle or shake his head when Mose said *we* like they lived the same life.

"You know where we are without organizations like the Brotherhood? Do you know, Hamond?"

"Where are we, Mose?"

"We're in the cotton fields, Hamond. We're in chains, Hamond. I tell you what it's like for me and my brothers on the train?"

"Everybody calls you George."

"Yes!"

"I been called worse than *George,* Mose."

"But George is not my damn name."

"I understand."

Hamond left the room when Mose turned his attention on Samuel. Samuel was the youngest and gentlest of the two Ferguson boys. He found it impossible to argue with Mose so he just sat back, listening and nodding. Simon left, stinking of liquor, to call on his sweetheart and her family. Addy worried, watching him wobble out the door, what the girl's folks would think of their daughter's drunken beau. *Merry Christmas,* she thought silently. *May the Lord bless us all.*

January came and Addy's birthday, and Addy's moon. The days were short, the nights long and dark and lonely. Mose would miss her birthday, but the boys showed up at her door that bitter cold morning with a gift wrapped in butcher paper and an invitation to dinner. Addy knew an invitation to dinner on Degge Street meant *she* was cooking, but she didn't care a bit.

As she'd been instructed, Addy waited until after Simon and Samuel left to unwrap the gift. Whatever it was, it was in a butterbox and she could smell the sour of it before she tore off the brown butcher paper. She pried off the lid and stared bewildered at the contents. Inside were family photographs, of Nora and her husband, of Hamond and Mary Alice, of the boys when they were small. There were tiny baby teeth in a medicine vial and locks of baby hair folded in parchment. There was a child's gold bracelet and Mary Alice's wedding ring and a note she'd written to Hamond when she must have been very young. The ink was so faded Addy could only read the words at the bottom of the page, *Always and truly your Mary Alice.* On top of the other things was a folded piece of paper with Addy's name in Hamond's writing. She unfolded the paper and was surprised when three crisp dollar bills spilled out. She read:

Dear Adelaide,
This is to say Happy Birthday to you and thank you for all you done for me and my family. It was hard to lose Nora this year and I don't know what we would have did without you. I found this box in the attic at her house and it's all the things I guess Mary Alice never cared about saving but her mother knew they'd be important to somebody. I didn't want to give it to the boys seeing they're still too young to care about old photographs and baby teeth but I bet they like to have it one day and I know you'll save it for them. The three dollars is for you to buy a trinket for yourself because Mary Alice said I never was good at picking things out. I wish it was ten dollars but it's three.

Hamond

Addy'd smiled and wiped her eyes and wondered about where to put the box for safekeeping. *The attic,* she thought, but knew she couldn't move the huge oak dresser by herself to get at the door. She strummed her fingers and looked around the tidy room, wondering what to do next. She decided to bake a cake for Hamond and the boys. Mostly she just wanted to keep busy, to stop herself from giving in to the feeling that Hamond was sick and preparing to die. She couldn't bear the thought of him leaving, for in her world he'd become a bridge to land. When the cake was cooled, Addy pulled on an old dress and didn't bother to fix her hair. It was only Hamond and the boys after all. And she was doing the cooking.

The house was spotless clean. Addy knew that was Samuel's doing. Samuel took care of the house. Simon took care of himself. The boys would be finished at the high school by spring. After that, Simon thought he might like to go up to Toronto and live with Olivia and take Darryl up on his offer to help set him up in a job. Samuel wanted to work the farm with his father, but Hamond wanted something better for his boy. Hamond thought he should go North with his brother and try his luck in Toronto too, but Samuel'd never leave Chatham.

The supper dishes had been washed, dried, and put away before Addy got back to the kitchen with her empty cake plate. She thanked Samuel and said she didn't mind he was heading off to go skating with his friend. Samuel's friend was a sweet and gentle boy and neither Addy nor Hamond could understand Simon's disdain. Simon wouldn't pass a word with the fellow, or even stay in the same room. Only reason Hamond and Addy could come up with was that Simon was tortured by his Grandmother's recent death. They noticed he'd become harder and more arrogant and guessed that was his way of coping.

With Simon gone off for the evening too, the house was quiet and empty except for the ghosts. Leam and Chester and Nora and Mary Alice had all showed up for Addy's birthday. Addy and Hamond sat side by side on the sofa, drinking tea, not feeling obliged to talk about the cold, the snow, the spring forecast from the *Farmer's Almanac,* or the spectres among them. There were no recipes to share, no household tips, no teasing, and no bickering. Hamond and Addy just sat, sipping in silence.

When an hour had passed, Addy stood and reached for her coat. As he always did, Hamond reached for his coat too so he could walk her the few blocks home. They said nothing as they moved down the street, heads bowed against the wind, and when they reached the door to the house on William Street, Hamond turned without a word and started off back home. Addy'd remembered then, there'd been something she'd been meaning to ask him.

"Hamond," she called, then again for he hadn't heard, "Hamond, will you move that big dresser for me so I can put that box of photographs in the attic?" As they climbed the stairs she reminded him, "That front leg's broke so be careful."

*W*hen Addy woke she was surprised to look across the room and see that the dresser had not been moved back in front of the little attic door. She was further surprised, and confused, to see that the dresser was nowhere at all in the room. She blinked, for it was still dark, and tried to focus her eyes. Nothing in the room was familiar to her. Where the old wine-colored sofa'd been, there now stood a long box made of glass. Addy cursed her eyes for telling her there was a mummy case against the sofa wall of her and Mose's apartment.

She heard his voice and recognized it before he came into her field of vision. There was just enough time for Addy to clear her thoughts and understand that she was sitting in a chair on the third floor of the Chatham Museum. Mr. Toohey was walking toward her, asking, "Are you all right, Mizz Shadd?"

"Oh yes. Fine. Mmm-hmm," she answered, smiling.

"I didn't know if I should call someone."

Addy looked around the room and saw they were alone except for the mummy in his sarcophagus. "Where they all gone?"

"They're downstairs having maple sugar fudge with Miss Beth."

Addy nodded and rose, feeling her hip buckle. Mr. Toohey took her arm. She looked at him. "Is this William Street? Number seventy-one William Street?"

He nodded.

"This house," she said, "I used to live here. This was my apartment."

Mr. Toohey cleared his throat. "Yes."

"A long time ago."

The young man nodded and watched her eyes swallow the room.

"I lived here with —" Addy stopped, having reached for his name and found nothing. It wasn't Chester. It wasn't Simon. How is it possible she could not recall his name? "My husband."

"Hamond?" Mr. Toohey ventured.

Addy turned sharply. There was fear on her face. Mr. Toohey answered her look, realizing she was still feeling confused. "You were talking a little. Talking in your sleep a little. Sharla said it's happened before."

Addy could hardly speak. "I was talking about Hamond? What'd I say about Hamond?"

"Nothing really. Nothing Miss Beth and I could understand. Just called his name a couple of times. Something about moving a heavy dresser." Mr. Toohey cleared his throat again. "Sharla said it was best not to wake you up. I hope we did the right thing?"

Mr. Toohey began to guide Addy toward the stairs and she was sorry, for it was a revelation to be in this room again, and to feel her old life here like it was real and happening. As she made her way down the stairs she wondered how she hadn't seen it earlier, the curve of the staircase, the original doors and knobs on what was once the Baldwin's apartment and was now the Aboriginal room on the second floor. The fancy molding at the foot of the stairs. The way Mrs. Yardley's door never quite hung right. How had she not seen? Even the entranceway was little changed. The wallpaper had been taken down and replaced by sickly yellow paint but the only other difference was that Miss Beth's big desk stood beside the sofa where she'd spent her time waiting and waiting. "My husband's name was Mose," she whispered to herself. "Mose."

Candy-Canes

The roast turkey was much too big for just the two of them but Addy wanted to give Sharla a homey old-fashioned Christmas. It was a utility bird, missing all four limbs and a good chunk of breast, and still it was too much. She'd have to move some things out of the freezer to make room for leftovers, and worse, there'd be that farty turkey odor every time she opened her fridge.

On Christmas morning, Addy was awake long before Sharla. In fact she hadn't slept a wink that whole long night. Krazy Kyle's had delivered the television the day before and she'd asked the man to put the huge thing in her bedroom closet. She wondered all night how she and Sharla'd get it back out and down to the living room. In the end she thought she'd bundle Sharla up and send her over to fetch Warren Souchuck.

Since that night Mum Addy'd suggested there was a special present coming from Santa, Sharla'd been sweet but certain in her insistence that she already knew what it was. Sharla'd been wrong, but Addy never guessed what she was thinking.

"Mr. Toohey says you musta had quite a life," Sharla had said that previous morning over breakfast.

"Don't talk with cereal in your mouth, Sharla. Look, Honey. You're getting your flakes all over the table."

Sharla chewed and swallowed. "He said you seen some things in your day."

"Did he?"

"Mmm-hmm. He said you had a life and seen some things and you must have a story to tell."

"What kind of story?"

Sharla shrugged. "We learned 'Oh Canada' in French. Want me sing it?"

"Not now, Honey. What else Mr. Toohey say? He say anything more about the museum?"

"You mean when you were talking at the museum?"

"Yes. That's what I mean."

"Were you talking to Leam?"

"Did you tell him I was talking to Leam?"

Sharla shook her head. There was a knock at the door then and Addy could see a big gray van parked out in front of the trailer. It was the fellow from Krazy Kyle's, she knew, and she didn't want to spoil Sharla's surprise. She hurried Sharla into the bathroom, explaining in a whisper that Santa Claus was dropping something special off a little early, and made her promise to stay inside till Addy said come out. Sharla went willingly, for her friend Lee-Ann had told her it was wrong to peek at Santa and he might not leave your presents if you caught a glimpse.

Finally, the television safely hidden in her closet and Krazy Kyle's big gray van gone off down the mud lane, Addy opened the door and let Sharla come out. There was a strange look on the child's face as she glanced around the room. "What's wrong, Sharla?"

"Nothing," Sharla whispered, peering down the hallway.

"Well, what are you doing?"

"Is he here?"

Addy didn't understand. "He's gone, Honey. I told you he was just dropping something off."

"He's coming back though?"

"He's coming again tonight."

"Where's he gonna sleep?"

"He won't *sleep* here, Sharla."

"I don't want him to come."

"Well you must be the only child in the world who doesn't want a visit from Santa."

"It wasn't Santa."

"Sure it was Santa!"

Sharla's voice was tiny. "I saw the van."

"Sharla Cody! Did you climb on the bathtub and look out that window?!"

Sharla nodded as fat tears began to roll down her cheeks.

Addy bent down. "What is it, Honey? You upset because you didn't see the reindeers?"

Sharla shook her head.

"You afraid? You afraid of Santa?" Addy asked with some surprise.

Sharla looked up into her Mum Addy's eyes. "I'm afraid of Emilio."

Addy didn't understand.

Sharla wiped her eyes. "I thought it was only my Mum coming."

"Your Mum?"

Sharla nodded. "I seen it was Emilio's gray van."

Addy felt her stomach drop as she understood that Sharla'd guessed wrong what the special surprise was. She eased herself into the chair and made Sharla look at her. "Sharla. Honey. Your Mama isn't coming for Christmas."

"You said though."

"No, Honey. I never did say your Mama was coming but I think that's what you thought when I said about the special present."

"It's something else?"

"It's something else."

"Can it be my Mum too?"

"No my little girl, it can't be."

Addy did not believe Sharla's mother would ever return to Chatham. Even if Collette did come back, she wouldn't stay long. Addy thought it would be worse for Sharla to know the truth than to infrequently remember her mother as a lost love. She squeezed the little girl to her bosom but Sharla pulled away. "Who will have me?"

"Who will have you what?"

"Who will have me be their girl?"

"What do you mean, Honey?"

"When you die?" she asked quietly, tears filling her eyes once more. "You told Leam you're gonna die. You told Leam you was just hanging on till you found someone to have me." She inhaled. "Who will have me?"

Addy rubbed her face and wondered what other frightening things the poor child had heard. "Look at me, Sharla Cody. Look at me. You're just a little girl and that's not things you should be worrying about. All right? The only thing you should be worrying about is did I find out you ate a candy-cane before breakfast today."

Sharla smiled despite herself.

"And you should be worried about if you can find your mittens so you can go on and play outside with Lionel and Nedda for a while. You don't be worried about nothing more than that, all right? I'll do the worrying and the figuring things out. And from now on, Sharla, you see I'm talking to Leam, or to anybody, you wake me up, all right? Nothing in my old chatter you need to hear anyway."

Sharla nodded.

"Now, as far as that gray van is concerned, I will let you in on a little secret. Did you see the fellow who climbed out of the van?"

Sharla shook her head and Addy was relieved. "Well, that *was* Santa but he likes to wear a disguise when he does his early deliveries and that's why he drives the van 'stead of bringing the reindeers." Addy winked. "They do make an awful clatter."

Sharla giggled. "What's his disguise?"

"A Red Wings hockey coat."

Sharla looked surprised. "Still got his beard though?"

"Mmm-hmm."

"And big black boots?"

"Mmm-hmm."

"Why ain't his van red though?"

"Well, red's no good disguise for Santa."

Sharla looked around. "Is the present here now?"

Mum Addy shook her head, deciding it'd be torture for the child to know her present was hidden in the house. "Santa just dropped by to say looks like he'll have enough room on his sleigh afterall and he'll just bring it tonight with the other things."

Sharla grinned and hopped on one foot. Addy tickled her and said, "But I told him, I said, 'Santa, don't be leaving the presents under the tree out here in the living room because Sharla's bed's right there and I just know she'll wake up."

"Where's he gonna leave 'em?"

"I told him leave the things in my bedroom. So soon as you wake up you can come in. Even if I'm still asleep you go right ahead and jump on my bed and say, "It's Christmas, Mum Addy! It's Christmas!"

Sharla hugged her Mum Addy and asked if she could bring candy-canes outside for Lionel and Nedda. Addy took six canes from the sparse little lean-to-the-left tree on the table near the window. "I got some of that ice cream, the candy-cane one Mr. Toohey likes. So when you get cold out there you kids come in and I'll make a Coke float out of it, all right?"

On Christmas morning, it was Addy who woke Sharla. At first Sharla was so groggy and annoyed she'd pushed Addy away and burrowed back under the covers. Addy'd laughed at that and it took a moment for Sharla to remember Santa had been to the trailer the night before and there were presents waiting for her in Mum Addy's bedroom. She threw back her blue plaid cover and raced down the hall and squealed when she saw the packages all over her Mum's already-made bed. She sat down on the bed and was set to open the first package when Addy stopped her. "First the special surprise."

Sharla looked at the presents, wondering which it might be. Addy said, "No, Honey, the special one's in the closet."

"In the closet?"

"Mmm-hmm."

"Why Santa put it in the closet?"

"Well, because it was too big to put on the bed."

"He put these other on the bed?" she asked, looking askance.

"Of course."

"How'd he do that with you under the covers?"

"He just did."

"How'd the bed get made though?"

"It just did."

"He make the bed with you *in* it?"

Addy glanced around mysteriously, then whispered, "Santa's a magical man, Sharla, and magic's a thing not to question. Now you want to get up and go look in that closet or not?"

Sharla rose and went to the closet. She opened the door slowly, her eye drawn immediately to the large color console with the huge ribbon and bow on the screen. She could barely say the words. "A television."

"Mmm-hmm."

Sharla was quiet for a long time before she said, "I never heard of Santa bringing no one a television before."

"Guess you musta been extra, extra good this year."

Sharla turned around. Her face was flushed, her forehead creased. "Maybe I did some bad things though."

"Oh, no doubt you did, Child. But you were mostly good, and I *know* that to be true."

Sharla grinned as it sunk in. "Santa brought a television for *me?*"

"Well, I hope you'll share it with me just a little."

"I will," she said.

Peas

*A**ddy could not help but think of her first baby* when she learned she was pregnant with her second. She'd been fifteen years old and horrified, that first time, that people would notice her swelling middle and guess at her misfortune. The second time, at twenty-four, she sewed five maternity blouses and wore them long before she needed to. She *hoped* strangers might inquire if she was expecting a baby, so she could tell them yes she was. Addy felt blessed to be having a child, and so grateful that God wasn't going to punish her after all, that she never complained about her sore back or swollen feet and never told anyone the baby kicked her hard enough one night she thought it had broken her rib.

Mose was away working for much of Addy's pregnancy, but when he was home he tidied their little apartment and shopped at the market, and reminded Addy every day — as if the forty pounds she'd gained wasn't reminder enough — that she had a baby coming and needed to take care of herself. There were days when Addy wished Mose was back on the train, for all his tidying and hovering and advising truly did pluck her nerves.

The child born to Addy and Mose that warm September night was a tiny, wrinkled baby girl. Mose thought the infant, with her wide black eyes and gaping mouth, looked like an insect, though he'd never say such a thing to his wife. He also wouldn't tell Addy that he'd nearly dropped the bleating bundle when the doctor placed her in his arms and whispered the word *deformity*. The doctor had pulled back the blanket to show him where a web of soft skin joined the large toe and the second toe together on each of the baby's tiny feet. Mose looked down and felt relieved. The webbed toes looked strange, but Mose thought the doctor'd been exaggerating when he said *deformity* and he reckoned Beatrice, named for Addy's childhood friend, would get along just fine in life with webs between her toes.

Beatrice grew from baby to toddler and took her first steps on the worn red carpet in their tiny apartment on William Street. She was barefoot and Mose could see the way the peculiar web of skin spread out between her round brown toes. "Look, Addy. Her feet look like a chicken." He scooped the baby up in his arms and made her squeal when he blew on her soft warm belly. "You're a chicken, Beatrice. You're Daddy's chicken!"

Addy'd laughed at that. "Chickens don't have webbed feet! You're thinking of ducks!"

Mose laughed too but he kept calling Beatrice *Chicken* or *Chick* and after a while Addy was calling her *Chicken* or *Chick* and soon no one called the little girl *Beatrice* at all. As Chick grew, Addy felt quietly jealous of the bond between her husband and daughter and envied the pure way Mose loved Chick. Chick was a different child, difficult and demanding, when Mose was gone, and Mose was always gone.

It was around the time Chick started going to school that Addy realized she was not likely to have another child. She ached at the thought she would never hold another baby of her own. Or nurse a baby at her breast, or rock a cranky infant to sleep for the fifth night in a row and not even mind. She searched her memory, wishing she could recall the details of Chick growing from new-born to now. All she could really remember about Chick being a baby was a sweet powder smell and short perfect sleeps.

Mose felt sick when he realized he would not be home for his daughter's sixth birthday. He'd tried to arrange the days off months in advance of the late-September date, and he wished now his employers had not been so reassuring it could be done. Addy'd be disappointed, but not cross, he knew. Still, his little Chicken would have her sixth birthday party without him. She'd weep when he told her, and cling to his neck, and beg, "Stay, Daddy, please. Stay, Daddy, *please*."

Mose hoped that's all Chick would do, for she was given to surprising dramatics. The pattern was unpredictable and all the more frustrating for that. For it wasn't each time, but often, when Chick didn't get her way, she'd throw herself down on the floor and kick her legs until she brought up her supper. Addy would watch, and, not knowing what else to do and not wanting to get the ammonia out for the second time in a week, give in and give Chick whatever it was she wanted. Mose hoped there would not be a scene about the birthday, and just to put the odds in his favor, he'd bought her an extra special present.

He'd first seen the doll in the window of a toy shop in Montreal. He'd gone in and asked the clerk, *"Combien d'argent pour la poupée dans la fenêtre?"* The cost of the beautiful porcelain doll was a week's wages. Addy'd be mortified, for much as she loved her daughter, she fretted they were spoiling their only child. *Ruining* was the word she used.

It took three trips across the country before Mose had squirreled away enough money from his porter tips to buy the doll. In addition to the doll, he'd come home that time with a pair of wheat sheaf salt'n'pepper shakers from Saskatchewan. Addy'd made a fuss about how well crafted and handsome they were. She didn't have the heart to tell her good husband that after nine years together she was running out of space for the knickknacks and was weary from the dusting. She'd started stashing some of the older ones in boxes and hiding them in a drawer. The fact was she wouldn't be sorry if during one of Chick's tantrums a few got knocked over and broke beyond repair.

Mose had been anxious to show Addy the special present but had to wait until Chick had gone off with her Uncle Sammy. He grinned as he brought the parcel to the sofa and took off the paper in which it was wrapped. He lifted the doll from the satin-

lined box and passed it carefully to his wife. Addy turned the doll
over, examining the perfect detail of costume and features. She
cleared her throat, returned the doll to the box, and said, "Take it
back."

Mose's grin left him. "I beg your pardon?"

"Take it back, Mose."

"Why would I take it back?"

"Because that's no present for a six-year-old girl."

Mose laughed. "She'll love this doll!"

Addy narrowed her eyes. "How much that doll cost, Mose?"
Mose shrugged and told her less than half the price he paid.
She knew he was lying. "That's too much to spend on a six-year-
old girl."

"Well it's said and done now."

"Take it back, Mose."

"I can't take it back, Addy. The place I bought it's in Montreal."

"You're stopping over next trip. Pick out something else."

"Her birthday's in four days."

"Well go on downtown why don't you then. Try Gray's Place.
Or see if Lyal Mulhern doesn't have some nice little something in
his shop."

"I'm giving her the doll, Addy."

"Keep your voice down, Mose."

"I'm giving her the doll."

"You're spoiling her, Mose. You're ruining her."

"It's just a doll, Woman!"

"She'll break it."

"What if she does?! Will the world end?!"

Addy'd taken a deep breath, determined to talk some sense
into the man's thick head. "It's a thing to be looked at, Mose. Not
played with. That doll won't last a week. Think of the money
wasted. We're saving up to buy a car!"

"I'm giving Chick the doll and that's the end of it."

Addy couldn't tell Mose, because she didn't know herself
and wouldn't figure out for years to come, the true reason she

hated that doll. The understanding hit her one day when she was working at The Oakwood Bakery. Her employer, Mr. Revello, opened a small velvet box and announced to his staff that the gold necklace inside was a birthday present for his eight-year-old daughter. "For my beautiful Fiorella," he'd said. Addy'd been within earshot of Mrs. Revello and heard her mutter to the bakery's accountant, "I been marry him twenty year and he don't gonna buy me nothing." Addy realized then that she'd envied Chick's bond with Mose because she had no such bond with her own father, but more because Mose brought *her* home salt'n'pepper shakers and never anything as wonderful as that porcelain doll.

Mose had left after the argument with his wife to go join his daughter, her Uncle Sammy, and Sammy's good friend Ben across the street in the park by the river. Samuel and Ben were Chick's favorite people, next to her Daddy and her Uncle Hamond, of course. On the short walk to the park Mose wondered if his wife was right. Maybe he had been wrong to buy the doll. It was costly, true, and they could have used the money for other things. Mose hated to argue with Addy and knew she felt the same way. They had precious few hours together, so he resolved to make things right when he got home. If Addy wanted him to take the doll back, he'd count on the fact she knew best.

It was unusually hot for late September, the kind of day that made people argue was it too early for Indian summer or not, and children were splashing in the river. Chick didn't like swimming, but would sit on the dock with her uncles and watch the other children frolic. It troubled her though, the way the children would dunk their heads, mouth, nose, and all under the murky green water. Chick was afraid of the water. Chick was afraid of dogs and darkness and thunder too.

Chick's sixth birthday was coming up and she was going to have a party. Her Uncle Hamond was going to bring the little Shetland pony from the farm where he used to work, and the children were all going to have rides. And her mother, though Chick wasn't supposed to have seen, was sewing the most beautiful dress of white cotton with an eyelet lace collar and shiny pink ribbon at the waist. Her father, she knew, would bring home a special gift. There was always a special gift from her father, and a special feeling of being adored by him.

The night before her party, her mother had laid down in the bed beside her and said, "I can't believe my baby's a little girl."

"I been a little girl for a long time, Mama."

"That right?"

"Since I been two years old I been a little girl," she said smartly.

"How you figure that?"

"Uncle Hamond said I was talking like a person when I was just two years old."

"Did he?"

"Was I?"

"Yes you were."

She'd snuggled in then, closed her eyes, and whispered, "Tell me the story, Mama."

Addy kissed Chick's cheeks and was glad her heart was safely contained in her chest, for she felt like it might explode with love. "Well," she began, "your Daddy was home with me and I know that was the Lord's doing because he wasn't scheduled then to have his days off."

"And I was impatient, weren't I, Mama?"

"Yes, Chicken. You always have been an impatient child. You were up walking at nine months and talking like a person at two. Nearly four weeks before you were supposed to come into the world, you give me a good swift kick and you said, 'Mama, you better wake up Daddy and send him down to get Mrs. Yardley because I am on my way *now*.'"

"Did I say that with my voice?"

"Yes you did."

"My word voice?" Chick asked, knowing the answer.

"Your inside voice, Baby. The one with no sound that comes from here," she said, touching Chick's heart, "and goes straight in your Mama's head."

"Or straight in my Daddy's head."

"Or other people you love too."

"And then what I say?"

"You said, 'Mama, I like to do things my own way so 'stead of being upside down on you, I think I like to try being birthed with my behind coming first.'"

Chick loved that part of the story and giggled. Addy kissed Chick's forehead and tickled her tummy. "I said, 'Child, I'm the mother here and you weigh all of six little old pounds so you let Mrs. Yardley put you the right way now. You understand?'"

"What's that cord called, Mama? The one attached to me and you?"

"That's the umbilical cord."

"That's the one the doctor cut?"

"Mmm-hmm. Still there though."

Chick lifted her pajamas to look at the twisted knot of her belly button. "No it ain't."

"Just invisible now is all."

Chick burrowed into Addy's chest. "How long before I came out and the doctor cut that cord?"

"Well, I pushed and I waited and I pushed and I waited and your Daddy and Mrs. Yardley could have cooked and ate a ten-pound roast of beef before you decided it was time you're ready. The doctor finally came, though I thought he was gonna miss the whole thing, then it seemed like it was just the one last push and there you were in my arms. You cried just a little and I took you to my breast and you was looking at me like you knew me and when your Daddy said, 'It's a girl. It's Beatrice,' you looked right at him like you knew him too. He said you even gave your eyes a little roll like to say, 'Well of course I'm a girl, Daddy.'

"Me and your Daddy loved you so much. We felt like you came as a gift from God and one we maybe didn't even deserve. 'Cept for when we have our problems with you, Chick, 'cept for when you throw your fits, I think I'm the luckiest mother in the world. Those fits we're just gonna have to work on and I think that's me and Daddy's fault for giving in to you too much. But aside from that, you're turning into a sweet and gentle person and

I'm very, very proud to say you're mine. And you know how your Daddy feels, because even though his work takes him far away, you're in every thought he thinks. Him and you like peas in a pod and you have been since the day you were born." As the night was still warm, Addy took the extra blanket off Chick's bed and kissed her sleeping lips good night.

In the morning, Chick had been grouchy from too little sleep. Addy kissed her cheek and said, "Happy Birthday, Beatrice Mosely." Chick complained about her breakfast and wouldn't drink her milk. She said, "I want my Daddy. Why can't my Daddy come to my birthday party?"

Addy'd thought to give Chick the gift from her father later, during the party at Hamond's, but she could see the child needed some placating now. Without a word she took the gift-wrapped box from its hiding place in the kitchen cupboard and set it down on the table. Chick looked up. "From Daddy?"

Addy nodded and watched her unwrap the present. She wasn't sorry, when she saw Chick's face, that she'd given in and told Mose to keep it. The porcelain doll was the best and most beloved gift Chick would receive in her life. Still, Addy was anxious such a costly thing would get broken, so she took it out of Chick's hands and put it back in the satin-lined box before the little girl had a chance to give it a hug.

Chick had loved the white dress too and it was a perfect fit. She'd pulled it on before the party and twirled in front of the mirror, asking, "Will you teach *me* to sew, Mama?" It startled Addy to think that she herself was already handy with a needle and thread by the time she was Chick's age. She realized she hadn't shown Chick much else in the way of housekeeping either. She hadn't even taught the child how to make Apple Snow. She'd do that, she thought, this fall, when the apples were crisp and plentiful.

There'd been some fuss over the pink bow for Chick's hair. Chick hadn't wanted the bow and Addy couldn't imagine why. "It pulls!" Chick had whined. Addy tied the ribbon tighter, then worried that the child would throw a fit. There would be no fits on Chick's birthday though. At least none of which Addy was aware.

There were ten children invited to the party and Addy'd feared ten was too many to handle. She nearly cried when Hamond showed up with the blonde Shetland pony and every child in the whole East End came over to see. She'd baked a white three-layer cake with butter cream frosting and decorated it with candy rose-buds, but the cake wasn't nearly big enough to provide for the extra children and neighbors who'd come to watch the pony trot up and down Degge Street.

Chick was the birthday girl, so she naturally felt entitled to special consideration, but when Uncle Hamond told the crowd that Chick would ride the pony first, she froze. She'd never ridden an animal before, pony or otherwise, and was afraid she'd look foolish, or worse, that she'd fall and hurt herself or spoil her beau-tiful dress. She let another child go first instead and Hamond pat-ted her back, whispering that he was proud to see her generosity.

Later, more than a dozen neighborhood children had ridden the pony and Chick still hadn't taken a turn. Sammy and Ben kept shovels at both ends of the street and tried to keep up with the Shetland's prolific output. Addy was in Hamond's kitchen throw-ing together a pan of peach cobbler, thinking about Jesus with the loaves and fishes. No one seemed to notice that Chick had disappeared.

A boy of eight, Abel Duncan, had three turns on the pony and was told he'd have no more. He couldn't complain, seeing he hadn't been invited to the birthday party in the first place. He was cutting through the Fergusons' backyard on his way home when he heard a banging sound in the woodshed by the big pear tree. He wasn't afraid, just curious, but he thought better than to go ahead and open the door. There was a small window on the side of the shed which he could just barely reach. He lifted himself up on tiptoes to see what was making the banging noise.

He didn't know what to think about what he saw inside the shed. Chick Mosely, dressed in her pretty white dress, teary and mad, was struggling to swing a hoe against the wall like a baseball bat. Abel started to walk away but came back, opened the shed door, and asked simply, "Why you doing that?"

Chick was startled to see the boy. She dropped the hoe before she realized he wasn't in a position to punish her. Abel watched her a moment longer, then said, "Why ain't you out there riding the pony?"

How could she tell Abel Duncan that she was afraid to ride the pony? How could she tell him that the Shetland pony had ruined her party? She picked up the hoe again. "Go away, Abel. You never was invited to my party anyway."

Abel looked at the shed wall where the hoe had splintered the wood. "If I *was* invited I'd say it was a good one. I liked riding that pony. And your Mama set out some cobbler and cake and fresh baked cookies too. If it was *my* party I sure wouldn't be here in no smelly shed." With that he turned and left.

Chick picked up the hoe and swung it again but she wasn't really mad anymore. She could hear the children in the kitchen and reckoned they must have been invited inside for cake so she set down the hoe and headed for the house. Her mother met her at the back door, damp with perspiration, her dress soiled from baking. She kissed Chick and said, "C'mere, Baby, I put aside a slice of cake for you."

Seeing the giant piece of white cake made Chick wish she hadn't splintered the wall in the shed. She asked, "Can Abel Duncan come have a slice?" Addy was not sure which of the Duncan boys was Abel or why Chick wanted to give him cake, but she nodded and watched her daughter race out the back door.

It being a Saturday, the majority of folks would be getting up early for church in the morning and Addy was glad she didn't have to shoo out any stragglers at the end of the day. When everyone was gone and Samuel and Ben had cleaned up the last of the mess, Hamond carried the worn-out little birthday girl the few blocks home to William Street. Addy confessed she felt bad for giving Mose so much grief about the doll. And bad for making Chick wear the ribbon in her hair. And bad that she hadn't thought to bake a larger cake too.

Before he left, Hamond kissed Chick's sleeping cheek, squeezed Addy's hand, and looked into her dark eyes. "You're just a person, Adelaide."

Addy nodded weakly, remembering the way Hamond had looked at her when he lifted her off the train at the Chatham station all those years ago. *You know me, Hamond,* she thought, *you know all about me.*

Mose came home a few weeks later but he was not himself. He'd been to Nova Scotia to visit his mother and this time there had been no quick recovery and no fluffy rice. "She's dying, Addy."

Addy had suppressed the urge to say, "She's always dying, Mose."

"She can't seem to catch a breath. Didn't even get up when I came in the room. Aileen, that friend who comes around every day to take care, she says this whole last month Mama's had to use a bedpan and last week there was blood in her urine."

Addy nodded. Maybe the old woman really was dying. Her heart ached for Mose. She sat down in his lap, glad that Chick was gone picking apples with her Uncle Hamond. She kissed her good husband's face and said, "We should go see her. You, me, Chick. She should know her only granddaughter."

Mose shook his head. "Cost a lot of money, Addy. It's a long way. I wouldn't like to be working with you and Chick on the train. I wouldn't want you to see me servile the way I have to be."

"Could we go together, on your days off?"

"Cost a King's ransom for three fares."

"It's your mother, Mose."

Mose nodded and smiled and felt so lucky to love and be loved by this woman. "I don't know how much time she's got left."

"We should go sooner than later then."

They could not afford tickets for the sleeper cars and would not have been welcome anyway. Mose couldn't in fact ever remember seeing a black face without a porter's uniform during his trips back and forth across the country. Still, even without the luxury of a sleeping berth, the journey would be far more costly than they'd expected. In the end it was Hamond who made a gift of the cost of Chick's ticket, waving off their thanks by saying,

"Child should know her family. That's gonna be a trip she'll remember the rest of her life."

There was a great deal of preparation in advance of the journey, and even with the extra work, Addy'd grown excited at the thought of traveling. Mose had warned her that Africville was no paradise though, and the more he talked about it, the more she worried and wondered.

"The place was settled by fugitive slaves but it's not like Rusholme. Least not the way you described Rusholme. The thing is," Mose said, looking ashamed, "it's a slum. That's just what it is. It's good people there, don't get that wrong, but the place is . . . it's right next to the city dump, Addy. The houses are shacks. There's no school nearby. Halifax won't provide water, nor sewer."

Mose was flushed, like when he talked about the Brotherhood. "When I was a boy we all used to go over to the dump to scrounge. Friend of mine found a pocketknife that must have been thrown out by mistake. I found a few treasures of my own. A man who lived up the street from us got caught there by the police. He told them he was looking for breakfast for his family and they took him to jail."

Addy shuddered. "Why'd your father let you grow up there? He was white. He had money."

Mose squinted and looked away. "My father gave my mother ten dollars a month to help out with raising me. My mother used to thank him like he really didn't have to do it. I didn't expect he was gonna move us downtown with his white family but I never did forgive him for not doing more."

"Well if it's so awful why's your mother still there?"

"I asked her to come live with us."

Addy tried not to cringe. "I know you did, Mose. I understand her not wanting to come all the way to Ontario, but why don't she move somewhere else in Halifax? Somewhere better?"

"Africville's home, Addy. She was born there. Her friends are there. It's all she's ever known. The shame is not on the people who live there but the city who'd let them."

Addy swallowed a dry lump in her throat. "Sure it's fine for us to go? Sure it's safe? For Chick?"

"It's safe. Nothing's going to happen. Not with me there. Besides, it's just for a few days."

Addy nodded, suddenly feeling a rush of cold air, surprised to find the window behind her closed.

Mose seemed not to have noticed the wind. "Maybe us being there will give my mother strength for a little extra living."

"What if us being there is just too much for her to bear?"

"Don't worry," Mose said, kissing her lips. "You'll like her. And I *know* she'll like you."

"I'm not worried," Addy bristled.

"Natural for a mother to feel jealous of her son's wife. And the other way around too. But once you get in a room together, you'll see. You'll like each other just fine."

"I'm not jealous of your mother, Mose," Addy said crisply.

It was the night before they were to leave. The November cold hadn't blown in yet and there were still three pink roses blooming on the bush out front of Mrs. Yardley's window. Mose and Chick had gone to the market to buy food for the trip and a few special things for his mother. Addy had awoken that morning with a sore throat and fever and brought up her breakfast before she chewed her last bite. At first Mose was thrilled to see her doubled over and whispered, "Why, Adelaide Mosely, are you . . . ?"

"No," she'd answered quickly. "No, Mose. I got a flu is all. Just a flu."

"You sure you're not . . . ?"

"I'm sure," Addy said, and she *was* sure she was not with child.

"Flu? You be fit to travel tomorrow?" He looked panicked.

"It's not a bad one. Ain't cold enough outside to catch a bad one. I'll be fine."

"Me and Chicken'll take care of the last-minute things. You just get in bed and stay there today. We'll be back in a hour or so. You just rest."

Addy was relieved to be told to go to bed, for there was no other place she could be. She felt too weak to stand and too nauseous to think of cooking or cleaning or shopping at the market. She was packed already and thankful for that. Chick's things and hers had just barely fit in the suitcase she brought from Poppa's all those years ago, and Mose had his own bag, of course.

Her fever had spiked and she was perspiring and shivering in her bed when she heard the knock at the door. She had not the strength to say "come in" and was glad when whoever it was took the liberty and turned the knob. Hamond stood in the doorway, looking grim.

"What's wrong, Hamond?" Addy croaked.

Hamond approached the bed slowly. "You don't look well, Adelaide."

"I'm not well," she said, relieved there was nothing more important that was troubling him. "But I'll be fine by morning."

"You won't be fine by morning and you know it. You'll be just as sick or sicker."

"Don't look at me like that, Hamond Ferguson. I'm getting on that train with my daughter and my husband." Addy could feel tears in her eyes. "I have to go, Hamond. I have to."

Hamond felt her forehead with the back of his hand. "I should call for the doctor."

"I just got a flu."

"Still."

"No." Addy sat up in the bed and collected herself. "Maybe you could make me a cup of tea, Hamond. I'd be grateful for a nice hot cup of tea."

"Cup of tea ain't gonna bring you back, Addy. I think you better get it in your mind you ain't going east tomorrow."

Addy ignored the comment and watched him make his way to the stove. She remembered, "I wanted to bring those photographs of Chick to show Mose's Mama. That one of her when she was two, sitting on Mose's shoulders. And them ones with the boys from the corn roast last year. And those photographs of our wedding day. Oh no. I best not bring those. Can't see nothing of a church in the background of any. You get them for me? Some's on the shelf right there but I been keeping most of them in the butterbox with the boys' things. You move that old dresser so I can get at the attic, Hamond?"

Hamond had wanted to tell Addy his back was aching worse than he could ever remember and it had been an effort for him just to climb the stairs to see her. He'd wanted to tell Addy she should just wait until her big strong husband came home and get him to move that old dresser. Instead he said, "I'll get the box. Just lay back down and wait for your tea. I'll get the box."

Mose and Addy had inherited the big oak dresser from the old man who'd lived in the apartment before them. They were grateful for the man's generosity, though they suspected the fellow mostly just couldn't see how to get the hulking thing out the door and down the stairs to take it with him. The right leg had been broken and it wobbled a little when it got pushed clear of the attic door, but it was sturdy and large enough to hold Addy, Mose, and Chick's clothes too. Each time Mose moved the thing to get Addy's safekept photographs, or to hide a present for Chick, he thought to get out his toolbox and fix the leg, but he never did. Hamond had thought the same thing over the years. He thought it again this time when he moved the dresser and saw the leg was near broke clean off.

One moment Hamond was planning how he'd come over while they were gone to Nova Scotia, for he knew Addy'd go, sick or not, and fix the leg for them. The next moment he was screaming in pain as the dresser leg collapsed and the weight of the thing landed squarely in the middle of his left foot. Addy flung the covers off herself and staggered across the room. She tried, with what little strength she had, to lift the dresser off his foot but couldn't budge it. Martin Baldwin from downstairs appeared in no time, heaving and pushing too, but he was a tiny man in declining health and his bird-thin arms offered nothing but good intentions.

They would all thank the Lord later that Mose arrived when he did. He and Chick had heard the screaming halfway down William Street and even with all their parcels had run home and bounded up the stairs, wearing that look of people afraid of what they'd find. Mose shoved Martin Baldwin out of the way, apologizing later if he'd been rough, hefted the massive dresser, and set poor Hamond's foot free.

They moved Hamond to the sofa and got a crate for his foot. They gently took off his old boot and everyone in the room wanted to weep for the state of his socks. Mose told Chick not to look when he pulled the cobweb of threads off Hamond's foot, so she buried her head in her Uncle's chest and wrapped her arms around his neck. Hamond was grateful Chick was there, for he had something sweet to cling to as the pain dug a groove from his foot to his brain.

Addy nearly vomited when Hamond's sock was removed. Martin Baldwin escaped downstairs to his apartment and put his music on loud. Mose had stared at Hamond's foot in surprise, for there was no blood at all but a two-inch crevice where the dresser had implanted itself. His bones were broken for certain and his toes were starting to swell and turn blue. They all knew he'd have trouble walking for the rest of his life, and he did.

Nothing much to be done for a broken foot. Mose carried Hamond all the way home and they laughed at what a sight they must have made. Especially Hamond, for in Mose's mind it was one man carrying his injured friend, but in Hamond's it was a white man carrying a black man. Samuel wept as he helped ease his father into the bed. Mose and Hamond pretended not to notice, as they thought it unseemly for a man to cry.

Mose made Samuel promise to look in on his Aunt Addy each day while he and Chick were gone. Mose knew Addy wasn't coming on the train. The look of her when he'd come in the room had frightened him as much as Hamond's screaming. In fact, after Chick finally fell asleep, he'd spent the better part of the evening begging Addy to stay, convincing her she was too sick to travel, and most of all, insisting she could not and should not bring her illness into his dying mother's house.

Addy had not the strength to argue and knew in the end he was right. Then Mose decided that he was staying too. He was suddenly afraid for his wife's health and gripped by a feeling he shouldn't leave her at all. She had to do the convincing then, and remind Mose of all the money they'd spent on the tickets. She urged him to go for the sake of his mother, and for Chick. "Go, Mose. Think of Chick. Think of how she wants to see the ocean. I'll be fine. I got Samuel and Ben to come and look after me. And Mrs. Yardley and the Baldwins too."

"I'm gonna miss you though, so much," Mose had said and recalled his shame for Samuel when tears formed in his own eyes.

"What's this?" she'd asked, quietly moved by his tears. "You're used to not seeing me. What's wrong, Mose?"

"This is . . . different."

She pressed her fever-hot lips to his forehead. "I'll miss you too. I always do. But it's Chick I'm thinking about. I haven't been separated from my baby girl for more than four or five hours in all the years she been alive."

"I'll take good care of her."

"I know you will, Mose. You're her good, good Daddy. Besides, I'm more worried about me missing her than her missing me. I'll be just sick from missing you both."

There'd been no tantrum, as Addy'd secretly feared, when she told Chick the next morning she was too sick to come along. "Just me and Daddy?" Chick asked.

"Yes, Chicken, but it's only for one week and then you'll be right back here and you can tell me all about the train and about what Nova Scotia looks like and all about Nana Mosely too."

Chick nodded and looked deep into her mother's eyes. "You gonna die, Mama?"

Addy'd been shocked by the question. "No. NO! Why would you ask such a question as that?"

Chick shrugged, looking too sad to cry. Mose had already taken Addy's clothes from Poppa's little suitcase, which considerably lightened his load. Addy smiled at Chick. "You suppose your Nana like to see your special doll?"

The porcelain doll was removed from her satin box so seldom that Chick had never even named her. She never dreamed her mother'd allow, let alone suggest, such a thing. "She can look out the window," Chick said, clapping.

She seemed so grown-up, Addy'd recall, when she pictured Chick standing in the doorway with her hand in her father's. She was wearing her good coat and hat, cradling her doll like an infant. She had a look on her face that said she'd changed, grown from one person to another all in a day, like she finally understood she couldn't always have her way. Addy'd been too weak to rise from the bed but had hugged Chick till the poor child lost her breath. And she'd let Mose kiss her mouth too, though she'd said he really shouldn't.

Mose had paused at the door and smiled, saying, "Don't you have yourself too good a time without us."

Addy cleared her throat a few times because she didn't want to start bawling and get Chick upset. "I won't," she said, and waved.

It had been a surprise to all of them when Chick ran back into the room and pressed the porcelain doll into her mother's shivering arms. "I got my Daddy for company. You have her, all right, Mama?"

Addy did cry then, and squeeze Chick again and whisper, "I love you so much, Chicken."

The train had been late from Windsor to Chatham and they'd lost an eternity switching tracks after London. Mose and Chick had been traveling for well over five hours and were still miles away from Toronto's Union Station, where they'd meet the connecting train that would take them on the longest leg of their journey. Mose was worried they'd miss the second train and wondered if they could impose upon Olivia and her husband, whom he'd met only briefly, to put them up for the night.

It was hot on board and Chick had been restless and whiny from the start. "How much longer?"

"It's a long, long way, Chicken. Be quiet now, so you're not disturbing other passengers."

"But I'm hungry."

"There's an apple in my coat pocket."

"I already ate a apple."

"Eat another."

"I don't want a apple."

"Chick."

"I want Mama."

"Chicken."

"I want to see Uncle Hamond and Sammy and Ben."

Mose had not been so confident as Addy that they'd seen Chick's last tantrum. He looked around the train and wondered what he'd do if she started up just now. His eye caught the land-scape flashing by. He knew the route and he knew precisely that they were approaching the trellis over that wide river whose name he couldn't recall. *We're moving too fast,* he thought. *They're trying to make up for lost time and they're moving too fast.*

Chick looked out the window and saw the train was about to cross water. *Don't be afraid,* she told herself and shut her eyes. When she opened her eyes again, she was looking at the bare arms of herself and her father, side by side on the armrest. As if it was the first time she noticed, she said, "Look, Daddy. I am darker and you are lighter."

Mose looked down at their arms and nodded. A thought flashed across his mind, and like a shooting star, where if you were a practical person you had to ask yourself did you *really* see it, Mose thought of Hamond Ferguson's broken foot and the way Hamond's big toe and second toe were joined by a birdlike web of brown skin. He decided that, like the shooting star, he had not really seen the web of skin at all. He looked down at his beautiful daughter — "Peas in a pod" is what Addy'd always called them — and said, "Your skin is beautiful."

She smiled at him. "And Mama's too."

Mose nodded, gripping her hand in his, and would have said, "Yes, Chicken," except at that moment the speeding train jumped the rail and left the tracks. The passengers, including Mose and Chick, died instantly, as the impact of the locomotive with the water was severe. It took only minutes for the river to drag the big train down.

Addy woke before dawn, not with a premonition or sense of doom, but because she'd already slept ten hours straight and couldn't sleep anymore. She smiled, imagining her husband and daughter side by side on the train. They're near Quebec City by now, she guessed. She remembered Mose last week, urging her to reconsider a move to Montreal. A porter friend named Rufus had opened a nightclub there called Rockhead's Paradise, a place where, Mose had kissed her and whispered into her ear, "We could dance all night long." Addy'd laughed at that because they had never danced all night long and hadn't danced at all since their wedding. Maybe she *should* reconsider Montreal, Addy thought. She was surprised to hear a knock at her door before breakfast. She read the words on the telegram that Mrs. Yardley brought up, then read them again, and again, and still she did not understand.

Hamond's youngest, Samuel, would carry his father to William Street and heft him up the three flights of stairs, neither man feeling ashamed of their tearstained cheeks. The three would sit in silence, Addy feverish, shivering, and numb, praying that Mose and Chick would rise from the dead.

The bodies of Addy's husband and daughter were never recovered. She imagined them, especially in those first few weeks, walking on the bottom of some silty lake or pond, meeting up with L'il Leam and Chester Monk, saying what a coincidence it was they all lost their lives to the water. Or she'd imagine Mose and Chick racing each other up the stairs to their apartment, drenched like they got caught in a spring rain, not caring they were soaked, thinking it was funny everyone believed them drowned. They'd be with her always, Mose and Chick. Not like some of the others, but steady and quiet and small, sitting alongside her, coupled together like train coaches, connected by that invisible cord.

Myrtle and Box

*T**he deliveryman had come and gone* before Addy thought to check the box. The eggs were in there, and the apples, though they were a sorry-looking dozen and not the tart kind that worked best. Why hadn't she done this in the fall like she'd planned, when the apples were crisp and sour? She knew before she set the water on the stove it wouldn't be the best batch she'd made. *Apples in April been sitting in cellars too long or they come from other countries,* she thought, sniffing a core. She remembered her mother used to garnish with myrtle or box and she'd told the man on the phone, "It's a shrub. Used to be called whortleberry too. And box is an evergreen. You have something like that in your garnishes section?" But the man had misunderstood and just put her groceries in a box instead of bags.

It was a beautiful spring day, the kind that fooled a person into thinking summer'd be along shortly. Truth was there'd be another snowstorm before the fresh leaves unfurled and, like almost every year, the daffodils would get buried, their short pretty lives blighted by white. After that there'd be the days of rain and Addy'd be reminded why hers was called mud lane.

Sharla'd been outside playing with Lionel and Nedda and was annoyed to be called into the trailer. "We're playing though, Mum."

"You're not going near them cows back there, are you?"

"No," Sharla lied.

"You're not throwing stones at them cows?"

Sharla wondered how her Mum Addy could have seen when not one window in the whole trailer faced the pasture. "We won't."

"No you won't."

"Can I go back out?"

"Later you can go out. Right now me and you are gonna make something."

"Make what?"

"A special dessert."

Sharla smiled and warmed to the notion of staying inside. "What special dessert?"

"It's a dessert my Mama taught me how to make and her mother taught her how to make it and her mother taught her."

"Is that a great-grandmother?"

"That's a great-*great*-grandmother and I bet it goes back even farther than that."

"Is it cake?"

"No it's not cake, Honey. It's more special than cake," Addy said as she checked the stove. "It's a dessert made with apples."

Sharla tilted her head. "Apple Snow?"

Addy turned from the stove, trying not to appear startled. "How do you know about Apple Snow?"

"You made that for Poppa. 'Cause of no teeth."

Addy cleared her throat and set the big strainer in the sink. "'Member what I told you about waking me up when I get to talking like that?"

Sharla nodded. "You were awake though. You were sitting right there," she said, pointing to the kitchen table.

"I was awake?"

Sharla's chin bobbed up and down. "Mmm-hmm."

Addy's stomach dropped as she wondered what else she'd said. "I was awake and I was talking about Poppa?"

"Poppa wasn't your Daddy though."

"No he weren't."

"And you did *not* want to get married to him."

Addy cleared her throat again but she couldn't relieve her panic. "If I was talking about Poppa like that, I was not awake, Sharla. I want you to wake me up when I get talking like that. Shake me a little. Or pinch me hard. Don't let me go on, Sharla."

"I did, Mum. I said, 'Wake up, Mum Addy.' And you said, 'I *am* awake, Child. I'm just remembering Poppa is all.'"

The apples in the pot were rolling with the boil. They wanted to be soft but not mushy. Addy watched them carefully, confident she'd know by the look of the fruit the precise time to take them out. "I say anything about Riley, Honey?"

"You said Riley like to walk around with money in his pocket acting like a rich, rich man."

Addy nodded and was glad she hadn't spoken more intimately about Riley Rippey. She even smiled, thinking that was true about him acting rich. She wondered where Riley was now, if he was in this world or the next.

"And you said that Camille Bishop had herself some nerve."

Addy caught her breath. She could remember none of it. She'd been preoccupied lately, thinking about her life, her past, but she could not remember talking out loud, especially not with Sharla in the room. She knew she should go see Dr. Zimmer just as she knew she couldn't. He'd tell her she was losing her mind, for what else could it be? They'd take Sharla away and then what? Addy wondered if she ought to try to collect her strength and make her way over to Krystal Trochaud's trailer and ask if she'd heard from Collette. She thought she might try Reggie Depuis again and see if the past year brought on any change of heart. She even wondered if Warren and Peggy Souchuck were having trouble conceiving and might love a child that was not their own. Addy tested the softness of the apples and prayed to keep her mind.

The apples were done. Addy found her burned-up old oven mitts and began to heft the pot of boiling water to the strainer at the sink. It surprised her and made her wonder how long it'd been since she made the dish, when she had not the strength to lift it.

"What's wrong, Mum Addy?"

Addy used a slotted spoon to lift the apples from the water and set them in her big bowl. "Just a little heavy is all," she said, and brought the bowl to the table.

"Does the skin stay on?"

"No. That's the next thing to do. Once you got the apples boiled soft. Be careful 'cause it's hot. Prick that flesh with your fork and feel how it feels. Soft, but not too soft."

"Soft but not mushy."

"That's right. That apple doesn't want to cook down to juice. It wants to stay meaty enough you're gonna taste the fruit when it's said and done. Now I like to run them under cold water just a minute so they're not so hot to peel and core. My Mama never did that, but she had so many calluses on her fingers she could use her bare hands to stoke the fire."

Sharla's little tongue found its place on her lower lip when Addy set half the apples in front of her and said, "Now you just pull the skin off like this. See. Just like that. Good girl. That's right. You got a knack for it."

"What's a knack?"

"Means you got a special skill at doing something. Means you take to something fast. Now after you get all the skin off, you cut it in half. Not you, Honey, me. You're too young to use a big knife. See, you cut it in half and you take that spoon there and you just scoop out the core."

"Like that?"

"That's right. Like scooping seeds out a musk melon."

"I hate musk melon."

"Get all the seeds out, Honey. All the seeds and all the core bits."

"Like this."

"That's it. Now set it down in the bowl there."

When they'd finished peeling and coring the rest of the apples, Addy clapped her hands. "I should have taught you this recipe years ago, Baby. Should have made it in the fall though. These apples been in the cellar too long. Your Daddy's gonna be so pleased when he gets home. Don't get a special dish like this on the train. 'Specially not one made by his good girl.'"

Sharla said nothing as she watched the stiff hands measure the sugar and pour it over the apples. She knew Mum Addy was confusing her with her own little daughter, Chick. It was happening more often, and though Sharla'd been frightened the first few times, now she just pretended along. Chick had a Daddy and three Uncles who loved her and was a good person to pretend to be. Sharla was confused by the pretending though, and knew it was not a game. She also knew her Mum was not sleeping like she claimed to be later, for she was standing and moving and talking too. Times like this, Sharla could do nothing but wait until her Mum Addy came back from wherever it was she went.

"Now," Mum continued, "I remember Claire Williams used to shake her head when she saw Mama like to beat the egg whites *before* she beat the apples and sugar but that's how I like to do it too. I don't believe it affect the flavor too much if you like to do it backwards, but that's for each person to decide. Now watch this, Chick. Are you watching? Watch, because you'll do the next one. You crack the egg on the side of this clean bowl. Not the one with the apples in it because you can't beat them all together at once. Might as well throw the whole of it out if you try. I did that once by accident and my mother make me set a whole new batch in cold water over the fire."

Sharla watched her Mum Addy crack the egg on the side of the large bowl and open it carefully, not letting anything but the clear Jell-O-y part spill out.

"Just back and forth like this and the yolk will separate from the white. You don't want to let any yellow in the bowl. Not even a drop. Not even a speck."

"Why though?" Sharla asked.

"Because you won't get a good whip," Mum answered, not looking up. "You just want the whites, Chicken."

"Why they call it whites when it's see-through?"

"When you cook it or whip it, it goes white. That's why. Now it's your turn."

Sharla took the egg in her hand and cracked it open. She was relieved not a speck of yellow leaked out as she poured the raw egg back and forth from half shell to half shell. She thought it was a miracle how the yolk stayed whole and separated from the clear part. Sharla begged to do all the eggs, for she enjoyed the cracking and coddling and thought she had a knack, but Mum Addy said it would take too long and, "Daddy be back shortly and we want to have it ready to surprise him."

When all the whites were in the bowl, Addy found the whisk and gave the eggs a good stiff beat. Sharla marveled at the speed and strength of the frail, thin arms which just moments ago couldn't lift the pot off the stove.

Addy drew the whisk up and made a high stiff peak in the egg whites. She was nearly out of breath from whipping. "See? Look, Chick. See how that stands up? If it can't do that you likely haven't beat long enough. That's just right. Like that is just right." Addy took a few deep breaths before setting the whisk in the apples and sugar, then she beat that mixture until it was firm. "Here, now, Baby. You do the last few minutes just so you get an idea how the whisk feels and how the apples should be just so. That's right," she encouraged, as Sharla whirled the thing around and around, "little faster though, so it fluff up right and look just like real snow."

Sharla spun the whisk faster and perspired for her efforts. She wondered if Mum Addy knew about them plug-in whippers she'd seen Krystal use to make Fawn's mash potatoes. Finally the apples were whipped enough and the egg whites standing proudly in the bowl. Addy lifted a spatula full of egg whites and said, "Watch now, you want to fold this in. Just this little bit, then another little bit, then another, then the rest."

"Why not all at once?" Sharla asked, watching the fluffy egg blending into the creamy apple.

"You don't want to dump the whole of one bowl into the other right off, Chick. You want to say, 'Eggs, I like you to meet apples, you two gonna be good friends.'"

Sharla giggled. "Can I do it now?"

Addy handed the spatula to Sharla and watched intently as the little hand worked the mixtures together. "Fold, don't stir. Fold means you're taking something from the bottom and moving it to the top. That's good. That's very good."

"I got a knack, don't I . . ." Sharla looked up and ventured shyly, "Mama?"

"Yes you do, Chicken. You got a knack."

There was a sudden loud pounding at the door. Sharla figured it was either Lionel or Nedda coming to get her and she said a couple of curse words in her head, for she knew, and she was right, that whatever spell Addy'd been under would be broken now. Addy went to the door and saw Lionel standing there, head bent, swinging his arms like he always did when there were adults around. She smiled at him. "Hello, Lionel. You want to come in and try some dessert Sharla just made?"

Lionel shrugged and stepped in the trailer and saw the fluffy stuff in the bowl. "You make that?" he asked Sharla, then took a seat beside her.

"Yes. Mum Addy did the cutting and whipping though."

Lionel grinned when Addy set a bowl of the dessert in front of them and presented the pair with spoons, saying, "This here's called Apple Snow, Lionel. You tell me if you like it."

Lionel took a too-big spoonful and shoveled it into his mouth. "I do like it," he said through the fluff.

Addy nodded and watched the children eat, then covered the bowl and set the mixture in the fridge. "My mother liked to garnish with myrtle or box," she said to herself.

"Can we go out after, Mum?" Sharla asked.

"Mmm-hmm. Just don't go bothering them cows."

Crescent Moons

*W*hen *she was a girl and pictured her future,* Addy Shadd imagined, as many girls do, a life just like her mother's. She imagined she would finish school, marry Chester Monk, and build a home with him on that land near the Rusholme crick where Chester said he would live and die. She imagined she'd have children to care for and love and that they'd be a source of comfort and companionship when she grew old. Addy had to remind herself that her mother's life was not really like that at all. Laisa had lost both her children tragically, her husband early, and then lived alone and lonely, in one way or another, the rest of her life. In the end, though it was not the one she'd imagined, Addy *did* have a life just like her mother's.

Hamond moved Addy out of her third-floor apartment and helped her find another, on the first floor this time because climbing stairs reminded her of Mose and Chick and their life together on William Street. It took her three days to sort through the drawers of the big oak dresser, which was left to list on its legless side, and three more days to decide what to do with the contents. She gave her husband and daughter's clothes to church charity and felt the better for it at the time. She'd regret it later though and wish she'd kept at least one of Mose's shirts so she could sniff it and dream she was with him. She was glad she had sense enough to keep Chick's porcelain doll and the pretty white dress, both of which were packed away. Addy wondered if she'd

ever see the things again and even thought to write down somewhere that the dress and the doll should be buried with her in the
casket.

In the days and weeks that followed Mose and Chick's death,
Addy would wonder, and always come to the same conclusion,
and finally never wonder again. She was sure Mose never suspected the truth. She knew that if something had caused him to
doubt, he'd ignore it. And if the Lord himself had told Mose
straight, he'd have figured the Lord was mistaken. She herself had
not been absolutely certain until Hamond injured his foot and
took off his sock. She realized she'd never seen his feet before and
reckoned he kept them hidden on account of his *deformity*. It comforted her to know that even if Mose had discovered for a fact it
was Hamond's seed that made his daughter, he'd forgive Addy,
keep a place warm beside him in Heaven, and just be grateful
Chick was made at all.

Addy and Hamond would never speak the truth about what
happened the night Hamond walked her home and moved the
big oak dresser so she could put the butterbox away. Addy had
pulled the attic door open and been sent reeling by a sickening
odor. It had shocked and horrified her to see the swarming insects
on a barely-there squirrel. She hadn't screamed. She'd been too
surprised to scream. But she'd fallen back against Hamond and,
without knowing just how sad she was, sobbed into his shoulder
until she ran dry and got the hiccups. Hamond had rubbed her
back and dried her face and she would wonder later whether it
was the nearness of him or the kindness of him, or because they
were both just so lonely. Whatever it was, she turned her face to
his, closed her eyes, and parted her lips.

The kiss was a soft one and tasted sweet, but Hamond could
not think it was more than a sisterly or daughterly kiss. Of course
he was in love with Addy. He had been for some years, maybe
since the day he lifted her off the train, saw she was that fool
Wallace Shadd's daughter, and guessed at all she'd been through.
But Addy could not love Hamond, not like that, and even when

she kissed him again, pressing against him and taking his face in her hands, he imagined she only meant to thank him for being there. It was after that second kiss, somewhere between the third and fourth, when her tongue found his and their breathing deepened, that Hamond allowed that this moment he'd imagined was truly happening.

As they kissed and stroked and Hamond moved slowly and tenderly inside her, Addy relieved him of his name, thinking only that he was a man whom she loved and who loved her. When he collapsed on top of her and looked like he wanted to cry, she knew it was because it had been years since he'd been with a woman and because he was sure now, if he wasn't before, that Mary Alice had never loved him. Addy kissed his face and whispered, "It's all right, Hamond. Shh. It's all right."

He rose then, and seemed a different man. Neither of them had to say a word to know what the other was thinking. What had happened would never happen again. They'd secretly cherish the memory and suffer for it too, but could not and would not regret. Hamond sat on the edge of the bed and pulled on his clothes. He didn't turn around when Addy set her hand on his shoulder. He did turn when he got to the door, and though his face was lost in shadow, Addy knew he was smiling and she smiled too.

The smell of Hamond lingered in the warm bed and Addy would think how strange a place for it to be. In the days and weeks to come, she'd feel sinful and guilty, but for the moment she felt nothing but pure and right. She would not think of Mose, or of Hamond, or herself. She would reach for the pillows at the head of the bed, place them under her hips, and sleep that way, not moving an inch until dawn.

Hamond would play that night over and over in his mind. He knew the night Chick was born that the baby girl was his. He also knew that Addy didn't or couldn't see the truth. After Mose and Chick died he dared to dream that one day he and Addy might come together under the same roof and share the same bed. As it was, they shared only their grief. For a long while, that was enough.

Samuel and Simon were sent overseas, but Hamond was too old for the war. When he came knocking on Addy's door early that Sunday morning, she knew something was wrong, and though she hated herself for it, she prayed if it had to be one of the boys it'd be Simon and not Samuel. "What is it, Hamond?"

"Darryl," he said quietly and took his usual chair near the fire.

Addy set the kettle to boil and thanked the Lord the boys were alive. *Poor Olivia,* she thought, then went cold when Hamond said, "I'm moving up to Toronto."

"You're moving up to Toronto?" Addy repeated, thinking if she said it out loud he would see how unthinkable it was.

"She needs me, Addy."

I need you, Hamond, she thought, but had no right to say.

"She's all alone."

I'm all alone, Hamond, Addy screamed in her head. "For how long?"

Hamond shrugged. Addy turned her back to him and watched the flames lick the kettle. "What about the house?"

"Thought you might take over the house. Look after it for me till I get back."

Even as Hamond said this, Addy knew he would never return. "What about the boys?"

"Well, if the Lord's willing, Simon'll go on back to Toronto, likely stay with us a while. I don't know if he's still involved with that woman."

"And Sammy?"

"Never could imagine him out of Chatham, but with Ben gone now . . ." Hamond shrugged again.

Addy knew she could make Hamond stay. She knew she could say she'd only live in the house if he were in it, and only sleep in the bed if he were beside her, and Hamond would tell Olivia he wasn't coming, and she'd be the one left alone, instead of Addy.

As if Hamond could read her mind he began, "Addy, if I thought . . ." But he stopped himself, or rather the look in her eyes stopped him, for he saw there was no hope. Hamond and

Addy both preferred to keep their memories in the butterbox. They could never do that and be together too.

The days and weeks and months passed and Addy felt a decade older than her thirty-two years. It was the weight of her grief and the winter, and the war of course, and as always, her loneliness. Mrs. Yardley and her husband and children had gone to live with her mother on the Prairies, but the Baldwins were still over on William Street and Addy went to see them when she thought she could bear being in the house. She would not pass through the big oak doors though. Instead she climbed the fire escape stairs, stepping around Mr. Baldwin's winter wood and kindling, intent on keeping her memories at bay.

It was Martin Baldwin who gave Addy her first cigarette. "Smoke one, Adelaide," he'd said, "calms the nerves." Addy had taken the cigarette, drawn the smoke into her lungs, and coughed so violently her eyes bulged. Mr. Baldwin had been encouraging. "Don't worry if the first one tastes evil, Child. Second one'll make you want a third."

"Just take in a little, Adelaide. Like this." Mrs. Baldwin inhaled shortly to demonstrate. "When you been smoking longer I'll show you how to draw it right up your nose, but for now, just take in a little. And don't be like Mr. Baldwin here. Just ten or twelve in a day is enough. Mr. Baldwin likes to have thirty cigarettes or so and I believe that's what's killing his appetite."

"Nothing wrong with smoking cigarettes. Keeps a lot of people around these parts in clover. How many tobacco farms we got around Chatham alone? There's Morpeth and Merlin, Tilbury and out to Leamington. There's some near Wallaceburg and Thamesville too. You know who brought tobacco here from the South? You know who showed the landowners how to grow it and cut it and hang the leaves to dry?"

Addy shook her head, watching the smoke curl up and disappear behind the man's yellow eyes.

"Our people, Addy. Negro people brought the know-how from the fields in the South. We brought the skill and we farmed the land. The tobacco in that cigarette you're smoking likely cut and hung by a Negro. I don't care if I smoke fifty cigarettes in a day, I believe I'm keeping my brothers employed."

The tip of the cigarette was glowing orange and Addy had an urge to plunge the thing into her eyeball. Instead, she brought it to her lips, liking how the acrid smoke punished the soft tissue of her throat. She smoked the cigarette down to her fingertip, impressing the Baldwins with her determination.

After a time it became a habit to leave her quiet little house on Degge Street in the evenings and go to the Baldwins' to sit near the fire, smoke, and sing along with the radio, never the phonograph anymore, for they were desperate for news from the front. The Andrew Sisters, Johnny Mercer, Kay Keyser, Harry James and His Music Makers, Nat and Ella and Billie. Addy and the Baldwins knew all the words to all the songs and they knew the arrangements well enough they might have conducted the orchestras too. They didn't talk much most nights. They just sang songs to forget and shrouded themselves in their cigarette smoke, hiding from the rest of the world and themselves.

It had been Mr. Baldwin, after sampling enough of Addy's baking and putting ten healthy pounds on his ailing frame, who suggested Addy for the job at The Oakwood Bakery. He knew a man who worked the bread ovens and that's how he heard about the opening in pastry. The Oakwood was a large operation and supplied bread and baked goods to all of the restaurants in Chatham and neighboring towns, not to mention the hospital and home deliveries. Mr. Baldwin's friend had gone to his boss, then his boss to his boss, with a box of sample pastries Addy'd baked in Mary Alice's unreliable old stove.

She'd been hired without an interview, though she'd heard Mr. Revello, the owner, wasn't pleased to be giving such a good job to a woman. Mr. Revello was even less pleased when she entered the bakery on that first morning. "What you want?!" he'd barked, blowing a whiskey breeze sharp enough to make her eyes water.

"I'm Adelaide. Adelaide Shadd," she said, shocked it was her maiden name that tripped off her tongue. She didn't correct herself right away and so she would be Addy Shadd again, from that moment on for the rest of her life. It was not that she meant to betray Mose, it was just that each time she said "Mosely" or thought "Mosely" she lost Chick and him all over again. "I'm Adelaide Shadd and I'm here for the job in pastry."

Mr. Revello had clearly not been told that Addy was a *Negro* woman and she nearly laughed at the look of horror on his face. She'd been informed that the bakery had a huge order going out that very day and she knew the man had no choice but to hand her an apron and point her to the pastry table. Revello hated women, everyone knew, and Negro women most of all.

The Oakwood had always enjoyed a solid reputation, but with Addy Shadd making pastry, orders doubled in the first two months. The workers showed her how to make the Italian pastry *cannoli* on her first day. Except that it was filled with custard, the sweet was not unlike the raisin horn Laisa'd taught her how to bake when she was barely six years old. Addy quickly took over the pastry department and discarded the bakery's recipes for shortbreads, walnut squares, and butter tarts, replacing them with her own. Her customers' favorite, which she would only make in the fall, was Apple Snow.

Unlike the other women, Addy mostly kept to herself. She found the lunchroom gossip tedious and couldn't help but wonder what all they'd say if they knew the truth about *her*.

Heather was one of the girls who worked in the back. Revello raged at the young woman one day, throwing a loaf of bread at her small red head. "Bastard," she said, and spit.

Addy'd been offended by the round of spit on the floor and scolded, "That ain't a clean thing to do in a food place, Heather."

"Sorry," Heather'd said and stepped on the spit with her boot. "You smell him though? He's pickled. Hope he crashes the truck. If I was his wife I'd kill him. You know he hits her?"

"I don't know that," Addy said.

"You don't see she's got bruises on her arms all the time? Remember last Christmas, the whole side of her face was purple and her eyeglasses cut into her eyelid. Remember? Remember she said she fell on the ice?"

"Maybe she fell on the ice."

"And maybe he beat the devil out of her. Maybe he beats Fiorella too."

Addy shrugged and didn't want to say that she suspected Revello *did* violate his daughter, but not with his fists. She didn't want to say she thought his affection for his daughter was unnatural. And she didn't want to tell what the little girl had recently told her.

"What's the tongue game?" Addy'd asked, already sickened by her suspicions. It was a few days ago. She was behind schedule and quickly, though expertly, shaping fruit-filled crescents to go into the oven. She'd been annoyed, as she always was, by the child's presence.

Fiorella was a coy little girl, and a loathing for women, including her own mother, had been passed down from her father to her. She licked her lips, stuck out her eight-year-old tongue, and said, "My Papa puts out his tongue and I put out my tongue and we touch and it's tickly."

Addy'd hoped the little girl would leave then and not say anymore, for what could Addy do with such knowledge? Instead the child went on, and Addy couldn't shake the feeling she was being taunted. "My Papa puts his tongue here and here too," she said, pointing at her neck and collarbone.

"Mmm-hmm."

"My Papa comes in my bed at night because he loves me more than Mama. He can't help it. I'm his *Bella*. I'm his *baby Bella*."

The mixers were grinding out back, people shouting as trucks came and went, heavy oven doors opening and slamming shut and, somewhere in the distance, Revello was drunk and ranting. Addy said nothing in response to Fiorella's last declaration, no longer hoping but *praying* the child would go away. Fiorella wasn't lying and she knew it.

Fiorella hated to be ignored though, and began to undo the crescent-shaped cookies Addy had so carefully placed on the baking sheet.

"Please don't do that, Fiorella." Addy smiled and ground her teeth.

"You can't tell me don't. You're just a colored lady. My Papa's the owner."

"Mmm–hmm."

"He's your boss."

"Mmm–hmm."

"And I'm your boss."

Addy looked up. "No, Fiorella. No eight-year-old girl is *my* boss."

Fiorella took one of the flaccid cookies off the sheet then, threw it on the floor, and dared Addy to hit her. They stared at each other a full three minutes before Fiorella stomped off to find her father.

As she knew he would, Revello appeared within seconds, looming over the table as she worked. "What you do to my Fiorella? Why you make her cry?" he growled.

Addy saw the child was standing just behind the door, watching her with red eyes and blotchy cheeks. "We're behind schedule. I told Fiorella don't throw my cookies on the floor."

"Fiorella doesn't throw cookies."

"Well I'm afraid she did."

"You don't talk to her no more."

Addy simply looked at him while her fingers continued to form the cookies into moons.

"Don't talk to her no more. You understand? You talk to her again, you gonna be fired," he growled, and waited to see what Addy'd do.

Addy held his gaze and answered him pointedly. "I don't believe I'd have any trouble keeping my mouth shut around Fiorella, Mr. Revello, but your *baby Bella* does seem to like to talk to me. She likes to tell me all sorts of things. Yes, all sorts of things."

The look on Revello's face was one of terror. Addy'd been right in her thinking that "baby Bella" was a *secret* name for Fiorella, and one only expressed in dark, depraved moments. Revello left then, without another word. Some moments after that, she heard glass break in his office and knew he'd thrown something at the window.

Still, that was not the end of it, for how could it be the end of it when Addy was aware the child was being betrayed, and worse by her own father? It had taken nearly a week for Addy to come up with the words. She'd waited till she was sure Revello was gone for the day before she headed to the office where his plump, passive wife was writing in the payroll ledger and counting dollars from a large tin box. "Mrs. Revello?" she'd said, after closing the door behind her. "I need to speak with you, Ma'am."

The woman looked up, then seeing it was Addy, shut the money box quickly and put it on the shelf behind her.

Addy cleared her throat. "Mrs. Revello. This is a delicate thing for me to say. A hard thing for me to say. But a thing I *have* to say because I haven't slept a night since this thing was said to me."

Mrs. Revello turned the pages of the big payroll book and though she still did not look up, Addy knew she was listening.

"Fiorella said a disturbing thing to me. It was a disturbing thing about her Daddy, about Mr. Revello."

Mrs. Revello lifted her face slowly. Her eyes were cold but her chin trembled slightly. "Fiorella makes lies."

"Yes, Ma'am, but I don't think she's lying about this."

The woman waved her arm. "Everything Fiorella lies."

"Yes, Ma'am."

"A husband and a wife gonna argue."

"Yes, Ma'am."

"Maybe sometime we gonna yell."

"What she told me wasn't about you and your husband, Ma'am."

Mrs. Revello folded the ledger and waited. Addy felt queasy and swallowed. "I feel obliged to tell you, Ma'am, that your daughter told me . . . your daughter told me that your husband kisses her in a way don't sound so fatherly. She told me, Ma'am, your daughter told me Mr. Revello sleeps in her bed."

The muscles around Mrs. Revello's mouth went slack and Addy felt sure the woman had no idea of her husband's sins against their daughter.

"It's what she told me, Ma'am."

"Fiorella lies," the woman whispered.

"I'll let you judge that, Ma'am, but I thought you ought to know what she said."

"When?" Her eyes were nothing but pupils.

"Guess it was last week —"

"When he go in her bed?"

"She didn't say, Ma'am. She just told me he sleeps with her."

"No." She shook her head resolutely and seemed ready to dismiss it.

"And she told me they play a game where they . . ." Addy wanted to sit down but didn't. "She told me she plays a game with her father, a game where they touch tongues."

"Tongues?"

To avoid Mrs. Revello's eyes, Addy looked at the wood planks and newspaper boarding up the still-broken office window. When the woman spoke again, her voice was not her own. "When I sleep? When I sleep he go to Fiorella? When I take my medicine?"

"I don't know, Ma'am. I just felt I had to say something."

Mrs. Revello was quiet for some time before she said, "You telling all the bakery this? Addy?"

It was the first time Addy could remember Mrs. Revello using her name. In the nearly six years she'd worked there they'd hardly exchanged a word. When Addy said, "Good morning, Mrs. Revello," her employer usually responded with a grunt or nothing at all. Addy looked into the woman's eyes now, wanting to be believed. "I wouldn't tell anyone such a thing, Mrs. Revello. Only I thought you should know."

The woman nodded, opened her book, and returned to her work. Addy didn't know what to think and wondered if she'd been clearly understood. "Well, guess I'll be getting on home now."

It was one of the bread men who delivered the news of her dismissal the next morning, just as Addy began icing her walnut squares. There was no reason given. There didn't have to be. Addy knew.

It was with no sense of relief that Addy left The Oakwood that day, for she knew her association with the Revellos wasn't over. Because she had not received her final pay envelope and had worked a full week, Addy went to the bakery the following Monday, steeling herself as she made her way toward the office. Mrs. Revello did not look up as Addy pushed through the half-open door. "I'm here for my pay, Mrs. Revello."

Mrs. Revello finally glanced up, silent and contemptuous.

"I worked a full week, Ma'am. You owe me my pay envelope from last week."

"I owe you *nothing*."

"I worked a full week. That's *my* earned money."

"You. Go. Now."

Addy took a breath and closed the door behind her. "Mrs. Revello, I know what I said upset you, and I know that's why you fired me and I guess I'll just have to live with that, but you owe me a week's pay and I'm not gonna stand for you keeping that from me."

The door opened then and Mr. Revello stood, glowering. "Why she's here?" he asked his wife.

"She wants pay."

"No pay."

Mrs. Revello looked at Addy. "Go now. Go. Go! You want I'm gonna call the police?"

Addy glanced at the money box on the shelf behind Mrs. Revello. She felt the urge to lunge at it, take it in the crook of her arm, and run. She felt the urge to run away from Degge Street and Chatham and find another place to live and another person to be. Instead, Addy Shadd lifted her chin and pushed past Mr.

Revello, holding his gaze just long enough to say she knew who he was. The devil closed the door behind her, and though Addy didn't understand their mother tongue, she had a good idea what he was shouting at his wife.

Addy wouldn't sleep that night, or the next or the next. The entire next month, as the Christmas season approached, Addy could not find her way to slumber. She lay still in the bed that was once Hamond and Mary Alice's and looked out the window at the same stars they'd seen. Her thoughts returned to Rusholme and that heat-wave summer night her family had gone to the lake for relief when no one in the little house on Fowell Street could get a wink. L'il Leam and Wallace were knee-deep in the cool water. Addy was stretched out on a scratchy blanket beside her nearly asleep mother. "Mama?" Addy'd said, pointing into the darkness. "That the moon? Mama?"

"Course that's the moon." Laisa was exhausted and annoyed.

"That right there?"

"You know that's the moon."

"Same one from our house?"

"What do you mean, Child?"

"Same moon I see from my window?"

"Course it's the same moon. Close your eyes and go to sleep."

Addy'd shuddered and could not close her eyes. She waited a moment, then whispered, "He follow us here?"

"Mmm?"

"He follow us, Mama?"

Laisa heard something in the tiny voice and turned to face her daughter. "You're not afraid of that big old moon, are you?"

"No, Ma'am."

"Good."

"Yes, Ma'am."

Laisa found her soft cheek in the darkness. "Why you afraid of the moon, Adelaide? How you think he can hurt you?"

"He was out my window before."

"Yes."

"Now he's here."

"Well the moon is always gonna be right there in the sky, Child. That's nothing to be afraid of."

"He gonna be out my window again when I go home?"

"Yes."

"Why he's gotta follow me?"

"He follows everybody. That's what the moon does."

"He gonna follow Daddy out to Mr. Bishop's in the morning?"

"Mmm-hmm. It's still dark when Daddy goes to work."

"He gonna follow Leam to Boy's Group at school?"

"Mmm-hmm."

"He gonna follow me when I get big?"

"Shh."

"Mama?"

"Shh."

"I don't want him to follow me."

"You got no choice in the matter, Adelaide. Now close your eyes and go to sleep."

But Addy couldn't sleep, not then or now. Addy was afraid for Fiorella Revello, and she was obsessed with losing her final week's pay. She was also plagued by the memories of Christmas past and longing for her loved ones. The man in the moon stared down at her, smiling and smug, reminding Addy what Laisa'd told her all those years ago. She still had no choice in the matter.

The streets were dark and deserted, and though Addy'd spent half her life wandering around Chatham, she was afraid this night and could not say why. Twice she'd spun around on her way to the Baldwins, gasping, heart thumping, tracked by a vanishing phantom. "Go away," she'd whispered toward a vacant house surrounded by a thicket of trees. "Leave me alone."

Addy'd been quiet in the little room on William Street and not in the mood for singing. She shook her head when Mrs. Baldwin asked if she was ill. "Have you been sleeping, Adelaide?"

"Not much since The Oakwood I guess." She glanced toward the window, lowering her voice. "When I was coming over here tonight, I felt like . . . I think a person was following me."

Mrs. Baldwin wagged her head. "I told you, Mr. Baldwin. I said Chatham isn't safe any longer. The whole world has gone bad. It's the war. I do believe it's the war."

At the end of the evening Mr. Baldwin offered to walk Addy home, but he was old and ill and the look on *Mrs.* Baldwin's face said it was not a good idea. He seemed relieved when Addy declined, saying it was just a short walk and she'd be fine. She waved as she made her way to the back door and out to the fire escape stairs. The firewood was stored under a musty tarp on the landing and the hatchet Mr. Baldwin used to make kindling sat rusty and dull on top. Addy had never noticed the hatchet placed in that way before, not in all the weeks and months she'd been climbing these fire escape steps. It was a sign, she knew, and though she wondered what exactly she would do with the hatchet if the footsteps followed her again, she snatched the thing up and rested it on her shoulder.

It was possible to reach Degge Street without passing The Oakwood Bakery, and this Addy had done each night since her dismissal. The indirect route meant going by the vacant house and the thicket of trees though, and tonight Addy was more afraid of the footsteps than she was vexed by the injustice done her at The Oakwood. It was at that moment, as she chose one path over the other, that her fear was replaced with something she might have called courage, if she'd been the kind of woman given to self-deception.

The bakers would not arrive until three o'clock in the morning and it was only near midnight. Addy looked into the sky at the wispy night clouds. She decided the man in the moon wasn't so fearsome after all and grinned, challenging him. She felt the weight of the hatchet, swinging it back and forth, recognizing what an unusual thing it was for a person to know precisely what she would do next.

It was quiet and dark as Addy made her way to the back of the big brick building. She dared to think it was the Lord on her side when there was no fierce barking and growling from the old guard dog behind the gate. Addy didn't know that Mr. Revello had beat and killed the animal a few days after she left. Like the broken office window, the dog just never got replaced. The back door would be locked, of course, but Addy would use her hatchet to pry it open and she hoped the wood was just rotten enough to give. The office door would be locked too, but she felt sure a few mighty swings could break the lock and was prepared to hack all night if she had to.

Breaking through the back door was even simpler than Addy'd anticipated. So simple it made her wonder what fools the thieves in town must be not to have got there first. She chose not to wonder about the thieves too much though, for she believed herself righteous and her action not a burglary but rather a recovery.

Except for the mewling cats who skulked in the halls and kept the mice out of the flour bags, The Oakwood Bakery was still. Yet Addy knew, even before she rounded the corner to the office hallway, that she was not alone. It did not occur to her then that the presence she felt was earthly. She imagined only that L'il Leam was there, silently horrified by what she was about to do. Addy set her sights on the office door at the end of the hallway. She swung her hatchet and wondered vaguely at the odor that was climbing up her nostrils.

She reached the office door and took a breath, thinking she heard the sound of a cry. *Go away, Leam,* she thought. *It's my money and I mean to have it.* Now the odor she noticed before was stronger and she knew, burnt. The ovens, she thought. They must have burned a batch today. She drew her hatchet up and again heard something like a cry. This time she did not wonder about Leam and knew it was only one of the hungry cats. She paused to listen for the cry again, then thought to put her hatchet down and try the door, imagining how she'd feel if it was never locked at all.

The doorknob fairly glowed in the darkness. She reached out to turn it and it took some time for her brain to decide that the smooth metal was not icy cold but burning hot. She withdrew her hand, made a fist, smelled the smell again, and knew it was smoke. She had no thoughts after that. At least none of which she was captain. She hacked at the door until she felt it give, then she followed her feet inside the smoke-choked office. The flames ate the walls at the far end of the room. She heard the faint sound of coughing. Addy fell to her knees, her hands searching the floor for flesh and bone. The other hand reached up to save her mouth and nose as she shouted, "Hello! Hello!"

Addy felt the flames licking the drapes behind her. She turned to beat at the fire, not sensing the scorch on her hands. Then she saw the girl lying on the floor, sooty and unconscious. She picked Fiorella up like she was an infant and not a child of eight, slinging her over her shoulder, moving toward the door, coughing and choking. She had a vision of herself then, melting into a puddle, like she was made of wax and had never been human at all. She reached for the door, but a wall of flames exploded before her and she saw in the firelight the bodies of the Revellos. She screamed.

The window was the only way out. Addy reared back, using her foot to kick out the wood planks that had replaced the broken glass. She leaned out her dying head to draw in air. Then she lowered the child from her shoulder to the ground before she climbed out herself and collapsed.

It was described in the *Chatham Daily News* the following day how Adelaide Shadd had saved Fiorella Revello from the fatal fire that killed her mother and father at The Oakwood Bakery. It was described how Adelaide Shadd was a hero and did not mention she'd ever worked there or had recently been fired. It also didn't describe the scarring burns to her hands, which would prevent her from doing common things easily for the rest of her life.

She'd spend the next two weeks in the hospital receiving thoughtful care and decent meals from whites in white. After that she'd go back to Degge Street and let the Baldwins look after her while the bandages remained on her hands. And when the bandages came off and her fingers were pulled tight and mottled white, Addy would cry, thinking of Mose and Chick and Leam and Chester, ashamed that she had survived.

The fire and the deaths were a mystery. Revello had a successful business and a nice family. The fire chief had scratched his head, wondering why the man would have doused the place with gasoline and set them all aflame. He wrote "accidental" on his official report and hoped the surviving child could one day lead a normal life.

Mr. Revello had no relations, so it was Mrs. Revello's brother, Umberto Folo, who would take over the business. Fiorella would erase her father's transgressions, grow up in the loving embrace of her Uncle Umberto and his wife, and become a very different girl than if her parents had lived. Addy was surprised when Fiorella showed up at her door on Degge Street shortly after her bandages had come off.

"Your hands went white," Fiorella said, staring.

"Mmm-hmm. That's from the burn."

"Nearly white as mine," she said, looking from her hand to Addy's.

"Mmm-hmm."

"My Uncle Umberto saved ten newspapers."

"That right?"

"He says only special people get their names printed in the newspaper."

"Special people and criminals, I suppose."

"He says it's a *complish* to have your name in the newspaper."

"You feeling fine then, Fiorella?" Addy asked, wondering how she could find no affection whatever for this saved-from-the-fire child.

Fiorella nodded and went on, peering past Addy to see the place where she lived. "Uncle Umberto says you should save a newspaper so you can show your children someday. Did you save a newspaper?"

Addy shook her head and held the door open with her foot, wondering why the child had come, as it did not appear it was to express her gratitude.

"Uncle Umberto wants you to come in for work tomorrow," Fiorella said, looking at Addy's hands once again.

"Work. I can't work. I don't believe I'll be able to roll a nice dough for a long time, if ever I can again."

"He knows. He said you're scarred for life and not gonna be much good in the pastry department now."

"That right?"

"He still wants you to come. He says he's gonna find some work for you."

"Like sweeping up kind of work? Like cleaning the ovens kind of work?"

Fiorella shrugged and skipped off and never did, and never would, say thank you for saving my life.

It was difficult, the next day, for Addy to fasten the buttons on her blouse with her stiff claw hands, and she felt vaguely foolish walking the few blocks to The Oakwood Bakery. It occurred to her that Fiorella was a mean-spirited child and this all could be a cruel joke. She was relieved when she reached the smoke-smelling building to find that Umberto Folo was expecting her. She was further relieved that he was a pudgy and kind middle-aged man.

He and his bug-eyed young wife had been living somewhere in New York when they got word of his sister's tragic death and had come at once to find they were to inherit the bakery and become custodians of their niece. Umberto took Addy's hands, careful not to squeeze. "You saved the life of Fiorella."

"Yes."

"It is not I can repay you, but to offer you a job."

"Thank you, Mr. Folo."

"Umberto."

"But you see," she said, holding out her paws, not for pity but to be understood, "I can't work the pastry. Not like I used to."

Umberto winced and touched his own heart. "What job you would like, Mizz Shadd?"

"What job would I like?"

"You can't make the pastry, you choose a job you like."

"Choose a job?"

Addy was suspicious, of course, for a Negro woman could not have just any job. She wondered if Umberto realized that with the war over there'd be throngs of men lining up to apply for work at the bakery. "Any job?" she asked.

Umberto smiled. "You like to work the ovens? You like to keep the books? What you like to do?"

The thought came to Addy like a craving, and she said it before she thought it through. "I'd like to drive."

"You like to drive?"

"Yes, Umberto, I'd like to drive. I'd like to sit myself behind the wheel of an automobile and press my foot down on the gas pedal. I'd like to be all by myself and go places too far to go on foot."

"You like to be my deliveryman?" Umberto asked, tilting his head.

"Yes. Yes. I'd like to be your deliveryman."

"You know truck? You know how drive bread truck?"

"No I do not. But I seen a good deal of driving done in my day and I have always wanted to learn."

There were protests at first, for few had seen a woman deliveryman and *never* a colored woman deliveryman, but Umberto was unruffled and told his customers if they didn't like his employees they should find another bakery. All but one or two got used to the idea of seeing Addy Shadd in their stores, restaurants, and homes, hefting boxes of bread and baked goods, trailing the scent of yeast and cigarettes.

Her job as deliveryman for The Oakwood Bakery would see Addy through nearly two decades. She kept up the house on Degge and stayed friendly with the neighbors but didn't get close enough to care. From time to time she'd head over to The Chicken Shack on King Street, mix with the regulars, and watch the young people dance to the jukebox. Mostly she worked and was thankful to occupy her time and mind.

One evening around Christmas, shortly before her fifty-first birthday, Addy'd just finished working a double shift when she climbed down from the truck and found she could not walk a step. Dr. Zimmer took some X rays and gave her some pain medication but said the long hours behind the wheel were stressing her already-troubled hip joint. He told her it was time to retire and that's what she did.

Years later, sitting at the kitchen table in her tiny trailer, Addy could close her eyes and feel the steering wheel. She could see the country farms and city streets, and recall each season of death and rebirth. She could see the people waving from the sidewalk too, for she'd been known to all, though no one knew her. Not until the Lord sent Sharla Cody did Addy realize just how lonely she'd been since Mose. Not until she embraced the child that first time did she realize it had been decades since she'd smelled skin and felt flesh. For the longest time, it had been just Addy and the moon.

Corn

A ddy Shadd was six years old and afraid her brother L'il Leam would die. Wallace was working as a handyman for Teddy Bishop and Laisa couldn't cope with both her sick son and her well daughter at the same time. Teddy had generously suggested Addy could come stay at his house on the lake until Leam had recovered. He said it'd be nice for the twins, Camille and Josephine, what with Addy and his daughters being best friends.

Wallace simply ignored Addy when she whined, "I hate Camille. I hate Josephine. I'm *not* going."

Laisa hastily packed some summer clothes and said, "You remember your please and thank yous at Mr. Bishop's house." She was set to leave the room when she noticed the quiver in Addy's chin. She bent to embrace her daughter, but Leam coughed in the other room and Laisa hurried to his side. The following morning Laisa was still fretting over Leam and forgot to kiss Addy good-bye.

Though she tried, Addy could not avoid the twins in her first few days at the Bishops. They followed her everywhere and watched her every move. She spent most of her time in the big barn, hovering over the crate where one of the cats had recently given birth. In the few weeks since they'd been born, the litter of kittens had grown soft downy coats over their pink wrinkled skin. Their eyes were no longer slits and Addy liked how they'd flick their raspy tongues to lick salt from her fingers and thumbs.

Camille brought the crate out to the front lawn one dewy morning. Addy asked could she hold one of the squirmy things and Camille considered a long moment before she said that was fine. Josephine already had two kittens hanging off her summer blouse and she laughed when Addy reached into the crate and came back not with a kitten but a bloody scratch from its Mama. Camille slapped the Mama cat's head, then tore a gray kitten from her teat and tossed it to Addy like a ball.

The kitten folded up like a curl-bug and cried in Addy's arms. Addy whispered, "Shh. S'all right. S'all right." Truth was she wanted to cry too, for she missed her little house on Fowell Street and had been torn, as such, from her own Mama.

Camille looked inside the wicker basket Mrs. Bishop had sent them out of the house with and announced there was no more jam and biscuits. Josephine looked in the basket too, for she never did believe her sister. Addy hadn't eaten a biscuit or anything else that day but didn't care there was nothing left. She felt sick and sorry because her brother Leam had a fever and her Mama'd be crying and her own front tooth was loose. She pushed at the tooth with her tongue, heard the tissue tear, and tasted blood. She stopped pushing and sucked on the blood, looking back and forth from Camille to Josephine, thinking how with their bigness and their matching summer dresses, they appeared to be four girls and not just two.

Addy brought the kitten to her cheek, stroked its bumpy spine, and wondered at the yellow crust in its eyes. She kissed its slippery nose, and then, because the kitten was still crying, whispered, "You want your Mama? You want your Mama?"

"Give him here, Adelaide," Camille demanded.

"He wants his Mama."

"Give him to me."

Addy handed the kitten to Camille and winced when she held him aloft by the scruff of his neck. "That hurts him."

"Don't neither. His Mama hold him like that in her teeth."

Addy'd seen Mama cats clamp their mouths over their babies' necks before, but she'd never seen a kitten squirm and pedal the air the way the gray one was doing now. She looked out toward the big barn set on the cliff near the lake. She could see Wallace high up on the ladder and she could hear the faint sound of his hammer hitting a nail. "Daddy!" Addy called, though she knew he couldn't hear.

With a short little yawn, Josephine announced she was tired of the kittens hanging from her blouse and tried to pull them off. Addy could see the poor things wanted to be rid of Josephine too, but their claws would not retract and they cried and clung even as they were desperate for release. "Get them off me," Josephine hissed.

Camille dropped the gray cat and laughed when it landed on its back and staggered for refuge under the porch. She reached for the kittens on her sister and yanked until one of them had lost a claw and the fabric of Josephine's blouse was frayed. "Go on," she screeched at the lost babies, and used her foot to guide them under the porch. "Ignorant things," she huffed and settled on the lawn.

Josephine found a place beside Camille and watched her sister select a plump clover flower, pull off a tiny tube-shaped petal, and suck the sweetness from it, sighing like it was a long cool drink of water. Camille watched Josephine do the same and envied her the plumper blossom. Neither wondered when Addy didn't join them and neither cared when the handyman's daughter began an idle stroll toward the barn out back.

Wallace had taken his work shirt off because of the heat and his white undershirt shone against the background of watery blue sky. Addy's mother would be horrified to see her husband in just his undershirt, though secretly she'd be pleased at how clean and bright his was, compared to other working men she'd seen.

"You don't tell your Mama I take off my shirt, understand, Daughter?" Wallace had warned on that first day three weeks ago.

"I know, Daddy."

"And you don't tell your Mama about Mr. Bishop's friends coming around neither."

"The ones with them big automobiles?"

"That's right. Don't be telling her."

"Can I tell Mama when Josephine and Camille get mean on me?"

"No."

"Mama told me I ought to tell her if they get mean."

"Just make her feel bad."

"Makes me feel bad."

"You keep that to yourself, you hear?"

"Yes, Daddy."

"Your Mama's got enough grief these days."

"Leam gonna die?"

"No," Wallace said sharply, like his saying so was enough.

"Can I tell Mama what Mrs. Bishop give me for dinner?"

"Only if it ain't a complaint. And don't say nothing about that shed near the water neither."

"What shed?"

"Never mind, Adelaide. Just don't say nothing about nothing."

The sun was sinking toward the horizon, and though she'd been told never look directly, Addy couldn't help but sneak a glimpse from time to time. The sun watched her, she knew, for her mother had told her so and the Pastor said so each Sunday at church. The sun was the son of the father. The son of the father was Jesus too, but he died on the cross for our sins and whether he'd become that big don't-look-at-it ball of fire in the sky, or that's just where he was living now, Addy hadn't quite figured out. She just knew that he was the light. And the light was the sun. And the son loved and protected them all.

It was hard to get a deep breath on a thick summer day and Addy didn't want to open her mouth too wide lest her loose tooth fall into the grass and get lost forever. She knew her mother would cry if she lost it, for baby teeth, like wedding linen, were to be saved in a box along with pieces of hair from the newly born and newly dead. She inhaled deeply through her nose and was about to call to her father again when out of the corner of her eye she saw a little gray ball. She giggled when she realized it was the kitten and that he had followed her.

She bent down to stroke the kitten but the gray ball rolled off toward the cornfield on the other side of the barn. Addy giggled again and watched the kitten stop and tilt its head at a flitty white butterfly. "Get him," Addy called out. "Get him."

The kitten jumped at the butterfly, swiping and nipping as it flew into the cornfield. Addy laughed and chased them both. "Get him," she called again. "Get him."

Within minutes Addy knew she was in trouble. "Don't you never, never, never go near the cornfield," her father had cautioned her. She'd said, "Yes, Daddy," but the warning had been administered along with a hundred other *don'ts* regarding Mr. Bishop's place, and until she was there, dwarfed by the stalks and crowded by the dense rows, she hadn't considered her father's words.

Addy had often wondered whose wrath was greatest, the Lord's or her father's, and she was afraid of how she might be beaten, particularly in front of Camille and Josephine, if her father caught her emerging from the field now. She scooped up the little gray kitten and turned to go back the way she came. Only she could not see the way she came, for each stalk and each row and each leaf that cut her arm was exactly the same. She stopped, listening for the sound of her father's hammer hitting the nail, but she could hear nothing other than her own heartbeat and the motor-car purr of the kitten clinging to her chest.

With a great sense of relief Addy looked through the slicing green blades and saw a patch of light. She went toward it, reaching the patch and finding only that it was a small area where the cornstalks had mysteriously withered and died. "Never, never, never go near the cornfield," she heard her father say, as she jumped higher than she'd ever jumped before. But Addy could not even begin to clear the cornstalks and it occurred to her she couldn't be seen among them either.

"DA-DDYYYYY!!!" she cried. But there was no answer and no feet running down the row to save her.

"DAAAAA-DDDDYYYY!!!" she cried again and made the kitten cry too.

The field was vast, Addy knew. She'd heard her mother talk about the acreage at the Bishops and wonder at how he was the only farmer in the county who seemed to do well regardless of floods or drought.

"He's a rich man, Laisa. He has other resources," Wallace had said once, meaning it was best not to speculate.

"I suppose we should be grateful we ain't cursed with wealth, Wallace. Harder for a rich man to pass through the gates of Heaven than for a camel to pass through the eye of a needle."

Wallace looked at his wife sideways and whispered, "Likely as not Teddy Bishop gonna buy the gates and fire St. Peter and don't matter if his wife and twins fat as camels."

Laisa had laughed and laughed. Addy thought of Laisa now and wondered if her mother knew never to go near a cornfield.

"DAAAAA-DDDDDYYYYY!!!!" Addy cried once more. But just as she was ready to weep in earnest, something got caught in her throat. She knew by the bloody taste in her mouth, it was her tooth. She gagged and swallowed and thought how it'd be another thing she never, never should have done. But even after she'd been walking for an hour, then two, then three, and was sore and cut and thirsty, she didn't know the true danger of being lost in the corn was that she might not be found before she was taken by the heat.

Parched and exhausted and wishing now she'd wrestled just one jam biscuit from the twins, Addy looked around at the long, same rows and let herself sink to the ground. It was shaded at least, she thought, then realized it wasn't shade but darkness over her head. The sun was making its final dip and she could glimpse the faint pink light in the sky above. "Red sky at night, sailors delight. Red sky at morn, sailors take warn," her mother would say, though Addy couldn't recollect Laisa knowing any sailors at all.

The kitten in her arms had been sleeping for some time and seemed unaware of their peril. Addy placed the animal on her lap, closing her eyes too. She wasn't just tired. She was near ready to give up.

She dreamed then, or at least she thought she dreamed, that she had wings and was soaring high above the corn. She could see everything and everyone, including her mother in their house on Fowell Street. She dreamed she called out, "Mama, I'm here. Look up. I'm here." But Laisa's eyes only left the face of her sick, sleeping son long enough to look at the clock and worry over what it was keeping her husband tonight. Out on the lake, Addy could see a large boat heading toward shore with men loud and drunk and pleased with their day's catch. In the field, she could see Teddy Bishop and two other men with kerosene lamps barrel past the body of a small brown child asleep in the corn.

She could see her father too. He was alone, with a lamp of his own, moving slowly through the rows crying out in a choked voice, "Adelaide? Addy! Baby?! ADDDD-DDDDYYYY!!!"

Addy dreamed that she flew downward, the tips of the corn-stalks tickling her tummy, to see her father's face. Even in her dream Addy felt confused, for it was not anger on Wallace Shadd's face, but fear. "ADDDDD-DDDDYYYYYYY!!!!" he called. And Addy cried back, "Here Daddy! Look up! I'm right here! I'm flying!"

And then, though Wallace did not look up, he stopped and looked down, and there he saw his daughter, curled up with the gray kitten in her lap. He lifted her and shook her gently, whispering, "Baby? Wake up, Baby. Wake up, Addy," until she opened her eyes.

He drew a flask of water from his pocket and brought it to her dry lips. When she drank greedily and wanted more, he knew she would be fine. "Daddy," she whispered. "You see me flying?"

Wallace nodded and hugged her to his chest and wept sound-lessly, for he knew he nearly lost Adelaide and he loved his daughter well.

"I forgive you, Daddy," Addy whispered.

"You forgive me?"

"I know you been waiting a long time to hear it."

"Adelaide?"

"I know you loved me. I know."

"Adelaide?"

Addy cleared her throat and looked down. She saw that her hands were not young and small but old and afflicted. She cleared her throat and looked up and didn't know what to say to Nedda's granddaddy from Detroit City, who was sitting at her kitchen table with a pencil in his hand, asking, "Are you all right, Adelaide?"

"I'm fine. Mmm-hmm. Just fine."

"Sure you're fine?" Earl Bolton looked uncertain.

"Mmm-hmm."

"You seemed to . . ."

"I was daydreaming is all. I was thinking about when I was a little girl."

Earl chuckled to take the chill out of the air. "I do that myself. I do that myself."

"Suppose it's natural, when you know there ain't a lot of forward steps left, to take a few back from time to time."

"Amen to that. What was it you was thinking of, Addy?"

"I was remembering a summer day when I got lost in the corn."

Earl Bolton shook his head, for he understood the dangers of the corn. "Someone leave you in the field?"

"No. I was by myself."

"You said *Daddy*."

"I did?"

"You said, '*I forgive you, Daddy.*'"

Addy looked down at her hands. "I said that?" She cleared her throat as she recovered the memory and the sawdust smell of her father's neck and the strength of his bare arms. "I suppose I do then. Yes, I do forgive my father."

"He didn't leave you in the cornfield though?"

"No," Addy said, and nothing more.

Earl was silent for a long time. He sipped the cold beer Addy set in front of him and drummed the pencil on the table. Addy took a moment, reading the upside-down words on the notepad. She remembered now. She'd sent Sharla to fetch Earl Bolton so he could write out some recipes. She'd been thinking of the bakery and the fire and how she never did teach Chick how to make Apple Snow or walnut squares. She'd been thinking how she wanted the recipes written out so Sharla'd have them after she was long departed.

From the moment she'd opened her eyes that morning, Addy sensed it would be a day to remember. She'd think on it later and wonder about the precise moment everything changed, when the clock started ticking in half-time and there was a slow-motion feel when she turned her head or drew breath. It was still dark when she woke but the flittering birds and fluttering curtains warned her there was a storm coming in from the lake. She closed her eyes and saw the storm approach and didn't fear or hate it, but recognized it was kin to all the other storms she'd ever known.

The bed was warm and the pillow soft and though she didn't want to move her tired old body, Addy shifted to make room, knowing Sharla'd be along any time. When the thunder roared and the lightning struck and a fierce rain assaulted the trailer roof, Sharla did come into her Mum Addy's room to snuggle in beside her and whisper, "I hate that."

"Hate what, Honey?"

"Thunder and lightning."

"Why you hate that?"

Although she knew she could tell Mum Addy anything, Sharla still hesitated. "Sounds mad. Sounds like somebody's gonna get it."

Addy caught one of Sharla's curls in her baby finger and twirled. "I like the thunder and lightning. You know why?"

"Why?"

"My Mama told me about storms when I was a little girl and I happen to know there's nothing mad about it."

Sharla loved when Mum Addy talked about her Mama and waited for the rest.

"My Mama told me lightning happens when new angels get to Heaven and God puts on their wings."

"The wings make a flash?" Sharla asked, her little fingers making an explosion in the air.

"That's right. And the thunder, well that's just the old angels clapping for the new angels."

Sharla rested her head on her Mum Addy's chest, breathing in her scent and wishing away the wheezy sound of her lungs. Together they listened to the storm and wondered fleetingly what lay ahead. After a moment, Sharla asked, "That *really* what thunder and lightning is? What your Mama said?"

"It could be that, and it could be some other things too. Few things got just the one explanation."

"What's the other explanation?"

"I recall something about the cold air meeting warm air and the two not getting on so well. That's a thing you best to ask Mr. Toohey."

"School's nearly over."

"Then we got a whole long summer with you underfoot. Have to get you some new sandals and whatnot." Addy looked out the window and said it again like she hadn't said it at all, "Have to get you some new sandals and whatnot. When Daddy's home next I'll have him take you downtown for your shoes then over to the parlor for some ice cream. Just the two of you. You like that?"

Sharla nodded and waited, but there was no more.

*A*re there more, Addy? Are there more things to write down for this here one on the butter tarts?" Earl Bolton had been careful about his accuracy and penmanship and since Addy had gone off again, he feared she might have missed a crucial ingredient. He imagined Sharla Cody in some kitchen of the future, cursing a recipe she never could get right.

"Just put down that the nuts is optional," Addy said, admiring his commitment.

Earl wrote out loud, "Nuts is optional."

Addy smiled. "I appreciate your help, Earl. I know you come to Chatham to see your daughter. She mind you having a visit with me?"

Earl shook his head and said, "I don't mind if she minds. Fact is *I* mind. I mind her man and I mind the way they're raising my granddaughter and I mind the way she minds me speaking my mind." He chuckled. "Bonita's never too happy to see me."

Addy nodded and glanced out when the sun appeared from behind a cloud. The window was open and Addy realized she could smell the strawberries growing in the nearby field. She wondered why the smell of the berries didn't drown her the way it did every other year. She started back for the answer but Earl Bolton stopped her. "What say we go for a drive, Adelaide?"

"A drive?"

"Sure. We'll get the girls and go for a drive. Lake's nearby, ain't it?"

Addy grinned, thinking of Earl's fine car. "I never rode in a Cadillac before."

Sharla and Nedda didn't enjoy the Cadillac the way Addy did. The backseat was so plush and low that neither could see properly out the window. The girls knew they were heading in the direction of the lake though, and instinct told them the precise moment they passed by the Sweet Freeze. "Maybe we'll get a cone on the way back," Mum Addy said.

They hadn't bothered with swimsuits or towels or a picnic basket so Nedda said it didn't feel like a real trip to the lake. Sharla had never been to the lake before and when that was announced, Addy and Earl just shared a look and hung their heads. Sharla wasn't eager to see the lake and worried, "Ain't the lake *polluted* though?"

Addy, in truth, didn't know. She cleared her throat. "Course not."

"Collette said the lake's *polluted* and there's fish eyeballs all over the sand."

"From time to time you'll find a dead fish in the sand. That's nothing to be afraid of."

Nedda kicked off her sandals, put her dirty toes on the back of the front seat, and was told for the fourth time to keep her feet in her sandals and her sandals on the floor. She slumped and whined, "Why we going to the lake if we can't even swim?"

By the time they left the sky was angry again, and without sun the June water'd be too cool for swimming. Earl and Addy agreed neither had the strength in their old bodies to wrestle a child from the undertow anyway. Sharla and Nedda fought for backseat territory, a hand gaining inches, a foot slipping over the wrong side of the hump. In the end, they retreated to their corners and quietly watched the gray sky above.

It would rain again, Addy knew, and likely hard. Earl studied the clouds too. "Should we head back?"

"Only if you care to."

"I don't mind the rain."

Addy stroked the leather seat beside her and thought she'd never known a chair that loved her back so well. "It's a fine car, Earl."

The lake road was long and winding and so close to the water in some places you could feel the spray when the window was down. In other places there were cottages separating the road from the water. Some were summer places, built new for the well-to-do, and some were old clapboard shacks that were home to poor folks all year long. Some of the dwellings were built up on stilts, protected from the lake and her unpredictable temper.

Sharla climbed onto her knees to look at the houses on stilts when Mum Addy said it was something to see. The child thought it looked like the houses could up and walk away if they had a mind. Nedda said the underneath part looked like a good place to play. Sharla imagined herself crushed beneath the weight of a tired-of-standing stilt house and said she'd rather play with the dead fish in the sand.

The lake road curved and straightened and curved again. Earl drove slowly and deliberately, his gnarled hands clutching the wheel in a way Addy knew they never had in his youth. Even with his glasses, Earl had to squint, and Addy wondered just how long it took the man to drive the fifty miles from Detroit.

When they reached a stoplight, Earl leaned down to turn on the radio. Addy liked the music and the way it masked their silence. For a moment she wished she was young and that Earl might reach across the seat, take her hand, and look at her with soft eyes. She surprised herself with her yearning and was startled when Earl did reach across the seat. He gestured for Addy to look in the back. The ill-tempered little angels were both fast asleep.

It was the first time since The Oakwood that Addy had been on the long lake road and the first time since she was a child that she considered traveling farther along it. They'd set out to see the lake and to look across at the horizon and never said how long they'd drive before turning back for the Lakeview. Earl lost track of the time, but Addy knew by the shifting land and the fragrant air and the quickening rhythm of her own heart that the gold Cadillac had made some decision on its own and was taking them all to Rusholme.

Addy heard it again, as she'd been hearing it all her life. "Rush Home, Addy Shadd. Thou Shalt Rush Home."

Rush Home Road

When the rain finally came, it pounded on the Caddy's roof like it was locked out and mad and somebody better open up *now*. Nedda and Sharla woke, wondering where they were. Addy could barely see through the lacquered windshield and Earl couldn't get the wipers working on fast speed. The road to a town was somewhere nearby, Earl knew, for he could make out a sign to his left, though he was too intent on driving to read the words.

The sign had not been there when Addy was a child. She was troubled to find no sentiment when she read it and she even wondered at its sincerity. WELCOME TO RUSHOLME it said.

Though the air-conditioning was on high, Earl Bolton was perspiring, and it was the first time, inching forward on the unseen road, he allowed that his eyesight might be poor enough he shouldn't be driving at all. He was relieved when Addy reached down to turn off the radio, for he badly needed quiet to concentrate.

Knowing how a woman's voice could grate on a man who's skitty at the wheel, Addy whispered and made it a question. "Should we pull over to the shoulder and wait till the storm passes, Earl?"

Earl didn't say that was just what he was trying to do except he couldn't see the road or the damn shoulder. Instead he said, "I'm fine."

Addy glanced into the backseat. Sharla and Nedda were straining to peer out the back window at a big farm truck speeding up behind them. Addy couldn't see the driver but knew he was young, for who but a youth would risk a life whose value he'd yet to learn?

Earl checked his rearview. He saw the truck and quietly cursed the fool inside. When he turned his attention to the road ahead and saw there was another car speeding toward them, Earl cursed out loud, "Damn."

The truck driver behind them leaned on the horn and flashed the bright lights on and off and on again, saying he would not or could not slow down. The second car was coming just as fast. Earl might have closed his eyes for all he could see as he swerved to avoid being plowed from the rear.

Addy would thank the Lord for many things on that day. The first thanks she would give was that Earl was old and blind and slow at the wheel. Otherwise they might have hit the ditch with enough force to throw the girls through the front windshield. As it was, Nedda was hurled forward and sent crashing into her grandfather's skull. Though neither was seriously hurt, it was no pleasure for Earl to reach back and find a sticky, bleeding wound where the sharp edge of a baby tooth had embedded in his scalp.

When she saw the truck coming up from behind, Sharla'd hidden on the floor and so was spared being thrown anywhere at all. Addy had braced herself against the dashboard. She knew what was coming and only lost her breath, for now. The truck had seen them take the ditch, Addy knew, but the driver didn't stop and come back. After the damage was assessed, the four sat quietly on the plush leather seats and realized the rain had stopped.

"My stomach hurts," Sharla whispered after a time. It didn't really, but she desperately wanted to get out of the car and thought if she said so it might sound like whining.

"Mine too," Nedda huffed. She folded her arms and licked the blood from her lip. "We're supposed to get a cone."

Addy reached into the backseat and squeezed Sharla's hand as Earl turned the key in the ignition. The engine wouldn't turn and for a moment he wished he'd never met Addy Shadd and never offered her a drive to the lake or anywhere. "How far are we from the trailer park?"

When Addy didn't answer he looked at the road sign behind him. "Rusholme," he said quietly. "Why's that sound so familiar?"

Addy gestured at the ignition. "Try again, Earl."

Sharla held her breath. Rusholme. Could it be the same place? She looked around at the wet green fields and the gray-blue lake and the quiet road to town. Was this the place where Mum Addy and L'il Leam were born? And where they saw the crickets, and had the church suppers, and watched Laisa in the kitchen making Apple Snow? Was it truly the place from the stories, the ones Mum Addy never even knew she told?

Earl cleared his throat. "How far we outta Chatham?"

Addy shrugged. "Too far to walk."

Earl mumbled and opened the car door, slamming it into the muddy ditch. "Damn. Damn."

Addy didn't care Earl was cussing, for she'd have done the same. She slid out the driver's side door and helped the girls get out the back. They looked at the surrounding fields and trees like they were in some faraway land and had never seen either before.

Earl's fine leather shoes squished as he slid up the bank of the muddy ditch. He looked at the sign again. "Welcome to Rusholme. Welcome to the damn middle of damn nowhere."

Addy nodded and didn't say that a mile or so past that clump of trees was the church and cemetery. And she didn't say that just a ways down the other road was the town and old Fowell Street. And she didn't say if they continued on a bit they'd pass Teddy Bishop's, and that way there they'd find the school. Addy held her breath a moment and wondered if any of the places still existed. She wasn't sure what to hope for.

There was a green smell that rode on the wind and snuck up Addy's nose, making her turn her head. The crick, she recalled, was just beyond those bushes. She closed her eyes, remembering the crick and the lake and the church and her house and she was puzzled why nothing was as she thought it would be. Addy'd thought often of her return, but she imagined it'd be tormented and sorrowful. Instead, here she was in Rusholme, and it just was.

Like a dream, Addy thought, *when you're facing down the devil and you're hardly even scared.*

Earl found a long stick and used it to wipe the clumps of mud from his shoes. Sharla and Nedda found sticks too but didn't bother about their mucky sandals. A few fat worms had struggled up from the earth and writhed, unsuspecting, in the gravel. The worms could never have foreseen that two little girls would take such pleasure in halving them with wood-stick swords.

"Leave them worms alone, girls," Mum Addy scolded and went to join Earl.

Earl used his stick to point at Rusholme Road. "That way there looks like the way to town. Imagine they have some kind of body shop or towing service. Could just wait here I guess." He focused on the long lake road. "Someone ought to be along."

Addy nodded and called back over her shoulder, "Come on, Sharla, Nedda." But the girls did not appear. Addy turned around. The girls were gone. *The water,* she thought, and hurried through the bushes. She was relieved to see the pair had not drowned in the swollen crick. "Girls!" she called, but they pretended not to hear.

"Girls!" Addy shouted again. Nedda was accustomed to being asked to do a thing four and five times. She stood there, poking at a clump of wet leaves, looking at something nearby.

Addy tramped through the wet bushes. "Nedda Berry. You come when I say come, you understand me?"

Nedda nodded absently and pointed to the yellow-and-black sign posted on a tree. "What's that say, Mizz Shadd?"

Addy turned to look. "That says 'Private Property. No Trespassing.'" She glanced around.

"What's trespassing?" Nedda asked.

"That's being on land that don't belong to you. That's what we're doing now. Trespassing on someone else's land. Let's go now."

"Who the land belong to?"

"Not us."

Nedda looked around. "I don't see nobody."

"Mmm-hmm."

"There ain't no house."

"You don't have to live on land to own it."

"How they know we're here then? How they know we're trespassing?"

"They just do, Nedda."

"What happens?"

"They don't like it."

"They kill you?"

Addy huffed and grabbed Nedda's hand. "Come on, Child. We got to find somebody to fix your Granddaddy's car."

"Mu-um . . . ?" Sharla called from behind a clump of bushes. "Look at this here. What's it say?"

Addy dragged Nedda through the bushes, her patience all used up. "Sharla Cody, if you —"

Addy stopped, seeing the thing Sharla was pointing at, and felt her stomach rise in her throat. She let go of Nedda's hand.

"What's it say, Mum?"

Addy opened her mouth but did not speak. She approached the thing slowly, like it was a hurt dog and she feared it might run away. The look on her face was one Sharla'd never seen before and it frightened the little girl.

Nedda stabbed the ground with her stick. "Mizz Shadd? You said we better go, Mizz Shadd."

But Addy couldn't hear the child, for she was staring at the thing, wondering now if the whole day, the storm, the lake road drive, returning to Rusholme, if it was all just a dream.

Sharla pointed. "How come there's only one, Mum?"

Addy brushed away the leaves and branches so she could read the words.

Nedda rolled her eyes. "Because this ain't a cemetery, Dummy."

"If this ain't a cemetery why's it here though?" Sharla shivered as she watched her Mum sink to her knees to touch the words on the gravestone before her. "What's it say? What's it say, Mum Addy?"

Nedda shrugged and pointed at the slab of stone. "Maybe he was *trespassing*. Maybe he got *killed* for it."

It might have been a moment or it might have been an hour before Addy rose and turned and found her voice. "We better be getting on, children."

Sharla dared not ask again what the gravestone said. Addy could not have told her anyway, for she could not believe the inscription in the gray granite, which read:

> *Shed not for me your bitter tears*
> *Nor give thy soul to vain regret*
> *'Tis but a casket lying here,*
> *The gem that fled it glitters yet.*
> CHESTER MONK
> *Born 1907–Died 1973*

Addy climbed toward the road, not sure and not caring if the girls were behind her. She was no longer anxious about Sharla and Nedda's safety, for she was certain now she was in a dream, and in her life, only the things she *never* dreamed came true. She did wonder though, as she watched Earl chat with an older man who'd stopped his pickup truck by the side of the road, if it was a daydream or a night dream. She preferred a night dream, of course, for then she would wake in her bed and it was just steps to the kitchen and a cup of hot coffee. But the daydreams frightened her because she never knew where she would wake or who she might be with or what she might have said. Wake in bed, she told herself. Wake in bed and know, because dreams are not true, that the sun will be shining and it will not storm today.

Earl waved when he saw Addy emerge from the bushes and didn't look worried she'd been gone so long. Nedda and Sharla ran up to the truck and told Earl about the no trespassing sign and the grave near the crick.

Addy approached the truck smiling, for even in her dream-world she understood the importance of friendliness and good manners. Earl gestured at the man in the truck, telling Addy, "Fella here says the man who owns the body shop gone until tomorrow morning. He thinks he can help me rig up a tow though. Least we can get her out of the ditch and see what all needs doing."

Addy nodded and hardly cared, since the Caddy wasn't really in the ditch and she not really here in Rusholme, and Chester Monk not possibly in that grave dead at sixty-six and not sixteen.

The man in the truck glanced at Addy, then looked again, hard this time, for there was something familiar in her face. Addy looked twice at the man too. She remembered him. It was his nose, the profile of his chin. Had he been on the bread ovens at The Oakwood? No. She remembered now. She'd seen him at The Satellite Restaurant on the night of Mrs. Pigot's accident.

The man looked at her sideways. "Addy Shadd?" he asked. "Are you Adelaide Shadd?"

It being a dream, Addy was set to shake her head no, for she couldn't be sure who she was just now. Earl looked surprised and asked, "You know each other?"

The man grinned and wagged his finger. "Yes. Yes. I saw you at The Satellite in Chatham a while back and I told my wife I couldn't place you but you looked awful familiar. Then driving home it hit me. That was Addy Shadd. That was my old neighbor, Addy Shadd."

In the way a person could flip through snapshots, Addy looked at the man and saw him as a boy bent over his reader at school. And she saw him in the yard next door, helping his Mama hurry the washing off the line before it rained. She saw him again, his face twisted and angry, launching chestnuts at her as she cowered on her front porch. "Isaac Williams," she said, and knew she was not dreaming, day, night, or otherwise.

Earl turned to Addy, puzzled. "You lived in this town?"

Addy nodded. "Grew up on Fowell Street. Right next door to the Williams."

Isaac nodded too and pretended not to recollect how and why she left. "That's right. We were neighbors."

Earl thumped on Isaac's truck. "Well how's that for a coincidence?"

Isaac laughed. "In a town small as Rusholme we don't call it coincidence. We just call it life. You're bound to run into someone you know when you know everyone." He turned back to Addy, asking casually, "What brings you back to Rusholme, Addy?"

Earl answered for her. "We thought to take a drive on the lake road and just never kept track of the time." He didn't mind the nostalgia except that there was the matter of rescuing his fine car from the ditch. "You say you think you can rig up a tow?"

Isaac gestured at the cab of his truck. "Got room for one of you up front here. Not such a comfortable ride in the back but it's mostly dry, and I'll drive slow. We can go back to my place and get some rope for a hitch while you ladies have a visit with my wife."

Earl couldn't picture himself sitting in the back of the old truck and didn't much want to leave the Caddy alone. "I'll wait here."

Nedda giggled and squirmed as Isaac lifted her up into the truck, but Sharla was quiet and serious. She'd seen the change in Mum Addy, from dreamy confusion to just plain confusion, and she wondered what the rest of the visit to Rusholme would bring.

The truck motor purred and the tires hummed on the wet pavement, but none of it seemed real. Addy sat quietly in the passenger seat thinking, *Yes, look at the strawberry fields dotted with plump red fruit. And over there, that army of young cornstalks. No one'd believe they'd grow taller than the tallest man in just a few weeks. And the old brick homes and the closed-by-the-rain fruit stands and the wide blue lake beyond. Yes. Rusholme. Yes.*

The truck rounded a curve and the church, preserved by the Lord and the generous donations of parishioners, appeared before them. Addy heard herself say, "Mind stopping, Isaac? Just for a moment?"

Isaac figured, rightly, that she wanted to visit her dead in the cemetery and he turned into the church parking lot like that had always been their destination.

Sharla and Nedda were told to stay in the back of the truck and they didn't mind. Neither was interested in the gravestones, and Sharla didn't want to see her Mum looking strange-eyed like she had before. Nedda amused herself with the stick she'd brought along. Sharla tried to ignore the prickly sensation at the nape of her neck.

Isaac helped Addy out of the truck but did not accompany her beyond the willow tree to the edge of the yard. He wondered briefly if she knew her mother'd gone down South and it was only Leam and her Daddy in the ground there now.

"Leam . . . ? Leam . . . ?" Addy called out silently. "Leam . . . ?" But he did not come. In all the years she'd known him, she hardly ever had to call Leam twice. He'd always been there, watching over her shoulder, just like he promised when they were children that first time he rose from the dead. A chill ran through Addy, for she didn't know what it meant that he was gone. She looked at the gravestone of her brother and, beside that, her father. She closed her eyes, remembering how they all once were, in the little house with the matching lace curtains.

This was something else she'd not expected. She'd longed to return to the cemetery to stand at Leam's stone again, but the thing seemed now not a dwelling, but just a stone. And looking at her father's grave, she felt not remorse or anger, just a little sad it'd taken so long for her to find forgiveness. She turned back to see Isaac Williams and the girls waiting in the truck. She whispered a good-bye, just in case anyone was listening, then, breathing in the scent of the lake, found her path back through the wet green grass.

In the truck again, with Isaac quiet and uncertain beside her, Addy watched for the landmarks. She pointed at the big house on the cliff. "Still there. Kept up nice too."

"Bishops?" Isaac said. "Oh sure. Teddy died years ago, of course, but Jonas and Camille kept it going till they passed on and now their son, my brother-in-law in fact, lives there with his wife and little one."

Addy looked at the big house, remembering. She heard what Isaac said like an echo and inquired, "*Camille* and *Jonas?*"

Isaac glanced at her, surprised she didn't know. "Jonas Johnson. Sure. Him and Camille got married young. Weren't you still around?"

Addy shook her head.

"He was bootlegging for Teddy over to Sandwich for a time, but then he came home. They always do."

"I suppose they do."

Isaac turned to look at her. "This can't be your first trip back to Rusholme."

"Mmm-hmm."

"But you been living in Chatham all this time? Since you left?"

"Mostly. Mmm-hmm. And out at the Lakeview."

Isaac didn't ask why she hadn't ever come back when she lived so close. He had a good idea why. Though he was younger by six years, Isaac knew the story of Addy Shadd like a parable from the Bible. He'd told the story to his wife, Rochelle, that night after dinner at The Satellite. Isaac also didn't ask why Addy was return-ing now, even though it seemed unlikely she and that man Earl just been driving and lost track of the time like he said. Isaac believed there was a reason for all things.

"What happened to Josephine, Isaac? She stay in Rusholme?"

"She got married off to a friend of Teddy's down in Chicago. She never had children, but she had some fine fur coats and liked to lord that over Camille. She came back about fifteen years ago, for Camille's funeral. She was skin and bones. Like a skeleton. You wouldn't have guessed it was her."

Addy thought of that Strawberry Sunday when she was fif-teen years old and Chester Monk broke her heart by asking Camille Bishop for a stroll. She mused, "Jonas Johnson and Camille Bishop. Jonas and Camille. I suppose they had a number of children?"

"Just had the two, actually. Rochelle, my wife, she was the first, then her brother, well he came along as a surprise, many years later. Some thought it a little . . . well . . . what with Camille being gray and Jonas so sick with the diabetes. Rochelle's been more a mother than sister really."

"Rochelle, that's your wife. That's Camille and Jonas's daughter?"

"That's right."

Addy wagged her head. "It's a small world, just like they say."

Isaac shrugged. "It's Rusholme."

As they drove, Addy wanted to beg Isaac to slow down, to let her out so she could walk, to stop the earth from turning altogether, for even though it was slow motion, time was still moving much too fast. Addy hadn't known she would say it until the words were already in the air. "Did I see Chester Monk's grave down by the Rusholme crick?"

"Chester? Oh yes. He came back here, when was that? Not so long ago. Sometime in the early sixties, I believe."

"But I thought . . . it was said that Chester drowned in the Detroit River."

"It was said wrong. Chester came back fit and fine. He'd been living down the States some place. His wife passed on and I guess he just longed to come home. He did well for himself. Built that big house for his daughter's and his grandchildren's summer visits. You see the place?"

Once Addy began to shake her head she could not stop. Chester had lived? Chester had *lived*. Not only had Chester lived, but he'd lived *here* for years, just miles away on Lake Erie, until not so long ago.

Isaac misunderstood Addy's puzzlement. "Oh it's hard to see all right. Pretty secluded back there with the trees and all. Nice house though. And when he died, well, he wanted to be buried near the crick instead of the cemetery."

Addy felt heat in her cheeks, remembering Chester and their youth and the things she'd thought about him and the way she'd planned for their future. She whispered to Mose in her heart, "Don't be mad, Mose. You're my true love, but he was my first."

Addy didn't know she was grinning until Isaac asked, "What? Something funny?"

"No," Addy said. "Just a little strange to be here after all this while. I believed Chester drowned with my brother. I'm glad to know he didn't and that he had a wife and children who loved him."

Isaac slowed down as they came into the town. "Few of the old houses left, Addy." He knew what she was thinking. "Yours is gone. Ours next door too. They got a museum going up on the Fowell block where we used to live."

"A museum? That right?"

"Government's designating Rusholme as a historical sight and putting up a museum dedicated to the Reverend Mills and the original settlers."

Addy nodded, impressed, and thought of what Verilynn Rippey'd snidely said all those years ago about how someone should write a book about Rusholme.

"Earl your husband?" Isaac asked.

"Earl? No. No. He's just a friend."

"You ever marry, Adelaide?"

"Yes. Yes, I did. I married a good man called Mose. He died some time ago."

"I'm sorry."

Addy nodded.

"And children . . . ?" Isaac asked. He'd known for sure about the one.

Addy couldn't tell him about her sweet baby Leam or explain how her beloved daughter Chick had died with her father. She smiled sadly and shook her head. Then she remembered suddenly, "Birdie? What about Beatrice Brown?"

Isaac laughed. "Birdie Brown? Well she taught school here for about a hundred years. She taught my children and their children and we all thought she'd go one more generation but she retired down to Florida last year."

"Married?"

"Never."

"Never?" Addy couldn't believe it, until she remembered the way Birdie had loved her good brother Leam. Addy was still thinking of Birdie when Isaac pulled into the driveway of a modest brick home. His wife, the woman Addy'd seen before in the restaurant, came out the door at once, curious about the strangers in her husband's truck. She recognized Addy right off and smiled in that easy way a person does when they want you to know they'd never judge.

Up close, the resemblance between Rochelle Williams and her mother, Camille, was uncanny. Addy had the sense she was being greeted not by a stranger, but a grown-up friend from her past, one ripe and sweetened with time.

"This is my wife, Rochelle. Rochelle, like you to meet Addy Shadd. You remember, I told you about her after we —"

"Of course." Rochelle Williams took Addy's hand, looked into her eyes, and scrunched her nose. "I know. I look just like my mother. I've heard it all my life."

"I bet you have."

"Thank the Lord I took after my mother and not my Aunt Josephine."

Addy nearly laughed, for Camille and Josephine were identical twins, but she saw Rochelle Williams was not joking.

Isaac went to find his rope as Rochelle caught sight of the suddenly shy little girls in the back of the truck. "Well who do we have here?"

Sharla and Nedda looked up, guilty.

Addy smiled. "That's Sharla there, and that's her neighbor friend, Nedda."

Rochelle smiled warmly but looked twice at Sharla Cody, like she was trying to decide something. After a moment she said, "Well, I happen to have some cookies just out of the oven." She turned to Addy, explaining, "My three-year-old nephew's coming over and he doesn't get cookies at home. Not fresh baked anyway." She smiled at the girls again. "You girls like a cookie?"

Nedda clapped her hands. "Yeah!"

Sharla checked in with Mum Addy and waited for the nod before she said, "Yes please, Ma'am."

The women settled at the kitchen table where they could see Sharla and Nedda through the big picture window. The girls were in the backyard munching cookies and taking turns on a tire swing hung on the limb of a huge old maple. Addy prayed the girls wouldn't start fighting and embarrass her. She listened, genuinely interested and not a little envious, as Rochelle described her children and grandchildren. "And of course there's little Otis. He's my nephew, but he's like my grandson. I couldn't say whose block he was chipped off, my brother or my sister-in-law, since they're both a trial, but he's a darlin', my little Otis."

"Is your brother's wife from Rusholme?"

Rochelle shook her head and poured black coffee into large mugs. "Windsor." She lowered her voice. "She's white. But she's all right. Not, well, not, you know, but she's all right."

Addy understood what Rochelle meant and nodded. She wondered out loud how things were progressing with Isaac and Earl and the Caddy in the ditch.

Rochelle rose to tend to the big pink ham in her oven. "We got plenty of room to put you up for the night."

"Oh thank you, but we'd never impose."

Rochelle basted her ham without turning around. "You'd do the same, wouldn't you? So if they can't get the car tonight, you'll stay over and take care of things in the morning."

The women sipped their coffee and watched the girls swing on the tire. The front door opened and the sound of a screaming youngster pierced the quiet. The child ran bawling into the kitchen and into his aunt's waiting arms. Rochelle kissed the head of dark curls and whispered, "What's wrong, Darlin'? What is it?"

The boy extracted his face from his aunt's ample bosom just long enough to point a dirty finger at the pretty young white woman who'd followed him in. He opened his mouth and unleashed his vitriol, but no one in the room could make out a single word. The young woman set a casserole dish of baked beans on the stove and plopped down in a chair after nodding to Addy, something between a greeting and an apology.

Rochelle spoke over the crying boy's head. "Addy, this is my brother's wife, Tracy Johnson. And this here is Otis, but I still don't know what's wrong with my baby? Do I?" She held him close.

Tracy offered her hand and said, "Sorry about the noise, Addy. We told our son he couldn't play with his daddy's jackknife. He hates us."

"I hate you!" Otis confirmed.

Tracy rolled her eyes. "Sorry, Rochelle. He didn't go down for his nap this aft'. He's been a bear. And," she added loud enough to be heard over the crying, "if he doesn't shape up we're going straight back home."

Little Otis turned again and wagged a finger. "No."

"Don't tell me no, Otis. A little boy does not tell his mother *no*." Tracy meant business and Addy liked her for it.

The man who entered the kitchen next was Rochelle's young brother. He was average height but had considerable girth and the same round face of his father, Jonas Johnson. Addy stared. There was something familiar about the young man, something more than his resemblance to his father. It was his build, his walk, the way he looked at her. She knew him. Had he been at The Satellite that night and she'd forgotten? Did he deliver her groceries? She studied the young man, wishing her mind was young again.

Rochelle's brother smiled and nodded to Addy like it wasn't strange to see her there staring at him.

Rochelle squeezed her brother's shoulder. "Addy Shadd, this is my brother, Cody."

"Mizz Shadd," he said warmly, and extended his arm.

Cody? Addy's hand stopped in midair. *Cody?* Suddenly, she saw it — the same eyes, hidden between fleshy cave of lid and cheek, the same crooked smile, the same walk, the same talk, the same splayed legs. She didn't know what to do or what to say, for how could she ask this stranger, whose acquaintance she just made, if he ever knew a girl named Collette and if the child playing out back on the tire swing could possibly be his daughter?

Addy Shadd was old and confused and wrong, of course. She had to be wrong, for it would be most unlikely to find Sharla's father when she wasn't even looking, in a place she'd never considered. Then again, her whole life had been made up of unlikely occurrences. She shook Rochelle's brother's hand and told herself stop staring.

Cody didn't stay long. When he heard about the Caddy in the ditch, he'd gone off to see if he could help. Addy would have put the resemblance out of her mind right then and there had not Tracy Johnson herself looked out into the yard and remarked on there being something familiar about Sharla.

Otis had asked to go play with the girls and Tracy said that was fine with her if that was fine with the girls. Nedda wasn't pleased to see the little boy, as it meant sharing another turn on the swing, but Sharla didn't mind and told Tracy, "He can take my turn."

Tracy saw that her son was in good hands before she returned to the kitchen, asking, "Who's that little girl?"

Addy knew she meant Sharla. "That's Sharla."

"She from Rusholme?"

Addy shook her head. "She lives with me at the Lakeview."

"She looks familiar."

Rochelle nodded. "I thought the same thing."

"You her Gramma, Addy?" Tracy asked.

"We're not blood related, but she's mine, much as anyone can be anyone's."

"Amen," Rochelle said.

"Where's her mother?" Tracy asked, her eyes on her laughing son.

Addy sighed and hesitated, then leaned back in the chair and told the women the story of Sharla. She told them how Sharla's mother came around her trailer that day asking a stranger to take in her own daughter. She told them what Sharla told her about Emilio and Claude and the others. She told them about Collette's letter, and how she knew she wasn't ever coming back. And finally she told the women how she worried about who'd take Sharla when she was gone.

"Well, Addy, you got a long time to worry about that," Rochelle said.

Tracy shook her head. "I can't imagine a mother just *leaving*. Poor thing. Poor little thing."

"What about the child's father?" Rochelle asked, just as the three men came tromping through the front door.

Addy was close to telling the women that all she knew about Sharla's father was his name was Cody, and that until today she'd always figured that was his *last* name. And she was close to asking didn't they think Sharla Cody bore a striking resemblance to Cody Johnson. She almost declared, *The Lord moves in mysterious ways,* as she thought how Poppa would have said it must have been Heaven, and not Earl Bolton, that brought them to Rusholme today. She was glad the men came home and interrupted though, for she realized what she was thinking was only wishful and certainly not a polite thing to bring up in conversation.

Earl was grateful to Isaac and Cody for their help, but Addy could tell from his face that his Caddy was still in the ditch. Earl figured it didn't make much sense to get a drive back to the Lakeview, then back again in the morning, and was grateful for Isaac and Rochelle's offer of a bed for the night. "Besides," Earl said, "it'll give Adelaide here a chance to talk about old times." Addy smiled at Earl and was glad for his friendship.

Over a dinner of honey ham, baked beans, and fresh green peas, Sharla watched her Mum Addy, troubled by the look on her face and the way she was staring at Otis's father. Sharla was even more troubled when she looked at Otis's father and found *he* was staring at *her.* She planned to tell Mum Addy about that later when they were alone. For now, she smalled her eyes at Cody Johnson and made him look away.

Isaac Williams was remembering the cold spring nights when the children would head down to the lake with nets and lanterns to scoop the running smelt. He recalled the time that Birdie Brown had felt so sorry for the caught fish she'd cried and Li'l Leam promised he would never eat a smelt again. Isaac wondered out loud if Li'l Leam kept his promise. If Addy had been paying attention, she would have told Isaac that her brother did keep his promise, as he kept all promises in his short life.

If she'd been listening, Addy would have laughed to hear Rochelle say her mother'd been shocked to find crates of liquor buried out near the barn after her father's death. Addy would have told Rochelle that Camille must have been the only person in Rusholme who didn't know Teddy Bishop was a bootlegger. As it was, all Addy could do was stare at Cody Johnson and pray that what she suspected was true.

It was the longest day of the year. The adults would brave the backyard bugs that evening and wonder at how it could be nine o'clock at night but still bright as afternoon. They would wonder about many other things that night too.

As the sun spilled her amber light into the big kitchen window, Cody Johnson gestured across the table at Sharla and inquired of his wife, "Do we know Sharla from somewhere?"

Tracy didn't tell him that she and Rochelle'd thought the same thing, for just then Otis spit a mouthful of peas across the table and Nedda begged, "Do it again!"

Tracy shook her head. "No. NO. Otis Johnson, we *do not spit* at the table."

Otis stuffed another green spoonful into his mouth. Tracy didn't look at him. "No one thinks you're funny, Otis."

Otis turned to Sharla and Nedda. The girls hid their grins and Tracy said, "Look how nice Sharla's eating. See how nice Sharla's manners are?"

Sharla decided to be helpful. "See, Otis? See how I put the peas in my mouth, then I chew with my mouth closed. See?" She chewed and swallowed. "No spittin'," she added sternly.

"No spittin'," Otis repeated and all the adults laughed in that unpredictable way they could.

Addy'd been watching Cody watching Sharla and she didn't know what to say or how to say it but something had to be said. "Sharla lives in Chatham with me. I'm her guardian." Addy paused. "Since her mother's been gone."

Cody nodded and returned to his food. Addy willed him to look up again. He stared at Sharla. "Something's so familiar about her."

She looks like you, Addy screamed in her head. *She looks just like* you. Earl must have heard her silent scream, for just then he remarked to Cody, "She looks like you, Son."

There was silence at the table as they all looked back and forth from Cody to Cody. Rochelle saw it next, then Tracy, and finally Cody himself. When the resemblance was considered, it was arresting.

Addy cleared her throat and didn't know what all would happen when the truth came out, if it even was the truth. "Funny thing, Sharla's last name is Cody. How's that for a coincidence?"

Sharla looked around the table and, because they were all staring, felt obliged to say, "My last name is Cody because my father's name is Cody."

Tracy was watching her husband keenly now, for something had occurred to her when she saw Sharla sitting alongside Otis at the dinner table. A thought had crossed her mind, one she'd brushed away like a bothersome fly, that the two could be brother and sister.

Cody Johnson couldn't take his eyes off the girl now. He knew, or seemed to know, before Tracy asked the question. "What's your mother's name, Sharla?"

Sharla looked around the table. Everyone was watching her, waiting. Earl and Isaac looked confused, but the women, even the two who couldn't know, seemed to know what she would say.

"Collette," Sharla answered in a tiny voice, in case anyone was mad. "My mother's name is Collette Depuis."

Cody did not drop his fork or his jaw as Addy thought he might. He simply nodded and returned to his dinner. Tracy smiled tightly at Addy and Rochelle and picked up her fork. Then she set her fork back down without taking a bite and rose from the table, scraping her chair.

When Cody rose seconds later and followed his wife into the living room, Addy and Rochelle had a good idea what he was going to tell her.

Earl Bolton shook his head, pierced a slice of ham with his fork, and remarked, "Funny them both being Codys," without a trace of awareness.

Home

*A*ddy *Shadd could not sleep that night.* The bed was comfortable but the house unfamiliar and too quiet and dark. She rose, tied the housecoat Rochelle had given her snugly around her waist, and padded down the hall to look in on Sharla.

Sharla and Nedda were asleep in the bunk beds the Williams kept for their grandchildren. Addy moved quietly into the room and eased herself onto Sharla's bed. Though she wanted to wake her and kiss her damp cheek, she knew it was best to let the little girl sleep. She watched Sharla's chest rise and fall, and knew when her brow knit and her lips strained that she was struggling to win some battle in her dream. *There will be more battles,* Addy thought. *That's just what is.*

Addy tried to remember the words to the song her mother used to sing. *Sleep Child,* was all she could recall. *Sleep, Sharla,* she thought. *And know that you are loved. Fight your dream demons and judge not and find joy living simply and simply living. I'll always be here,* Addy whispered silently. *I'll always love you.*

It was a cool night. The sky was cloudless and the moon and stars lit the Rusholme sky like they never could in Chatham. Addy wondered if she would wake the whole house if she tried to step outside to take the night air. The door creaked a little, but no one inside stirred as she made her way, barefoot, out to the lawn.

If someone had seen her standing there, watching the sky as she was, they might have thought she was crazy, but if they'd ever done such a thing themselves, they'd know what she was looking for. There were no cars on the roads, no lights in the homes, and Addy thought how pleasant it would be to take a little walk around the town in her housecoat and bare feet. It wouldn't be a proper thing to do, of course, but Addy didn't care anymore what was proper.

When she reached Fowell Street Addy was puzzled, for Isaac had said the house was gone and there it was, the rocking chair on the front porch and the apple tree out back and the tea-stained lace curtains in all the windows, looking just right from the street. Addy nodded when she realized she was dreaming and was only glad to see her home again. She did hope her Mama and Daddy would not intrude on her dream though. She mostly just wanted to rock in the chair and think her thoughts about Sharla Cody and Cody Johnson and what tonight was going to mean to them all.

Addy settled into the chair and remembered the last time her body felt the rocker, and her eyes saw from the porch, and her heart had been broken by the betrayal of all those she loved. But tonight she didn't feel sorry or sad. She even changed her mind and wished her Mama and Daddy were inside the dream house and might come on out and talk as they did, about the neighbors, or the weather.

When the front door opened, Addy wasn't surprised to see L'il Leam there in his nightclothes. He looked as he'd looked the last time she saw him, small and spry and grinning. Addy giggled and felt like a child again herself.

"What are you doing out here, Sister?" he whispered.

"Just dreaming, Leam. And rocking. Just sitting here catching a little breeze."

Leam nodded and studied the sky. "You still scared of the moon, Adelaide?"

Addy thought about that for a moment. "No. Right now, I don't feel scared of anything atall."

"You know Sharla's gonna be fine, don't you?"

Addy surprised herself when she answered, "Yes. Yes, I do know. Cody Johnson's a good man. And that wife of his, she could love any child, you can see that."

"Sharla'll have a brother. She'll like that."

"Mostly she'll like that," Addy teased. "Sometimes she'll wish she was a only child." Addy turned her face to the moon and inhaled deeply before she realized she hadn't done so in many years. "That old butterbox is in my closet. There's the photographs of Hamond and the boys and there's Poppa's ring and that curl of baby Leam's hair and Chick's first shoes and a love letter from Mose and the recipe for Apple Snow. That butterbox is to go to Sharla."

Leam settled on the front step and leaned back on his elbows. "Isaac Williams'll see that she gets it." He turned to look at his sister. "You saw Chester's grave."

"I did. I was shocked, Leam, but mostly because I was right. Mostly because a part of me knew his death wasn't true."

Leam nodded. "Mostly we know the truth."

"Leam?" Addy waited until her brother looked at her. "You think Mose knew? About me and Hamond?"

Leam tilted his head and didn't have to say yes.

Addy felt her heart skip. "You think he forgave me?"

Addy shivered when she felt the hand on her shoulder. Leam glanced up and smiled as Addy followed his gaze. "Mose," she whispered.

Mose leaned down, taking Addy's face in his big hands, saying, "My wife. I've missed you, Addy."

Addy wanted to rise to embrace her husband but felt rooted to the spot. She saw the moonlight in his good green eyes. "Oh, Mose, look at you. How come I never dream you old like me?"

Mose kissed her lips. She smelled his smell and tasted him like it was real and happening. She reached up to touch his face and laughed to see her hand was not old and scarred but young and strong. "Mose," she said again, then quietly, "Did you know, Mose?"

"I knew, Addy. But only for a second, and only in the end."

"You forgive me?"

Mose nodded. "I been waiting on you an awful long time."

"Waiting on *me*?" Addy laughed. "All the time we were married I was the one waiting on you."

Mose squeezed her hand. Addy inhaled and whispered, "Chick?"

"She's here. Everyone's here." Mose pointed inside the house. There were lights suddenly, and the sound of Ella Fitzgerald on the Baldwins' phonograph, and the trill of laughter and the aroma of roast beef and strawberry pie.

"Is it a party, Mose?"

"That's right, Adelaide. It's a welcome home party." He held out his hand.

Addy took Mose's hand and felt no creak of age in her bones as she rose. She waited, pausing at the door. "This is no dream, is it?"

Mose touched her cheek.

Addy took another deep breath. "Not what I expected atall."

Mose offered his arm to Addy like he did that first time at the station in Chatham, then he opened the door and guided her through.

"Rusholme," Addy whispered.